BOUNTY

BOUNTY

JASON PCHAJEK

RaveN
STONE

Bounty
© Jason Pchajek 2023

Published by Ravenstone, an imprint of Turnstone Press
Artspace Building, 206-100 Arthur Street
Winnipeg, MB. R3B 1H3 Canada
www.TurnstonePress.com

Turnstone Press gratefully acknowledges the assistance of the Canada Council for the Arts, the Manitoba Arts Council, the Government of Canada through the Canada Book Fund, and the Province of Manitoba through the Book Publishing Tax Credit and the Book Publisher Marketing Assistance Program.

This novel is a work of fiction. Names, characters, places and incidents are either the product of the author's imagination or are used fictitiously, and any resemblance to actual persons living or dead, events or locales, is entirely coincidental.

Printed and bound in Canada.

Library and Archives Canada Cataloguing in Publication

Title: Bounty / Jason Pchajek.
Names: Pchajek, Jason, author.
Identifiers: Canadiana (print) 20230448097 | Canadiana (ebook)
   20230448135 | ISBN 9780888017741 (softcover) | ISBN 9780888017765
   (PDF) | ISBN 9780888017758 (EPUB)
Classification: LCC PS8631.C53 B68 2023 | DDC C813/.6—dc23

MANITOBA ARTS COUNCIL
CONSEIL DES ARTS DU MANITOBA

Canada Council   Conseil des arts
for the Arts   du Canada

Funded by the Government of Canada
Financé par le gouvernement du Canada

Canada

Manitoba

To our planet, with love.

On Spaceship Earth there are no passengers;
everybody is a member of the crew.

—Marshall McLuhan
"At the moment of Sputnik [...]"

BOUNTY

ONE

I try my best not to kill people. Believe me, I do.

Usually, I give them a chance to surrender, come quietly, let me slap the cuffs over their wrists and end things without bloodshed. There's no point in spilling blood if you don't have to—and I wasn't in the habit of taking lives unnecessarily.

But making sure everyone gets out alive is tough when your job is dangerous.

It's even harder when you're a bounty hunter.

A soft hiss announced the arrival of a fresh spray of mist over the bustling city, adding to the humidity and the scent of wet stone and steel. The airborne water reflected the LED and holoprojected billboards dotting the buildings, pooled on the surfaces of glossy solar catchers, and danced off the slowly rotating personal wind turbines, making the already shimmering metropolis glow even brighter. But while the watery haze gave the nighttime glow of Winnipeg a dreamlike quality, it did little to relieve the suffocating heat trapped down here, in the bowels of the city.

I was perched atop a sign, crouched low and invisible within a darkened alcove, scanning the area below, waiting for my target to emerge.

The guy had led me all over the lower levels of the city on a wild goose chase that finally brought me to the core, the devil's den: bounty hunter territory.

A police cruiser rumbled slowly through the air ahead of me, turbine-powered engines in place of wheels baying out in the night, spotlights scanning left and right over the crowd below. They wanted the populace to know they were watching, but everyone knew they wouldn't dare put boots on the ground this far down without a good reason.

As the cruiser rumbled out of sight, I could hear the cops call down to a pair of teens peering over the edge of a walkway, warning them they'd be fined if they kept throwing things down below. In response, the pair gave the cops the finger and walked off. The cruiser kept moving. If it had been ninety years ago, that slight would've meant the kids eating pavement with a boot on their neck, but in the 2120s, the police knew they should just take it.

These were the sublevels, after all.

Kilometres below the surface, on Sublevel 11, the lowest habitable level of the city, the police presence was no more than a token force, buzzing around but rarely setting foot outside their flying cruisers to do any real "peacekeeping." You were more likely to get shot by a shop owner when robbing a store than get cuffs slapped around your wrists. Then again, it was equally likely the same shop owner would be shot while the perp escaped, only for the judgement of their crime to fall, eventually, to people like me.

With my target taking so long, I finally got a chance to catch my breath and look at the city I called home. From the alcove where I crouched, between a pair of residential towers, I drank in the claustrophobia-inducing crush of glass and steel that comprised the sublevels. Huge spire-like buildings extended from the floor of the sublevel to the ceiling in uninterrupted blocks, connected by a web of walkways, roads, platforms, and railways, filled with people skittering across the floor like ants or buzzing through the sky in transports on AI-determined flight lanes. The building I was perched on faced perhaps the most open of spaces in the immediate vicinity: one of the surface shafts that stretched, from the surface above, down to the bottom level of Winnipeg.

The tangle of residential buildings and sprawling civic districts picked up again on the other side of the shaft, but from where I sat, the real stars of the show were the hundreds of towering black Argite columns, gleaming in the light. Wherever in the city you were, these trademark mineralized-carbon supports would be near, extending the entire depth of the metropolis, through each sublevel ceiling and floor, all the way to the surface. Argite cores could be found lining the city's outermost walls too, improving the structural integrity of the bedrock and allowing the existing geology to hold up the ever-expanding mass that was Winnipeg. Long Argite supports that braced the columns at various angles provided further surface area for buildings and walkways to cling to, giving the city the distinct appearance of an attic taken over by a hive.

It was an impressive sight, but after spending most of my life here, I was used to it. The Argite. The heat. The tension. The cramped space. Breathing recycled air, drinking recycled water, using recycled ammunition. It was all normal. Natural. Home.

I relaxed slightly, shifting the rifle slung across my back, sliding down the wall into a sitting position, and letting my feet dangle in front of the flickering LEDs below me. I propped the gun on my knee, sliding the barrel shroud forward to inspect the internals. The small electromagnets that lined the barrel hummed quietly with energy, ready to fling the rounds of recycled metals at whatever I decided to point the weapon at. I'd learned long ago to inspect my weapons carefully, as a buildup of debris could stunt the charge and leave the gun unable to fire. Satisfied, I pulled the shroud back, hearing an audible click, and turned the weapon to check the status light, which held green. Charged, primed, and ready to rock.

I'd fired an old gas-operated firearm once, probably a decade ago at this point. They were almost nonexistent, phased out in favour of the greener electromagnetically propelled weapons so ubiquitous now. And cartridge bullets weren't made anymore anyway, so even if you had such a firearm, you'd have to find a stockpile of old ammo to make it worthwhile.

Pulling the weapon up to a near-ready position, I took a deep breath. The thick, humid air around me filled my lungs, giving me a sensation of drowning. The rain was so tantalizingly close, imminent relief from yet another heat dome that had settled overtop of the province. Clouds had been gathering at the surface, ready to burst and bring forth the torrential downpour that always followed. It was like the city was holding its breath, pressure rising, the sublevels a metal-and-stone box of sweltering heat, the whole place crying out for release.

Or perhaps that was just me.

Each deep, calming exhalation pushed a blast of warm air through the skull-like mouthpiece of my mask. Beads of perspiration streaked down the sides of my face. My clothes were soaked through with sweat from a day wandering the humid alleyways and rooftops of the sublevels, pelted by the routine sprays of recycled moisture meant to stem the wretched heat, chasing a guy I was sure would be coming along this way. My wrist-nav sputtered to life with a couple of flashes, and the heads-up display within my helmet blinked on to show the image of a hawk-faced man, scowling at the lucky officer taking his mugshot. His hair came together in a widow's peak as sharp as the point of his nose, accentuating the piercing stare of his black eyes.

"The Bounty Commission has sent along an update for us," the computerized voice of my AI companion ODIN began, sounding a tad annoyed. "They want to remind you that our target's name is Ivan Sobotka. A mid-level fixer with ties to multiple anti-establishment groups, wanted for tampering with probation implants and illicit sale of corporate property. Same conditions as before …" ODIN paused, before he gave a slight, satisfied hum. "Well, now we know why he was given to us. Apparently, he was hired to broker the sale of a tablet stolen from an Argo-employed contractor who was testing recycled water samples on Sublevel 7."

"Good to finally know," I replied. High-quality corporate tech was a big-ticket black-market item, especially when it came from Argo, the gatekeepers of the city's environmental infrastructure. "The Commission know who the seller and buyer are?"

ODIN paused again, reviewing the data. "The buyer is

unknown, but according to recent CCTV footage from Sublevel 7 the seller was someone connected to the Plainswalkers."

That made sense to me. The Plainswalkers essentially had the run of legitimate and illegitimate business on Sublevel 7. It was their turf. But what sealed it was the footage itself. Pulling up the clip on my HUD, I was met with a local security feed outside a known Plainswalker greenhouse and watched as a man exited the front door, right into the path of Ivan Sobotka, where the pair collided. The angry shouting that followed—complete with rude gestures tossed back and forth—did nothing to hide the pair bumping their wrist-navs together to complete their clandestine transaction.

Unfortunately, the Plainswalker was in a spot where the camera feeds couldn't see his face clearly, so getting a positive ID was impossible.

Regardless, it was a fixer selling corporate tech stolen from a contractor working in the city's environmental maintenance infrastructure. Standard Eco-Terror Taskforce job.

Underneath the description and last known location of Sobotka, in big red text, blinked the words *Wanted: Dead or Alive*. For the kind of crimes Sobotka was wanted for, legislation dictated his bounty should be alive-only, but with a rap sheet longer than my arm, Sobotka wasn't given as much leeway. This wasn't his first rodeo fencing stolen corporate tech and tampering with implants, not by a long shot, but he also had some more serious crimes in his history. Assaulting peacekeepers— like myself—was the big one, so the Bounty Commission was assuming there'd be more risk and wanted to give me an option to do this quickly, quietly, and safely.

Safely for me, that is.

Despite the "dead" option, I had every intention of taking Sobotka alive. It was a matter of principle. Dropping him here from across the street with a well-placed rifle round would've been easy, but I wasn't known for taking the easy road. Besides, as a member of the Bounty Commission Eco-Terror Taskforce, knowing who was trying to get their hands on Argo property, and why, was part of the job.

And you can't question someone if they're dead.

In any case, after a day of tracking through oppressive heat and moisture, a chase would be just enough to knock me out when this was all done.

And Lord knows I needed sleep.

Sobotka sure wasn't making it easy for me. Normally, I would've set ODIN to comb through security camera footage and the social feeds to try and find him, but it seemed that along with tampering with his probation chip to dampen the signal, he'd installed ID-masking tech—a dermal implant that seamlessly hid the man within the pixels of every frame of footage.

It was expensive black-market tech, not to mention annoying as hell for hunters, so I was out of luck. Until I got a tip.

It was Tuesday.

A somewhat innocuous detail on the surface, but growing up the son of a lawyer, you learn to appreciate small details, especially when you hunt people for a living. After a brief conversation with his probation officer—a stressed-out, overworked, and underpaid young woman on Sublevel 8—I learned that Sobotka had dinner with his mother every Tuesday. Come rain, snow, sleet, or bounty hunter hot on your tail. Following that lead, I hedged my bets and came up golden. He was inside.

So, it seemed my persistence would finally pay off.

Down below, the door of the apartment complex opened, and the hawk-faced man stepped out onto the walkway of the sublevel. He walked to the railing, gazing down to the level below while taking a long drag from a vaporizer, slowly turning back to join the crowd moving like a river down the walkway. In a few seconds it became evident that Sobotka had a tail, as two bald men slipped out from between adjacent buildings to follow close behind him. The pair bore intricate tattoos that covered their heads, and I rose enough to tug my rifle around to the front and pull the scope up to my eye, studying the designs. I hadn't seen their faces before, and most of the ink was just generic enough to not offer any clues, but small matching sigils on the napes of their necks, etched in black and green ink, caught my eye. It depicted a falling star or meteor of some kind.

A stream of mugshots flowed down the left side of my HUD as ODIN checked their faces and tattoos against known offenders in the Bounty Commission's database. He let out a disappointed sigh.

"No dice. They're not in the system."

"What about the tats? Any anti-establishment affiliations?"

Same answer.

Could these be Sobotka's mystery buyers? Or had he simply hired some muscle to look after him while he made his way to the buy, knowing there was a price on his head? If the former, I needed to know more. If the latter, they were about to have an awful night.

But regardless, I needed Sobotka to talk.

Sobotka and his tail took a right down the next street and would soon be out of sight, so I began to follow, using the railings and pipes above the sublevel's walkways to remain in the shadows. Where I couldn't find a direct path to go through, I clung to grooves in the walls of buildings, sliding along swiftly, experience and skill keeping me from plummeting to my death. Sobotka was walking fast, and so were the trailing mystery men.

A few blocks down, the three took a left, and I followed, quietly and unassumingly stalking from above. A low growl of thunder echoed through the sublevels.

They entered a plaza filled with artificial sunlight—realistically, just certain levels of UV rays pumped in through secondary lighting from the streetlamps. The sprawling plaza and park stretched across the open surface shaft, exposed to real rain and, when it wasn't raining, a few precious minutes of sunlight, though it was nowhere near enough to sustain the plants and stunted trees that lined the plaza, hence the late-night dose of UV rays.

Oxygenation proved to be a major problem the farther we expanded downward. Having so many people crammed tightly together, increasingly removed from the plant life of the surface, meant breathable air became hard to come by. The solution was creating these underground parks, which often amounted to nothing more than lining many of the walkways with trees, and having low levels of UV light fed through the sublevel streetlights to keep them alive. The alternative used for many years was having people walking around with oxygen masks, which some people still preferred for the extra boost of O_2.

I hopped the railing and landed on top of a rusted public airbus, riding it up onto a walkway above Sobotka. The different sublevels were layered more or less identically—long streets arranged in a vague grid, a main sublevel floor with multiple smaller streets, paths, and platforms built above in a patch-work way—meaning that I could slip into the crowd and follow my target closely and easily, watching from seven-odd metres above their heads, keeping as low a profile as possible.

Anyone who saw me would know I was a hunter—I didn't exactly try to blend in. Hunters styled themselves in distinct and different armour, helmets, masks, capes, and colours, and I was no exception. Wearing my combat vest, there were dark grey plates of fibre-reinforced ceramic adorning my chest, shoulders, and back, along with extra padding on my thighs, and thick armoured boots that came up to my kneepads, gaunt-lets that covered my forearms, and a stylized skull helmet with glowing red lenses. Behind those glowing red eyes were the equally bright top-of-the-line cybernetic replacements for the flesh ones I'd lost years ago. Then there was the military-grade cybernetic right arm, the pistol on my hip, and rifle slung on my back.

Although people noticed when a hunter was around, they wouldn't say anything, and many tried to pretend they didn't see us. It would be nice to get a smile, but those were hard to come by so close to rock bottom.

Whether they hated us, respected us, or feared us, ordinary citizens wouldn't get in our way.

That's when I spotted Mack, call-sign "Strigi," though he was never called that by anyone who knew him personally. The name was derived from "Strigida," the taxonomic family for owls, envisioned as smart and silent predators. It was a moni-ker he wore proudly, adorning himself in lavish coats of a vari-ety of colours, often billowing in the wind like some intelligent and dapper professor. On his head he wore a simple helmet with two circular lenses, set above a long V-shaped protrusion that looked like a sloping beak and contained an air filter.

He nodded as he passed, closing his right hand into a fist, slamming it into his breastplate over his heart before sliding the fist across his chest. This was the hunters' salute. I returned the gesture and continued moving.

There was a crackle in my helmet's comms as we moved apart.

"Nikos, you've got a bounty-snatcher ahead," Mack said. "The next crosswalk, dude with the goggles."

"Always look out for me, eh Mack?" I responded.

"Always, brother," Mack said with a chuckle. "Take a few teeth out for me."

The snatcher was standing at the railing, brushing long dark hair from his eyes so he could put his goggles on. Green as grass following April showers. He had no idea the trouble he'd put himself in, from both the fixer down below and the much more experienced hunter sauntering towards him.

Stealing someone's bounty was not illegal, per se. As long as it was marked as a public bounty by the Bounty Commission, it was first come, first served. And while there were a lot of contracts, there were even more hunters, so there was nothing stopping any green kid from jumping onto a bounty and trying to sweep it out from under you, getting the payday and the all-precious points on the Bounty Board. Every monetary score equalled points on the leaderboard. And when you were starting out, like this guy clearly was, the bigger scores were the best way to catch the eyes of specialist groups like the Eco-Terror Taskforce.

Like it or not, bounty hunting prospects were treated exactly like athletes in professional sports leagues.

While I wasn't opposed to sharing bounties, tonight I needed to be sure it was done right—my brand of right. No unknown variables. So this kid needed to be put in his place.

Besides, this was a private bounty, sent directly to me for first dibs before the Bounty Commission would need to try it on the open market. How this kid might've caught wind of it I didn't know, and I really didn't have time to find out.

The slamming of my boots against the concrete caught the kid's attention and he looked up just in time to see my fist coming for him. I connected hard with his nose, causing him to spin back with an audible pop as his nose broke. I stood over him, the glowing red of my helmet's eyes reflected in the water around us, studying the would-be hunter grasping his nose, which was gushing crimson.

He was young, probably not much older than eighteen, and his now-cracked goggles lay next to him in a puddle. I recognized them from ads on social feeds and street advertising projectors. Not the type hunters would necessarily wear, but they had enough features to be useful to us. The goggles synched to your wrist-nav, and neural or dermal implants, and provided live updates on messages, news, weather, maps, social media— you name it. You could, however, find someone to hack the device and make it close to the tech in the masks worn by hunters, but there was a reason we usually covered everything—as his bloody nose showed.

The kid was dressed in black, wearing a rec-leather jacket and slick, dark pants with a holster on his hip containing what looked like a charge gun—capable of lethal and non-lethal

BOUNTY

shots, but the energy was short-range, meaning he'd have to get right up on Sobotka and his buddies to use it. Energy weapons were still a way off from being totally useful outside of close-range encounters, and hunters stayed with convention, preferring modern magnetic weapons that fired caseless ammo made from recycled metals. One day, like gas-operated firearms, the magnetic-propulsion ones would be overtaken by their energy-based successors, with dialable power settings and completely rechargeable ammunition, and I could commend this young guy for taking the non-lethal option into account.

The young hunter spat out a mouthful of blood and looked up at me, a river of red trickling from his nose and highlighting the spaces between his teeth. He looked astonished; his anger had left him, and a mixture of fear and excitement flooded his face.

"You're Wulf, aren't you? Are you hunting Sobotka too?" he asked excitedly. "I didn't expect to meet someone like you tonight."

I wasn't surprised he knew who I was, but that didn't mean I liked it. Stories of everyone in the Top 10 were passed around everywhere hunters went. If he had started bounty hunting recently, his little head would've been flooded with tall tales of exploits from me and Mack, to someone like Ravager. Not the type of thing to keep a young kid from going out and chasing glory on their first night. I had no problem with the kid working, but it was more getting him away from such a dangerous target, and out of my way. Whether he passed his certification or not, this was not the best contract to start with.

"Well, kid, I'm the reason you're going to stop today," I said

15

through the voice-changer in my mask. "You're in way over your head, chasing a guy like this. You read his file?"

A naive smile was plastered across his face. "Yeah, and I thought it would be a good start," he replied. "I want to be someone like you; get on with a task force. I'm not going to get there nabbing drug pushers and small-time aug-hackers."

The kid was young, hungry, stupid, and on his way to an early grave.

"Hunting a guy like Sobotka is a bad idea when the ink on your licence isn't dry. That's not how I started, kid," I replied, voice forced into dual octave by my mask's exterior speaker. The sound was causing the kid to look worried, and even a bit scared. "Listen, I don't know how you got word of this bounty, but you need to walk away now and start smaller. This is for the Eco-Terror Taskforce, not the general pool. Believe me, I'm trying to save your life."

"Well, how about I come with you? You could teach me," the kid said eagerly, wiping some blood from his nose. "We could split the cash and the score."

I stepped towards him, and the kid flinched as I knelt next to him and placed a soft hand on his shoulder. He wasn't getting the hint, and I needed to hammer it home.

"Not tonight," I responded quietly. "I'm no teacher, even with this. Now do yourself, and whatever family you have, a favour, and get the hell out of here. Start small, corp-crimes and alive-only contracts. Build it up the right way." I slipped the broken goggles back into his hand. "And get yourself some proper gear. Something that won't fly off and break after a single punch, even if it's a good one." My soft grip turned into a crushing one, highlighted by the pained grimace on the kid's face. "From one hunter to another: go home, kid. I probably just saved your life."

The kid's smile faded, and his jaw clenched as he weighed his options. He let out a sigh, realizing that chasing down *this* target wasn't worth me being on his tail. Hopefully he had internalized my advice and was going to be smarter next time. I helped him to his feet and the kid brushed past me, walking down the road with his hands in his pockets.

The young hunter had cost me some time, but luckily my mark wasn't too far gone. I looked down to the lower level, scanning the throng of people milling about, just in time to see Sobotka round the corner again, heading towards a market.

These markets popped up all over the sublevels: scrappy stalls packed wall-to-wall in an open area, where those who couldn't afford a shop of their own would peddle synthetic food, recycled and modified clothes, and cheap electronics. Making scraps—but down here that was enough. The cramped quarters and crowd cover also masked some of the more dubious business going on. Not surprising, considering how desperate some of the peddlers were just to eat. If you didn't have in-demand skills, the right credentials, or powerful and connected friends, you were never going to taste life on the surface. Throw in the influence of anti-establishment groups offering a helping hand to like-minded—or at least, willing—individuals, and this packed market would be a hotspot for a guy like Sobotka.

I slipped over the railing and onto a staircase leading alongside one of the buildings, walking around to find a perch overlooking the market.

Sobotka had stopped at a stall to admire some comms tech being sold by a young man.

My target said a few words to the man, pointing towards a tablet on the wall. It was a thin sheet of transparent material, likely recycled plastic, that could be folded and curved. The clerk complied, pulling the tablet down and handing it over. After inspecting the tablet in his hands, Sobotka shared a knowing look with the young man and began walking away, not a single credit exchanged. It was a solid bet that the tablet was the same one nicked from the Argo contractor, that the young guy running the stall was a proxy hired by the Plainswalker seller to rendezvous with Sobotka and give him the goods, and that Sobotka was now on his way to deliver the stolen tablet to the unknown buyer. It was a decent plan, but it wouldn't go any further. It was time to collect.

I swung down to intercept him, my boots hitting the ground with a thud, sending collected water flying in all directions.

Sobotka's eyes flashed with pure terror as he stumbled back. He squeaked orders at his two tattooed companions, pushing them towards me.

Bodyguards, then.

The first man up snarled, green cybernetic eyes ablaze as he wound up for a punch with his right that surely could have taken my head clean off. I dodged the swing, balled my cybernetic right hand into a fist, and with a slight pneumatic pulse, struck forward. As he lurched over me, the punch connected with his knee, and a loud pop and groan of pain followed the strike.

Carried forward by momentum, I moved towards the second guard, slipping past his own punch and driving another jackhammer right up into the bottom of his jaw. The bone cracked and blood pulsed from between his clenched teeth as his jaw shattered from the impact. The attacker let out a single grunt and went slack as he crumpled to the floor, unconscious. I shook my prosthetic hand, a ripple of simulated pain working its way through the appendage as its finely tuned tactile sensors pretended at the real thing.

I turned in time to see the first attacker coming at me again with a left jab, stumbling forward on the broken knee. A slight shift of my head let his fist pass harmlessly over my shoulder. With my left hand, I grabbed him around the wrist and twisted his arm, so his palm faced the sky, then brought it down over my shoulder with an audible crack. The green-eyed guard howled in pain, and I swung an elbow back and up, burying it in the big brute's throat. He fell to his knees, clutching his neck, gurgling and choking. With a swift kick to head, he fell over, the green light fading from his cybernetic eyes as he blacked out. Turning around, I found Sobotka still there, gaping at his quickly dispatched security detail currently out cold on the sublevel floor.

His eyes flicked up quickly to meet mine.

"Ivan Sobotka!" I called out, confidently striding forward. "Stay right where you are. My name is Nikos Wu—"

He took off running.

I bit out a curse and took off after him.

The chase through the market was a tough one. The market grounds were packed with vendors' stalls and tables, arranged in organic disorder. Benches, carts, and people filled the empty spaces between them, and service robots cleaned the ever-mounting piles of garbage. Sobotka took off like bat out of hell, knocking a woman into a kiosk selling knock-off brand-name clothes, sending the wares scattering behind the table.

For all time this guy spent in and out of prison, he had

great endurance. The market stretched the length of a football field, and having to cut left and right around tables and kiosks in a zigzagging maze of vendors only made the distance longer.

Luckily for me, I had ODIN, who was tracking Sobotka's position in real time, displaying the optimal pursuit path directly into my helmet's visor.

Sobotka bumped into another person, sending them straight into me. I flipped, rolling over them back-to-back, keeping my momentum moving forward. I was quickly closing in on him, and Sobotka knew it, so he knocked down part of a newsstand, which I jumped over like a hurdle. Next he hopped over a table of fruit grown on Sublevel 7, sending apples, cantaloupes, and oranges spilling all over the market floor, drawing swears and yells from their seller. I dodged past a young guy who crossed my path—too busy staring at his smartglasses—dropping to slide underneath the fruit vendor's table.

My target turned right, and I jumped on top of the kiosks to cut him off, but he was too fast. I saw Sobotka knock a couple down, then barrel through another, prompting swears and threats from the offended parties; however, they stopped after catching sight of the bounty hunter chasing him. They knew he was in big trouble and would take solace in the fact that he'd have more to answer for than their wet clothes and bruised egos. I was beginning to regret this whole chase idea as Sobotka took a left and another right to go down a path out of the market.

A combination of mist and condensed humidity had collected on the floor here, making the ground slippery. Sobotka knocked over a couple of service robots sweeping trash from the streets and sent refuse skittering across the floor of the sublevel. The chase went left again, past a row of small independent shops, holoprojected signs advertising authentic diamond jewelry, communication implants, and genuine cotton clothes—things way out of the price range for people down here.

This path ended at a large maglev train track. Trains were the main mode of public transport in the sublevels, and this meant a crowd. Within seconds, Sobotka was gone. I had followed him up the steps to the train station but he had disappeared into the crowd of commuters waiting for the next train, creating a forest of humanity for my target to hide in. My eyes scanned the platform, looking for any sign of him, but found nothing among the mass of life.

"ODIN, hack into the station's security cameras," I barked into my comms. "Small zone, short scan. Within regulations. And start recording."

"Certainly, one moment," ODIN's computerized voice responded. The edges of my vision pulsed red to signal the recording was in progress, and after a few seconds, video feeds began playing across my mask's HUD. "The bounty target Ivan Sobotka was last seen heading through a maintenance access door to the ground level."

The door Sobotka escaped through was across two tracks, and with the 10:30 evening trains about to arrive, I had to act fast. Breaking into a sprint, I cut through the crowd, hopping over the barrier to the first track, and onto the walkways in between the two. The station's speakers crackled to life, announcing the imminent arrival of the trains. With a running start, I jumped from the median to the crowded platform on the other side. From there I was able to crash through the maintenance door, and instead of following Sobotka down,

ODIN stepped in, tracing the optimal path to a walkway that carried me above him.

I wouldn't be able to catch Sobotka travelling on the floor of the sublevel. He was too fast and too far ahead for that.

I needed to go another way.

I took off, hopping between walkways to close the distance as he cut left down a side street.

On the next jump, I looked down in time to see my target below, still running. He hooked a right down an alley and passed through a large archway that led to a dead end.

That's where Sobotka stopped, at the railing beyond which was a massive expanse of the sublevels under construction, a wide surface shaft reaching above our heads.

I dropped down behind the thug, who turned to stare down the barrel of my pistol. The gun whirred to life and various ports began glowing blue, illuminating Sobotka's terrified face. Behind him, the world was glowing a warm orange, the earth being blasted and melted to make room for more life. The distant hum of lasers cutting through rock was accompanied by an electric whine of large construction machinery, working to extend the city down even farther. Sobotka was shaking, beads of sweat glistening off the prism-shaped neural implant embedded in his temple, and breathing hard from the chase. The added heat of the construction going on just beyond where we stood thickened the already oppressive air to a soup that screamed for relief. Far above us, the sky emitted a deep rumble.

He looked me in the eyes. "Whoa-whoa-whoa, hold on. Whatever they're paying you, I'll double it," the fixer begged. "Just let me go."

My HUD zoomed in to measure biometrics, allowing me to

see my masked face reflected in Sobotka's eyes. Two massive dark pools, dilated by pounding adrenaline and fear, reflecting a motionless red gaze. My heart thrummed as my focus and edge returned.

"Sorry, that's not going to work here," I replied, adjusting the grip on my pistol as my HUD display zoomed back out. "Ivan Sobotka, my name is Nikos Wulf, from the Bounty Commission Eco-Terror Taskforce. I am the bounty hunter assigned to your case. You've got a lot hanging over your head and it's time that bill was paid, but not by whatever credits you're offering. My bounty hunter licence number—"

"Come on, man." Sobotka interrupted as he backed up, bumping into the railing. "I'm just the middleman. The Plainswalkers needed a buyer, and I had one waiting in the wings. I didn't know it was so important."

Behind the mask, I smirked. He wasn't wrong there, but it didn't matter. I needed to bring him in.

"Well, that's unfortunate for you, then. A contract is a contract. You are brokering the sale of stolen corporate property—and beyond that, you tampered with your implant. That's an automatic violation of your parole." I stepped forward, closing the distance while reaching for my cuffs, only barely catching what happened next. "But the real thing I want to know is who this mystery buyer is."

"The … buyer?" he stammered, blinking sweat from his eyes. "Why would you? No. No-no-no-no, I can't. You can't stop it. They won't let you stop what's coming. All will be steel and sun."

Sobotka's next words lodged in his throat, as if the air was suddenly stolen from his lungs and the tension seemed to evaporate from his limbs, as he was overcome with a look of acceptance, his voice shifting slightly, calm like a still pool.

"And I will not betray them." His hand whipped to his hip. I only now spotted the matte red finish of a charge gun that at this range would melt right through my breastplate. The resigned look in his eye told me exactly how this would end.

"Thanatos take me," he bit out, and before I could reach for my pistol, he jammed the charge gun under his jaw and pulled the trigger. A brief orange flash filled the space between us as the lethal burst sliced through, and the man dropped to the ground, dead.

I exhaled and looked down at his body. The charge pistol was still cradled in his hand, power slowly fading as Sobotka's grip went slack. The tablet, meanwhile, was peeking out from inside his jacket. At least I'd be able to get that back.

A peal of thunder tore through the dense sky as the storm finally broke overhead. As if Sobotka's shot had popped the bubble over Winnipeg, the first droplets of rain—real rain— struck my shoulders, before the pace picked up in earnest, hammering down hard, soaking the rapidly cooling body of Ivan Sobotka.

A cocktail of guilt and frustration roiled through my insides as I stared down at the corpse. This wasn't how this job was supposed to go. I'd been sloppy—careless, even. Picking the chase over doing this the right way. I tried not to think about how easily our roles could have been reversed, had he aimed the gun at me instead of himself, a smouldering hole burned into my combat vest right where my heart was.

Turning my eyes to the sky, searching the kilometres of open air above me that stretched in a giant chasm towards the surface, I removed my helmet to feel the rain on my face, the dead fixer's words echoing in my head.

They won't let you stop what's coming. All will be steel and sun.

I had no answer about his mysterious buyer. But something told me Sobotka's death wasn't the end of this.

For now, though, sleep. Pouring rain and sleep.

"ODIN, send the recording in. Time to collect this bounty and go home," I muttered quietly, more to myself than to my AI partner.

"Certainly," ODIN responded, sending the kill confirmation and required recording to the bounty officials. A bounty retrieval crew would arrive shortly to collect the body. "I will chart a path to the back to the Bounty Commission outpost so you can change and will find the quickest transit route home."

"Thanks, ODIN." My gaze drifted down to the body, and the blood pooling at my feet. "Good job today, bud. As always."

TWO

The door slid open, and a burst of cool air rushed out to meet me from the open window at the other end of the room. Along with the gentle, rain-soaked breeze came the discordant clatter of the city, and the scent of damp steel and ozone you only get down in the sublevels. The space was orderly, clean, and functional, just like a soldier should have it. The single rec-leather couch was spotless, wiped clean; the armchair sitting opposite was similarly pristine, but from where I stood, I could see a small condensation ring on the coffee table. As ODIN hopped from my wrist-nav to the apartment's internal computer systems, there was a small chime, and the space came to life. The projected fireplace along to back wall of the living room began to silently flicker. The holoprojector descended from the ceiling, and off to my left, dim orange lights in the kitchen began to glow, illuminating the oxygen-giving vine-covered walls. The window that comprised the whole outer wall of my neat one-bedroom apartment shifted from opaque to transparent.

Beyond the glass was a picturesque view of Winnipeg's Sublevel 4, billboards and hologram displays flashing and changing, sending shimmering light through the rivulets of rainwater on the glass in a vibrant display of dancing colour. Being next to a surface shaft meant that the rain pattering against my window was mostly real.

Elsewhere on Sublevel 4, however—where rain droplets had the almost impossible task of dodging countless walkways, mag-lev tracks and floating transports—the vast majority was recycled. Rain, river runoff, or other moisture from the surface was contin-ually collected through vents and runoff drains on buildings and walkways and reused to simulate real-world surface conditions and maintain some kind of moisture. All done to keep the city cool during the deep droughts on the prairies. The intention—but not always the result—of climate mirroring was that whatever happened up on the surface also occurred down below it.

This far down, though, it was almost all artificial. While the surface got the real deal—full seasons, rain, snow, lightning, thunder, and real sunlight—after you hit maybe Sublevel 5 or 6, the concept of seasons stopped mattering. Unless you were near a surface shaft, the deeper you went, the thicker the air got, following the density of the city itself. The precipitation down here amounted to a spray of recycled rain. Sunlight, a blast of UV-infused streetlights. Winter breeze, a gust from cooling ducts. Whether it was January or the dog days of August, the sublevels felt the same, and one could go their whole life never seeing a flake of snow. Sure, it could get cold, but only the air, never a lick of snow at your feet. The geothermal temperature of the sublevels saw to that. Whatever moisture was hanging in the air got blasted by reflected UV rays and turned to sleet and mist, so climate mirroring could only make it rain.

Good thing I loved rain, then.

There was a clattering thud as I dropped the duffle bag containing my gear on the floor, and I descended the steps from my front door, down through the living room, to take up a position at the window. I breathed deeply, filling my lungs with the cool night air, and listened to the city. Away from work for the moment, I could enjoy the sound: the thundering bass swelling from one of the dozen or so bars and restaurants close by; the distant melody of conversations drifting up from the street below; the warble of transports floating through the open air; and the ever-present hum of electricity being drawn from solar catchers and small turbines hanging off buildings, spinning in the winds that bounced through the city. If I'd had the right neural augment, I could have heard the colours.

I didn't have any, though. The thought of neural implants freaked me out, and my father's lifelong paranoia around the technology didn't do anything to assuage that discomfort.

That wasn't to say I had anything against enhancements in general. As I raised my right hand and placed the cybernetic appendage on the glass, its tactile sensors fired electrical signals up the black carbon-and-metal arm to where it connected to my flesh at the shoulder and the nerves therein. Sometimes the augmentations were necessary, helped human beings become better than they were, or, in my case—and as was the case for billions of others—returned us to what we had once been. But as I gazed out at the recycled rain, mingling with the real stuff coming down from the chasm-like surface shaft beyond, I caught a glimpse of the glowing blue of my machine eyes, and was reminded of the fact that I'd never truly be wholly human again.

At least I was alive, and able to see this view.

Sublevel 4. It was a nice place, nestled beneath the earlier sublevels, which retained the city's middle class, while the breadth of the sublevels hung below, being what most people think of when the word "sublevel" escapes someone's lips. Part entertainment district and part metropolitan destination, Sublevel 4 was always lively, young, and colourful.

I could've picked anywhere to live, but something had brought me here. If pressed, I could say the more central location made it easy to traverse between different parts of the city when need arose, or the proximity to the surface brought fresher air, some real sunlight, and true weather without direct exposure to the harsh storms the surface sometimes saw. But really, I wasn't sure why. It was a sublevel between the two worlds, caught in the middle. It was loud and bright, the middle ground between the Ivories up top and the sublevellers below, while truly belonging to neither.

For the second time that day, I found myself looking closely at the city that was my home. The metal and Argite pressing in around me, that had shaped me into a tough but—I hoped—fair person. A city once sliding off the edge, into the nation's basement, which had now become a shining beacon of progress in a hundred-odd years.

When my great-grandfather was growing up, Winnipeg was struggling. Economic stagnation in the 1990s gave way to government cuts, and then growth led to rampant spending with no clear direction, which brought about even more years of social programs being slashed, health care being picked apart by vultures, and lives getting more expensive. It was an endless cycle of political jockeying and citizens not knowing what they really wanted from their leaders. Throw in a couple economic recessions brought about by deregulation and one massive global pandemic, and lives got more difficult for the common folk. All the while, the very planet we lived on revolted against us. For a century, extreme storms battered cities, waters rose around our ankles, deserts grew unchecked, and plague-like diseases popped up with such regularity we began to run out of catchy names.

But that all changed when my great-grandfather, Demetrius Wulf, founded the Argonaut Group.

From my window, I could see a constant reminder of his legacy: an arm of thick Argite running perpendicular to my window, emerging from the limits of my vision to the right and disappearing into the mass of buildings and supports on the opposite side of the vast subterranean atrium. In the multicoloured glow of Winnipeg's nightlife, the glassy black sheen of the compressed carbon shimmered, our salvation borne from millennia-old rock. But where most saw stone monoliths upholding the city and reinforcing the walls that held its historic Red and Assiniboine rivers overhead, bisected by tunnels and carefully carved hollows to allow people and traffic through, I only saw the gleaming carbon, and the story it told.

My great-grandfather started the Argonaut Group with four of his best friends, and their goal was simple: beat back climate change and make the lives of others greater in the process. They wanted to lift this city above the clouds. Little did they know that the future lay underground, and their thesis project would create an empire.

In the early 2000s, global temperatures were steadily on the rise, due in large part to an excess of greenhouse gases—carbon dioxide, methane, nitrous oxide, and other fluorinated gases—trapped within our planet's atmosphere. By the 2020s, the effects in Canada had become obvious. Intense storm systems battered coastal communities, washing away homes, destroying infrastructure. Further inland, droughts left crops stunted, while flooding created millions of dollars in damage, and arable land began to grow fallow, exacerbated by frequent heat domes that settled over much of central Canada. Something needed to be done. Someone needed to step up and provide tangible solutions to remove the gases turning our planet into a prison of heat and storm.

The ability to recapture carbon from the atmosphere and turn it into usable material was a pipe dream. In Iceland, other eco-minded companies had found success in capturing and storing carbon in existing rock by dissolving gaseous CO_2 in water and injecting the substance into porous basalt, which was abundant across Iceland's geology. The chemical reaction that resulted from CO_2 meeting basalt saw the previously airborne carbon remineralizing within the pores of the rock, allowing it to be stored in a solid form, thus diminishing its impact on the atmosphere.

Storing carbon was one thing, but the question on the Argonaut Group's minds was whether the science could be modified to result in a purer, stronger remineralized carbon that could fortify stone and be repurposed in countless ways—a solution to climate disaster and the next great scientific and economic boon. Experts in the field believed it impossible. Yet when my great-grandfather and his friends tested the hypothesis in the Manitoba Whiteshell, on a tiny island nestled in West Hawk Lake, the entire world was changed.

Even now, decades later, I could remember the story I was often told as a child. The project—known then under their chosen code name of "Architect"—was spearheaded by two of the other founders, Madran Roy, a mechanical engineer, and physicist Guy Beauvillier, while Demetrius Wulf used his legal expertise to help navigate the Argonaut Group through the complex legalities and patents needed to safeguard their plans.

Picking up where the Icelanders left off, and looking to stick close to their hometown of Winnipeg, they'd collectively surmised that the basalt beneath West Hawk Lake—an old meteor impact crater—was conducive to reliable carbon injection, and had the best likelihood of producing the denser remineralization results they were hoping for with their re-engineered machines and formulas. They spent three years pulling and testing large core samples and tweaking their methodologies, failing at almost every turn, but just weeks from their funding running out, and with their investors threatening to pull the plug, they suddenly made a breakthrough that was far beyond what any of them had hoped for. They had somehow found a way to bypass the need for a host rock and were instead able to remineralize atmospheric carbon directly into the cavities left behind from earlier core samples, creating impossibly strong, pure carbon cores—which were now manufactured en masse to support multitiered cities around the globe. Something no company since has been able to replicate.

They called their remineralized carbon Argite, and it made them trillions.

Not only did they prove it was possible to pull excess carbon from the atmosphere, but they were also able to find a way to do it cheaply, taking a little startup called the Argonaut Group—now simply referred to as Argo—and turning into a global enterprise that helped companies and countries smash emissions targets, while creating the dense and strong material that held up the city beyond my window, and many others like it.

Winnipeg was one of the first cities to begin expanding down, putting level after level beneath what was once Portage and Main, excavating kilometres of subterranean city in all directions under this landmark intersection, until they hit Sublevel 11, the lowest habitable level—for now. The scientific community concluded that climate change could be slowed further by expanding cities vertically, rather than horizontally, leaving ample land to grow vast forests, protect wildlife, maintain ecosystems, and install huge swaths of solar- and wind-power generators. The massive carbon recapture machines created by Argo quickly pulled the gases choking our planet out of the air, compacting them into dense, solid Argite that reinforced the earth and now served as the building blocks to enhance global infrastructure in the face of climate doom. Taking the thing destroying us and using it to build us back up.

Once Argo showed the world how much profit could be made by thinking this way, other major cities put their own spin on it, and Argo was always there to make those plans a reality. In ultramodern Shenzhen and Shanghai, Argo's technology was used to continue each city's expansion skyward, with layers of full metropolis stacked kilometres into the air. Coastal cities jumped on board with the idea too, with places like Abu Dhabi and São Paulo building up to escape rising sea levels. Others like Moscow, Phoenix, and Las Vegas chose the so-called "Winnipeg model" and built down, boring deep into the ground to escape worsening conditions on the surface.

But Winnipeg did it first. And we did it best.

In the century following its founding, the Argonaut Group—and the subsequent generations of the five founding families—threw this country into the forefront, and with it, Argo diversified, stretching its influence into every possible market. Looking out across the surface shaft to one of the streets below, I saw a few small cars zip along one of the electric roadways that covered the nation, generating power during the day, lighting the cities at night. Here it had the bonus of scattering the glowing lights of Sublevel 4 across its shimmering, translucent surface. Another reminder of Argo's influence, making the world a bit more green.

Toss in with those their investments into eco-friendly travel, green energy, sustainable food production, cybernetic prosthesis, neural augmentations to curb cognitive decline or improve human productivity, and disease prevention, and the Argonaut Group had rewritten the history books on what entrepreneurs could do if they prioritized climate solutions and made new markets. As reluctant as some governments and societies were to turn themselves over to "corporate saviours," few could deny we were better off now than a hundred years ago.

Even now, despite my family's expulsion from Argo's orbit, I got to continue my great-grandfather's legacy in my own way, working for a task force I felt was making things safer, bringing justice for crimes that could not only hurt people, but also threatened the tenuous climate gains that began with Argo. This was the reason I was soaked through, muscles burning, and with specks of blood still visible on the gear in my bag. Nobody cleans your gear for you, even when you're on top.

My trance was broken by ODIN.

"Good evening, Nikos," ODIN said, his voice coming simultaneously from everywhere and nowhere. "The bounty has been collected and the credits have been deposited into your account."

"Thank you, ODIN. Is there anything else?" I asked, slipping off my jacket.

"You have a message as well, from Mr. Castor Roy," he said with almost human-like apprehension. "Shall I play it for you?"

The name rang in my ears for a moment, and I let out an audible groan. It had been months since I'd last spoken to Castor—six months, to be exact, as ODIN would undoubtedly remind me—and for a while it appeared that he had gotten the hint. Each time he'd pinged my wrist-nav or called my comms, I neglected to answer. Each time he told me to come in to exchange data on ODIN so he could give my companion the newest firmware update, I declined, sending him the data dump instead and requesting the update sent back. ODIN was complicated, being comprised of a set of interlocking blocks of code that were themselves millions of lines long, but after a decade, I knew the AI probably better than Castor did. At least on a personal level.

I exhaled sharply. "Again?"

"Yes. And it appears urgent. He has called twenty-six times in the last twenty-four hours. The latest one just came in. I thought you'd want a moment to breathe before I bothered you with it."

"What does he want?"

"I'm not sure. He …" ODIN paused.

"He what?" I kicked off my boots and stretched out my toes. The cool air of the apartment felt great on my hot and sweaty feet. "Did he offer me a job? Say he's fixing things? Did he tell Zara to go fuck herself?"

ODIN chuckled. "No, I'm afraid not. He … well, he's encrypted the message in such a way that I *can't* tell you what it says. The only way to know is by playing it to you."

There was a chorus of crackles as I flexed my back, working out the tension and pain from the stiff joints. "Are you joking?" I asked, eyebrow cocked in a direction I knew ODIN's sensors could see me from. "Is this some trick of yours to try and get us talking again?"

"Of course not," ODIN replied, tone hinting at indignation. "I completely agree that Ms. Kravchenko was exceedingly rude in her assertions and very much out of line in her appraisal of your character."

The memories came back in flashes. A screaming match between myself and Zara, two childhood friends dressing each other down in the Argonaut Building lobby, her hand waving away security before clocking me in the nose. As the memory faded, my own hand drifted to my face and the spot where she'd hit me.

I shouldn't have said what I did. But she didn't have to punch me.

"Well, in that case, ODIN, sure," I said, taking a deep breath.

What could one of the richest men in the country want with me at this ungodly hour?

The projector flicked on to display the call screen, a holographic projection of crystal-clear quality hanging in the air an inch from the living room wall ahead of me. The message began, and a firm and professional voice spoke from the same purgatory as ODIN.

"Hello, Nikos," Castor started. I could almost hear the smile hiding behind the executive tone, which only lasted a moment, his professional airs bleeding away swiftly as he continued. "It's been a while. And I know why—honestly, I'm pretty sure the whole company knows—but we've both known Zara our whole lives, and this wasn't the first time she's gotten in your face about your relationship with Argo. Not that it makes her comments any easier to take ..." His voice caught, and he paused, breathing softly. "Listen ... I've discovered something, something *huge*, and it seems like all that time you've been spending with ODIN has turned into something that could be a game-changer for humanity ..." He paused again. "I know you're mad. And I know it won't be the last time, but trust me, you need to come to Argo to see this, Nikos. And at the very least to update ODIN. I haven't seen his code for a while, and there are six months' worth of data I need to reconcile.

"I'm not promising an apology—that's not my place—and I'm sure Zara won't offer one, either. Just please come in."

I walked over to the bar along the wall the living room shared with the kitchen, contemplating the situation, and poured a drink for myself. Manitoba rye slid generously from the bottle until my glass was half full. I took a swig directly from the bottle before setting it back down on the freshly polished surface of the bar top, watching the liquid slosh inside before settling, just like the burning liquor working its way through my system. I perched on the edge of the coffee table in the middle of the room, bent forward, fingers tracing the edges of the frosted glass in my hands as Castor's words tumbled over in my head, eyes locked on the simple phrase holding considerable weight now being projected onto the wall: *Delete message?*

In all my thirty-three years on this spinning ball of a world, Castor had been my friend through almost the whole thing— but so much had changed. Following years of mental deterioration, my father, James Wulf, had been forced out of the company his grandfather had helped found, taking the whole Wulf family down with him, and because of that, I hadn't been part of Argo in any meaningful way since I was a child. This little project, living and working with ODIN, was the closest I'd ever gotten, periodically stopping by Argo to debrief with Castor while he collected data and made small tweaks. The AI was a gift, really, and the project was a way for two friends to reconnect after a decade apart. But then again … my conflict wasn't with Castor, or with Argo, despite what they'd done to my father.

It was with Zara. For someone like her, the ODIN project still brought me too close. Years of passive- and not-so-passive-aggressive comments bubbling up to a screaming match where her true feelings had been unleashed. Words like "leech" and "outsider" and "fake." So maybe my absence was for the best. Zara got me out of her hair, no longer "tainting" the company with my presence after my family was cut off from it before any of us were old enough to understand what that meant, and I got to be away from it. Able to continue building my own life.

Besides, being an Ivory wasn't for me. Not anymore.

"Shall I make an appointment with Castor?" ODIN piped up, noticing my silence, but giving me time to think.

"No," I said curtly, flicking my eyes up as if I were speaking to a person. "I'll leave it for now. Whatever he wants to talk about can wait a day or so. And if it's so important, then he can come to me." I stood from the table, legs aching from a long workday, and collapsed into the armchair. "You recorded the game tonight, right?"

"Can't miss a rivalry match," ODIN replied.

"Damn right. Bring it on, Minnesota."

The projection flashed in ODIN's silent response, showing the hockey game I had missed chasing Sobotka all night. Home players in navy jerseys and visiting players in an earthy green danced along the ice, crashing into each other hard one moment, pulling off slick dekes the next. They were part ballerina and part gladiator, moving around the ice at blistering speeds. Well, not ice, but a synthetic alternative that didn't need the energy and emissions old hockey rinks had once used.

The recording quickly lost my attention as I stared into my drink, spinning the glass in my sleek metal-and-carbon hand, noting the way the swirling liquid caught the light. I could feel the warm buzz of the liquor gathering at the base of my skull before it splintered out across the firing neurons in long tendrils. I felt myself relaxing, so I downed another swig, letting the buzzing neurons take my mind where it wanted.

My thoughts wandered from the message I'd just received, to the bounty just completed, and to the final moments of Ivan Sobotka.

The scene replayed on a loop in my mind's eye. His features, held stiff by fear, suddenly slackening into a resigned gaze, with full knowledge of what would come next. Yet there was something unnatural in his movements, even distracted as I was by the weapon I was sure would be turned on me. Had I sensed some hesitation? A slight hitch in the arm, apprehension in his fingers? The man had been willing to kill himself rather than be arrested by a bounty hunter. The question was why: Then there were his words.

They won't let you stop what's coming. All will be steel and sun.

He'd been so afraid when I'd asked about the buyer, and if Sobotka had been willing to kill himself to protect that information, then who were these people? And what did they want?

But the answer to those questions, and a whole host of others, had died with him.

By now, he'd probably already be undergoing aquamation, his body enclosed in a capsule of hot water and alkali that would dissolve his flesh, leaving only a skeleton behind to grind up and prepare for burial, as national policy dictated. His family had no hope of paying the extreme cost of a real burial, or even something as simple as a wake. That cost millions of credits. The best he could hope for was to be interred in one of the sublevel mausoleums, placed within a tiny niche built within the stone walls that contained the city itself, where he'd stay forever, along with all the answers to my questions.

A dead end. Or was it?

"ODIN?" I called out, still peering into the swirling liquid in my glass, as if I would find the truth behind Sobotka's words there.

The volume on the projected hockey game dropped to a barely audible mummer. "Yes, Nikos?"

With a small groan, I leaned forward, tired muscles giving me grief. "Did WPS follow up on the note we sent about the bodyguards? Find out who they were?"

ODIN paused for half a beat as he retrieved the report from the Bounty Commission database. "They did, but unfortunately by the time Winnipeg Police Service officers found a place to land and reached where I'd tagged their location, they were gone. According to eyewitness reports, soon after you took off after Sobotka, an unmarked transport came and scooped them up. Same for the market vendor. The owner of the stall said he'd closed up shop for the day and didn't have any employees. The young man was probably hired to break in to get the goods to Sobotka without raising suspicion."

Damn.

"So someone else was monitoring Sobotka," I said, taking another sip.

"Seems so," ODIN said. "Likely our mystery buyer. It would also indicate some kind of organization."

"And influence, if Sobotka was willing to kill himself over the deal."

If I had been quicker, been able to grab the gun, maybe I could've stopped him. Saved his life. But instead he was gone, and I was powerless to change that. Sobotka's mother and girlfriend would probably be hearing now that he was dead. What would they think? It shouldn't come as too much of a surprise—after all, the deep sublevels offered few options for honest employment, and Sobotka had a record longer than the sublevels were deep. This wasn't his first sale of stolen goods either. But to die for this particular buyer, willingly? It didn't make sense to me. And certainly wouldn't to them. I'd been tracking him all day and he'd stopped in with each of his loved ones before I finally caught up to him—had he been notifying them that he likely would not see the sun rise?

Was he expecting to die all along?

I lifted the glass to my mouth, taking a long swig before setting my now half-empty drink down on the table beside me. With an exhale, I stood and walked to the windows, peering out into the mass of glowing buildings before my eye settled on a small wind turbine lazily rotating in front of a large holographic ad for Argo-branded cybernetic prostheses.

Jaeger had once told me that death was an inevitability when it came to being a bounty hunter. That, contract status or not, there would always be someone who'd rather die than be taken alive. People get desperate. People act stupid. People believe so much in their ideologies that they'd kill and die for them. So we needed to be prepared for death. We had legal authority to defend ourselves—lethally, if necessary—which only served to muddy those waters.

But right now, I had to question whether that was possible, or even sustainable. In fact, with the Eco-Terror Taskforce, I went out of my way to avoid bloodshed when I could, often taking jobs where death wasn't the only option.

Tonight, though, it didn't matter. My personal moral standards had been violated, and despite a decade of seeing people die—and sometimes taking lives myself, however unwillingly—the image of Sobotka's lifeless corpse lying in the rain was hard to shake. His strange behaviour, the unknown buyer, and the answers that died on his lips before he pulled the trigger. His final moments of life were dogging me, swirling around in my mind like the rye in my glass. With every turn around the bounds of my mind they did not dissipate, nor did they grow. They just sat, festering.

I walked back to the chair, polished off the last of my drink, and told ODIN to stop the game still projecting against the wall. I had no idea what the score was. I stood in the suddenly dark room and looked back over my shoulder at the glittering lights of Sublevel 4 pulsing under the curtain of precious rainwater.

Whoever Sobotka's buyer was, how many lives were they willing to give up? And how would the great Nikos Wulf keep up?

After all, I'd spent most of my life with people's lives in my hands.

THREE

Gunfire and the thump of explosions resounded in the distance, and humidity hung around me, thickening the air until it was nearly suffocating. A moaning wind blew through the broken windowpanes, providing only the briefest respite from the heat.

The magnets in my gun barrel stopped vibrating, and I looked at the two dead men lying at my feet, their eyes glossed over by the new arrival of oblivion. I exhaled and slowly moved back, keeping an eye on the doorway down the hall that led to the final pair of combatants.

The classroom they were in was missing the back wall, and the two men—not much younger than me—were standing with their helmets off, admiring the view. Far off in the distance, fires were burning, plumes of jet-black smoke streaking towards the heavens like cracks in the glowing sky. It was still early morning here, the hot sun peeking over the fields surrounding the village, oceans of wheat and barley stretching farther than my eyes could see. It would be a beautiful place to live, if not for the rumbling engine of war trampling this part of the world.

One of the men had short black hair and the slightest hint of a beard. The other soldier's longer brown hair was blowing slightly in the breeze.

"Beautiful, isn't it?" the black-haired one said, my earpiece translating his Argentinian Spanish into perfectly accented English. "It reminds me of home. My family has a field like that, but if I were home, the sun would be to my right, and the rows of wheat would be flanked by solar strips. Also, we don't grow wheat like this; ours is stubby, engineered to grow fast in a shortened harvest season, before the floods come. This is real wheat, thick and tall. Still, it's beautiful."

"It is beautiful, I agree," the brown-haired one replied.

"How long do you think we'll be fighting?" The black-haired one asked. "The harvest would be soon, and then the holidays … We might miss it all."

"I don't know. Every time we take a town, the Brazilians and their private military company allies take a different one, and once we take that one back, they reclaim the first. It just keeps going, and nobody seems to be able to push hard enough."

"How did this happen? I mean … there's so much land. Just look at it!" The black-haired one gestured out to the rolling golden fields of unharvested wheat, craters still smouldering.

"It happened the way it's been happening since before we were born," his companion answered, solemn. "It's land—and fertile, beautiful land at that." He paused. "It's not like this every-where. Brazil is lucky. Many of the other nations have lost their good land, just like us. Nothing can grow, or grows short and weak. They were lucky enough to have it—have this—but not lucky enough to stop other people from taking it. The Northern corporations want this land now, though, so our little fight here is probably lost."

"Why don't we just share? If we all need food, why don't we work together, as people. No one needs to steal it, right?"

"I wish it were that easy …"

It felt like an immense weight, my body fighting against me as I raised my rifle. This felt wrong, like a bad dream. If only I could change it, not be here, and save myself from what I knew was coming—but then I saw it. Streaks of white smoke soared into the air, the sound of distant cracks reaching us a half second later. A lump dropped in my stomach, and I gazed out to the field, letting my rifle clatter to the floor, the noise echoing off the concrete walls of the abandoned school. The soldiers turned, saw me standing there, unarmed.

I'd seen this play out a hundred times before. I just needed to take it.

A blinding flash of white and orange light illuminated the room, followed by a wave of heat and energy that knocked me off my feet, sending me across the hall and out the window. Shattered glass, debris, and the cold hard ground came up to meet me.

I shot up in bed, a searing pain burning through my right arm up to my shoulder. I clutched my forearm, the fingers of my left hand wrapping around the cool metal and polymer of the prosthetic appendage.

Phantom pain. It was always the fucking phantom pain.

The throbbing heat began to fade while I sat in bed—the light outside my window hinting it was almost dawn—and reflected on the Brazilian tour that had cost me my arm. The physical scars had healed long ago, but the mental ones still lingered, biding their time in the quiet and unseen corners of my mind.

"Nikos?" ODIN asked. "Are you all right? Do you need a sedative?"

I slid back in bed and leaned against the cold wall, feeling the coolness on my sweat-drenched skin. For a moment, I let my fingers glide across the surface of my cybernetic arm again, pausing at the seam in my shoulder where the doctors at the Argo-funded rehab facility in Texas had amputated the mangled tissue and dead nerves. In its place, they'd attached a new limb directly to my bone and muscle tissue. Electrical impulses from the muscles and nerves went down the arm to move it, tactile sensor and motor data went back up to confirm to my brain its messages were received, and all came together in perfect symbiosis.

Almost like the real thing. Almost.

It took me a while to answer, and the words came out breathless and quiet.

"No, ODIN, thank you. I'll be okay."

I could feel him observing me from multiple points in the room, scanning my vital signs, making calculations, and diagnosing me based on my medical history—along with our personal history.

A word on ODIN. The name was an acronym that stood for "Operational Diagnostics and Insights Network." It was also an allusion to the head of the old Norse pantheon, who was associated with knowledge, healing, war, and victory, a fact

Castor swore up and down was unintentional. But I knew better. Besides, it fit.

"Which one was it this time?" His voice was warm, understanding.

"Brazil."

ODIN hummed in acknowledgment. "I thought so."

"You know me better than I know myself, ODIN," I chuckled.

I could hear the smile behind his computerized voice as he replied, "I think that's a bit of an exaggeration, but it's good for us to revisit these therapy modules from time to time."

"Lucky me." I directed a pained grin at where I knew one of ODIN's scanners was.

It had been years since I'd left the world of private military companies. So long that I had forgotten my ID number. If I ever wanted to go down to the Tempest Security headquarters and get a look at my deployment records, I wouldn't know where to start, even if those records weren't scoured with redactions. Knowing what they had us do back then, I wouldn't be surprised if they'd destroyed my records as soon as I'd handed in my resignation papers.

Strangely enough, it was Argo that sent us to Brazil. They'd signed a deal with the Brazilian government to finance the mission on their behalf, hiring Tempest to get the job done—repel the Argentinian invaders trying to annex Brazilian farmland to replace what they'd lost to climate change decades prior. In return, Argo was able to set up shop in the area, and now supplied wheat and coffee across South America, establishing and funding automated farming operations across the region that now fed millions. I remembered the trucks parked near our barracks, ready to swoop in and begin the process of rebuilding with every town we took, not stopping to worry whether the Argentinians would come and take them back—it wasn't until after the conflict ended that we learned Argo had swung a deal with the Argentinian government to maintain their hold on the country. So no matter which side "won" the war, Argo would remain. A corporation spreading, like a parasite ready to feed on healthy flesh, or a scab ready to begin healing it. Whichever side you were on, you believed one narrative or the other. I just remembered the flames and shrapnel.

"Nikos?" ODIN said, breaking my recollection. "Your heart rate is still elevated, and your breathing is irregular. May we enter a grounding exercise?"

We'd gone through these exercises and therapy sessions more times than I could count—as often involuntarily as voluntarily—but I still trusted my AI companion. One of the many gifts Castor programmed into ODIN, these modules were meant to help me adjust to civilian life at first, while also managing my PTSD after Tempest cut me off from my flesh-and-blood therapist. But ODIN was better than any shrink I'd met. It's amazing how good you get as a therapist when you essentially live in your patient's head.

I pressed the tips of my left hand to my carotid and damn him, he was right. My pulse was pounding, and I was breathing like a frightened rabbit.

"Okay," I said, resigned. "Lead on."

"Good," he replied, sounding pleased with himself. "Now, what is the first step?"

"Aren't you supposed to be the one leading the exercise?"

"Nikos …"

"Fine," I exhaled sharply. "Name five things you can see."

With my soldier's level of cleanliness and minimalist design sensibilities, there wasn't much to be seen. Every surface was pristine and orderly, with nary a speck of dust in sight, despite the fact I'd left the window open overnight and some asshole kid could've tossed something in—as was known to happen. They needed only float up close in a personal transport and hurl something messy into the gap, then speed away. But luckily for me—and them—it seemed nothing of the sort had happened.

I scanned the room, fingers still pressed to my neck. "I see a black duffle bag." My bounty hunting gear, which only counted as one item according to ODIN's rules, was on the floor next to my bed. "A tablet ..." My tablet was plugged in and charging on the desk. "A re-breather ..." A small silver mask sat next to the tablet, its two saucer-shaped filters recently replaced and ready if I ever got caught in a dust storm on the surface. "Larry ..." I smirked at the tangle of silver satin pothos that had started as a single stem a few years ago, but, thanks to ODIN's minding, had taken over the small trough which comprised my window-sill. "And I see the window. Does that count?"

"I don't see why not."

On the other side of the glass, I could see the beginnings of a sunny morning on Sublevel 4, or whatever passed for sunny down here. If I stuck my head out the window and looked up, I might be able to catch a narrow glimpse of the sky, but enough early morning sunlight bounced off glass, metal, and other reflective surfaces that the light reached at least this far down, bringing the morning's warmth with it. Already, there were transports moving past, and a window-cleaning service bot was hard at work on the building across the surface shaft.

The pounding in my veins persisted, but had noticeably slowed.

I cleared my throat. "Step two is …"

"Four things you can feel," ODIN finished.

"Right," I closed my eyes and turned my focus inward. "I feel my pulse," a dull throb in my chest now. I ran my right hand along the covers, the soft fabric sliding against my bionic digits, sensory receptors communicating with my nervous system to simulate the feeling. "And the sheets."

"Good, and what else?"

I flexed the joints of my prosthetic, small servos buzzing and whirring as the forearm moved up and down, wrist rolling and fingers fluttering. "My arm."

I inhaled deeply, breath filling my lungs as the tightness in my chest softened. Eyes still closed, I extended my arm laterally until my fingertips met a hard surface. "And the wall."

"There. Now three things you can hear."

This was easy, as a police transport zipped past my open window, sirens blaring.

"I hear the city." I smiled, inhaling deeply again. "And my breath, and …" A familiar rhythmic ticking caught my attention from the other side of the apartment. "The clock," an antique analog timepiece my mother had left for me when she passed. An item I couldn't fathom being rid of.

"I'm not surprised. It's quite loud," ODIN chuckled. "Almost done. Now two things you can smell."

I angled my head towards my armpit and quickly recoiled as I breathed in again. I'd neglected to shower after last night's job, and I had the stink to prove it. "My sweat," I croaked, and sniffed tentatively at the air again. "And coffee?"

"I started brewing it as soon as you woke up." ODIN was chipper to start the day. "You're running low on the Oregon grounds, so I've ordered more. The genuine Colombian is still too expensive."

"You beautiful bastard." I threw the sheets aside and swung my legs over the edge of the bed. "Lord knows I need it. My head is pounding."

"Which brings us to our last question." ODIN was solemn now. "What do you taste?"

I knew it was coming, but that didn't do much to dull the sting. My mouth was as dry as the Oklahoma desert and tasted rotten.

"Alcohol."

There was the briefest pause. "About that," ODIN said. "I really think you should stop drinking, particularly after work."

The thought had occurred to me—I would be lying if I said that it hadn't. But it was a habit, like many things I did, that stretched back years, and was particularly hard to break. There was something about drinking that was built into hunter culture. No matter whether you were toasting a big score, clattering glasses together with your friends, or sitting and stewing over a pint, remembering the ones that you'd lost, or the mistakes you'd made along the way. A lot of us did it. It was just a thing. And for me, it came naturally. I rarely thought about it when I was squeezed into a booth with Mack and Trapper, chatting about something stupid the former had done, or insane for the latter. We just drank.

"Well, Dad did it for long enough." I stood up, defiant. My muscles shuddered softly in the cool morning air.

"And what did that get him?" ODIN pressed.

"A one-way ticket to the aquatorium," I mumbled.

Not exactly true. My father often drank after work when I was young, but he stopped once he was ousted from Argo, and booze wasn't what destroyed his mind. It just … fell apart. Neurodegeneration. Something that happened to my grandfather and great-grandfather before him. Something that would probably happen to me too, someday. Alcohol or not. Still, it probably hadn't helped my father's condition.

"Listen, Nikos …" ODIN paused, choosing his words carefully. After a decade together, I could see where the two of us blurred. The AI mimicked my speech patterns and thought processes, so I knew what he was going to say next, and I wasn't sure how to feel about it. "I'm just a bunch of code, so I really can't do much. Honestly, I'm a glorified butler. But I know you. It's hard not to think that your nightmares and the drinking are connected somehow. Maybe you should try quitting for a while?"

A single puff escaped my lungs and I reached up, running my thumb along my lip, feeling the water-starved flesh. "I dunno, ODIN. Maybe."

"Maybe you should take the day off?"

We both knew what my answer was. It had been a few years since I'd taken any extended time for myself. I didn't count times when a metal round or particularly rough fall would put me out of action for a short stint, because I'd just spend that time in the weight room or shooting range, keeping on top of my game while also making my doctors tear their hair out. There were a few of those medical leaves on the résumé, but I'd had a run of good luck recently, nearly four months without any major injury, so I might as well keep going.

My wrist-nav buzzed on the nightstand and the small

holo-display flickered to life to reveal a waiting message from Castor. He still wanted to meet.

I wasn't going to take that distraction at this point either. There was precious little that would steal my interest from work.

The floor was ice-cold, and cool conditioned air streamed from the vents overhead, accompanied by rays of light pouring between the blinds on my bedroom window, the heat of the day kept at bay for now. Fall was encroaching on summer faster each year, it seemed, as the seasons continued to warp and stretch in the lingering throes of climate change, but down in the sublevels, temperature always lagged behind that on the surface. With this most recent heat dome gone, relief would be fleeting, but enjoyed, A/C and climate controls working overtime against the heat absorbed by the rock encasing us.

And when winter rolled around, we would be complaining about the cold. Such was the Winnipeg way.

Reflexively, I stamped my feet and shivered, my body trying to recapture some of the warmth it had left behind in bed. Whatever panic had gripped me from the nightmare had melted away, but I still felt off.

"Going back to bed is always an option," ODIN half mumbled. "It might do you some good."

"Yeah, I'm good, ODIN … thanks for asking."

"Of course, it is my duty to assist in any way I can." The AI dropped the conversational tone and kicked into his morning routine. Or at least the one that didn't involve coaching me through a mild panic attack. "It is 7:15 a.m., September 18th, 2120. The current temperature is nineteen degrees Celsius, and the daytime high will be twenty-seven. Would you like me to read out the new bounties for today?"

"Give me a minute, please." I waved my hand limply. "I just got up and haven't even had coffee yet."

I strode slowly towards the bathroom, rubbing grit from my eyes. I grabbed a neatly stacked outfit from the top drawer of my dresser. Old and worn pants with a strange stain that was likely blood—mine or someone else's; it was hard to tell—along with a black V-neck shirt that hugged my frame tightly. The shirt was a breathable smart material that was programmed to provide airflow in the heat and could seal tight to your skin in the cold to prevent heat loss. Meanwhile, the pants were a simple recycled material, similar in feel to those I wore during my Tempest days, that were comfortable, flexible, and provided good airflow. I'd learned a long time ago to trust ODIN, and today was no exception. This snap of cool weather wouldn't last much beyond morning.

In the bathroom mirror, a ragged and tired stranger stared back at me with glowing blue eyes. When they'd been real, I'd often been told they had a certain "oceanic" quality, but the cybernetic replacements seemed cold and emotionless by comparison. The lenses shimmered as they spun and adjusted to the light in the room. My eyes were another casualty to the blast that had taken my arm and scarred my mind.

A piece of shrapnel had embedded itself in the left, and the heat and pressure had mangled the right, taking much of my face with it. But thanks to cutting-edge dermal treatment, the scarred tissue had either been replaced or healed. All at Tempest's expense.

My beard was a mass of untidy whiskers, sticking out in odd directions and nowhere close to uniform, while my long dirty-blond hair was its usual brand of morning crazy. Nothing a quick shower and a trim wouldn't fix.

I stood in front of the mirror for a few moments, letting the hot steam from the shower billow out to fill the room, and watched the mirror begin to cloud, smudges of condensation obscuring what I could see of my torso reflected in the glass. The creases and curves of my musculature, covered in scattered scars. An ex-girlfriend used to run her fingers along them while we were lying in bed, but that was so long ago I barely remembered her face, let alone the touch. Now it was just me, ODIN, and a lot of work needing to be done.

Shower and grooming complete, I spent the rest of the morning drinking coffee, skimming through bounties on the display set into the table with the news playing in the background. There were a lot of cheap and easy contracts on the open market—murderers and the like, for a couple thousand credits a pop, nothing spectacular—but I kept looking. I didn't often stray into the general market, where most hunters made their money until specialist units came calling, but I liked to keep an eye out just in case. You never knew who, or what crime, had slipped through the specialist cracks to land on the open market, though long gone were the days where I'd swing in and pick off a few such contracts in an afternoon when things were slow on the Eco-Terror side.

Most of my time was spent on the Eco-Terror Taskforce's

private board. Contracts were meant only for members or select freelancers who were on a probation period pending full membership, if they could prove they had the chops for it. The board was stacked with available jobs, and the list kept getting longer as the definition of "eco-terror" crimes widened seemingly by the day. Years ago, most of the board had been contracts for dangerous anti-establishment group members, folks who felt something had been taken from them when society took a hard turn away from the old oil-guzzling, emission-spewing ideologies of the twentieth century in favour of greener ventures—and stricter penalties for non-compliance. Unable to evolve with the times, or unwilling to change, they'd lashed out by destroying solar farms, holding hostages at climate mirroring facilities, and the like. Then at some point it flipped, and contracts were now primarily aimed at protecting the operations—and more importantly, the interests—of the corporations who held back climate disaster.

Chief among them: Argo.

Scrolling through the available eco-terror jobs, it was much more of the latter. People violating agriculture regulations, stealing and reselling outdated augments, trafficking modded tech, even a few wanted for tampering with the climate mitigation measures on the surface. Nothing special. But the work would need to be done by somebody, just not me. Not today.

I also noticed nothing that hinted at Sobotka's mystery buyer from last night.

But eventually something would catch my eye. Without a private bounty popping into my inbox, it needed to. I would never say it out loud, but I was feeling as bad as I looked, though that didn't mean I was going to stop any time soon.

Meanwhile, the local news blurred by on the apartment's sound system, to which I was only half paying attention. The big news of the day was in Ottawa. The prime minister was embroiled in a scandal involving Vertex Coms—a megacorp out of Turkey that had started as a media conglomerate—and was being urged strongly to resign. Her family, as it turned out, owned part of Vertex, so I wasn't remotely surprised.

Every politician was taking money from a megacorporation. If it wasn't Vertex it was Ravencrest, or Loki Security, or Typhoon Navigations, or any other number of big players. Though I'm sure if she were taking money from Argo, the national newscasters would change their tune. Everyone likes a homegrown name.

In truth, the government basically *was* Argo at this point. Almost every service the feds and provinces offered was now filtered through a subsidiary of the corporation. Even the hospitals.

I was completely lost in thought when ODIN finally chimed in.

"Uh, Nikos, I believe your toast is burn—"

"Shit!" I jumped up so fast that the chair toppled over, and I almost tripped on the table leg. I was quick enough to stop my breakfast from turning to charcoal, but not quick enough to stop the smoke detector from going off. The sublevel-harvested eggs and synth-bacon turned out much better, so I was able to salvage part of the meal. "I thought you said you had that!"

ODIN scoffed. "I didn't think I had to monitor the toaster for a grown man."

Okay, he wasn't exactly wrong.

Righting the overturned chair and sitting down with my

breakfast, I flipped to my personal inbox and found what I had been hoping for.

"How about this one, bud?" I said, tapping the bounty to bring up the details. "Private bounty. Maxwell Van Buren, sought for petty theft, civil disobedience, and destruction of corporate property." If ODIN wanted me to have a quiet evening, then this would be a good compromise. I got to work, while he got the fact I probably wouldn't be shot at.

ODIN hummed quietly. "Seems fine to me. But what's put it on our desk, so to speak? There's nothing about this young man that screams our usual targets. Should probably be something open to the Eco-Terror taskforce, not marked out just for us."

Had to admit, he was right.

The first two charges on Van Buren's record were petty crimes, nothing even close to what put a person's name on the Bounty List, but the third one—destruction of corporate property—was an automatic bounty. A relatively new offence, to say that destruction of corporate property was a controversial topic would be an understatement. The legislation had been put through in secret, provisions snuck into a larger omnibus bill that was hidden from public scrutiny. It didn't get a public reading, the debate was truncated, and the vote held in private. But beyond the scummy process, what got people really riled up was its use. Proponents argued it was a provision meant to ensure that valuable corporate property wasn't destroyed by disgruntled employees or to protect small businesses from violent riots, but in practice, it had been something else entirely. It was a hammer swung at anti-establishment protesters, where even cracking a window, or scuffing the steps of a building, meant the threat of having a bounty hunter tracking you down in the dead of night.

Ultimately, though, most corporations, like Argo, had their hands so deep into the ecological and climate protection cookie jar that one could not exist without the other. Any act that could damage the functioning—or more crucially, the bottom line—of a corporation engaging in climate change negation and control work was seen as an attack on the climate infrastructure itself, bringing it onto the Eco-Terror table where contracts for burning crops and destroying solar farms sat.

I didn't like it, but looking at Van Buren, I knew the charge wouldn't amount to much. He was a young guy from Sublevel 2 who'd gotten caught up in a protest last night against a plan for Argo to take over anti-desertification efforts in Alberta. The fact it had a bounty attached was moronic, but the legislation was clear. Destruction of corporate property is automatically worthy of a bounty. Pushed right through. The fact it was private, and the Bounty Commission had sent to me directly, probably meant his parents had money and wanted this handled quietly, and the Commission wanted someone they trusted to handle it that way. It would be easy credits and a good excuse to spend a night wandering around Sublevel 2, so I wouldn't complain.

It still didn't explain why it had come to me, because ODIN was right. This wasn't something you put your top hunters on.

Then I checked the conditions.

First up, my suspicions were confirmed, as under the "alive-only" status was a short message stating that the young man's parents had been in contact with the Commission and agreed to cooperate if the bounty was handled privately, and that the capture could take place at the family home this evening. Simple enough. Probably some wannabe-Ivories looking to climb the social ladder. But under that was evidence—a lot of evidence.

Chat logs turned over by his parents, and posts from forums and social accounts traced back to Maxwell, all uttering threats to Argo, the city, bounty hunters, and a host of other corporations. Specific threats. The thing that caught my attention, though, was the final line: *Anti-Establishment/Eco-Terror affiliations: Unknown (See image).*

That image in question was a crudely etched green emblem on a jacket Maxwell had been wearing the day of the protest. The same one I'd seen on the two guards from last night.

A falling star trailed by curving and cutting lines.

Bingo.

With a smirk, I confirmed my claim and leaned back, deftly balancing my chair on its rear legs.

"The only issue is time," I said. "Any idea how to kill an afternoon?"

FOUR

Thank God for air conditioning.

That was my only thought as I wove my way down the crowded streets of Sublevel 3, popping in and out of various shops, checking on what new wares the various boutiques had to offer. Not for the purpose of buying anything, but rather to enjoy the cool breeze from fans and A/C units flowing out of the open-front shops.

Although fall was certainly on its way, and the sublevels were always slow to match the seasonal temperatures enjoyed on the surface, the last few days had been especially bad. The rain last night had been a welcome change, as the final heat dome of the summer had finally broken over western Canada, ushering in the slow procession to cooler temperatures that would also be felt down below; but here on Sublevel 3, which served as an economic hub—dubbed the New Exchange District—there was always a crowd, which meant less air circulation, which meant more heat.

And I hated the heat.

The memory of my nightmare still clung to my body, sweat beading at my temples and soaking my back between the shoulder blades. Brazil had been its own kind of hell, disrupted only by the loss of my arm and eyes, which earned me a brief stay at a U.S. recovery centre, but after that I was back to the heat, setting boots on the ground in Mexico.

Maybe that would be the next nightmare.

I'd made good on my promise to ODIN about taking the day off, making my way up to Sublevel 3 to browse, have a late lunch, and generally just get out of the apartment for a few hours. If not, I'd probably be kneeling on the apartment floor, furniture pushed to the outer walls, firearms in pieces and splayed across the ground around me in a well-organized system as I set about cleaning the parts and checking them over before reassembling the weapons all over again. It was tedious work, but worth it. I'd had too many experiences with firearms failing at the worst possible moment—Mexico came to mind again, and the Tempest-issued rifles that sputtered and died in one of the many sandstorms that kicked up daily.

But, to be fair, it would be the second time I'd cleaned my weapons in the past forty-eight hours, so it would be ultimately pointless.

No, instead of that, I was currently standing in a warmly lit jewelry store, eyes dancing across rings and bracelets, countless glittering gemstones catching the soft orange glow to scatter colour across the room. They were very nice.

"They're all synthetic," ODIN chimed in through the earpiece I used as my comms, admiring the gems using our shared vision. "But you wouldn't expect so, based on the prices."

"Are you a gemologist now?" I mumbled in response, smirking.

There was a brief pause as my companion considered. For all intents and purposes, he could very well be an expert in gemstones. It would only take a few minutes for him to scour the net for all available information, but realistically he wouldn't. It wasn't something ODIN was interested in.

Finally, ODIN replied, "I could be if you wanted, but I don't see you needing my expert opinion on engagement rings anytime soon. I'll catalogue it for later."

"Ouch, catalogue that in the list of times you've hurt my feelings, pal," I scoffed, leaning back to glance around the rest of the shop. It wouldn't surprise me if most of the shop's stock was synthetic. Gemstones of any size, colour, or cut had fallen out of favour nearly a century ago, as the ecological and human impacts of mining operations became too much for consumer sensibilities of the time, and cultural beliefs around rings changed. "Besides, I know where the real gemstones are."

"Hmm." ODIN paused again, considering. "The jeweller?"

"Bingo."

It hadn't taken long for me to notice. The main desk, located at the back of the shop, doubled as a small display case with a payment terminal located behind. While you could process a payment anywhere in the shop with mobile terminals, this place had one hardwired into the desk, meaning you had to go back there, right in view of at least three cameras, to make any transaction. But what tipped me off was the jeweller, who hadn't bothered to speak to any of the six patrons in his shop. Rather, he was pacing around the rear desk, never stepping more than four paces away, conveniently when someone walked within his range. Odds were all the necklaces, brooches, rings, and bracelets in those big cases at the back were the real deal.

"Not that the average person would notice," ODIN mumbled in my ear. "They are very convincing fakes."

"Weren't you supposed to be helping me choose a lunch spot?" I asked, turning back to the heavily overpriced engagement rings, trying to look like I had a reason to buy one and wasn't just killing time. "Maybe you'd have found one instead of scanning gemstones through my eyes."

ODIN sighed. "Fine … just thought we were having a nice day browsing."

"We are. I'm just hungry."

"Go out the front and turn right. Two hundred metres, you'll hang a left, which brings you into the food concourse, there's a nice bánh mì deli you've never eaten at before. Do you like the sound of that?"

I smiled, put my hands in my pockets, and turned around, heading towards the front of the shop. "I certainly do, ODIN, old pal. And don't worry, we can keep browsing after."

Happy with the agreement, ODIN hummed contently in reply. It was only natural for him to enjoy these little jaunts around the city, particularly to places we rarely went. Since his entire being was effectively built around a complex machine-learning algorithm, new experiences and stimuli were the ideal way for him to refine himself, creating an exponentially larger knowledge base to draw from when the need arose.

Plus, I honestly thought he enjoyed window shopping.

Stepping out into the street of the open-air mall, I was blasted by a swell of hot air, the raucous noise of urban chaos no longer drowned out by white noise emitters in the shop. Sublevel 3 was always busy, being a prime meeting place between the more residential level of Sublevel 2 above, and the more metropolitan Sublevel 4 below; it was also a major commerce hub, filled with high-priced clothing stores, boutique shops, specialty grocers, and a smattering of luxury transport dealerships, all collected into clusters of open-air markets and malls. It attracted the wealthy, semi-wealthy, and wannabe-wealthy of Winnipeg, who could rub shoulders and window-shop for things the average person couldn't afford.

This shopping centre was a few blocks from the nearest surface shaft, which only exacerbated the issue of temperature, meaning air flow was stymied. Along with that, the climate mirroring and climate control measures used across the city to make life outside comfortable were conspicuously missing in these open-air malls, meaning the only way to get relief from sweltering heat in the summer months and frigid cold in the winter was to pop in and out of shops, just like I was doing.

More traffic. More potential sales.

But it was just a coincidence, right?

As I continued down the street, eyes flicking between faces, checking what people were holding, I began to hear a noise over the din of Sublevel 3 life. A familiar jingle I'd heard throughout my life, which grew louder as I approached a holo-display positioned right outside an aug clinic. The familiar tones of the Argo corporate jingle—the first three notes of which played every time I entered my apartment and ODIN came online—now played in full over the tail end of an ad for Argo's Generation 4 Nu-Breathe Artificial Lungs.

Once that finished, another immediately fired up, showing

a distressed-looking middle-aged woman being consoled by someone who appeared to be her daughter. The same peppy narrator returned. "Experiencing bouts of memory loss? Finding yourself losing the dexterity and mobility you used to enjoy? Preventing cognitive decline and improving neurological functioning is easier than ever with the IR-9 Neuro-Enhancer, the newest neural augment from your friends at Argo. Ask your local augmentation specialist today!"

As the advertisement faded, I let out a small snort, hardly convinced by the sales pitch. Something about having a chip lodged in my brain, playing with the signals in my squishy grey matter, didn't sound appealing. The science was astounding, of course. Neural augments had initially been developed to treat degenerative neurological conditions like Alzheimer's and Parkinson's in the aging population, and once they'd proven successful, and scientists realized they essentially held the keys to unlock our minds, innovations flooded the market. Now we had neural augs to enhance focus, to improve VR experiences, to pair with communication tech in wrist-navs, to treat concussions and cancer. The list went on. They were ubiquitous, but that didn't mean I had to believe the hype.

Call me old-fashioned, but I was wary of such heavy-handed mods, an attitude I'd undoubtedly inherited from my father, though I knew I was in the minority.

I was about to turn away from the holo-display and move into the crowd, but was met with a flash as the display cut to a rolling news broadcast, showing footage of … me?

"Stunning footage is gaining traction on social feeds today, stemming from a high-octane chase last night on Sublevel 11," the broadcaster said over jittery smart-spec and ocular cache footage of me, in hot pursuit of Ivan Sobotka through the market last night. One person caught the moment Sobotka took off, footage showing me standing between the two unconscious guards, slightly crouched and ready to go after my target, while another captured the moment Sobotka hurdled the table, before panning back to follow me as I slid under it and kept the pursuit going. "The CBC has confirmed the hunter shown is Winnipeg's top bounty hunter, Nikos Wulf.

"While the conclusion of the pursuit was not captured, Bounty Board records do indicate Wulf was awarded forty thousand credits for the contract, and sources within the coroner's office confirm the target, who will remain anonymous, is deceased. We are not able to confirm cause of death at this time."

Not that it matters, I thought. Bounty hunters had authorization to defend themselves with deadly force when justified, and it would be hard to argue against that when Sobotka's guards had swung at me, and the man himself was carrying a weapon. My only wish was that Sobotka were still alive.

"Whoa!" a small voice erupted from below me, and I looked down to see a small cluster of kids, probably no older than eleven or twelve, eyes locked on the amateur footage. The speaker was the smallest of the four, standing slack-jawed, hand gripping the sleeve of one of his companions who—judging by appearance—was probably his sister. Both were dressed in breathable mesh tops, meant to wick away sweat, and had identical shaved spots on their heads where I could see a small green light blinking from prism-shaped neural augments. Same clothes, same facial structure, definitely family.

The sister turned to look at her brother, face pulled into a soft, understanding gaze. "I know, right? He's so cool."

"Yeah!" the brother replied, with a slight hop of excitement. "Did you see how quickly he dropped those goons? And when that guy threw that person at him?"

"He just flipped over and kept going like it was nothing …" another boy said. He was short, with curly black hair, and his eyes were still glued to the footage on display. "How do you think he does it?"

"Probably some kind of enhancements," the sister said as she ran her fingers along the smooth surface of her augment. "All the hunters have them. I bet he has so many neural augs his brain is like a big computer."

"Nuh-uh!" the fourth kid chimed in. She was the tallest, with bright blue eyes that held all the confidence she could drum up in her little body. "My brother says Nikos Wulf only has an augmented arm. The rest is one hundred percent human! He's just *that* good at being a bounty hunter."

The curly-haired boy turned to her, his face screwed up in confusion. "Well, I heard he's got no augments at all. Somewhere on the net said he was trained by Argo to be a bounty hunter."

With that, the blue-eyed girl stamped her feet, fists balled angrily, and began to argue with the curly-haired boy, contending that I was just born skilled at hunting, and didn't need any artificial help, while he maintained the opinion that I was made to be this way. Meanwhile, I watched the young boy tug on his sister's sleeve, stealing her attention fully away from the footage of a bounty hunter tearing through a market kilometres below them.

"Do … do you think I could be like him someday?" He pointed at the screen, which was now fading into a different story.

His sister only smiled. "Of course you can."

"You going to tell them it's you?" ODIN chimed in with an audible smirk.

"No," I mumbled in reply. "Best not give them that satisfaction. It'll only lead them in the wrong direction."

Besides, I'd worked hard to make my mask the real face of Nikos Wulf. No need to toss that aside for a few minutes of glory, and maybe a few photos shared on social feeds.

I turned away from the kids, stealing one last glance at the young boy. Whatever his sister had said next was making him smile with the kind of glee only a child can feel. But truthfully, it twisted my stomach into a knot.

Bounty hunting was a dangerous and messy profession, one that required a special kind of person to succeed in it. But that didn't mean only particular, special individuals were allowed to try.

It also meant hunters did it for different reasons.

If I were like Centurion—an English hunter and friend who was all flash and flair—I would've probably tousled the one kid's hair, introduced myself, posed for pictures, and made sure they'd followed me on socials and one of the many Bounty Board trackers.

One of the benefits of bounty hunting being a public system in Canada was that everyone had access to the Bounty Board— for better or for worse—and with it, a community of supporters, and even admirers, had grown up around the industry. Originally meant for transparency, so you could know how many hunters there were, how much they were making, what amount of public funds were being pumped into the industry for contracts, and to track the actual impact of bounty hunting in your community, all the public information about the bounty hunting system was repackaged, commodified, and given the same treatment athletes and sports leagues had been getting for centuries. Except instead of scoring goals for a hockey team, we were tracking and catching criminals.

People like Centurion embraced it, leaning into their celebrity status for all it brought—hell, more than a few bounty hunters had become reality-show stars—but then there were people like me. Those of us who hated the idea someone could look at what we were doing as something other than a necessary vocation, and one that wasn't very nice. People died, on both sides of the coin, and to me, that wasn't something to celebrate.

Kids like the ones I'd just seen often became like the bounty snatcher I'd met last night, and while on some level I was happy there were people willing to take up the job, I couldn't square the reasons why some did it.

Besides, wouldn't celebrating people who carry guns cause more harm than good? As I walked away from the kids, who took off down the street pretending to be me, I wasn't quite sure. Going out of my way not to take lives was my style. It's what made me sure I was doing the right thing every time I stepped out the door. Despite the fact bounty hunters had kill authorization, able to act in self-defence, even when that meant taking a life in the process, it was something I tried to avoid.

We didn't carry guns to be vigilante gunslingers in some Wild West crusade against lawlessness. We were state-sanctioned criminal justice agents in a democratized public safety system. I got into this job so I could help people, not put holes in their chests and cash a cheque. Like every major city in the world, Winnipeg was far from safe, but I wanted to do my part to change that, to make sure every person in the sublevels, no matter who they were, knew that if someone wronged them or they needed help, someone was on their side, ready to lend a hand.

But maybe there were fewer hunters like me, and more like that kid from last night. I chewed on that thought as I waited in line at the bánh mì place.

Nestled into a cavernous alcove was the food court, a raised platform that curved around the outside wall of the space. The air was thick with scents wafting out to chase the light bleeding from glowing displays, signage overhead advertising the various food vendors, large and small. Along the rim of the raised section was a long counter, with equally spaced stools for people to sit, arranged in clusters of three, each divided by small planters built directly into the counter. Food in hand, I took a seat there, overlooking a mass of cluttered tables and people milling about, stopping their day's shopping to grab a bite to eat. As I usually did, I picked the spot closest to the street, where I could easily keep an eye on the crowd to my right and the folks ahead, close enough to respond to either if necessary.

Through the cacophony of sights, sounds, and scents, my eyes drifted from person to person, table to table, unable to turn my brain completely off to enjoy the day—sorry, ODIN. Years of military service, then over a decade as a bounty hunter, meant I was just wired this way.

It didn't take long for this situational awareness to ping on something.

Midway through my meal, movement caught my eye. A signal in the noise. There was a woman, middling height, long black hair shorn on the left side to leave room for a series of serious neural augments that blinked purple—matching the glowing strip of purple LEDs around her jacket collar. The complicated mass of hardware arrayed across her scalp was definitely above and beyond what a standard civilian would normally have. Typically someone with a neural augment had one or two, but this woman had a half-dozen or more packed onto the side of her head.

There was nothing about her appearance that would normally give me pause. Outfits rarely did, unless they were clearly bearing signs of an anti-establishment group—like the HRF patches of the Human Reclamation Front, or long blades of wheat sported by the Plainswalkers. What caught my eye was her movement. It didn't match the leisurely pace of those around her. Actually, she was walking too slow. Hands in her pockets, feigning a comfortable, relaxed gait, she was simultaneously too aware, head flicking around to check her surroundings

She looked like a person up to no good, trying to make sure she wasn't seen doing whatever she was about to do, and her eyes confirmed this. With a quick zip, my eyes zoomed in so I could see magenta irises hidden behind her thin sunglasses, pupils small as pinheads, focused, trying to pierce through all the visual stimuli she was getting to ensure she saw everything she needed to.

Then she hung a sharp right and cut down a small alleyway between two buildings.

ODIN sighed. "Please don't."

"I have to," I replied through a grin. "Y'know, out of curiosity."

Another sigh from ODIN and I was up. Affecting an appropriate calm demeanour, I weaved through the crowd of people lined up at the various vendors in the food court and quickly balled up the wrapper that had held my lunch. Without breaking stride, I tossed the ball towards a paper recycler, and it bounced of the rim and down into the receptacle, earning a happy chime from the small bot.

Cutting across the street, I entered the same alley the woman had disappeared down, now slowing my pace. As I crept along, mindful of the debris at my feet, the street noise dimmed slowly, until all I heard was the whir of climate mirroring emitter above and the idle whistle of wind fans collecting scattered energy.

ODIN returned with a whisper.

"I thought we were taking the day off."

"Yeah, and we are," I said. "I didn't see a contract for this on my ledger. Did you?"

Another sigh. "No. But that doesn't mean we have to keep throwing ourselves into situations like this."

"I'm just taking a look. We'll be back to browsing in no time."

The alley ended in a small open courtyard. There were scattered benches and tables where employees would presumably take their breaks throughout the day to puff on vaporizers and chat, and in the centre was a sad and very poorly maintained garden. It rose half a metre out of the metal and stone floor of the sublevel, and while the grass seemed to be doing all right, the oddly spaced flowers were stubs, overgrown by rampant weeds.

Beside the garden was the woman with the magenta collar, joined by four other people.

It didn't take long to determine they were members of the same anti-establishment group: NetDreamers. They all had a similar look: clothes covered in strips of glowing purple LEDs, heads shaved in places where neural augments poked out from their skin, gaunt frames that were far more used to lying in VR rigs, and eyes ringed with dark circles after hours spent hooked directly into the net, staying up day and night while poking around for new ways to cash in. It was impossible not to notice, especially now that they were clustered together. This realization made the woman—who was now talking very animatedly to her fellows—even more obvious, though none of them noticed the figure crouched in the alley, watching. Neither she nor any of her friends were used to being outside.

I'd had run-ins with the NetDreamers on more than one occasion, but those were still exceptionally rare. Their group was a hacker collective, spending more time in the digital world than the real one, rarely doing anything to find themselves on the Eco-Terror Taskforce's radar. Typically, NetDreamer activity was under the watchful eye of the Bounty Commission's cybersecurity unit, unless they needed a bit of help from the other sections of the Bounty Commission for special cases.

Once, years ago, a member of the group had broken into one of Winnipeg's gardening systems that maintained the green roofs on the surface, meant to consume UV radiation before it reached the street, cooling off the city while it munched on CO_2 He'd used it as a back door to hook into the internal system of a surface condo complex, en route to a bank located on the building's main floor for a quick fraud job. He'd taken the money and gotten out. But while he left no trace on the bank systems and had nothing to tie him to the crime, he hadn't closed the hole he'd made in the gardening system, which left some of the horticulture drones offline, and made for a few unhappy bushes.

The justification behind the bounty against him was that he'd threatened local ecology, so I got tossed the contract for a quick cleanup job. When I kicked in his apartment door, the guy put up no fight, just asked to disconnect from his devices properly before I took him to the Bounty Commission outpost for processing. NetDreamers weren't fighters—usually.

I scanned the area, making sure to stay hidden from view, crouched low and pressed against the wall to my right. Aside from the five NetDreamers, whose conversation was quickly devolving into an argument, with flailing arms and barely contained hysteria, there was nobody else in the courtyard. No employees, no random passersby coming from one of the other alleys to find a spot to sit, smoke, or whatever else; in other words, no backup for this group of upstanding young individuals.

"Nikos?" ODIN whispered. "We've looked, now can we go?"

I waved my hand at the invisible presence of ODIN. "Hold on," I said. "Now they've got my interest piqued. NetDreamers almost never gather in person, right? I want to know what they're up to. I'm going to go talk to them."

"Why?"

"Because that's what people do. We talk. They don't know who I am or what I want. You never know, maybe they need help. What's the worst that could happen?"

There was a brief pause as ODIN considered—or calculated. "Do you want me to answer that question?"

My answer was simple. I stood, dusted off my pants, and strolled into the courtyard, hands in my pockets as I angled towards the NetDreamers.

"Hey!" I called out, hand raised. "I think I got a little turned around. Can any of you tell me where the nearest electronics shop is?" I raised my wrist-nav and pointed to it. "This thing is on the fritz again and really need it fixed. Could've sworn it said there was one ar—"

"And why the fuck would you think we could help you?" spat the woman I had followed. "What do we look like? A fucking navigation service?"

I snickered, feigning humour. "Clearly not. You folks just look pretty tech-inclined."

One of the others spoke next. They were wearing a very thin mesh top, under which I could see exposed augments jutting from their skin, likely connected to synthetic lungs, maybe even an augmented stomach—often NetDreamers altered their organs to facilitate longer time spent skimming through the net, bypassing pesky bodily functions. They also had a long, silver neural augment running down the middle of their scalp like a metal mohawk, framed by fine blue hair, and spoke with a hoarse, weak voice.

"Well, we'd better be. We're NetDreamers." They stepped forward, in front of the woman, who had turned away slightly and now peered back at me with a wary, magenta-toned side-eye.

In response, I smiled, hands held up in a placating gesture. "Oh, I know that." This snapped the other three to attention, while I continued. "I also know that you …" I pointed at the woman with magenta eyes, "are really bad at looking inconspicuous. What's your name? Maybe I can help you out."

The woman turned further away, now looking back at me over her shoulder. She took up a defensive stance, arms crossed, unconsciously covering her vitals.

"Nikos," ODIN started, wary. "Something's wrong."

It only took a moment, all the NetDreamers' eyes flashing as their neural augments went to work.

"He's a fucking bounty hunter!" one of the others yelled, as he pointed at me with a wavering finger, yellow eyes wide. "He's *the* bounty hunter. The one from last night, the top one. He killed that Sobotka guy. He's got a hunter ID badge on his wrist-nav!"

Ah, shit. Of course they would hack me. So much for doing this quietly and anonymously.

Again, my hands went up, showing I was unarmed. "Hey, I'm not here as a bounty hunter, I don't have a contract for any of you. I'm just trying to figure out if I can help you."

In unison, four of the five NetDreamers turned, taking on aggressive stances with fists balled, shoulders squared, and at least one pulled a knife. The only one not to turn was the woman with magenta eyes, who seemed to shrink away, moving closer towards her friends for safety, long strands of slate-black hair falling over her face. Still, she kept her gaze on me, with a soft purple glow shining from the shadow that enveloped her face.

"Well," said ODIN quietly. "What's that thing they used to say about curiosity and cats?"

A faint but shrill sound cut through the muffled quiet in the alley, causing everyone to freeze. It was a whoosh, or pulse, like small transport engines firing in the distance, followed by a whistle as whatever had made the sound began to fall.

Its impact in the courtyard caused the ground beneath our feet to tremble slightly, and the NetDreamers wheeled around to face the source of the noise behind them. Slowly rising to full height was an armoured hunter, tall and lithe, but strong, and the very last person I'd expected to see. Dressed head to toe in thick silver plates that mimicked medieval plate armour—but which I knew were made of an extremely light but ultradurable Argite alloy that did nothing to hamper her mobility—Valkyrie stood tall, chest flared, light glinting off the burnished armour surface as she stared down at the group in front of her. The NetDreamers stood stock-still as they watched the two small cylinders behind her shoulders fold down like wings and lock back into place, the sound of rushing air dissipating to leave us in silence. Valkyrie slowly scanned them, sharp eyes hidden behind a bright yellow, T-shaped visor, set within a round, silver helmet with small fins that rimmed the crown of her head.

Her masked face hid all emotion, but when her eyes landed on me, there was a slight, nearly imperceptible nod.

One that screamed "I've got this."

With a confident, powerful stride, Valkyrie moved towards the group and the fight began. Three of the NetDreamers made a beeline to meet the armoured hunter. The first swung a wild haymaker left that Valkyrie met with her forearm, spinning to wrap up the attacker's arm with hers before she landed a heavy right cross. Her fist met his face with a loud crack, and the NetDreamer crumpled to the ground. Valkyrie released him before wheeling her right elbow around towards the next attacker. Another crack echoed throughout the enclosed courtyard as Valkyrie slipped her strike through a pitiful defence by the woman attacking her and drove her elbow right into the woman's cheek. The impact rippled through her skull, throwing her hair in all directions, and the second attacker was down.

The third was the man with the knife, thinner than the

rest. I dived for him, shoving past magenta-eyes and the other NetDreamer who hadn't joined the fray, but I wasn't fast enough to catch the guy before Valkyrie got there. The knife went forward, and Valkyrie twisted, blade stabbing nothing but air. With military precision, Valkyrie wrapped her hand around his and snapped the guy's wrist to the side, slapping the knife away. With a quick turn back, she seized him by the throat, the NetDreamer's eyes going wide as he probably began to reconsider his life choices, waiting for what came next.

Punctuated by a shrill ping, Valkyrie produced a blade of her own that jutted from her armoured fist, just above her knuckles, and hurled her fist towards the NetDreamer's face.

A loud crack rang out, followed by silence broken only by the sound of struggling, and metal grating against metal. I hadn't been fast enough to separate the two, but I'd been able to catch Valkyrie's arm before she put a blade into the guy's eye. My cybernetic fist was vice-like, clamped down on Valkyrie's forearm, our faces centimetres apart as I looked through her visor, able to catch a faint glimpse of two eyes, not focused on me, but fully aware I was there.

"Maria. This is a street fight, not a firefight," I bit out through clenched teeth. She was exceptionally strong, stronger than I remembered her ever being.

She took the hint, blade retracting back into her glove. Satisfied, I let go.

Fist met face with a resounding crack, and the third NetDreamer joined his friends on the sublevel floor. Unconscious, but at least not stabbed.

"Whew," I said. "That was—"

The words died in my mouth as Maria shoved past me, her

shoulder clipping mine, a shot of pain reminding me how thick her armour was. Without sparing a glance in my direction, she approached the magenta-eyed woman, but not before her gaze suddenly snapped towards the other conscious NetDreamer, who was rooted in place, eyes flicking between their friend and the bounty hunter who had just laid waste to their group.

Valkyrie growled, her voice filtered and projected through external speakers in her helmet. "Leave. Now."

Not needing any more encouragement, the NetDreamer took two meek, stumbling steps back before turning to run across the courtyard. Their footsteps on the stone and metal sublevel floor echoed off the high walls surrounding us until they were long out of sight. Meanwhile, Valkyrie's target tried to stand tall, arms crossed over her chest again, chin held high, attempting to look down at the hunter who'd just beat up her companions like they were made of paper. Despite her clenched jaw, muscles visibly taut, and her tough persona, the remaining NetDreamer was trembling slightly, angled a bit away from Valkyrie, betraying her fear.

Still, she held on.

But Valkyrie wasn't buying it.

"Bo Richot, my name is Maria Lindgren, and I am the bounty hunter assigned to your case," she stated. "My licence number is 27441877. You are wanted for illicit sale of malicious software and tampering with corporate property. Please …"

Her voice trailed off as tears began streaming down Bo's face. Whatever veneer of confidence she'd tried to maintain melted away, and the NetDreamer seemed to shrink before our eyes.

Maria sighed, and continued, gentler this time. "Please put your hands behind your back. A bounty retrieval crew has been called, along with EMTs, but I'd like to treat your friends. Can I trust you to sit there …" she pointed to the stone edge of the garden, "while I work? I don't want to have to chase you, and trust me, you won't get away. I've also got him here now." She jabbed a thumb in my direction. "And I can guess you know who he is."

Bo nodded. "Yes … to all of that," and moved towards the garden. She didn't resist as Maria snapped the cuffs on her and sat her down without a word.

While Bo waited quietly, Maria stepped back, finally turned to me, and slowly reached up to unlatch and remove her helmet. A sheet of short silvery hair cascaded down to just above her shoulders, and Maria shook her head, letting the strands catch the light, shining a faint pearlescent blue, before she finally looked at me with amber eyes I hadn't seen in years.

A few beats passed before I spoke. "That hair doesn't look like standard regulation. Even for a PMC."

"Two years since I've seen you," Maria replied, "and that's the first thing you say to me?"

I smirked. "Well, thought it was going to be four. Don't Ironways contracts run that long?"

"Ironways got bought out and they gave us the chance to walk away. Anyone who didn't want to stick around could go, so I left." Her voice was calm, and she finally cracked a smile. "Now Corporal Maria Lindgren is back to being Valkyrie."

Maria was one of my oldest bounty hunting friends, third only to Mack and his older brother, Trapper. When I'd returned to the city after my tours with Tempest and began hunting, Jaeger took me under his wing, and soon after that Mack and Maria came along. The three of us were entirely more than the old man had bargained for: idealistic, headstrong, and extremely reckless. Over the years, much of the first was tempered, as we all began to realize the gravity of what we were doing, but Maria was still headstrong, and we all still had a bit of a reckless streak.

It was the latter two traits that got Maria involved with Ironways.

Maria was one of the best, and had even challenged me for a spot at the top of the Bounty Board, but sometimes even the best need a change. For Maria, that change was joining a PMC.

The night she told us hadn't ended particularly well. We all sat in a private booth at Haven, the hunter-only bar on Sublevel 5, sharing drinks after a long night out on contracts.

But that night, the energy in the bar made it feel like anything but its namesake.

It was the four of us: Mack, Jaeger, Maria, and me. We all knew Maria was getting restless with the hustle of Winnipeg bounty hunting. She was clearing contracts left and right, but it never felt like enough, and that night the conversation was no different. Maria brought up how meaningless the work seemed, how burnt out she felt following the same cycles, facing the same groups, for the same reasons. Jaeger told her she needed to find a hobby, Mack said she needed a vacation, and I told her to put her head down and work through it. Then she dropped a bomb.

"I joined up with Ironways. I deploy to Africa in two weeks."

I thought Jaeger was going to keel over from a heart attack from all the yelling he did, and Mack was like the placating parent, working hard to calm Jaeger but also reason with Maria. Their opposition only made her dig her heels in deeper.

I'll give her credit: she didn't budge, not one iota—and with each word from Mack and Jaeger, she became more and more insistent. Meanwhile, I didn't say a word, because I knew it wouldn't help. Besides, I understood. I'd been there before, and wasn't about to try to change her mind.

Maria stormed out just as Trapper arrived, finding the old man fuming and his little brother frantic, and it was one of the few times I'd seen Trapper display an emotion that was not stoic indifference.

That had been two years ago, and now Valkyrie had come home.

"They haven't reinstated you to a task force or specialized unit?" I asked.

"No," Maria replied, not looking at me as she crouched next to one of the still-unconscious NetDreamers and began treating his injuries. "I'm on probation. General contract pool for thirty days until they're certain I'll stick around, then they'll reassign me. I guess they want to penalize hunters for coming and going. Maybe save themselves the paperwork. Got told I had a spot on the serial crime unit if I wanted, and was also asked if I wanted back on the anti-establishment prevention beat, which ..." she indicated to Bo and the three unconscious NetDreamers lying around us, groaning quietly in pain, "I seem to be doing anyway."

She turned back to the man she was tending to. With one hand prodding his face to check the damage, she produced a small medic kit from her utility belt with the other and popped it open. "Seems like a fracture of the zygoma ..." Faster than I could register, Maria flipped through various medical implements, finally settling on one that I knew well. A small pen-sized device that helped assess skeletal and soft tissue damage. One used on me more times than I could remember. The device flared on with a click, bright blue light radiating from the end, and as Maria swept the cool blue beam over the unconscious man's face, her expression screwed up into a look of concentration, now seeing the extent of the damage. "Hmm … I got this one good. Crack runs up from the zygoma and into the orbit, while the main damage is a horizontal break that follows the curve of his cheek, going from the maxilla, all the way to the temporal bone, which …" she studied the spot for a second. "Yeah, the augment he's got there seems to still be in place."

I snorted quietly. "And in English, for the rest of us?"

"I broke his face," Maria replied, turning to give me a smirk. "Cracked his cheekbone and part of his eye socket."

"Nasty." I placed my hands back in my pockets and sat on the garden's edge, Maria's amber gaze following me the whole way. It had been a while for both of us, so she was probably assessing me too. Trying to see whether anything had changed over the past two years.

"Nicer than what would've happened if you hadn't stopped me," she said, attention back to her patient.

With paramedics on the way, along with the bounty retrieval crew coming to snag Bo—her companions would be booked on "assaulting a peacekeeper" charges and processed once they were treated at the hospital—there wasn't much that Maria *had* to do. She was a trained medic, though, having gotten a solid medical education from her father, who was a well-known trauma doctor in the city, so this was in her nature.

Maria was a tough hunter, working a dangerous beat before

she'd taken off for Ironways, but her empathy towards people in the city never took a back seat. To her, keeping the peace and protecting the public went beyond simply roughing up bad guys like some armour-clad superhero, to being able to treat those who had been injured, being both a sword and a shield for those who needed her.

But for Mack and me, it was also nice having someone around to patch us up after we'd done something stupid, and Maria was always that someone.

Now, our trio would finally be back together.

"Well," I said, leaning in to watch as Maria removed a small medical graft from its packaging and carefully placed it on the NetDreamer's broken cheek. "Speaking from experience, it can be hard to transition back when you've been overseas. Things are a little different when you go from soldier to bounty hunter."

"Well," Maria answered, "if *you* of all people can do it, then it'll be a breeze for me."

Directing a finger towards the unconscious man beside us, I replied, "Tell that to the guy you almost stabbed."

A slight groan escaped the NetDreamer's lips as Maria pressed the graft onto his skin, but that was the least of his worries. There was a quiet hiss as the graft sealed onto his flesh, and the healing process began, small pulses of energy that would open pores and inject medical compounds, meant to stimulate cellular growth. It was a miracle of science, but it hurt like hell. Bones, specifically, are repaired slowly for a reason. It's painful. This would not be a fun time.

With one patient dealt with, Maria moved to treat the rest, and I followed.

We crouched down next to the woman Maria had elbowed.

Even I could see from a glance what had happened. A severe kink in the bridge of her nose screamed that it was broken, a slow trickle of crimson escaping each nostril, along with a quickly darkening ring around her right eye and a long gash open just below it. Maria, though, would see more, and she flipped through her medkit to find the right tool for the job.

"How long have you been back?" I asked, holding the NetDreamer's head in a firm grasp, ready for what Maria had to do.

She gave a slight sigh before she placed her left hand under the patient's head, cradling it, with the other grasped onto the broken nose. "I got in two weeks ago."

A wet snap punctuated my shock.

"Two weeks?" I blinked hard and the NetDreamer screamed. She began to struggle but I held her as Maria readied a small painkiller, unable to look me in the eye. "As in fourteen days. Fourteen days where you never even thought to reach out to us?"

"Yes, Nikos, fourteen days. Three hundred and thirty-six hours. Twenty thousand, one hundred and six minutes." A thunk signalled that the needle found purchase and was able to administer the dose. After a couple more seconds of thrashing, the NetDreamer calmed, and Maria began tending to the gash. "But I've been kind of busy. My entire life was still at my parents' house. I had to find a new place to live. My sisters wanted to spend time with me. Then there was all the severance paperwork from Ironways, the reinstatement paperwork from the Bounty Commission, all the certification renewals, and—"

"You couldn't find time for a call, a message? Maybe ask us to help out?"

Maria sighed again. Louder this time. Finally, she looked back up at me, golden stare holding frustration. "No."

The look said "quit it." And I knew Maria well enough that I probably should've. But I also wasn't the kind to listen. Not about this.

"Why?"

We sat there in silence, eyes locked in a staring contest, two friends who'd been through literal and metaphorical fire together for over a decade, daring the other to blink first. Impressively, Maria maintained eye contact while stitching up the NetDreamer's wound. I wanted to steal a glance to see how well she was doing it, but I also didn't want to relent.

Maria did first, looking down to verify her work.

Her reply was a growl. "Because."

"Because?" I scoffed. "What are we? Twelve?"

"I'm certainly not, but pestering me like that gives me doubts about you." Maria stood, and for a brief moment I caught a hint of a smirk on her lips. "Now come on, we have one more to deal with. I want to be done before the EMTs get here. Show them Valkyrie is back in business."

We set about checking the last NetDreamer, the one who'd started the whole brawl. Like his companions, he had some facial damage, but nothing more severe than a small crack in his cheekbone. Scans also showed his implants were still attached and in working order, which was good news since a punch from Maria in full armour, even without the help of her jump-pack, could seriously cause some damage—something I knew from experience. Throughout the whole process, nothing was said between us, but as I stole glances at Maria, working diligently, I could see she was pleased to be back to work. Back home.

The EMTs arrived soon after, with a few bounty retrieval crew members—or "retrievers" as hunters called those tasked with transporting bounty targets to the nearest outpost for processing and transferring them to the local police—following right behind. I didn't know the two working today. One was a bit older, obviously more experienced, and the second was a trainee, judging by the upright posture and devotion to following protocol to the letter.

Retrievers made the bounty hunting world go round. Although it might be easier for bounty hunters to call cops directly—having them pick up a perp in one of their fancy flying cruisers and process them directly at a local precinct—retrievers provided another added layer between bounty hunters and police, the two entities distinct and separate until the cell door closed on an offender. It also meant more money and jobs in the bounty hunting system, and even less burden on police. We did the hard work, while they chased away loiterers and acted as first responders.

As we watched the back door on the retrievers' transport slam shut, I turned back to Maria, who was sliding her helmet back over her head, her eyes locked on the transport, as if to make absolutely sure everything was going off without a hitch. I cleared my throat audibly, which got her attention. Her visor hadn't lit up yet, giving me a yellow-tinged look at her through the bulletproof glass.

I let the silence hang a second longer, just enough to make her shake her head emphatically, holding out her arms expectantly. "Can I help you, Mr. Wulf?"

"Who else knows?" I crossed my arms and leaned against the wall behind me. "Aside from your family."

Maria sighed. "Nobody."

"You know you need to call Jaeger, right?"

"I'm not calling him," she replied, crossing her own arms, gaze directed back at the transport, its engines starting up softly. "And I'm not apologizing."

I pushed myself from the wall and delivered two quick bangs on the back of the transport, signalling to the driver, who knowingly popped a side door. Maria would need a ride. "Who said you needed to apologize?"

Maria sighed. "We both know how it went before I left. I'm not going to sit there and have him lecture me about how he knew it wasn't going to last, that it was a bad idea, that I was being selfish, that I was needed here the last two years. He'll probably pull crime stats to throw at me."

The thought made me smile. Jaeger flicking through two years' worth of Department of Justice stats, pulling up every major anti-establishment incident from the day Maria left to the day she returned. The man took bounty hunting as seriously as any doctor, engineer, or lawyer takes theirs, and he demanded the same from us. His kids. He still saw us as kids, and I assumed that's why he'd been so angry about Maria leaving. He didn't have anything against PMCs, corporations, soldiers, or trying to make some good money—though he had strong opinions about all those things—but it was the fact she was going somewhere to get shot at where he wouldn't be there to watch over her. As big as he was on being a good person, and an honourable hunter, he was bigger on the relative safety of Mack, Maria, and me.

The transport's engines began to whine, so I had to shout to be heard. "Give him a little more credit than that, Maria. At least try. Also, call Mack. I'm sure he'd be happy to hear you're home."

A nod in reply, and suddenly I was being crushed by Maria's amplified strength as she closed her arms around me. At this distance, I could just hear her whisper, "You haven't said it, either."

Before I could respond, Maria released me and stepped back, patting me twice on the cheek. We hammered our chests in mirrored hunter salutes, and Maria disappeared into the Retrievers' transport, off to cash in on a contract closed.

FIVE

The trip up to Sublevel 2 was a short one, the Commission-owned shuttle transporting me from one Bounty outpost to the next so I could get geared up, but looking around as I stepped from the squat, grey building, I was reminded just how different this place was. Like moving from Sublevel 4 to Sublevel 3, jumping one level closer to the surface meant a starkly different environment.

While the lower sublevels—basically everything below Sublevel 6, save the industrial Sublevel 9—had a similar, neon-drenched, urban-monolith feel, every level above had its own unique character. If you kept your gaze below the rooftops on Sublevel 2, you'd almost forget you were underground at all. Block after block of one- and two-storey homes that looked like they'd been plucked from the surface and placed here on mid-sized lots, forming small neighborhoods on long, winding roads. But if you looked up, you'd see the massive, cavernous roof, with clusters of thirty-floor condo and apartment towers visible in all directions, looking like hundred-metre tall pillars holding up a dark steel and Argite sky—which, in fact, they were.

For some, it felt like a slice of the surface, with individual lots and open air over your head, but to me, it felt isolating. Exposed.

This wasn't the *real* sublevels.

As I walked down the wide streets on perfectly aligned side-walks, personal transports passed with the low hum and whir of electric engines, the occupants inside directing strange glances at the man in a rec-leather jacket puffed up by the ballistic vest underneath. At the pistol holstered at his hip next to a bounty hunter's mask. I gazed up at the empty air of the cavern above me. How many thousands of people could be housed here if they just used the space, instead of trying to approximate sur-face living for the city's middle class? Over the past century, as the country had been ravaged by climate change, some tried to escape out, building small communities off in distant parts of the prairies, not wanting to be sucked into the endless urban depths of the burgeoning metropolis. Some of those towns survived, becoming quiet spaces for the ultra-rich, lining the surviving lakes to the north and east—the Wulf family cabin being one among them—while others withered and died as the occupants flocked back to Winnipeg, chasing work, culture, and the creature comforts that came with being in the centre of the national orbit. Those homes they abandoned were left to rot, falling to splinters as time and nature reclaimed them.

It was that pull to keep people here that resulted in Sublevel 2, with its quiet streets, quaint homes, and heavy weather sim-ulation that often created small clouds to obscure the sublevel roof above. This was where I would find Van Buren, the son of a financier and homemaker.

I turned down Van Buren's street, stepping deftly around a bike left idly on the sidewalk by a gawking child, then dodging onto the road to avoid a pair of masked joggers, giving them a curt nod which they returned with a skeptical glance. Hunters rarely came this high up, and almost never armed, so it was extremely likely the joggers had never seen one of us up close. Doubly so for the slack-jawed kid, who kept his eyes locked on me as I made my way down the street.

I stole a glance over my shoulder and gave him a thumbs-up. A toothy grin replaced the awed gape.

At least someone up here liked us.

Van Buren lived in the sixth house down on the left side of a long, looping cul-de-sac, in a wide two-storey home with a driveway that sloped a tad too sharply, in which sat a small two-door luxury EV. A quick check of my wrist-nav confirmed this was the house.

When people cooperate with hunters, things go much more smoothly.

I wound my way up the front walk, between a set of freshly watered desert shrubs that swayed softly in the evening breeze that rippled across the vast open space, and approached the front door, knocking lightly. Off to my left, I caught the faintest flash of movement behind the drawn blinds but didn't look up or react. Instead, I lowered my hand and listened, trying to sense any movement inside.

I heard the rattle of a lock disengaging and the door jerked open to reveal the worried face of a balding older gentleman.

From social feeds and available records, I placed him as Otto Van Buren. Maxwell's dad.

He was short, maybe five-foot-six, with black hair that was quickly receding, a sizable bald patch on top hastily combed over, to no avail. Thin wire-rimmed glasses with circular lenses sat tightly on the bridge of his nose, and the thickness of the glass amplified the size of his eyes somewhat. A bead of sweat worked its way down his left temple.

I met his worried face with a smile. No need to be gruff with a man who desperately wanted to avoid a scene.

"Good evening," I said, keeping my voice low. "My name is Nikos Wulf, from the Bounty Commission Eco-Terror Taskforce, and I am the bounty hunter assigned to your son's case. My bounty hunter licence number is 27441026." Behind Otto, another face emerged, another male, slightly taller than his partner, with sandy blond hair, shaved to the wood around the sides and slicked back on top. His grey eyes flicked between Otto and me. I could see he was trembling slightly from worry and some level of adrenaline. I assumed this was Walter Van Buren, Maxwell's other father. "Now if you could please direct me to your s—"

"He's in the back," Walter said curtly. Rigid shoulders and tightly gripped hands betrayed his stress. "But please be quiet, and fair. He's a good kid."

"I understand. If you check my record, you'll find I am quite capable."

"We've checked your file," Otto said. "When we were informed of the bounty, it was the first thing we did."

"Not that we needed to," Walter continued. He swallowed hard, watching me from the doorway. "Your name is well known, even up here, so close to the surface, Mr. Wulf. Some of the young people, like our son, follow your exploits on the news feeds. It is—"

"A bad idea," I finished. "We shouldn't idolize people who carry guns."

"Unfortunately, the people with guns often become idolized, whether they want to or not," Otto said. "It has occurred for generations. Though, thankfully, you at least acknowledge the harm. Please, just get this over with."

Otto stepped back and the door swung open noiselessly to reveal the foyer. The space was spartan, opening to a long hallway that led towards the kitchen, with the den off to my left and a wall to my right that had a hollow stairway protruding from it, leading up to the second floor. As I'd approached the house, I'd spotted the personal transport parked up on a flat section of the roof. Many of the homes on Sublevel 2 had landing pads on their roofs, the second-floor offices and bedrooms providing quick access to a flying vehicle used to bypass the thrum of morning traffic to the surface. It seemed the Van Burens were of the same ilk. If Maxwell ran, he might go there, so best to take him in the yard. But I wasn't expecting much resistance.

Resisting meant attention, and attention was clearly the last thing the Van Burens wanted.

Peering down the hall, through the kitchen and dining room that glowed with orange light bouncing off the shiny black walls of the home, I spotted Maxwell, pacing on the backyard patio. I'd expected him to be stressed. Instead, he was oddly calm, pacing more to stretch his legs rather than out of nerves.

Odd, given the circumstance. He was barely twenty-one and already had a bounty hanging around his neck. Regardless of the fact it was an "alive" one, it wasn't a situation anyone would want to be in.

But then again, the image of the falling star sigil in his file was enough to raise red flags for the Bounty Commission. Having seen it myself on Sobotka's security detail, their suspicions—and my own—seemed justified. Especially with the nature of the group still unknown. Hopefully the kid could provide some answers.

Before I could put one foot in front of the other, I felt a firm grip on my shoulder.

"Wait, please ..." Walter Van Buren choked, eyes drifting to the young man still pacing in the backyard. "I just need to say something."

I stepped back and motioned for him to proceed.

Walter released my shoulder and took an unsteady breath. "We have tried hard to help our son stay on the right path. Please understand. Our son is not a bad person. He just ... slipped away. He's been cold and distant, and now we find out that he's joined those people, those—"

"Terrorists," Otto chimed in. "You know the type."

"Yeah," I replied. "I know the type quite well." I paused, thinking over my options. "Did Max happen to share any details about last night's protest? Say who he was there with, or why?"

"No ... unfortunately not," Walter began again. "Max had mentioned a few times that he's been hanging around with some new friends. Some 'real activist types' as he put it. But this ... this is so—"

"Militant," said Otto, finishing Walter's sentence again. "Not that our son has said anything about it. He comes and goes as he pleases, won't find work—says that whatever he's been doing *is* his work—then, when he does come home, he's shut up in his room, eyes glued to his screens. Up all night on video calls, speaking in whispers when he knows we might be listening, stonewalling us when we confront him about it."

"Otto …" Walter's faced screwed up into a pained look. "We don't know that they're militant."

"You look at what our *son* has been saying online and tell me it's not militant."

Walter sighed. "They're words."

"They're *threats*. Now we find he's been going to protests, assaulting Argo security, throwing bricks, posting pictures of politicians' homes. Bringing home hunks of scorched scrap metal the same night as that trawler incident on the surface."

I felt my body tense. I'd seen those same reports. A few weeks ago, a cluster of Argo's carbon trawlers—small autonomous drones that dredged the Red and Assiniboine rivers and monitored the flow and structural integrity of their Argite-reinforced riverbeds—had been sunk by a set of coordinated explosions. It was all over the social feeds and news stations, Argo saying it was a spontaneous malfunction, but the rumours flying around hunter circles spoke of something else, especially after we learned that a few Argo techs had been found murdered on-site—seemingly a case of wrong place, wrong time.

If Max and his "friends" were somehow involved, this had just gotten more complicated.

I'd been in plenty of scuffles with anti-establishment group members before, and questioned my fair share of them as part of working the eco-terror beat, but their ideologies were always contained. A collective sharing personal beliefs. They often only strayed into eco-terror by accident, or to further their aims through relatively harmless means. Groups like the Plainswalkers, who wanted to take back control of the land from corporations, might strip agriculture drones on the surface to rebuild in their greenhouses, splicing new plant varieties, or diverting water illegally from the city's water recycling infrastructure to sustain their crops. Or Cyber Volition members, who went to extremes of bodily augmentation in search of some synthetic perfection and who legislators claimed were wasting valuable natural resources and creating unnecessary emissions through the demand for augments they created, resulting in a bounty hunter showing up at their doorstep to "politely" bring them in.

Sure, sometimes anti-establishment groups could be dangerous. There was a reason we bounty hunters were licensed to carry firearms and given leeway to defend our lives if necessary—the mortality rate for bounty hunters was high enough that it scared off some new recruits while it drew others in like moths to a flame.

But there was something about this new group that was hard to shake.

Sobotka had been so afraid of his mystery buyers that he was willing to die, rather than potentially give up information leading to them. Then there were the tattooed meathead bodyguards who attacked me without question and were whisked away by some unknown associates while I was chasing down the one I thought was the important link in a deal gone wrong. And now Max, who had all the makings of a newly radicalized youth and was nothing like Sobotka or the guards who shadowed him. Could they all be linked to a new brand of violent domestic eco-terrorism that was targeting Argo and willing to kill innocent techs just doing their jobs?

I realized both of the Van Burens were staring at me expectantly. I tried to give them my best reassuring smile.

"I understand," I said, looking between the two terrified parents. "Destruction of corporate property may carry a heavy price tag, but I'm sure this will go smoothly. It's an alive-only bounty for a reason. I'll bring him in, he'll sit in a cell overnight, have a virtual appearance in front of a judge in the morning, and then he'll be back home by noon."

That seemed to satisfy them, and with a nod from Otto I started walking towards the garden. As I made my way down the hall, among the semi-reflective black surfaces of the walls, I caught images in my periphery. Framed pictures, some stills, showing the small family on vacation or posed together during the holidays, a slow progression of Maxwell alone as he aged from a pink-faced infant, through his childhood at school or playing sports—specifically, a short-distance sprinter, which was something I noted—to the young man he was today.

Among the stills were also framed video clips, playing soundlessly on a loop. One showed young Max, maybe eight or nine, standing next to a massive California redwood on a family trip. Attempts had been made to grow those wooden giants in other locales to limited effect, with the intention of preserving the redwoods in case the annual wildfires eventually tore through the forest. Another of the silent, looping memories was Maxwell walking across the stage at his university convocation, being lucky enough to gain such an education. Then there was another of Maxwell in what looked like a cancer ward, head bandaged after surgery, pointing at the familiar angular shapes of a fresh new neural augment.

The images tickled at my mind, nudging me forward. I wanted to get this over with as quickly as possible so the Van Burens could go back to their lives, but also caught my thoughts wandering elsewhere. To the picture-laden halls of my childhood home on the surface, to flashing cameras in my face as my mother and father rushed me to the transport clutching a bag filled with a week's worth of clothes.

Where were all those pictures now? All those memories?

There was a faint pneumatic puff of air as the patio door slid open, the sounds of a quaint Sublevel 2 evening crawling into the vacuous stillness of the Van Buren home. I could hear Maxwell breathing, deep and measured. His parents moved to join me as I stepped through the open doorway, but I held a hand out, not looking away from Maxwell, signalling for them to stay put.

The evening air was hot, but thankfully not thick. Though we were still in the sublevels, being just a level below the surface helped remove some of the moisture, and Sublevel 2's construction allowed nearly unabated evaporation, which meant the air wasn't as humid, and I was glad for it. The breeze carried the faint scent of freshly cut grass and watered flora, accompanied by the distinct smell of barbequing synth-meat somewhere nearby. My target froze at the sound of my shoes on the patio tiles.

"You're here for me, right?" Maxwell asked, his voice hoarse, wavering slightly. He had his back to me, but I could see his hands starting to shake with adrenaline.

"Yes, I am," I replied with a step forward. "My name is Nikos

Wulf, and I am the bounty hunter assigned to your case. My bounty hunter licence number is 274—"

"They told me you'd come."

There was a pause, and Maxwell looked at me over his shoulder. "You spoke to my fathers?"

"I did. They told me you're a good man, but that you got caught up in the wrong crowd." I gestured towards the set of patio chairs arranged around a lonely glass patio table. "Why don't you sit, and we can talk about this."

I knew Maxwell would be questioned once he was in the hands of the Bounty Commission, but with the promise of more information hanging between us, I was hoping I could get him talking about his new "friends"—and see what stress and adrenaline of the moment would let slip from Maxwell's mouth.

Maxwell exhaled sharply through his nose and chuckled bitterly. A single bead of sweat ran down his neck, betraying his fear. "Will that change anything?"

"Unfortunately not," I replied with a sigh. "These things are kind of set in stone, especially in this instance. Not much legal wiggle room with what you're wanted for, I'm afraid. Kind of cut and dried."

Silence again as I considered how best to press him for information, while Maxwell looked out towards the back fence—a two-metre-high stone wall that ran the perimeter of the sizeable yard, at the foot of which sat small stone gardens filled with the same desert plants I'd seen as I approached the house. Following Maxwell's sightline, I looked beyond the wall to the vast open expanse of Sublevel 2, with its high roof leaving so much of the area in view. Off in the distance, large towers of Argite met a thin layer of misty cloud that stretched across the sublevel roof above. Small service lights were visible through the cloud, winking on and off—markers for transport pilots in the night to keep them from hammering into the roof itself. The occasional service drone and personal transport buzzed through the fading light of the evening sky. Mixed into the scene was silence. As if up here, the din of the city didn't exist, like we weren't even in Winnipeg anymore. There was just the sound of wind, the distant chatter of people enjoying their evening, the laughter of children playing in the streets, and the soft chitter of birds that had found their way down here. The scene was idyllic. If you woke up and weren't told the contrary, you'd swear you were on the surface in the early 2000s. Just before the climate scales tipped in a disastrous direction.

I was starting to see the appeal of this place.

Maxwell let out a long, deep exhale and straightened his back, looking every bit like his father Walter, but with a demeanour that screamed Otto. "To think I'd die at the hands of a bounty hunter …"

I closed the space between us in a few quick steps and placed my human hand on the young man's shoulder, feeling the tension in his muscles. "Maxwell, I'm not—"

The elbow came out of nowhere, cracking me across the face with a loud *thwack*, pain radiating throughout the right side of my face. Flashing lights and stabbing pain filled my eyes and I staggered back. Through the haze of my vision—my cybernetic eyes mimicking my former real ones *too* well—I saw Maxwell running for the fence. The sound of yelling filled my ears as Walter and Otto sprang from the house, screaming after their son. Striking a bounty hunter was a bad idea, and they knew it—Maxwell, hopefully, did too—but luckily for them, use of force was legally my call.

Instead of pulling the pistol from my holster, I took off running too.

The surprise elbow had given Maxwell enough of a lead that in the time it took me to shake the momentary shock and cobwebs from my brain and start running, he was already scaling the rear wall. I covered the distance, legs firing like pistons as I watched him disappear over the top and land with an audible thud on the other side. Stepping up on the lip of the rocky garden, I leapt up, my hands grabbing hold of the stone barrier and biceps flexing to catapult me over easily.

Shouts erupted from the house ahead of me, the residents likely not used to seeing a bounty hunter chasing someone through their backyard, especially not their—up to this point, I'd assumed—nice and polite neighbour. Ahead, said neighbour was making a break for the side of the house. Scrambling forward in a panicked sprint, he overshot the turn and slammed hard into the house next door with a loud bang, which bought me a few paces as I tried to close the distance. This was my second chase in twenty-four hours, and my legs were already burning from the exertion, my body moving on autopilot to carry me forward, chasing after a target I had started the day assuming was going to come with me quietly.

Maybe the universe was punishing me for making last night harder than it needed to be.

As I rounded the corner to head between the two houses after Maxwell, I looked up just in time to see a small flowerpot flying in my direction, and ducked. The projectile shattered against the wall behind me in an explosion of ceramic and soil, and I kept moving, undeterred, catching a glimpse of Maxwell as he burst through a small bamboo gate and made for the street. He wasn't as fast as my usual targets, so when I shouldered through the door, I found myself a few paces behind the young man, who made the unfortunate mistake of looking over his shoulder.

It cost him precious seconds, and I sprang forward, wrapping my arms around his waist and taking Maxwell down hard onto the grassy lawn.

We rolled, bodies looped together, falling awkwardly over one another until we landed in a freshly landscaped flower bed. Our collision sent a shower of dirt into the air, and I felt my mask slip free of my hip and roll along the grass in the opposite direction. There was a slight crunch, and I felt a sting of pain in my knee as it twisted the wrong way. I let out a loud grunt but kept hold of the kid. Maxwell struggled, driving his elbow hard into the side of my head, and I caught the follow-up with my hand, but in the process had to let go, allowing my scared target to scramble forward and out of my reach. I swiped forward feebly, trying to grab hold of his pant leg, but found air, and Maxwell was able to stand, looking back at me with fear in his eyes.

The whole scene brought screams from the scattered suburbanites going about their evening, who turned to watch the display, eyes trained on the bounty hunter rising to a knee. A thin rivulet of blood was running down my cheek like a bloody tear from where Maxwell had hit me, and I wiped it away, spinning back to grab my mask and slip it on.

I turned and locked eyes with Maxwell, holding out my hand in a placating gesture. His eyes had gone wide as the full reality of what he'd gotten into started to hit home.

"Kid," I started. "I can excuse you hitting me. Now can we just—" Maxwell took off running down the street. "You've gotta be fucking kidding me."

The first step was fine, but the second sent pain radiating up my leg as I put weight down to continue my movement. I swore under my breath, but kept going, taking off after Maxwell.

"ODIN, cue the recording," I said through gritted teeth.

"Certainly. Bounty recording is live." The telltale pulse of red filled the edges of my vision.

"Good. I'm in pursuit of bounty target Maxwell Van Buren. Wanted for destruction of corporate property. Currently on the run in Sublevel 2. Previous point of contact was unsuccessful. Bounty is alive-only, and I will attempt to apprehend." It sounded silly to say it all out loud, but the recordings were an important part of the bounty process. Like the recording of Ivan Sobotka's suicide, this would be proof that I was the one to apprehend Maxwell, despite the fact it was a private bounty with my name on it. It also acted as legal protection, as the recording could be used in court to prove guilt of impropriety on the part of a hunter, or use of unreasonable force—though the statutes around the latter were quite flexible.

The only thing on my mind, though, was making sure the recording didn't show Maxwell getting away.

Whatever had happened to my knee, it was slowing me significantly, and making the pursuit longer than it otherwise would've been. Also making this chase particularly annoying was the terrain. I was out of my element.

Hunting down in the sublevels—the real sublevels—there were crowds, elevations, back alleys, barriers, twists, and turns. Things that could slow down the target or give a hunter the ability to quickly close the distance. But here, in the suburbs, there was none of that. While they were quaint and clean, the streets were wide open, the houses close together and hard to pass between, and the only changes in elevation were the vary- ing slopes of people's lawns.

The chase continued down the street for two blocks, Maxwell running ahead and me limping behind, before he ducked between another set of houses. Maxwell burst through the side gate, tossing the weight aside with a heavy shoulder and cracking one of the hinges free to let the door dangle loose. I followed through easily, catching sight of him slipping over another fence, like the one behind his house, and disappear- ing over the other side. This time, I didn't have the speed or strength in my step to leap, so instead I had to clamber over, landing hard in a small back lane. As my feet hit the ground, a spike of pain rocketed up to my knee. I doubled over for a moment, but kept on my feet, letting out a long and deep groan, before turning to follow Maxwell down the lane.

Spotting my target, I noticed he too, was limping, favouring his left side, legs bounding to minimize the weight put on his right ankle. I could also see the sweat running down the back of his neck, long streams emerging from his messy hair to stain his shirt with dark patches that seemed to grow by the minute.

He was gassed, and now he was hurt too.

From there, the chase petered out, the two of us injured and exhausted—me from a lack of rest and him from lack of con- ditioning—limping down this damp and uncharacteristically cluttered back lane.

The lane opened to a small square, high walls from the surrounding properties ringing the area and forming a dead end, closing us in. As we moved farther in, the space seemed to shrink, my vision growing more constricted as the walls seemed to rise up around us. My heart was pounding, and my busted knee was beginning to throb in earnest.

Visibly exhausted, Maxwell hobbled over to the wall ahead of us, and tried unsuccessfully to find a foothold. His injured ankle gave no ground, and his jump amounted to a limp hop, hands grasping desperately for the top of the wall but falling more than a foot short. His palms slapped the stone quietly, and the young man fell hard, clutching his ankle. As the shadow of the bounty hunter in pursuit covered him, he rolled, sliding backwards to slam his back hard into the stone barrier. Like a cornered animal, he lashed out, grasping for rocks and scattered refuse and flung them at me, his energy all but spent. The projectiles flew in pitiful arcs, landing halfway between the two of us with uninspiring thuds.

I was breathing hard as I limped towards him, chest heaving, and could barely speak. So I just stared at the young man in front of me. How the hell did we wind up here? He had everything. A comfortable life with loving parents, a roomy house on spacious Sublevel 2 where he could look up and at least pretend he was staring at the sky.

My voice came out as a raspy whisper. "Why?"

Instead of responding, Maxwell pressed himself harder against the wall, the heels of his hands digging deep furrows in the patchy grass at its base. Then, with the same breathless whisper, he said, "The sky is fake. No matter what I do, I can't forget the fact the sky is fake. Nobody seems to care. They live their lives in the dark, but we were never meant to be down here."

His eyes locked on the pistol in my hand, finger off the trigger, but the weapon was still powered on, a round in the chamber and blue light pouring from the vents.

Maxwell braced himself, muscles tight. "At least make sure they pick a mausoleum on the surface for my ashes. I don't want to spend eternity in the dark."

I inhaled deeply. "Maxwell, I'm not here to kill you. That's not how this was ever supposed to go."

Van Buren scoffed, youthful arrogance taking over despite the position he was in. He hoisted himself up to a low crouch, favouring his left leg. "Then what's with the gun? Oh, right, because I'm a dangerous eco-terrorist who wants to destroy the world—or at least that's what your corporate masters believe."

Typical self-righteous twentysomething. I had been the same when I was his age, but that didn't mean it wasn't annoying.

Warily, I let myself relax, shifting pressure off the injured leg that pulsed with pain, though I kept a solid grip on my pistol. Maybe I could make use of this youthful smugness.

"So, what *do* you want?"

"Salvation." Maxwell spread his arms wide. "Salvation from this fake world. Humanity in a box, with corporate logos slapped over every surface not covered by reminders of what they did. How they destroyed this planet. Instead, they get to act like they saved it, and send people like you …" an accusatory finger jabbed in my direction, "to enforce their whims. So that's what I'm doing here: playing my part, so we can raise humanity back up, to our true purpose, our true place. To Eden, and a world that is once again ours, forever. From the depths we will rise. The time of steel and sun has arrived."

My pulse pounded harder within my ears as the familiarity of his words struck me. So similar to what Sobotka had said before he died. And if Maxwell truly was involved with the same group Sobotka seemed to have killed himself over, I was in a good position for some real answers. Now for the most importance piece.

"You and who, Maxwell?" I asked. "What anti-establishment group are you running with? The people with this." I raised my wrist-nav to project the logo—a green circle with stylized lines jutting up and left, like a falling star—spinning in the air.

There was a slight chuckle from Maxwell, who continued to smirk. "Why? Want to join?"

I cocked my head to the side. "Not exactly. Give me a name, Maxwell."

"No. You won't be getting that out of me."

There it was: the stonewalling. But at the very least, he didn't seem in as deep as Sobotka. That, or his lack of experience with bounty hunters meant he didn't know how long interrogations could go, and how we could get the answers we needed.

Eventually.

"Fine," I replied with a smile Maxwell couldn't see, but it felt good nonetheless. "You'll just have to come to one of the Bounty outposts on this sublevel so we can have a nice long chat. ODIN, send our location to a bounty retrieval crew and get them to prep a cell for Maxwell. We can put in a request to have his court time delayed ..." I glanced towards the now aggravated young man, "citing 'Urgent Eco-Terror Threat.'"

"Of course," ODIN replied. "I'll get ri—"

The rest of his statement was garbled, fading to static. Then nothing.

"ODIN? Copy last."

No response.

"ODIN! Copy la—" A heavy weight slammed into my stomach as Maxwell launched himself at me, his hand clawing at mine, fighting for the gun. Awful situational awareness. I'd gotten wrapped up in ODIN for just a moment and lost focus, giving Maxwell an opening.

It also appeared his injured leg was a ruse too. Kid was smart.

We slammed hard onto the ground, and another spike of pain rocketed out from my knee as it was crushed by Maxwell's weight. Stunned for a moment, I kept a firm grip on the gun, which was clenched in my right hand and pinned to the ground. I caught Maxwell's right arm when he attempted to reach across for the weapon. The pistol was clenched in my metal fist, so would be hard to get free with one human hand.

Maxwell drove his knee down into my injured one and my vision flashed white with pain, allowing the young man get free of my grasp and deliver a strong right to my cheek. There was a dull crack and Maxwell howled in pain, hand recoiling after striking the protective mask.

Using the opening, my left hand darted out to shove Maxwell over, throwing us into a roll, both with a hand wrapped around the gun. Carried by the momentum, I swung overtop to crouch over Maxwell, foot finding good grip, trying to keep the pistol barrel aimed away from him. Recovering, Maxwell's hand slapped overtop of mine, clutching the gun tightly with both his hands, and despite the strength advantage given by my prosthetic arm, it began to drift closer to Maxwell. While the younger man tried working at my fingers to pry to gun loose, he was also pulling it into a dangerous angle, pointed perilously close to his heart.

I tried to reach over with my left to push the gun in the other direction, but Maxwell only made it worse. He kicked me hard, foot glancing off my chest to pin my right shoulder, his foot giving him leverage, while also keeping my pistol-carrying arm out of the reach of my free one.

I had to give the kid credit. He could fight.

But that didn't mean he knew his way around guns.

It only took a moment. My finger was on the trigger guard, as soldiers and hunters are trained to do, which meant the opening was empty when Maxwell's thumb—reflexively looking for a spot to find leverage as he tried to pry my fingers off the grip—jammed itself into the trigger.

The crack drowned out any attempt to warn him.

A small bloom of red confirmed it was too late.

Immediately, Maxwell's grip dropped away. I pulled myself free, still crouched over him, momentarily frozen by shock.

"No-no-no," I said, holstering my weapon and stooping low. The kid had gone slack, arms falling to his sides. "Maxwell! Hey, stay with me, kid." Putting pressure on the wound, I could feel his heartbeat—faint and weak. The kid had minutes. Not even. The shot had entered his chest, and judging by the angle and location, it had either barely missed his heart, or just nicked it, but the weakness of the pulse told me it was probably the latter.

I reached over and tapped into the emergency line on my wrist-nav.

"This is bounty hunter Nikos Wulf. I have a target down and in need of emergency medical treatment. He's sustained a gunshot wound to the chest, and I need—"

A choking cough produced a spurt of blood from between Maxwell's lips, which were pulled into a sickening grin. He was dying, quickly, and I didn't have the tools, or the knowledge, to keep him alive. The kid was going to die here.

And he was smiling.

Lazily, his eyes drifted to me, and with the last breath in his lungs, Maxwell Van Buren whispered, "Told you. No name."

SIX

Silence. Pure, uninterrupted silence. Everything that needed to be said in that moment left to the whims of the air, the vacant eyes of the inert mask staring back at me from where I'd placed it on the table. The two dark voids of darkened crimson glass reflecting a doubled image of myself, reclined back in my chair, framed by the expansive picture window through which the hustle of another Sub-level 4 night was visible. Transports floated through the air, carrying occupants to and from various sites—judging by the time, most likely off towards home for the evening. Down below, people milled about, their chatter blocked by the soundproof seal of the apartment's outer walls and windows. A lively night, like most on this level, juxtaposed by the quiet solitude that washed through my home like an expanding force.

I slowly spun the glass in my hand, brown liquor lazily swaying within like dense tides against a shore made of solid glass.

I'd filled it, but hadn't taken a drink just yet, the voice of my now silent, slumbering AI companion still echoing in my mind from this morning.

Maybe you should try quitting for a while?

The silence was invaded by the crinkling of fabric and slight pop and crack of my hip joints as I leaned forward to stare into the vacant eyes of my mask. I reached up and rapped my knuckles on the bridge of its carbon nosepiece and smirked.

"Even when you're silent you find a way to speak."

I'd tried every option I could think of to restore ODIN and bring him back online. I'd plugged the mask into the apartment systems, thinking the mask itself was the issue, and that ODIN was locked behind a hardware malfunction, but no dice. Then I tried hooking it up to my tablet and computer to see if the mask's internal OS had buggered things up, but that didn't work either. Neither did checking my wrist-nav, in the event ODIN lost data or had corrupted files while connected between it and my mask. I'd turned the mask off and on so many times I'd lost count of the attempts, spending an hour or more with my eyes locked on the ever-spinning circle, where my trusty AI's symbol should be.

There was nothing I could do to fix this issue, but I wasn't emotionally ready to use my last bullet: Castor.

He'd mentioned in his message that ODIN needed an update—was that the reason behind the apparent software crash? Some bug or hole that Castor had missed since the last time we linked up? Or had he purposefully sent ODIN offline somehow to force me into a meeting? Castor wasn't a petty man, but he would know how to do that, and would be the only one holding the key to bring my AI pal back. I grabbed my wrist-nav, intending to refresh Castor's message history, but when my eyes met something else, I froze.

Sorry for earlier. Wasn't expecting to see you just yet. How's your night been?

Maria.

I stared at the message, lungs tightening in my chest.

What should I say? What *could* I say? The truth was the contract had gone as badly as it could've. What was supposed to be a simple snatch-and-drop job—picking up some kid from the suburbs and dropping him off at the nearest bounty office for processing—had ended with a body bag and a squad of retrievers polishing blood from a back lane in Sublevel 2.

But then again … it wasn't my fault. Right? Maxwell's thumb had slipped in the scuffle and pressed the trigger. I hadn't shot him. I hadn't even *intended* to shoot him. It was a complete accident, and the footage from my mask would show that. Not that it would make much of a difference to Otto and Walter Van Buren. Their kid was still dead.

But what haunted me most was how receptive he'd been.

Maxwell had died with a smile on his face.

He was expecting to die on the patio—the way he'd spoken said as much—and he'd acted just like anyone with a dead-only bounty would. He'd smashed me in the face and taken off running. Like he'd been forcing an altercation, or trying desperately to get away, making a snap decision with more information than I'd had at the time.

There was something I was missing. Hopefully something that would put my conscience at ease. Something I needed ODIN to help me find.

But ODIN was currently occupied being fast asleep.

I tapped the mask again and placed the glass of rye beside it. "Y'know, this better not be some ploy to get me to work through these issues on my own. You're still my therapist, after all. Didn't Castor put some kind of Hippocratic Oath into your code or something? That you can't trick your patient or abandon care or something?"

There was no response, so I leaned back, sighed, and stood up.

"Some help you are."

I walked to the kitchen, the pain in my knee still a source of discomfort, causing a slight limp. The stairs up from the sunken living room and around the corner to the kitchen were a particular struggle, as putting weight on the tweaked joint sent a jolt of pain through my leg. The stimulant shot the attending retrieval crew had given me had already worn off, and I could feel the angry swelling coming back. I moved towards the cabinet where I kept some medical supplies, my thoughts returning to Maria's message.

What was I supposed to say? That it went okay, but I fucked up my knee and accidentally shot the guy I was there to take alive? That my last two bounties had ended with body bags instead of jail cells? That I might have been able to prevent both of their deaths if I had been faster, smarter, more alert, not so far into my own head?

I grabbed a stim pack and hobbled back to the chair. The pack had a gel layer that warmed up to generate blood flow and relax muscles, which went to work as soon as I sealed it over my knee. That was the nice part, then I braced myself and cracked the tab, which sent a set of tiny injections into the flesh to pump CBD and multiple other natural anti-inflammatories and pain relievers into the swollen joint. It felt like a hundred tiny bug bites.

I'd rather have the shot again. The retriever at least was quick.

I picked up my wrist-nav again, still turning around a response to Maria in my head. But instead of seeing her message on the screen, I was met with a deposit confirmation for the Van Buren contract.

Lovely. The Commission clearly didn't find anything wrong with how that bounty shook out. The footage spoke for itself, and to them it was just another bounty. An alive-only contract that had gone south when the target ran, struggled, attacked a peacekeeper, and gotten shot through the chest for his trouble. And it just had to be Argo, didn't it? It was not lost on me how the story could be spun on the socials. Nikos Wulf, child of Argo, killing the poor saps who protest and throw rocks at Argo-owned windows and gloat about it online. I choked out a laugh. That'd look good.

I tossed my wrist-nav aside.

Propping my bad leg up on the coffee table, I nudged my inert mask with my foot. I hated being alone with my own thoughts, which was one of the many reasons I needed ODIN around.

I paused, suddenly aware of the uncomfortable tension in my muscles, a headache brewing around my temples. What would ODIN say if he were here?

Focus on what you know.

I forced myself to take a deep breath, which came out more like a heavy sigh, and began to pick at a loose thread in the armrest.

"Okay, so the facts," I said aloud, more for my own benefit than ODIN's. At least I could pretend I wasn't alone with my thoughts. "First, the Commission has documented new iconography on the streets, which I've also seen firsthand, pointing to a possible new anti-establishment group. Unfortunately, we have no information about their group structure, origins, or even a damn name.

"Second, two of their members were accompanying Ivan Sobotka the night he took the stolen Argo tablet into his possession—which gives me a strong suspicion they were, in fact, the buyer.

"Third, Sobotka's last words before he killed himself were echoed by Max Van Buren, a known associate of this new group, based on video footage that shows him wearing their logo. And if the Van Burens are to be believed, this same group could also have been responsible for sinking those carbon trawlers a few days ago and killing the Argo techs responsible for monitoring and maintaining them. Meaning this group, so far, has been targeting Argo-owned property."

I successfully—or unsuccessfully, depending on how you perceive loose threads—loosened the one I was picking at, and it unravelled further. "And fourth, both Sobotka and Van Buren were willing to die rather than give up more information about this new group."

And I had played a role in both of those deaths. Sitting here now, mulling it over, flipping the issue back and forth like a tennis ball, it felt like those points on the Bounty Board were tainted.

From there, I was stuck. Hopefully Max's seized tech—wrist-nav, smartglasses, tablets, computers—now in the hands of Bounty Commission, would yield some answers, so *something* positive could come from this.

I picked up my wrist-nav and slipped it on. Opening Maria's message, I resolved to avoid drawing others into this mess until I knew more.

It was okay. Another payday.

I sat for a moment before turning back to the mask.

"How was that?" I said, the skull staring back with the two glass voids. "Yeah, I know. Lying to Maria never works out."

I sighed hard and switched over to the thread with Castor. As I scrolled, the wall of unanswered texts loomed large, flying by as my finger flicked through, scattered messages sent intermittently over the past few months, with exceptionally rare responses.

My current relationship with Argo had always felt weird, almost like a betrayal of my principles. Dad had railed for so long against Argo as our betrayers, and after witnessing his mental decline, with no help from our supposed friends, on some level, I bought into it too. Then again, my work with the Eco-Terror Taskforce essentially meant I was enforcing laws that helped Argo maintain its stronghold on the world, keeping those supposed betrayers in power, able to hold back the climate clock from ticking forward any further. I resented them for abandoning us with one breath, but respected them for keeping the planet alive with another. My fallout with Zara had been a good excuse to maintain some physical and psychological distance from Argo.

Yet, in a way, I wasn't that far from serving Argo. Working the eco-terror beat meant contracts bringing justice to those who threatened Argo and their bottom line. The last two jobs had only confirmed that. No matter how far I tried to go in the right direction, and get away from the company that had thrown us to the curb like we were a hunk of trash worth forgetting … even now, I was a loyal soldier. Serving corporate interests over those of the people.

It was a mess. A big fucking mess.

And from the looks of things, I couldn't avoid it any longer.

I shot Castor a quick message, to which he replied almost immediately— which was very out of character.

It was confirmed. A meeting at Argo, tomorrow.

At least ODIN would be happy. He'd get his update and I'd finally take a day off.

That was the plan, anyway.

SEVEN

What had been another blistering morning down on Sublevel 4 was forecasted to give way to a warm—even pleasant—afternoon on the surface. Despite the medicinally dulled protests of my injured knee and a fitful night that held little sleep, I chose to walk to the nearest surface elevator, taking a meandering path through the sublevel, an extra-large coffee in hand. The massive elevator column ferried people between sublevels, and even all the way to the surface. The elevator cars were spacious, laid out with long rows of seating, and were three-levelled to ensure they could cram as many commuters in as possible—though only legally rated for three hundred. It was dangerous, but hey, there were millions of people in this city, and with fifty shafts and four cars each, you had to make do somehow.

For some people, airbuses were too cramped, and the flights too chaotic. Ride-share transports were too expensive at peak times. Personal transports even more so. Which left the surface elevators as the only easy public way between levels, and the cheapest of all up to the surface.

I'd nabbed a window seat for the smooth ascent up the side of the surface shaft towards the sun and sky above, grateful to take the weight off my still-sore joint. We rose quickly above the late-morning buzz of Sublevel 4 and slipped swiftly through Sublevel 3, stopping to pick up a healthy throng on the journey up. The stops at Sublevels 2 and 1 were brief, and I counted fewer than a dozen suburbanites stepping on, most of them likely opting for personal transportation of some kind.

A thought came unbidden. *Like the Van Burens. Undoubtedly grieving the son they'd lost.* I quickly quashed that train of thought before it could go any further.

Next came the surface. As the elevator door opened, the tempered glass gave way to an eruption of light, like stepping through the gates to Valhalla, and a blast of warm afternoon air washed over the commuters inside. The sunlight and warm breeze on my skin provided an instant hit of endorphins, and my lungs rushed to greet an influx of potent, unfiltered oxygen.

Even after spending more of my life down below than up above, there was a sense of comfort at the surface that never leaves you. Something intrinsically human about fresh air and sunlight on your skin.

Flashing my hunter ID got me around the security checks and lineups that accompanied the surface-level exits of the elevators, saving me the annoyance and time lost to slowly trudging through the long lineups to go through body scanners and bag checks that awaited everyone else.

My queue-hopping earned me a few nasty looks, but I paid no mind.

Recent protests had made surface security even tighter, as pearl-clutching Ivories worried about who was coming up from below, and for what reason. Between protests about airbus and maglev fare hikes, and the city's stingy use of climate control misters in the sublevels during another brutal summer, there was a long sit-in protest over the province's decision to buy out some independent solar farms near Swan River and transition ownership of them to—who else—Argo. A few months back, activists had a row with some very ill-equipped police during the prime minister's recent visit. It seemed the whole country had descended on the Manitoba legislature to protest the government's decision to provide financial backing to conflict in South Africa. The money was used to hire my old crew over at Tempest, a favourite of the feds, so it was only fitting I was dragged up to the surface on a general order when some of the anti-establishment groups decided to join in on the fun and start a riot.

In response, security guards at the surface elevators were checking IDs a lot more closely and being a little less careful with people's belongings. There had been little news when, like the destruction of corporate property legislation, provisions were snuck through allowing the city to track and count when people came to the surface.

Just another piece of privacy being eroded in a world where everyone was already a data point, so nobody batted an eye.

I knew from past experience that the closer to the surface you lived, the easier and smoother it would be getting through surface elevator security, but being a hunter meant that you had the easiest access. Despite the ire people like me got from Ivories about the nature of our work, and how we almost all universally lived below their feet, having a few of us close at hand probably helped them feel safer.

I just had to flash the digital ID card on my wrist-nav and I was let through a secure side gate and onto surface soil. The world of the Ivories.

This particular surface elevator opened into the Osborne District.

A century ago, the intersection of Portage and Main had been considered the economic heart of Winnipeg, and that hadn't changed. While the layout of the city's main arteries had remained relatively unaltered in the last hundred years, Argo's ability to recapture pure carbon from the atmosphere meant they were now suppliers of Argite, the world's strongest building material. As construction began on the sublevels, The high-rises of the early 2030s were quickly razed and consolidated into towers and large complexes, engineered with Argite to withstand the harsh surface storms. Designed with a series of angles to let wind and debris glance off near harmlessly, they looked like geometrically complex obelisks rising out of the prairie soil. The buildings were connected by supports, each tower a node in a larger chain to help keep the spires on the green, lush surface standing during even the harshest winter storms.

Like most regions of the city, the Osborne District took its name from the neighbourhood that had once sat in this area, immediately south of the Assiniboine River and a mere two kilometres from Portage and Main, and closer still to The Forks, the historic centre of Winnipeg where the Assiniboine joined the Red River. In the time before European settlers arrived on Canadian shores, the area had been a critical trade hub for Indigenous peoples—as well as the settlers that eventually established the city—and it remained an important hub for commerce. The indie shops that had once dominated the area had long ago given way to large business towers. The Canadian headquarters for Ravencrest and Loki Security, the technology and transportation firm Verosight, finance powerhouse Theta Limited, and the Bulgarian hedge fund that now owned naming rights at Winnipeg's soccer stadium, Georgiev Holdings, all called the area home, and those were just some of the signs I saw.

As I walked down the sidewalk, throngs of people streamed out of office buildings for their lunch breaks, the welcome drop in temperature after the last few weeks drawing them all outside their carefully climate-controlled office spaces. Small parks and patios were filled with people in collared shirts, suits, and neatly pressed pants wandering between healthy surface greenery, eyes locked on holoprojections and wrist-navs, or peering through smartglasses. Looking around, the difference was stark. Down in the sublevels, people wore vibrant colours to match the buzzing LED neon and bright holographic signage clinging to the sides of buildings, but up here, everyone was dressed in a cascade of greys, tans, and whites, complementing the glistening black of the Argite skyscrapers and dull grey of the translucent solar roads.

To my right, expensive matte silver EV cars were parked in diagonal stalls and plugged into charging stations, each sleek, streamlined, and bearing luxury manufacturer logos on their grills, while holographic displays showed battery charges and the time left on their parking—a few of the times flashed red, noting their parking had run out and a fine was on its way. Then, to my left, were the owners of such luxurious vehicles.

The young ones at least seemed to have some interest in speaking with one another, but while they chatted about the latest hockey game, or what bar they wanted to visit in their off hours, the older Ivories spoke in hushed tones, and from what I could gather, mostly about business.

This was the Winnipeg I knew from my early childhood. A city of high tech and even higher finance.

On the surface, if you'd ask someone what they did for a living, they'd often say one of three things: tech, finance, or politics. Tech drew in the dollars, finance moved those dollars around, and the politics ensured that those dollars passed between hands unimpeded. It was a system that everyone was okay with because everyone profited, and all the problems were pushed out of view. If I were doing this walk down in the sublevels, it would be a different story. I'd be walking past checkpoints, hearing the ever-present thump of music, through crowds of industrial workers with cybernetic appendages, old folks wearing rebreathers to help their ailing lungs not used to the dense recycled air, and teens not in school because they had to make money for their families to have something to eat.

The future always looked utopian when companies like Argo arrived to spur our world forward, promising clean energy, medicine for all, cures for diseases, and to save the world from its anthropogenic demise. But standing in the midst of it, I wasn't so sure.

When your city—and later your country—was increasingly built on those big three industries, there was an even bigger incentive to keep them exclusive. To keep the money in the same few pockets. So say goodbye to affordable education, paid internships, and any protections for industrial work. If they thought it had been bad when my grandfather was young, it had only gotten worse.

I guess there were some things Argo couldn't fix.

As I walked, the stares became more apparent—and I expected as much. I was an outsider here in all the ways that mattered.

Amid the crowd of people in fancy name-brand clothes, I stood out like a lighthouse beacon. For one, I was physically larger than most of the people here, owing to my profession and exercise habits, but otherwise I had a larger presence, like I had "bounty hunter" in shiny LED lights above my head. I didn't dress like them, or walk like them, and if I opened my mouth, I certainly didn't talk like them. It didn't matter that if things had gone to plan, I would've been just another one of them—a cog churned out by the same money-printing machine. The fact I was the son of a former executive and had a sizeable bank account didn't matter, because I was different.

Not one of them.

Luckily, it had been twenty years since my face had graced tabloid articles and exposés on the biggest news sites around the world, so nobody could recognize me as Nikos Wulf, an expelled heir to the Argo dynasty. They just saw me as a brawny guy with glowing eyes, and sublevel air hanging around him like an invisible energy field that deflected everything "surface."

Moving through the crowd, I crossed a bridge over the Assiniboine and continued towards Argo. The path took me past the Manitoba legislature, one of the only buildings not torn down and replaced on the surface. Instead, it looked the same as the day it was built. Limestone with slopping edges, columns, intricately carved engravings, and the same golden statue atop.

And just as the building stood the way it always had, the lawn was filled with protesters, just as it always had been.

To save time, I decided to cut across the legislative building grounds, which also gave me a chance to see who was protesting what this time. There were plenty of signs on poles and recycled-cloth banners emblazoned with slogans. Along with the usual protest fare were international flags, but not ones that I'd seen in years. Singapore, reduced so much it had been swallowed by neighbouring countries. Ditto for Philippines. Zambia, meanwhile, reduced to nothing but blowing sand and scattered shrubs. There were too many to count, and some I couldn't identify. They were countries that no longer existed, now covered in water or vast desert, with all signs of human life erased from their surfaces. A large holoprojector contained a scrolling list of names, some in yellow, others red with dates written next to them. Another flashed faces. Ones I had seen on social media and in news coverage.

I looked back at the signs and banners, seeing slogans like "We are all Canadian" and "Save the Scotians." People were draped in Nova Scotia flags, and a young woman with a thick East Coast accent was on a small stage shouting, her cybernetic fist raised in the air, talking about losing family to hurricanes, of the fishing industry dying on polluted oceans, of homes and businesses being dragged into the sea by massive waves, and large sections of the province now underwater. Angrily railing against the premier for passing the buck to Ontario and Quebec.

The names on the holoprojector were missing persons, and in red were the names of the dead.

The primary target of Argo was always climate change. They had done all they could to solve that problem, shifting away from fossil fuel by buying up all the oil reserves and switching the world to cheap, clean energy, but all they could do was slow the progress and dampen the impact. Island nations still sank below the waves, coastal areas were ravaged by storms, and already dry regions became near uninhabitable. Even here in the centre of the nation, our climate had worsened. We had always dealt with huge extremes in temperature, ranging from minus forty degrees Celsius in the winter to forty above in the summer. But now, swaths of the Canadian prairies had been reduced to desert, annual wildfires raged hotter and hotter, and a destabilized polar vortex left us at the mercy of extreme winter storms; the increased ice and snow meant harsh flooding. Every dire warning from scientists the world over was coming true: we were too late to stop it entirely, and it would be likely a century before the situation began to stabilize.

But at least it *would* stabilize.

Not that it gave climate refugees any solace. Their homes, businesses, and even entire countries were demolished and sunk, or reduced to miles of unlivable desert. They'd probably never get to go back.

Now it was on our doorstep.

For decades, we had been warned that the East Coast was next. The wealthier West Coast had time and money from self-preserving international investors to prepare for rising sea levels, but the East Coast had not been so lucky. Climate disaster hit the Maritimes hard and fast in the 2020s, with warming ocean waters exacerbating storm systems, causing them to increase in intensity and frequency, while rising sea levels caused ocean swells that destroyed communities thought once to be safe, along with their repeated efforts to rebuild. Now the East Coast was being wiped off the map, one city at a time.

I scanned the crowd and spotted a young man wielding a

worn but functional tablet, trying hard to stop onlookers and get their signatures for a petition. On his cheek was the image of a flag for the now nonexistent Ethiopia. Desertification had worn away arable land in the west, leaving drought-riddled deserts in its wake, only for sea levels to rise and consume the eastern half of the country after it had swallowed what was once Somalia. Eventually, what was left of Ethiopia was annexed by South Sudan and Kenya, for similar reasons to those that had brought me to Brazil all those years ago.

I angled in his direction, flashed my wrist-nav to sign mid-stride, and kept walking, listening to the young woman's booming voice fade into the background, replaced by the chittering of birds flying amongst the tall and solid trees on the legislative building grounds. My eyes drifted up and I made a mental note of how far I had to look up to get a clear view of the sky. Next to the smallest building in the city, it felt strange, like a hole opened in the middle of a field of cornstalks, and looking up, it was hard not to feel small.

Glass walkways connected many of the skyscrapers, allowing people to walk from one building to the next without ever having to step outside. You could theoretically go from one end of the city to the next without ever setting foot on the ground; you just needed the right QR codes or access codes from dermal implants. Some of the most high-priced condo towers contained all the amenities a person could need. Before I'd signed the lease for the apartment I lived in now, electing to live among those people I claimed to protect, I remembered touring one, and being taken through open-air parks, shopping centres, and recreational facilities. I tried not to bristle when the young realtor mentioned how I might never have to step outside again, and it's probably what got me to accept the somewhat dingy digs I'd transformed into a comfortable outpost.

My gaze flitted from building to building, taking in the city, feeling wonderment for the first time in years.

I was fixated on the sky, and the personal shuttles that zipped around in clear, AI-determined pathways. These weren't the boxy rustbuckets that transported goods and people throughout the sublevels, nor the aggressive-looking police cruisers, but sleek and shiny executive shuttles, meant for at most four passengers plus the driver—or just the four if you wanted to ditch the driver. They weaved from building to building, ferrying rich financiers or tech execs from meeting rooms to exclusive taprooms and five-star restaurants.

I exhaled sharply and kept walking, spotting at least one executive shuttle flanked by two larger shuttles that looked a bit more formidable. From so far down, I couldn't exactly make out the logos on the side, but once the trio landed on the Argo building's landing pad, I had my answer. Castor had arrived, and I needed to pick up the pace.

EIGHT

I still arrived at the Argo building on time, walking down the stone path flanked by beautiful floral arrangements, well-kept shrubs, and healthy trees. Winnipeg had always loved trees, lining sidewalks and boulevards with natural shade long before we ramped up efforts to combat climate disaster with photosynthesis. Despite their exposure to the sometimes harsh elements, the obvious benefit of more oxygen, sunlight, and real rain meant these specimens were far more robust than their sad, stunted cousins down in the sublevels.

Beyond the rows of arbour, the Argonaut Building loomed large. The company's full name, "The Argonaut Group," was projected in large glowing gold font above its front doors. The tallest tower in the skyline, the building had a strange, prismatic shape, where, looking dead-on, you could see it bowing slightly in the middle. This was not as much an artistic choice as a practical one. Like the other buildings around it, Argonaut HQ was angular, the edges letting debris and heavy winds whisk off, and made from durable recycled glass, Argite, and green-sourced steel. The building itself sat in a cleared plaza, with stone paths arcing out in rings from the base of the building, lined with lush plant life, small gazebos, and covered seating areas where employees could work outside.

I ascended the stone steps and passed through the big glass doors of the main entrance to find it empty, polished black stone floor reflecting the stark white LED lights above, and the click of my solitary footsteps echoing throughout the spacious room. The potted plants and ferns hanging from the ceiling did little to dampen the sound; neither did the large, leafy green wall behind the sleek black reception desk. As usual, a smattering of service bots zipped around and under empty couches and chairs in the waiting area, tidying up. The only other human in the atrium was the receptionist. When I stopped at his desk, he slid a plain white card in my direction, not bothering to look up from the thin glass display of his computer.

"Please use whatever interconnected device you'd like to scan this, Mr. Wulf."

I frowned. This was another one of the reasons I hated coming back to the Argonaut Building. Despite the decades that had passed, and the churn of employees in a place like this, people always knew me. And here, in this building, it was always as "Mr. Wulf." I wanted to be known as Nikos Wulf, the bounty hunter, not Nikos Wulf, disgraced castoff of the Argonaut Group. The receptionist's words conjured up memories of my father. Of his pressed suits and glittering cufflinks, striding up and down the carpeted halls upstairs. Of the flashing cameras and reporters screaming questions, asking how it had all gone so wrong. Neither memory was much fun.

Before I could answer, the receptionist reached out with a perfectly polished fingernail and tapped the card impatiently. An illuminated Argonaut Group logo appeared on its surface, an etched hologram, along with a scrambled barcode glowing through the transparent material. Apparently, he was done with the niceties and wanted me out of his hair.

Yeah. Feeling was mutual, buddy. I didn't want to be here much longer either.

I leaned over to scan the code with my wrist-nav, and as not expecting what happened next.

I jerked back as my vision suddenly flashed green. As my eyes refocused, I could now see text floating midair, letting me know I had direct access to Castor's office.

I didn't like that. Although military-grade cybernetic eyes like mine had the ability to overlay information on top of normal vision, hanging in the air like a hallucination, I had those settings turned off, preferring to keep my eyes functioning as, well, eyes. With no added features. Normal. I didn't want to feel any less human than I'd been before a mortar shell blasted parts of me out of existence.

Knowing Argo had the ability to override that bothered me.

I noticed a pulsing trail to my right that led along the floor and around a corner. My directions, I presumed. Sighing heavily, I shot the receptionist one last look, but his eyes were locked on the computer screen again. I guess we were done here.

The trail led me around the corner and down a hall of stone walls lined with some of the earliest remineralized carbon samples that Argo had produced before its big breakthrough. The first fifteen floors of the building were made of the stuff, large slabs of basalt from the Whiteshell as a monument to the company's own history, but as you got higher, naturally, its next step in history was on display—Argite. The entire frame was a skeleton of recycled metals surrounding Argite cores, holding up each floor that was made to move independently, allowing the building to flex within tolerable bounds to withstand storms. It was a marvel of design and engineering, but it still felt weird being here again.

The hologram took me on a meandering path through the labyrinthine halls of the Argo building, passing innumerable Ivories in business attire, all staring at tablets or looking through smartglasses and too busy to notice the dutiful cleaning drones buzzing around their feet and along the walls. Offices and conference rooms lined the walls around me, and I could've sworn I'd gotten turned around and would be spat back out in the lobby, until the holographic path led me around another corner, towards what at first appeared to be a dead end. As I approached, a section of the wall slid to the side to reveal a private elevator that closed and began moving as soon as I stepped aboard.

As the shiny box ascended, I took a moment to analyze the situation, the hunter within remaining ever vigilant. Moving up meant good things. Just a meeting. Probably. Though the upper floors of the Argo building housed various important arms of the Argonaut Group—floors for Argo's finance department, one for its subsidiary hedge fund Kravchenko Capital, and multiple floors where Argo lawyers bent, or in some cases, intentionally broke, legislation and red tape—the work that mattered most was underground.

Floor upon floor of labs extended down through the surface and into the roof of Sublevel 1, nestled within the thick slab of carbon that held the juncture of the Red and Assiniboine rivers aloft. There, Argo-funded scientists and engineers toiled to develop the next great breakthrough, pushing humanity forward with each discovery.

A trip down to the labs would mean Castor was looking to drag me into whatever latest project was consuming his attention. No thanks. My sole reason for agreeing to this meeting was to get in, get ODIN fixed, and get out as quickly as I could. So going up was good.

As the elevator passed beyond the topmost floor accessible to the average employee, it began to slow down. It passed two more floors of private offices before the doors opened. This was my first visit to Castor's private office, and there was no announcement from the elevator to signal which floor we were on. As we came to a stop and the doors opened, the ghostly text in my vision flickered "Thank you" and dissipated, hopefully forever.

I stepped into an open space walled entirely with glass, with a mirror finish to hide the activities occurring on the other side. A quick glance around the room told me it was an ill-used but clean waiting room. To my right was a pair of small, low-backed, and uncomfortably firm-looking black couches, with a glass coffee table between them, beyond which was a neatly organized counter with a tea station and water cooler. To my left was a small walk-in closet where visitors could leave their coats. In front, meanwhile, there was another receptionist's desk, helmed by a woman in a uniform almost identical to her counterpart in the main lobby, and with matching laser-focus on her computer screen. As I approached, she said nothing and motioned to a blind corner on my right. I paused to take a breath, centring myself for the meeting ahead, and headed right ready to face my old friend.

As I rounded the corner, I came nose to nose with a massive human being. Although I was over six feet tall, I barely reached this behemoth's chin.

Allister Brown, the head of Argo's security team, was wearing the standard Argo guard uniform: a long-sleeved black-and-yellow jacket, black military pants, and a protective vest with a horizontal stripe made of flexible material that turned out to be a display, as the words *Argo Security* scrolled along. He had a pulse gun slung from his shoulder and resting slack at his abdomen, one hand gripping the upper receiver. A beefier version of the one I'd seen on the bounty-snatcher kid. Brown's military-grade version emitted a wide burst of energized plasma that, like charge guns, could be dialled from non-lethal to lethal. The relatively short range meant it was good for crowd control, which Argo security had a lot of experience with. The slab of meat and testosterone looked me up and down with his mismatched eyes. His left was a cool blue, almost sapphire, while the other was the colour of an exploding star, red and orange fire in the pupil of his cybernetic eye. He didn't seem thrilled with what he saw.

"Nikos," he grunted, arms crossed.

"Al." I smiled wide.

"Don't call me that."

I could see his jaw clench, and knew why. He hated being addressed by anything other than his last name—at least by me. While being here wasn't what I'd call fun, that didn't mean I couldn't find a bright spot.

With feigned shock, I stepped back slightly. "And how come? I thought we were pals after all that time you spent walking me out of the building, standing between Zara and me as we insulted each other."

Somehow, I got the brute to chuckle. "Yeah, but that doesn't mean we're friends, and certainly doesn't mean I won't put you out on your ass again."

"I'd like to see you try." I gave another big smile, and Brown stepped aside. Taking a deep breath, I steeled myself, mind focused on what was coming next.

The glass door parted silently, and I stepped through, admiring the space around me. Like the lobby, Castor's office had natural light pouring in through windows on all sides. The room was divided into sections by mobile partial walls, which I assumed could be moved at a moment's notice to create meeting rooms or huge workspaces, depending on what a project called for.

At the moment, Castor had organized the walls to form four distinct spaces. There was a small area with couches and a holoprojector. Another contained what appeared to be a design studio. The third room held a small table with a coffee maker. And the last was against the outer windows, empty except for a small prism in the middle of the floor, standing around a metre tall, surrounded by blinding sunlight, washing out the skyline beyond. An imposing slate-black glass desk sat in the middle of the room, at the epicentre of this spatial representation of Castor's mind.

The man himself was sitting at the desk, glasses on, scribbling on the screen that comprised the top of his desk. His head rested lazily on an open palm, elbow propping him up as he barely listened to the person shouting at him from the other side of the desk. Even from the door, I could tell he wasn't listening, not letting this latest lecture get in the way of whatever ideas were being moulded in his mind.

Of Argo's current reigning families, the Beauvillier family were generations of physicists, the Abara family were medical geniuses, and the Kravchenkos were born financiers. Castor Roy and his forebears, meanwhile, were artists, not of pictures but of technology and engineering. The family had revolution-ized artificial intelligence and robotics, with many of the service and personal assistance bots in the world being the brainchil-dren of his lineage. It was Madran Roy's machines that brought Guy Beauvillier's theories and plans to life on that island in the Whiteshell generations ago. An island chosen by Demetrius Wulf, who went on to legally incorporate the Argonaut Group, which eventually grew influential enough to bring in Aboyami Abara to head up its medical research division, allowing Argo to become the all-encompassing research and development giant it was today.

All, in a way, so those five childhood friends could work—and dominate the world—together.

By rights, I should be here as well, as the next link in a long chain of legal experts that started with Demetrius all those years ago. I had been trained for it. Readied for it.

At Argo, personal choice and personal interests really didn't matter. Those of us in the founding families were raised for a specific specialty, to do what your parent did before you, or to at least be good enough to lead the best and brightest in that field, given Argo could effectively hire anyone they wanted. If you weren't up for it, or weren't performing well enough, one of your siblings might.

It was your duty to fulfill your role.

Innovation had its price, though, and Castor was wearing it plain as day. He was a young man but looked much older—dark circles under brown eyes that stared intently at the documents displayed before him, small grey whiskers peeking from his skin, face slack in boredom as he was being chewed out by the one person I didn't want to see today: Zara Kravchenko.

As I approached, I caught the tail end of their conversation.

"Castor, I don't give a shit what they're protesting, or why we're the target." Zara's voice was fried, but still sharp and venomous as always, attesting to how much biting the snake had done today. Wearing a sleek and slightly glossy grey suit jacket that clung to her slender, sloping shoulders, Zara looked every bit like a cobra, ready to strike out at her fellow Argo leader, each biting word causing her short black bob to flare out like a serpent's hood.

"It's just a few broken windows, Zara," Castor retorted, his voice like silk. "The province will hand out some bounties, people will go to jail, the fines will cover the damage, and the storm will blow over. It's protests, not an Alberta dust storm. These walls will hold. Eventually they'll turn their attention to some other issue. That's the way it's always been."

"I don't give a fuck about how many panes of glass get replaced. These protests are scaring our investors, and that means bad things for our bottom line," Zara snarled. "You are the head of this company and your cute little smile is the one saving grace we have right now, so get out there and use it. Win that public favour back, because bounties are piling up and the province will only pay for them for so long."

Finally spotting me over Zara's shoulder, a slow grin crept across Castor's face, his eyes glinting mischievously. When she noticed she'd lost what little of Castor's attention remained, Zara whipped around, fury melting to childish irritation.

"Oh, speaking of bounties," Zara jeered, leaning back to perch on Castor's desk. The roboticist threw his hands up in annoyance.

"Hi, Zara," I chirped. "Having a rough day?"

She smiled, barely hiding her contempt. Her piercing grey eyes locked onto me, hardly wavering as she tracked my movements. "Oh, it's just peachy, Nikos. You know how it goes, we sit on our asses all day and let the economy of this country chug along like it's going to keep running forever. Never had to work a hard day in my life. What about you? Living the good life killing people?"

I let the last jab fly past like the weak punch it was. There was no way she'd know about my last bounty, and it was just meant to insult my station. "Mm-hm, yes, so great. Love putting the boot to the little people so you folks up here can enjoy the fresh air and have plenty of room to sunbathe. But if you ever took the time to check my record—which, let's face it, I'm sure you've done a thousand times—you'd find it relatively blood-free. Which would be important to know, seeing as the Eco-Terror Taskforce is clearing out all the people you lot don't seem to agree with."

"Oh! Did you hear that, Castor?" She looked down at him, and he turned to scribble feverishly on his desk with a stylus—quick, deft movements that betrayed his discomfort. "Apparently, it's our fault people get bounties on their heads. It's almost as if Nikos forgets where he comes from and who he really is. Careful, old friend, you might fall getting off that high horse you've planted yourself on."

A quick scoff from me earned a sour look from Zara, and knowing exactly how she would take the gesture, I caught a smirk from Castor. "Oh, don't worry Zara," I replied. "I wasn't planning on sticking around long. I can only stand so much of you."

"Well, good. You're ruining the air in here with your sublevel stink."

With that, Zara hopped up and strode out, intentionally clipping my shoulder as she did, sucking the air from the room in her considerable wake.

Without looking up, Castor broke the silence. "I was afraid you wouldn't show," he said to the desk, rather than to me. "Can't imagine why. How are things?"

"Life is good," I said, taking a few lazy steps towards Castor's desk. "Well, as good as it gets when you chase people down alleyways and get shot at trying to collect bounties."

The young CEO finally lifted his eyes. The look on his face was tired, but warm, showing he was genuinely happy to see me. "I hope you know Zara came in unannounced. The protests have her all jumpy. She can't see the forest for the trees."

"Yeah, she looks out and all she sees is green."

Castor laughed. "Unless she's looking at you. Then it's all red."

"Been that way since we were little, so why stop now?" I leaned against Castor's desk, studying the knick-knacks splayed across the touchscreen display that comprised its entire surface. Among the half-finished blueprints and other digital documents arrayed on the desktop were small items meant to fidget with, something Castor did constantly when his hands weren't otherwise occupied with something mechanical or digital to work on. I plucked a small baseball from the top of his desk and started tossing it from hand to hand, thinking.

It was true. Zara and I had never seen eye to eye, even as children when her take-no-prisoners ambition clashed with my more relaxed and inquisitive nature. Where Castor and I would spend hours tinkering or plotting fantastical and childish world-altering inventions, Zara had been laser-focused on being the best successor to her father. The oldest of three, Zara Kravchenko was mean, sometimes downright ruthless. She'd use her analytical mind to manoeuvre around the successes of her brothers to always position herself as the best, the most successful, and the unquestioned favourite to succeed her father as chief financial officer of Argo, and leader of its investment and money management subsidiary Kravchenko Capital. By all accounts, growing up in the Kravchenko family was tough, but fair, though Zara's ruthlessness came directly from her father, who had been one of the first to close ranks, turning on my father at his lowest point.

So it was no surprise that my reintroduction to Argo, even in this limited capacity, irked her. Ousting my father was part of her family's legacy, and to Zara, that legacy meant more than anything.

Castor stood. "You'd be surprised how often she screams at me," he said, snatching the baseball out of the air. "Her dad? Never raised his voice more than half a decibel. But Zara is a different breed. Every time there's another protest, or a funny rumour on the social feeds about one of our products, or another conspiracy spiralling out into the dark corners of the net, she comes barging in here, demanding damage control. Instead, I tell her not to worry, that these things always blow over. And they do."

That was the Castor Roy way. Calmly tread forward and see where the chips fall.

A light toss sent the ball back my way, and I snapped my hand out to grab it. "Well, I would prefer we never cross paths again." The ball went back to Castor.

"Well, I would prefer it if you were around more often. That, though, incurs the risk of running across the indomitable Zara Kravchenko." He chucked the ball back my way, a bit too far to the left, but I managed to grab it with my fingertips.

"Well, if she would apologize and stop giving me so much shit, then maybe I would consider it." I put some backspin on my return pass, but Castor caught it easily. Knowing the kind of goalie he'd been when we were kids, I wasn't surprised.

"Noted. But that doesn't help me with the PR problems." He placed the baseball back on his desktop next to what looked like designs for enhanced viral filters for synthetic lungs, like the one I'd seen on the ad yesterday. He gestured to the drawing. "If I went in front of the media every time there was a rumour or protest, I'd get nothing done."

I grimaced. "Yeah, if only there was someone within Argo's inner circle whose job it was to help the company save face whenever things got too … controversial."

If not for Zara's dad … and mine.

My father, James Wulf, had had no chance to build a similar legacy as those before him, as startlingly early-onset neurodegeneration took hold and he downright refused to get neural implants to stave off the condition, eventually leading to his ouster. Zara's father and, unfortunately, Castor's, had been the ones to give him that shove, citing the public risk and unsuitability for the job. Rumours abounded on online forums of the day, with supposed "insiders" citing scandal and infidelity—an assertion anyone who knew my father would have laughed at, owing to his adoration of my mother—while some other, stranger theories pointed towards unethical experiments my father had caught wind of, or the stock-standard claims of embezzlement, collusion with competitors, and even supposed plans to break away a segment of the company into an independent enterprise. What mattered was that my family was out. All of us. And Argo's remaining board moved swiftly to close off any claim I would ever have of regaining my father's lost position. To me, it was a simple power grab. From that point, he became a shell of what he had once been, my mother died, and I took off for Tempest.

Sensing my shifting mood, Castor sighed. "Yes, but just to be clear, that's not why I called you."

"Yeah," I said, watching him from the corner of my eye. "Despite what people like to say, you don't actually perform miracles."

To say being reinstated would take a miracle wasn't an understatement, and Castor knew it too. It would require a unanimous vote by the Argo board of directors, and despite a cordial relationship with Jaheem Abara, a tenuous friendship maintained with Castor, and an easily convinced Andre Beauvillier, Zara was never going to let me back in.

She'd made that perfectly clear to me.

"Well, how about you perform at least one, so I can get out of here," I said, removing my wrist-nav and sliding it across the desktop. "ODIN went dark last night, and I couldn't get him back online. Update him, take the data dump, maybe we can do a bit of our usual debrief, then I'll be gone."

Castor looked down at the wrist-nav and back up to me with a confused squint. "Is that the only reason you came?"

I nodded, trying to block out the hurt expression that flashed across Castor's face.

"Ah … well, then," Castor sighed. He tapped quickly on the desk's surface monitor and set the wrist-nav on a glowing circle where it would connect to the secure system Castor had to himself.

"Well, this will take some time …" he muttered, the mischievous glint returning to his eye. "So screw the debrief, I have something more important to show you."

He turned on his heel and waved for me to follow him to the room behind his desk that contained the gleaming prism. I groaned inwardly.

"It's true that I can't perform miracles," he said, his quick footsteps echoing off the shiny floor. "But this might be the closest I've gotten in a while. To be perfectly frank, I've had a tremendous breakthrough."

"Castor, come on, let's not do this," I said, following reluctantly behind. "I have things to do."

Ignoring my protests, Castor reached the far side of the room and turned to face me, his back to the glass wall and the shining prism between us. He was grinning ear to ear. At the sight, all hope for a quick and easy exit turned to dust on an Alberta highway. Somewhere, ODIN was smirking.

"Do you remember when we made ODIN?" he asked. "I mean the one we made when we were kids. How we thought he was the pinnacle of artificial intelligence?"

I couldn't help but chuckle. "Everything you make, you call the pinnacle of something, Castor." In truth, ODIN was always more of Castor's creation. The program had started out as a few lines of code that could solve semi-complex puzzles. Castor built it, and I was the ever-willing Turing test, a role I took on with every new iteration of the synthetic intelligence.

"And what amazing progress we've made. Smashing the plateau every AI before him hit," Castor waved his arms around emphatically, willing his enthusiasm to latch on to me. "Could you have ever imagined ODIN would have grown into what he is today? How long has it been now that you've had him?"

I knew Castor was baiting me, but I played along, if only to humour him.

"Twelve years," I replied. "You gave him to me at the funeral, asked me to help him learn."

Over the decades, AI had advanced close to a point that had once been deemed only theoretical: the singularity, and true intelligence. Argo had had a big hand in that, turning its eyes towards AI and automation in order to make processes more efficient. The tech was currently used to find optimal engineering patterns for cities, ways to construct buildings to withstand shifting climate and weather patterns, predict storm conditions more accurately to prepare people for when they would hit, and even to manage transportation, maintenance, agriculture, and climate control in population centres in a way that reduced inefficiencies while also maintaining comfort for people living in them.

Consequently, AI had been able to learn for a long time, but ODIN was different. Sure, many hunters had AI companions they worked with, purpose-built to aid in navigation and administration for the 2100s' favourite peacekeepers for hire. But they were just fancy personal assistants, scripts and code, same as you could get right off the shelf in any tech shop. ODIN, though? He could anticipate things, take what he saw or heard and develop complex and nuanced pathways of knowledge. He wasn't reactionary like the AI of old, following a clear set of instructions at increasing levels of complexity. He was faster and smarter than that. ODIN could understand me. He was, as close as could be scientifically stated, alive.

"Well, get ready," Castor said, raising his hand overtop of the prism, which caused the windows around us to darken, dimming the lights. "Because ODIN may now be obsolete."

With a gentle tap of his hand, the prism came to life in a flash of aquamarine light. I couldn't help leaning in for a closer look. Lines of blue light danced across the surface, spiderwebbing deep into the centre of the prism, where they ricocheted and pulsed at a dizzying speed. There was something uncanny about the way these lines of light moved together, and as I brought my nose even closer, I realized I was staring at what was essentially a synthetic brain. I stared at the mass with a mixture of awe and confusion.

"This," Castor continued breathlessly, "is the culmination of decades of research. A set of complex neural pathways mimicking the mind of a human being, created through billions and billions of interactions and self-referential thought processes."

I took an unsteady step backwards as the realization struck me. "It looks like it's thinking, but that's not possible," I said as pulses of light flew down the streaking blue roadways. "Even ODIN's cognition is just a set of algorithms playing out to find the optimal or most likely outcome of any situation based off calculations or previous information."

"They said AI could never learn," Castor answered smugly, "but a true artificial intelligence has technically never been impossible, just extremely difficult to produce. My father laid the groundwork, but I gave him form. It's a 'him', by the way. I call him Prometheus."

"Seriously? Greek Titan, sibling of Zeus, the one that gave man fire?" I fought the urge to roll my eyes. Castor always thought highly of his creations, so it came as no surprise he'd chosen to name this one after yet another god. "Isn't that a little heavy-handed?"

"Prometheus was the beginning of man, so this will be the beginning of something else," Castor said. With another tap, the lights within the prism slowly faded away, leaving behind an eerie afterglow in the darkened room. I could still make out Castor's face hovering behind it, grinning widely. "Now, follow me."

NINE

We were going down. Fuck me, of course we were. I should've known Castor would turn this into a field trip.

The worst thing was, Castor said nothing the entire ride down. He just stood there, hands in his pockets as he rocked back and forth on his heels gleefully, smiling at me out of the corner of his eyes. In contrast, I was silent, arms crossed, leaning against the wall of the quickly descending elevator, absentmindedly gazing down at the wrist-nav that wasn't there. It—along with ODIN, the only reason I'd come here today—was still upstairs "updating and repairing," as Castor put it.

Apparently, my suspicions had been partly correct. There was a hole Castor hadn't patched; it had just taken a large data buildup for it to show itself.

The least Castor could've done was save us some time and *explain* the next part of our journey, but no, of course not.

The elevator doors glided open noiselessly to unveil a long, glistening white corridor stretching out before us, lined with large windows made of ceramic reinforced glass, displaying the work going on within the various rooms. These windows created the feeling of a shopping mall, where you could stroll around and browse the latest creations. Or perhaps, more aptly, it was like a theme-park attraction, where children could gawk at the spectacles of the near future. Men and women in lab coats milled about the hall, talking, staring at their tablets, or rushing off to some important task.

Castor led the way with a confident and determined stride, while I trailed, hands in my pockets, peering into the labs to avoid eye contact with anyone who might know me. Eventually, one of the labs caught my eye. Within, there were three people, wearing masks and bodysuits to keep dust and contaminants out of the room, working on a machine projecting a wall of light about four feet wide. Without a word, I stopped. It took Castor a while to notice, but he happily jogged back to join me.

"These are physicists from the floor above," Castor explained. "Their labs lack the equipment necessary for this project, so we are allowing them to work here," Castor said, giving one of the scientists inside a curt but affirming nod.

"What are they doing? Do they really not have lightbulbs upstairs?" I asked sarcastically.

"They're trying to alter the properties of light to make it more solid," Castor answered, gesturing as one of the physicists tossed a few stones and a stylus at the light-wall. Amazingly, they seemed to slow down midair as they passed through the shimmering golden sheet. "Suffice it to say they are trying to make 'hard light,'" he continued. "The plan is to have large beam emitters installed around cities in areas hit hard by storms. When one rolls in, the emitters fire out subatomic particles, while also condensing those particles in line with each other to create a protective bubble around human settlements. The B.C. government also wants to test whether it could replace the sea walls along the Pacific Coast. Significantly cuts the maintenance costs, ecological costs, and gets rid of a particular eyesore for property owners."

I was about to ask more, but Castor heel-turned and kept walking.

Near the back of the corridor, far from the elevators, we came to Castor's personal lab. It was the only one that had two-way mirrors for windows, allowing him to see out but no one to see in. As we approached, a small scanner above the door swivelled in our direction, a bright red ring around the lens blinking slowly before flashing green. There was a heavy clunk within the wall, followed by a few smaller clicks as the locking mechanism unwound to give us access. Castor swept a hand along his head and torso, signalling that it was programmed to his biometrics. As with the elevator that I'd ridden up to his office, Castor had taken great pains to ensure only those he deemed worthy could see his work.

The thick metal doors of the lab slid open to reveal a black void within. We had to walk a couple metres in before the motion sensors activated the lights in a blinding white flash. I jerked up a hand to shade my vision. My eyes struggled to adjust, automatically filtering out some of the incoming light, but not fast enough. When I was finally able to see, what I found around me was astounding. A workshop for a genius mind.

Countless projects, from fully completed prototypes to piles of seemingly random scrap, were littered around the room. Cybernetic prostheses in varying stages of completion were laid out alongside different parts of robots. Castor seemed to be pulling the former apart for use within the latter. The largest project was what looked like an early prototype for a scorpion-like tank, which sat in one corner of the room. It was missing a couple legs and its back was bleeding wires. Thankfully its tail—which looked like a large mining laser—was lying a few feet away, unattached.

Many of these projects would never see the light of day, or even make it out of this room, but those that did could be worth a fortune. I had to admit, it was impressive. Their creator was now at the opposite end of the room, by a set of massive sliding doors almost camouflaged into the wall.

With the press of a panel, the lights dimmed, and the doors began to creak, shuddering under their own immense weight as they opened. This was a vault inside of a vault, and the most valuable thing in this entire building was likely tucked away within.

Standing at the ready, watching me with a knowing smile, was Castor, and then it clicked. The persistent calls. The messages. Maybe even ODIN's blackout. It was all to get me into this room, to this moment. A captive audience for Argo's next big breakthrough, courtesy of CEO Castor Roy.

Clouds of vapour began to pour from the cracks in the wall like water from a dam. Lights from within had flicked on and were seeping through the widening space.

"Always the showman, Castor," I mumbled, trying to mask my growing awe.

The doors parted to reveal a small set of metal stairs leading up to a platform. Suspended from wires above it was a figure illuminated by bluish light. A sleeping metal behemoth, seven feet tall, slender, built for speed and manoeuvrability.

"With this platform, we will make ecological destruction

and eco-terror a thing of the past," Castor began, sounding every bit like a proud father. "He will be the greatest and most complex artificial intelligence ever seen by humankind, within a frame that is stronger, faster, and more agile than any human could ever hope to be. With a form able to withstand the worst storms, unaffected by the elements, and sustained by sunlight and gaseous compounds useless—or even poisonous—to humans, he will never tire, will never worry about the risk of death, and will always find his target."

As I listened, my throat began to tighten. "What the hell is this?" I said, more to myself.

Castor was unfazed by my shock. "It's a way for us to make the world safer—to make your job safer." He walked over to stand beside me. "Prometheus is the answer we need. Eco-terror work— hell, even bounty hunting as a whole—has become dangerous, and it's only a matter of time before things get worse, Nikos.

"I wish we could let people run roughshod over the countryside like it's the 2020s, but we can't. Eco-terror laws protect the structure we've put in place to protect humanity, to protect this city, and we need assurance that the worst of the eco-terror groups are under control. Things will continue to get worse before they get better, and having Prometheus means we'll have a bulwark against that flood."

I crossed my arms and gave my friend and hard stare.

He wasn't wrong. Whether I wanted to admit it or not, I did have to carry a lethal weapon, and for good reason. Anti-establishment groups, including those deemed eco-terrorists, operated in a strange grey area, unhappy with the new, post-climate-crisis world order in a variety of ways, committing acts corporations like Argo had flexed their muscles to criminalize, in an effort to "protect our assets," as Zara would probably say. But the fact the acts were deemed criminal didn't stop the groups from carrying on, wanting to achieve their ideological aims.

Most anti-establishment groups had started up innocently enough. Small collectives of people resisting the changing world, aligning on issues and experiences that came up against the work corporations like Argo were doing. Pushed to the margins of legality while corporations strode forward, carving out control of the planet in the name of "progress," "growth," and "ecological stability," the anti-establishment groups gave people a chance at survival, pushing back against a world that was leaving them behind. So Cyber Volition would keep modifying their bodies illegally through friendly clinics. The Human Reclamation Front would still sell illicit human enhancement meds to keep humans level with machines. The Plainswalkers would still synthesize illegal crops. And lately, it was starting to look like a certain demographic was willing to kill to for it. That was a cause for concern.

And it wasn't just Argo that was suffering as a result. The Eco-Terror Taskforce was also spread dangerously thin as the definition of what constituted "eco-terror" continued to grow in lockstep with the growing number of violent crimes, and this past month alone had seen two good hunters—Gregor and Glasgow—killed on the job. Gregor had been shot by two Cyber Volition members who were buying illegally modified neural implants, and Glasgow had been tossed through a window on Sublevel 5 after being ambushed in a high-rise apartment block when he tried to apprehend a Plainswalker accused of stealing agriculture drones from out near Brandon. Both had been hunting for years, and both had spent time in the top ten of the Bounty Board.

And both incidents were an uptick in violence for both groups involved.

Sure, hunters had died fulfilling contracts for Plainswalkers and members of Cyber Volition—and the groups weren't squeamish when it came to trading fire with me and my colleagues on a good day—but what Gregor and Glasgow had been there to serve certainly didn't necessitate the response. Those deaths were weird. Even unprecedented.

Then there was what I had seen the last two days. A new player in the market. While I knew the histories of groups like the Plainswalkers and Cyber Volition, their aims, and generally how far they were willing to go to protect their own "assets," this new group was something else. They had an experienced middleman fixer like Sobotka willing to die before revealing what they were after, and a young guy who seemed to have it all—and no previous record—threatening politicians and corporate execs, then ready to try and kill a bounty hunter for getting in his way.

They were connected, violent, and worst of all, anonymous. There was no telling where they would go from here, and Sobotka's words still echoed in my mind.

They won't let you stop what's coming. All will be steel and sun.

My gut told me they were dangerous. And I'd be lying if I said the outcomes of my last two bounties hadn't shaken my confidence as a hunter.

But the technology Castor was proposing was something else.

I stepped closer to the behemoth, studying it like dog

inspecting a new scent. Its seven-foot frame was made of aluminum and steel, long and slender arms ending in massive, three-fingered hands larger than my head, tipped with a glistening ore I knew from a glance was diamond-hard Argite. The thing's legs were likewise long and thin, perfect for loping steps and generating immense force. The casing of its left leg was off, exposing the mass of wires and servos underneath, a soft blue glow emanating from within. The eldritch figure hung in front of me, a soulless husk suspended by wires and chains like a caged animal fallen unconscious, small clouds of vapour descending from the vents above, chilling the air and sending shudders through my body. Its lifeless eyes—two short slits positioned on either side of its narrow face—were two black voids.

On its chest, "001" was stamped. This thing, the first of many.

Prometheus was supposed to be some sort of saviour; that was Castor's intention. A noble pursuit for a noble young mind, but I couldn't see this thing fulfilling his lofty expectations.

Sure, it would be precise, powerful, and unflinching in danger, but it lacked the character and humanity that human hunters possessed. Was it capable of reasoning with a desperate target for the sake of gathering important intel on a group's inner workings? Could it show mercy? How much resistance would it be willing to take from its targets before it took a life in self-defence? All the information in the world didn't matter in those moment-to-moment decisions.

Then my mind returned to Maxwell Van Buren, how he'd died because I'd lost focus, had been hurt, and was overpowered by him—a kid. Would Prometheus, all metal and Argite, mind and will of a machine, have been able to prevent Maxwell's death?

"Nikos," Castor said. "I understand your reticence to even consider this, but my hands are tied here."

Unwilling to waver, I swallowed hard. "So you're going to put this thing out on the streets and do what? Quash any protest against Argo because you've decided human farmers wasted too much fuel and didn't use the land efficiently enough, or because human transport drivers spent too much time idling? Maybe shake down a small-time repair shop on Sublevel 6 because they use scrap from the Human Reclamation Front?"

"If that's what it takes to protect everything our families worked to create, then I just might," Castor said, standing behind me, arms crossed. "Whether we like it or not, this is the world previous generations left us with. Governments privatized and purchased with the promise that Argo would save the planet from a disaster we, as a species, made, and we did. We kept up our end of the bargain, and that necessitated us taking some measure of control. So now if Argo goes down, the country goes with it." He paused for a moment. "We're on the same side here, Nikos. You have to see that."

"Even if that's true, hunting requires a certain level of ... well ... humanity," I replied, turning back to him. "Castor, this is a machine, meant to do a complex human job, and we know humans are unpredictable, almost random. You can't control entropy."

"Well, you'll just have to teach it humanity," Castor stated, as if it were a forgone conclusion.

I gaped. "You want *me* to teach this thing?"

"Of course, who better to teach him than the famous Wulf?"

Castor said, eyes locked on me expectantly. "I mean, over a decade of data from you and ODIN working together only goes so far. He needs to see you in action."

I could only stare at the machine in front of me.

There was an undeniable cost. It was a project that could upset the balance of power in the city—in the country. Train an artificial intelligence to do what I did better than anyone else, a job that, after the last few nights, I was beginning to question whether I had the stomach for, or, more accurately, if it had outgrown me.

If this new player in the eco-terror world was as serious as I thought they could be, a lot of people could die—so was Prometheus worth it?

Or was this just Argo stepping into another market it had no business in?

I needed time to think.

TEN

I didn't take a copy of Prometheus with me when I left the Argonaut Building. However, I did not leave empty-handed.

When I returned home, a discordant chime rang throughout my apartment that eventually coalesced into the melodic hum of ODIN, back in action.

"So," I began, "Castor get everything sorted out?" I tossed my jacket onto the kitchen table and descended the steps to the living room, splaying out onto the couch while watching Sublevel 4 life through the window. The natural afternoon light from the surface was gone, but the last vestiges of it remained, reflected down here off buildings as evening lights began to flick on outside the window. I kept the apartment dark so I could enjoy the view.

"On our return trip, I ran some diagnostics," ODIN replied. "It all seems to be fine, though I'm seeing some cluttered files in your mask. Nothing to worry about, just some duplicated data from your attempts to restore me, but otherwise we seem to be in the clear."

The fact ODIN was playing data janitor was a good sign he was back to his old self. I, however, was not. Not mentally, at least.

I propped my leg up on the coffee table and rotated the appendage, feeling out the injured joint to see if there was any lingering pain. Aside from some residual tightness as the swelling continued to dissipate, it felt better now. The meeting with Castor, and the mental flurry it had kicked up, was the sore spot now. I'd much rather deal with physical pain than this Gordian knot of morality.

Guilt still hung around my neck as I thought over the Van Buren contract. But now, as I rolled the thought around, I wondered about Prometheus, a machine acting on a script, following orders without the compulsion to feel guilt like what I was experiencing. I couldn't settle on whether it was a good or bad thing. Maybe guilt and regret were integral parts to being a hunter, breeding compassion and mercy, but maybe that was part of the problem.

I thought about it again. The Van Buren contract. I'd done my job, but that didn't mean what I'd done was right. That it hadn't had to get to a point where we were fighting over a loaded gun. If this became the new normal ... could I continue being a hunter?

Sensing my warring mind, ODIN broke the silence. "Do you want to talk about the meeting?"

"How much did you hear?"

"Enough." Once Castor's diagnostic and repair programs had restored ODIN to a point where he could get his metaphorical feet under him again, he'd hopped into the Argo building systems and followed the trail of my security clearances to join us for part of Castor's little sales tour. "It is an interesting, yet troubling, proposition."

I let the thought hang.

"I mean, he's got a point," I eventually replied. "The Bounty Commission is swamped. It's always been bad, but before, it was this tide around our ankles, sometimes lapping as high as our knees—but still a pool we could wade through no problem. But now?" I blasted air through my nose, a half-hearted laugh, just thinking about it. "We're drowning in contracts, and if I were a younger man maybe I'd enjoy it, but—"

"You're not a young man anymore."

"Exactly," I snickered. "But … beyond that, it's different. Prometheus was made to take over bounty hunting, and in some ways, it might not be a bad idea."

"How so?" ODIN asked.

"Because it's starting to feel different. Or maybe *I'm* the one that's different." I shifted uncomfortably in my seat, suddenly aware of how worn out I was. "I've been in the line of fire plenty of times and taken out perps with rap sheets longer than my arm. That's the job. I signed up for it."

In my mind's eye, I could see Sobotka jamming the pulse gun under his chin, his hard eyes as he pulled the trigger. Then Maxwell Van Buren's smiling face, his blood leaking between my fingers as I tried to compress the wound in his chest.

"But these bounties we're seeing lately … There's something different going on. Like the city is changing. Yeah, Castor is right—it's getting more dangerous. But why?"

My meeting with Maria came to mind. A simple job—handled in moments, and nobody died—just like they always had been. Juxtaposed against my last two jobs, it looked like a totally different world.

"We've now had back-to-back deaths. One guy, a fixer, with no solid connections to any anti-establishment or eco-terror group, killing himself so he won't have to sell out his buyer. A buyer, mind you, who sent guards to escort him to the pickup, then scooped them up off the pavement when things went south. Then we've got a second guy—er, kid," I corrected myself and shifted uneasily again, a pit forming in my stomach. "A kid from a happy family, good education, financially secure, who suddenly falls down some rabbit hole and turns into a wannabe eco-terrorist, who jumps at the opportunity to fight and try to kill a bounty hunter."

ODIN hummed softly. "And both espousing some very poignant ideological rhetoric," he said. "Destruction and salvation—it all sounds rather ominous."

"Maybe Prometheus is the way out? Up the ante on the right side of the law?" I asked, glancing at one of the sensors ODIN saw through.

"Maybe. But didn't the police say something like, that once upon a time?"

My eyes followed scattered transports making their way through the evening din outside. A bit of fog hung in the air, a mix of evaporation and synthetic clouds pumped out by climate mirroring, so everyone was flying just a bit slower, being careful not to collide, letting the AI co-pilots keep them clear of buildings and each other. I traced lines between the scattered sublevel ceiling lights that pierced the fog, stars visible through the murk of a cloudy night sky.

"Thanks, ODIN," I mumbled. "Take a break, buddy. You've had a long day."

"Certainly. Let me know if you require anything."

And with that, ODIN winked off, leaving me alone with my thoughts, Castor's words echoing in my mind.

You'll just have to teach it humanity.

The way he'd said it. The look in his eyes. The certainty. Like my acceptance was not up for debate. But was it even worth it to try? Did I really want to get tangled up with Argo like this?

I was raised to see our expulsion as a betrayal, plain and simple.

At the time, I didn't understand what was happening, the forgetfulness and impulsivity overtaking my father's mind. His flat-out refusals to accept neural implants to slow the same degeneration present in the two generations before him, and the failure of any other treatments they'd collectively tried. But it didn't excuse the way we were unceremoniously cast out, swamped by tabloid reporters, hack lawyers, and countless competitors ready to scoop my father up at the earliest convenience. Yet he turned everyone down. He never made comments to the media, never sued his old partners; it was almost like he wouldn't … or couldn't.

I pitied him—how could I not? His mind had rapidly failed him, and his demeanour would swing from panicked confusion to silence and distance. Lost to the condition eating away at his mind, too late to preserve what was left. He often mumbled to himself about something he'd forgotten. Then, in the end, especially after my mother died, he was a wraith, silently haunting my childhood home.

I understood why they did it. It was cruel, but I understood. As Zara would say, it was just business.

Could I really trust a corporation like Argo to have a hand in bounty hunting, though? Supplying these drones to the Commission in place of people? My father had been family to them … What would they do to people who opposed them, given the chance?

As I gazed out to the swirling fog, it began to clear, revealing the sublevel beyond, the picture coming together. This was my home; those who lived in it, my people. What would it say if I left it all behind? Even worse, what if I left it in the hands of Argo?

Rising, I turned and moved towards the bedroom. I don't know why, but I felt a pull towards it—the desk drawer—and the memories contained within.

It took a second to remember the code, but I found that my fingers responded eagerly, punching in the four digits quickly, like they'd been preparing to do so, despite the fact I hadn't opened the thing since I'd moved in over a decade ago.

At the time, after selling or trashing most of what Dad had left behind, I'd shoved the things I couldn't bring myself to get rid of into the drawer. Literally locking away the past so it could be forgotten.

God, Mack would rip into me if I said that out loud to him.

But it was true. I came home after my father died to nothing—nothing except this city and a tidy inheritance—and decided to build a new life. A new me. A new legacy for the Wulf name. Which meant that everything in this apartment had to be new too. Nothing from the old Wulf family home made it inside these walls, except for me, my mother's analog clock … and the contents of the locked drawer.

A small click echoed through the quiet space, followed by a mechanical pop as the drawer jerked open suddenly. I pulled it the rest of the way, revealing a small framed photograph—the only one in the condo. The compartment had an airtight seal, so there was no dust inside, giving the sight an eerie quality, like I was looking at a pocket out of time.

I delicately picked up the photograph, and was swallowed by the memories it, too, contained.

There was one time my father had allowed me into his office at Argo for more than a few moments. He always told me there were special things lying around that nobody could know about. When you're working with politicians and lobbyists, there would always be some secrets they would not want the world to know.

This time, though, had been an exception.

He brought me in and let me sit in his chair, to look over the desk that, one day, was supposed to be mine. I remember sitting there, barely able to look over the damn thing, with my dad standing right beside me, his hand on the back of the chair. Across from me, off to the side a bit, was the photo I now held in my hands, containing the image of a happy family.

This was not one of those stuffy photos, where we would all get dressed up so we could blow the picture up to a ludicrous size and hang it above the fireplace to be admired by men and women in business suits at fancy parties. It was a picture of Mom, Dad, and little me, sitting on a dock together during the summer. Dad's skin was pink, with the beginnings of sunburn, his sandy-blond hair swept back, sapphire eyes scrunched so tight from his smile they almost looked closed. Mom was smiling in a way I hadn't seen since years before her death, hazel eyes calm and content, the small mole on her left cheek ringed with sunscreen. Her head was leaning on my father's shoulder in a small moment of intimacy, auburn hair cascading down her back. Then there was me, small, with messy blond hair, wearing Dad's massive sunglasses. I was smiling in the photo, caught mid-giggle, trying to keep the sunglasses from falling off my face.

There was a quiet snap.

"Oh shit," I whispered, as the old frame, made from wood collected from around the water where the picture was taken, fell apart in my hand, the pieces tumbling into the drawer.

Despite the desk drawer seal, after so long, the glue holding the handmade frame together—despite my mother's expert hand in crafting it—had disintegrated, and the whole thing fell apart with it.

I gently pushed the glass to the side, so I could free the photo pinned beneath, and picked it up. It felt oddly worn, the corners slightly bent, as if it had been removed from the frame multiple times throughout its life, but despite all these years kept in the same spot, sandwiched inside the frame, the corners still curled in. I'd never given the photo more than a second glance as a child, but now here it was, in my hands. I turned the photo over, and on the back it read: *They are your prize, your pride, and joy.* A note my father left for himself. The kind of cheesy line Ivory suits need to make their work seem worth it while the whole world, and their whole lives, move on outside their office doors. But below that was something more puzzling. Two sets of numbers and letters, scrawled hurriedly in red ink, which my PMC-moulded brain identified as coordinates.

Eyes locked on them, I pulled out the chair from my desk

and dropped into it, spinning the seat around so the light filtering in from the window behind me illuminated the object in my hands.

"ODIN?" I mumbled. "Are you seeing this?" I angled the photo towards one of his sensors.

"Yes," he answered. "Looks like one set points to West Hawk Lake—specifically, a small island on the northwestern side—and the others are right in the middle of Lake Winnipeg. Up near the northern shore."

"Why would Dad bother to write these on the back of a photo?" I wondered aloud.

"I don't know. I never knew the man. That's something only you could answer."

But honestly, I didn't know either. Two locations, and the only thing tying them together was the fact they were in lakes. Why were they so important that my father had written them on the back of a family photo, and then repeatedly taken that photo out to look at them, like he was afraid he'd forget? Or—knowing where his mind ended up—maybe he *had* forgotten.

By the time I'd left for Tempest, he'd grown so frail, so paranoid, like he'd aged decades in the space of a few years. Maybe once his memory started to fade, he'd thought writing the coordinates here would help him remember. On the back of something he would presumably see every day, so he could maybe hold on to that knowledge for a little bit longer.

Racking my own brain, though, I was also coming up empty. The ones in West Hawk, at the very least, were pointing to the island where the Argo founders had first tested their carbon remineralization technology. It was also a short canoe trip from the family cabin, so their experiments had been in close proximity to comfortable lakeside accommodations. All told, it made some sense why Dad would write it down. It was an important piece of our family history, and if his memory had gotten so bad that he couldn't remember exactly where it happened, it stood to reason he'd write it down *somewhere*.

The other coordinates, though? I pulled up my wrist-nav and plugged in the coordinates myself. Oddly, they didn't point anywhere. Just to a spot in the top half of Lake Winnipeg, smack in the middle of the water. No islands in sight. Just water.

So why? There had been one time my family rented a cabin out there, on the shore of Limestone Bay. It was the last trip we'd ever taken with my grandfather, who died a few months after, so maybe that's why Dad wrote it down. So he could remember the last time he'd gone fishing with his father? Then why where these numbers not the location of the cabin?

Great, that's just what I needed—more questions.

A notification banner dropped down from the top of my wrist-nav screen.

It was a message from Mack.

You. Me. Maria. Haven. Tonight. We need to celebrate.

I couldn't help but smile. The magic of Mack. Always able to brighten my mood. Good thing, too. I needed to clear my head, and there was no better reason than getting the gang back together.

ELEVEN

ike every night, Haven was packed. This was its normal state, hunters filing in and out throughout the day,
whether they were working or not, to take a few moments and
be around our kin. Conversations ranged from loud to soft,
hunters swapping stories or trading information, stopping by
other tables and booths to shake hands with old friends or grab
a quick word with any of the top trackers in the game.

To say Haven was a bar would do it a disservice. It wasn't the
kind of place with thumping music, people gyrating their hips
on stage in various states of undress, and service bots making
sure your cup was always full.

No, Haven was a hunter bar.

Nestled under a Bounty Commission service station on
Sublevel 5, it was the perfect place to blow off some steam following a contract. It wasn't uncommon for a hunter to walk
out of the station, gear slung over their shoulder, and pull a
near one-eighty to descend the steps a metre to the right of the
station door.

The music was quiet, barely audible tracks from the 2070s and 2080s played on a loop, just how Fayola, the bartender, liked it, and enough to set the mood without interfering with conversations. The lights were low, moody, and easy on the eyes, changing brightness throughout the day to match the outside so you could tell roughly how long you'd been there by how much—or how little—you could see. Furnishings were exactly what you'd expect in an old pub, with booths around the outside walls, tables of various sizes, and chairs that never seemed to be in the same place from minute to minute. Along the back was the bar itself, glass-topped with a small rim of LEDs that faded between colours, surrounded by circular bar-stools, and above it was the main attraction: the Bounty Board.

The board had many purposes, manifest and latent alike. Though the Bounty Commission maintained the Bounty Board for taxpayer transparency—contract payments were split seventy-thirty between the federal government and the provincial governments, for folks who paid attention to that sort of thing—but all we hunters cared about were the bragging rights.

I sat at the bar, idly swirling the drink in front of me, watching the screen. Actually, there were three screens set into the wall, with font large enough to be read from any corner of the barroom.

Regardless of specialization, task force, unit, personal skill, or moral standing, every single hunter was on this board, and it was how we measured ourselves against each other. Eco-Terror Taskforce, Homicide Unit, Arson Group, General Pool, it didn't matter. We were all equals when it came to the Bounty Board.

The leftmost screen showed the daily leaderboard, names sliding up and down as bounties were closed and credit counts rang up. It wasn't legal to bet on the standings—yet—but that didn't stop hunters from wagering big sums that they could finish somewhere on the daily list before it reset at midnight.

The rightmost screen showed the big movers of the month. Hunters who were climbing fast, and falling faster, had the honour of being on that list.

But it was the centre screen, biggest of all, that was the source of everyone's attention: the Top 150. There were thousands of registered bounty hunters in the city, but the cream of the crop got their name on that middle screen. Names in massive font, next to headshots and flags showing their country of origin, and their career point totals. At the top of the list was my name, with career earnings displayed in nine digits—not that it was a fair comparison, seeing as I was handed specialized contracts with credit values that some hunters couldn't reach in a year. Closest behind me was Mack, in the eight digits, and Maria should still have been in third, but right now her spot was occupied by a Filipina hunter named Sophia "Harpy" Neves. She'd been born in Davao City, on the shores of the Davao Gulf in the country's south. But after her hometown had been wiped off the face of the earth by a massive storm, taking more than half a million people with it, Sophia's family wound up in Winnipeg, where she made her name bounty hunting.

"Are you going to finish drinking that? Or am I going to have to finish for you?" Fayola said.

She was cleaning out a glass with a bright yellow cloth, smiling as always. Her name meant some variation on "lucky," but you would swear she was blessed, given her bountiful energy and limitless empathy. I'd been a hunter for twelve years now, and that whole time, Fayola had been here at Haven, ready to lend an ear and fill up a glass. Of everyone in this building, I was probably the only person who knew her real age, since I'd won a bet with her one night and the only prize I would accept was that little tidbit. But for a woman pushing seventy, especially living in the sublevels of a city like Winnipeg, you'd never know it. She was tall, more fit than some hunters, and her ochre skin was clear of even a single wrinkle or blemish.

I smiled, knocking back the drink and placing the glass gingerly on the bar top with an expression that said, "Are you happy?" to which Fayola nodded approvingly, before exchanging my empty glass for a full one. Thankfully not vodka—although it was the cheapest spirit on the market, often made from potatoes that were part of huge carbon farms—but good old Manitoba rye.

"So you heard Valkyrie is back in town?" I asked, spinning the glass with my fingertips, the LED light flaring from the bar top changing the colours in a strange and almost hypnotic way.

Fayola nodded. "And thank goodness. I swear, if that little one had stayed with Ironways one more day, I would've tracked her down wherever she was and dragged her ass home myself. PMC be damned."

I had no doubt that she would have. Though not a hunter, Fayola had become like a mother to thousands of them. She knew the game as well as anyone, and the gunslingers paid to play it, but although she'd never picked up a contract in her life, she knew every trick in the book. Often you'd find hunters at the end of their rope trying to chase down leads, leaning over the bar here at Haven, begging Fayola to help them out. Which she always did. Because we were her "little ones"—except Jaeger, of course. The old man had been hunting as long as

Fayola had been tending this bar, and despite decades of cama-
raderie, Jaeger would never allow her to give him the title she
gave the rest of us.

She leaned on the bar, relaxing further. "And before you go
getting sour on me, yes, I did keep it from you, at her request.
Now as soon as her probation is over, I can restore her career
totals to the board and you'll finally have some good competition … unfortunately."

I snorted. "Unfortunately? You want me getting complacent
up there?"

"Oh, believe me, if I had my way, you'd quit while you were
ahead." Her hands got to work fixing up some drinks after a
hunter behind me signalled for another, but Fay's eyes and
attention remained on me. "Now, you know I've got my ears
to the ground, and I get confirmation about how all bounties
finish up, so you can be damn sure I notice when things get a
little too hot."

Nodding slowly, I picked up my glass and took a sip, pressing the cool rim to my forehead when I was done. It was getting
hot indeed, on the streets and in the air. "So you know how my
last two bounties ended."

"Mm-hm." Fay placed a pair of green-tinged drinks on a service bot's tray, which zipped off to deliver its payload. "Suicide
and accidental shooting. When I noticed you were the one
cashing in, it made me uneasy, to be sure. Not usually how your
jobs end." She slid a beer down the bar top to a waiting hunter,
who nodded in thanks. "You got any idea why things have gone
so poorly?"

Suddenly, I felt that familiar roiling weight in my gut, the
one I'd hoped coming here would help soothe, but luck like

that was in diminishing supply, apparently. It seemed this topic would follow me wherever I went. "Sort of. And by 'sort of,' I mean not at all. But maybe you can help me out here." I brought up the falling-star sigil on my wrist-nav and turned it towards Fay. "You know anything about this?"

The bartender threw the yellow washcloth over her shoulder and leaned in, balancing on her forearms, brow scrunched tight as she studied the image. "Well, shit." She shook her head slowly. "You know I always keep my ears open when people come through my bar, And I can tell you this: you're not the only one who's been seeing this, these—"

"New guys," I finished. "The ones with the falling-star sigil."

"Exactly," Fay continued, her eyes going hard and focused, and I could see her tense. "Hell, I've known every single anti-establishment group in this city—some who got snuffed out or splintered long before you picked up a gun and bounty hunter licence—so when I catch a whiff of new blood on the street, I pay special attention. From what I've been able to gather, sightings of that logo only go back about six months. Apparently, the very first was from Gregor's helmet feed before he …"

I sighed. "Died."

"Yup. Apparently, there was someone in the room with Cyber Volition that day, sporting that symbol."

Fay stood back as another hunter cut in for an order and got to work on it while I waited eagerly for her to continue.

"We both know Cyber Volition has never been the nicest of people, so whatever deal they were in the middle of must have been major—enough to kill a hunter over. And now I see you with two contracts, a day apart, going sideways, and you tell me both were connected to that strange logo? Can't say I'm too keen on seeing where this trend goes."

Unlike Fay, I *was* keen on following this trend. From what I'd heard about the night Gregor died, he was busting a couple Cyber Volition members who'd been trafficking modified neural enhancements, which was big business for them. The group often fell under eco-terror scrutiny, so I'd had enough experience to know they could get violent, being more fanatical and ideological compared to their anti-establishment peers. So when Gregor died, I had chalked it up to the general misadventures of being a bounty hunter in Winnipeg.

But now, I had more questions. This mystery group had been around six months, and were operating largely under the radar, perhaps in the circles of illegal augmentations—until now, when they'd kicked things up a notch, targeting Argo. Regardless, Fay was right; things were getting hot.

"Hey," Fayola said, knocking on the bar in front of me to break me out of my ruminations. She smiled. "Don't be so down, hun. I know you'll be able to figure it out. Besides, the three of you are back together, which should put these wackos on notice." Fayola reached under the bar and pulled out a large green bottle, the label in German and sporting a deer logo etched into the glass. Our eyes met for a moment; my confused gaze matched by her cheeky grin. "Oh, you thought for a second I believed you'd be here drinking alone? You're out of your mind, little one."

As Fayola grabbed a fresh pair of glasses, a cheer rose from the hunters around me, and amidst a chorus of claps and friendly insults, in walked Mack. Always the crowd-pleaser, he mimicked a regal wave, like one the Queen would make on her tours around the former Commonwealth.

And beside him was Maria, back in her street clothes, with a bag slung over her shoulder bearing the glowing holographic sigil of the Valkyrie: a golden representation of her own helmet, flanked by unfurled wings.

I turned back to the bartender, finding her with one of the two drinks in her hand, laughing at her favourite patron.

"Mack told you about our little reunion celebration, didn't he?" I said.

Fayola only winked, then turned to serve another patron. The sound of an old cash register rang out over the music, and every hunter in the bar raised a toast, cheering, eyes trained on the main Bounty Board screen where Mack's earnings turned green and spun up to his new number. The man was twenty thousand credits richer—a big payday. There was no celebratory animation for Maria, though. Until her probation was done, her name wouldn't be up there again.

By the time I got up from the barstool, Mack was already on me, wrapping me in a hug. Today his long coat was emerald green, glittering like something he'd stolen from the Land of Oz, and had white trim to match the white pants he wore—accented with a few splotches of crimson on his thighs. His helmet was tucked under his arm, so I could see the transparent healing pad pressed over a new mark on his cheek, and although hunters were required to turn our weapons in at the door, Mack's revolver was still strapped to his hip, tucked nicely into its holster.

There were perks to being the owner's favourite.

"How's it going, brother?" he said through the tight embrace. Before I could answer, he placed the helmet on the bar top and flopped onto the stool with enough force it spun him halfway around. Once he'd twisted back to face me, Mack held his hands up to his face, framing what would soon be a thin scar on his high and pronounced cheekbone. "You like? I think it makes me look tough." From the angle and straight edge of the cut, mixed with the bluish tinge his olive skin was taking around the wound, I surmised that it was a laceration caused by blunt force trauma, likely from getting hit in the face while wearing his helmet.

Maria rolled her eyes. "I told him it looks like he should stop grandstanding when he's trying to cuff a bounty target." She was in a black windbreaker, zipped up the middle, that bore the Commission logo on the breast and read: *Community Protecting Community: Manitoba Bounty Commission* underneath. It was part of the introductory package all new hunters got when they were certified.

I also happened to know the Bounty Commission sold them for a tidy sum. Everything got merchandised, apparently.

"I think it makes you look like you got punched in the face," I replied, shaking off the worry of the past few hours. Mack and Maria had that effect. "I hope the poor bastard who hit you was wearing hand protection. Punching a helmet would fuck someone's digits up pretty badly."

Fayola snorted, sliding the glass of brown German booze towards Mack. "Well, I don't like it, little one. But you knew that already."

"Of course, Fay." Mack smiled at her, teeth white as fresh January snow. "And no, Nikos, the bastard wasn't wearing hand protection. Not that it matters, because he hit me with his elbow, which *did* break, but still, I got a nice facial scar that I can show off to all the lovely ladies and gents at the Breather Club."

"Breather Club?" I leaned on my elbow, fist propping up my head, eyeing my friend with complete skepticism. "Since when do you go to a Breather Club?"

Maria blew a jet of air through her nose and sat down on my other side, dropping her bag at her feet. "Please, don't get him started. He was talking all day ab—"

"What's the issue?" Mack interrupted, arms held out in a grandiose gesture. "A guy can't start being more sociable? Sit in a dark room, take in fancy oxygen, and rub shoulders with Ivories in virtual reality? I just think it might be a great place to make some friends, or—y'know—more."

Breather Clubs were a little bit more than that. Building on the concept of oxygen bars of the 1990s, Breather Clubs hooked customers up to oxygen lines, which mixed in small doses of hallucinogenic drugs, and plugged them into a virtual reality playground. Some transported themselves into the Roman Forum, or a Jurassic-era jungle, or simply a nice park in nineteenth-century London, where they could mingle. Part social club, part commodification of the purest oxygen, part virtual escape—and all unaffordable to the average person living in the sublevels, where we made do with recycled air and scrubby plant life.

There was nothing illegal about it, per se, and it was something I could see Mack enjoying on his time off. But I also saw his real game.

"Uh-huh." I snatched up another drink that Fay had left beside me and took a swig. "Or what you mean to say is, you want to build up some more high-profile surface contacts. Influential and well-connected Ivories loosened up by microdosing hallucinogens, primed for you to endear yourself to them using your usual charm. Might be good intel and financially valuable connections for you." Aside from being one of the best bounty hunters in the city, Mack, like Fayola, had become well known for being something of an information broker, always knowing who to ask or where to look to find whatever you're after. It helped that he was a charismatic and deeply likeable guy. The complete opposite of his brother, leading many to question how two seemingly perfect opposites could be cut from the same cloth.

"That's exactly what I said," Maria mumbled. "Not that there's anything wrong with it, but he kept trying to say it was all for the fun of it." She took the glass Fayola offered her with a grateful smile, which the bartender returned.

"Okay, fine, it's for *both* reasons. You figured me out. Not all of us have the simple dumb luck you have, sir." Mack took a healthy swig of his drink, hummed in satisfaction, and gave Fayola a thumbs up. "What I mean to say is, with your rugged good looks, fame, fortune, and somewhat compulsive cleanliness, it's a wonder you've stayed single so long."

He cast a glance over to Maria, whose attention had turned to the Bounty Boards, before leaning in close to me with a conspiratorial grin. "But that works out perfectly, now that *someone's* ba—"

I jabbed my hand out, covering his mouth, leaving his words to die in my palm. "Consider the subject changed," I said in a measured, forceful tone. Mack winked, but seemed willing to leave it—for now—so I withdrew my hand. "How'd the contract go today?"

"Well, aside from this ..." he pointed to the healing pad, "it went swimmingly. Had a bounty broker contact me this morning, said they had twenty thousand credits lined up for me if I went and grabbed a transport thief for them."

Yep, that sounded like a Mack job. Despite his standing in the community—and on the Bounty Board—Mack had decided against joining up with a single specialist group. No task force or unit could catch his eye for long enough before the call to another adventure wormed its way into his mind. So he was always taking offers from bounty brokers—those who handed out privately-placed bounties, rather than the ones coming to the Commission through Manitoba Justice.

The one constant for Mack was his preference for the Eco-Terror Taskforce, so we could always find a way to share a contract, a payday, and spend some quality time together.

"You got twenty grand for a transport theft? That's a bit steep, even for Ivories. And it even passed muster in the court?"

"Apparently! But hey, it happened in Tuxedo, so maybe the guy knew the judge who approved it. Wouldn't be the first time. Anyway, a few nights ago, some rich banker was up late on some VR golf course when he heard a noise from his garage. Went to check, and the guy cracked him across the face, tore open the garage door with his bare hands, and flew right out in the transport while the poor sap was concussed on the ground. And that's where the perp made his mistake, because if it was a simple theft—"

"It wouldn't meet the minimum requirement to set a provincial bounty," Maria finished, taking a long drink, her attention back on our conversation.

Made sense. Isolated instances of theft were typically a police matter, and bounty hunters were only brought in if there was some serial nature to the crime. Clearly, this Ivory wanted retribution.

Mack took another sip. "Exactly. But with the assault thrown in the mix, the last victim found a sympathetic judge and got a personal bounty pushed through."

If something didn't meet the minimum requirements for a provincial bounty—which varied by the type of offence, with violent crimes having a lower requirement compared to property crimes, and eco-terror crimes having the lowest requirements of all—members of the public could set one for a fee, which, these days, ran you around five thousand credits. That is, if you passed the background checks—the government didn't want anti-establishment members using the bounty hunters as their personal revenge tools—and then there was the approval committee. Sixteen randomly selected "upstanding" individuals were brought in to comb through the proposed private bounty, the reasoning behind it, and whether there was any reasonable doubt that the person targeted had committed any crime. It was a time-consuming and costly process, making it almost exclusively an option for Ivories. But by greasing the right palms and knowing the right people, the process could take a few hours—sometimes with disastrous consequences.

"Still doesn't explain how a five-thousand-credit fee gets pumped up fourfold," I said.

Mack smiled, shrugging. "What can I say, Ivories love their fancy luxury transports. Can't take public transit or walk like us sublevellers, right?"

I nodded. "But how'd you get dragged into this?" I turned back to Maria, who was leaning on the bar, the zipper of her windbreaker held between her teeth.

"Easy five grand" she said, looking bored. "We showed up at the guy's doorstep, he said he wanted to grab a different shirt—which Mack agreed to for some fucking reason." She shot a disappointed glare Mack's way. "So when he didn't come out, Mack went in, got clocked in the face, and I took the guy down as he made a beeline for the fire escape."

Confused, I raised a hand and looked towards Mack. "Hold on. You only gave her twenty-five percent? Aren't we equal partners? That's the rule."

"That's *Jaeger's* rule. Not mine." Mack polished off his drink and turned to get another, but Fayola had disappeared.

The music slowly faded away, and so, too, did the disparate conversations as hunters began to notice something was going on. I cast my eyes up and down the bar in search of Fayola. I saw her leaning against the far wall, one hand on the volume dial for the sound system, the other pressed down hard on the communication implant in her neck. I couldn't immediately see her expression, but as she turned slightly to the side, in what appeared to be a one-sided conversation with the person on the other end, I saw all I needed to. Her eyes were glassy and unfocused, her face drained of colour. From so far away I couldn't hear what few words she was saying, but the look said enough.

Suddenly the weight of the whole room was on her, eyes locked on the bartender, owner, and confidant. She released the implant, placed her palm down on the counter beside her, and turned her head up to look at the Bounty Board, just like everyone else.

On the centre screen, within the top 150 bounty hunters in Winnipeg, one line flipped from white to red, and then was gone. Number 87, Hugo "The Judge" Richter. All the names from 88 down slid up, with a new name joining the list at the bottom.

Hugo was gone, like he'd never been there.

Mack hung his head. "Shit. Just like that, eh?"

"You know him?" I turned, looking briefly at Mack, then gazed out at the rest of the bar. Most hunters had turned back to their drinks, while others sat staring at the screen, or had heads bowed in prayer—or grief—and still others carried on like nothing had happened.

"No, not really," Mack said. "Ran into him here a couple times, and a couple times while working, I think—can't really remember—but, all told, I never heard anything bad about the guy. Did you?"

"Nope. Never met him. But if he got up to eighty-seven, that means he was one hell of a fighter."

"Yep, but that's the life we lead, right? You either die early or you die old. Hunters never retire."

The phrase rang in my head. Hunters never retire. It was one so common to us it had nearly lost all meaning. Back in the early days, it was what Jaeger would say to us, something to get us to think, maybe be a little safer; but it just as often came as a retort to our mentor when he'd chew us out for being too reckless. After all, if hunters never retire, then what do we have to lose? But today it was sobering. You live your whole life dodging bullets, and eventually your luck runs out, and death catches you. We had to be lucky every day, but death only had to be lucky once.

My thoughts drifted back to the Argonaut Building, to my conversation with Castor and the reason why I was here.

Hunters never retire … but what if they could?

I finished my drink and set the glass down. Searching for the words, I spun the vessel around with my fingertips, letting the bottom glide along the shining condensation on the bar top. In the past, the three of us could talk about anything, but this was something different. It was a change so radical to the fabric of our society that I had a hard time seeing all the ripples. Sure, I knew the problem, and I knew Castor's proposed solution, but I didn't know how it would shake out. What ripples now would turn into a tsunami later? Would this even work? Could we really capture the best of bounty hunters in this Prometheus AI and not have any of it tainted by the worst?

When legislators had first tabled bounty hunting laws in the late 2020s, it was purely theoretical, creating a freelance structure around justice, overseen by the state, that gave citizens more control. We could dispense with chunks of massive policing budgets and turn that money towards other things, like schools, addictions treatment, housing projects, job training, and universal basic income, while offloading the boots-on-the-ground work to private citizens and communities. At the time, it was seen as too radical an idea, but by the 2030s, when the war against climate change ramped up and the government needed money fast, they took that idea and ran with it, taking a hatchet to federal, provincial, and even municipal policing budgets, and replacing it with a democratized alternative.

Money came from those cuts, the open market meaning it was done at a fraction of the cost to the provinces and feds, with the provinces being allowed to fund it however they liked. Choice for the provinces and choice for the people, that's how it was billed.

Then, when it got near-unanimous approval in Ottawa, reality set in. Laws were drafted, the Charter of Rights and Freedoms was amended, and whole structures for overseeing, vetting, and operating the bounty hunting system had to be created essentially from the ground up. Winnipeg was the test case, and in the beginning, it worked. Communities and citizens were happy to handle issues themselves, and governments were happy to redirect huge funds towards Argo and other corps trying to save the world. Now, though, almost a century later, we were back somewhere approaching square one. Would Castor's proposal be the next step in an evolution of justice? Or was it more of the same?

"Hey." Mack's hand flew past my face and I jumped. "He asked if you want another drink."

Kwame was behind the bar now, wearing his grease-stained kitchen apron and the biggest smile I'd ever seen. Probably compensating for his boss's dour mood, but also partly fuelled by the fact that he loved people, Kwame had stepped out of the kitchen to assume bartending duties while Fayola took a minute. The young man hailed from Ghana, a nation now half reduced to desert, and half covered in ocean water, aside from the Volta and Oti regions, which still had land enough to support a small citizenry. Rarely given the chance to test out his bartending skills, Kwame looked at me eagerly.

I ordered another rye and turned to Mack. "If you could retire tonight, what would you do?"

Mack laughed, picking at a plate of fries Kwame had brought over while I had been lost in thought. "You're kidding, right? Retire? In this city?"

"Humour me, please. What would you do? Same for yo—" I went to nudge Maria, but she was gone. I saw her standing over by the door to the kitchen, talking to an obviously emotional Fay. I turned back to Mack.

He grinned good-naturedly and popped a few more fries in his mouth. I could tell he was considering my question while we sat in silence, watching the names rise and fall on the daily board.

Our profession was part of a multibillion-credit industry, but not many of us still had money lying around. So as not to have the bounty hunting system take up the same swelling budgets of police forces up until the 2030s, since the service had been individualized, so, too, were the costs. In our world, money went out just as fast as it came in for most. Aside from regular bills, you had to supply your own weapons, ammo, armour, transportation, and tech, none of which were cheap. Then there was the upkeep of those things, and the costs of going through physio, paying for counselling to deal with all the trauma, and the fees you needed to pay just to ensure that you kept your licence—plus the firearms and legal certifications you needed on top of that. While bounty hunting was easy to get into, the costs made it almost impossible to leave, so while many hunters might have made millions in their careers, there was no guarantee those credits would still be in our pockets when we wanted to say goodbye.

The only thing we *didn't* have to pay for were medical expenses—universal health care was one thing that the people of Canada downright refused to let the government privatize.

Mack wasn't like that, though, as despite his lavish trappings, his family had never been wealthy, so he and his brother Trapper cherished every single credit they earned. The fact they lived deep in the sublevels was out of pure pragmatism—it was leagues cheaper—plus they didn't want to live apart. I knew that Mack probably had seventy to eighty percent of the credits listed next to his name on the Bounty Board, so obviously he wasn't hunting for the money—not anymore, at least. Like me, he'd joined as an idealist, wanting to make the city safer. Growing up, his family hadn't had much, and he knew what it was like to grow up poor, live poor, and do anything it took to survive. It was part of the reason he took so many private contracts. Taking money from the rich instead of from the average taxpayer's pockets appealed to him more—and same with me.

Yet even knowing he could walk away, I could tell the thought weighed on him.

"I guess … I would leave," he finally said. "Bounty hunting was the reason I came to the city in the first place. I never would've convinced Trapper to come here if it wasn't for the fact I was certain this is what we were meant to be doing. Like, I spent *months* coming up with reasons we should go, appealing to everything in him to convince him it was a good idea, and eventually he wore down."

Knowing how stubborn Trapper could be, I understood the task Mack had undertaken. The elder brother was extremely private, hated the noise of the city, hated the lights, and was a deep traditionalist to his core, but in the end, he could never say no to his little brother.

I did know that, very quickly, leveraging the family name and whatever good that brought them in this city, Trapper had begun to work on the periphery of the bounty hunting system, taking contracts he could ensure were for a noble purpose. As part of the Bounty Commission criminal intelligence and recovery unit, he took the jobs nobody wanted—snatch-and-grab, intel collection, recovery of stolen goods, counter-surveillance, even got out of the city on occasion for agricultural production violations—and would always answer the call if a subleveller needed a private contract fulfilled, often paying the fee himself and forgoing any compensation. He would never show up in the top tier of the Bounty Board, but he kept his soul clean, and in this city, that was a rare feat.

"If I had to pick something, though," Mack continued, "I'd probably pack up and go somewhere else. Where bounty hunting isn't a big deal and corps like Argo can't find me."

I smiled, picking up the glass of rye Kwame had deposited beside me. "Good luck with that, Mack. Your options there are pretty limited, I'd say."

Mack waved away my point. "Beats working for a PMC. I'm not interested in travelling around the world, toppling governments, or ensuring Argo, or Vertex, or Ravencrest, or whoever the hell else has exclusive mining or agriculture rights to wherever catches their fancy."

"You should try toppling governments, gave me a lot of good stories ..." I wiggled the fingers of my cybernetic hand. I hadn't exactly been doing that in Brazil, per se, but it had been a shitshow all the same. "Where would you go?"

"Not sure. They've done a lot of rebuilding in Greece, and what's left of the country is moving to get back out of the European Union. Maybe I'll take my credits there, build a cottage on Mount Olympus, spend my days tanning, drinking wine, find a sweetheart and settle down. I have enough that I could find somewhere to go and just go. Not that I want to."

The thought of Mack living a nice, quiet life in the mountains made me smile. In his youth, life had been simple like that, so it stood to reason he would return to it someday. He really enjoyed the flash and adventure of being a bounty hunter, though, so that dream was likely quite far off.

"And if you had to start working again? Would you be the next great poet? Writer?" I continued, stealing some of his fries.

"Fashion designer."

"Okay, yeah, I can see that." We both laughed, but I couldn't escape the nagging feeling that maybe I was the only one thinking about finding a way out, and everyone else was fine riding out this whole bounty hunter experiment to its conclusion. Maybe like with the PMC, my path was going in a new direction. It was just that, this time, the path laid out for me was one on which I'd take every bounty hunter with me. But was it really the right thing to do? Maria had come home to pick her arms back up and join the fight, Mack saw it as his calling, and for me, it had been the only way I could see to make a difference for people in this city.

Then there was this new faction of the anti-establishment. If they were able to turn someone as privileged as Maxwell Van Buren into a ready-made radical, and get an experienced fixer like Ivan Sobotka to kill himself for them, then what else were they capable of? Could I really think about walking away with something like this brewing?

"Why are you asking? Thinking of hanging up your guns? Finally letting me take over the top spot up there?" Mack pointed to the Bounty Board screens. The right screen had flipped to show open contracts with credit amounts.

Keeping my eyes on the Bounty Board, I couldn't find the words. What could I say? Castor's plan was still so unbelievable, and I wasn't even convinced the Prometheus AI was a good idea either.

Bounty hunting was a such a lucrative industry, it was no surprise that a megacorporation would want its grubby hands in there, but the credits involved supported people. Not only the millions of hunters around the globe, but people like Fayola and Kwame, places like Haven. The industry meant real things for real people. How could I even begin to explain what Argo had in store for us, let alone that I had had been asked to play a role in it?

Then I thought of the names on the board, flashing red before dropping off entirely. Mack and I had sat on these same stools countless times, watching names wink out of existence with startling, and sobering, regularity. Names like Hugo's, disappearing like he'd never been there at all, to be forgotten, his records left on a server in some government building.

I turned and looked around the bar again, at all the faces, the people laughing, drinking, swapping stories, catching up. There were fresh-faced hunters sitting shoulder to shoulder with grizzled vets, some of them parents, readying themselves to head home to their families and loved ones. If Prometheus could save even one of them from dying, would it be worth it?

Then again, if I took bounty hunting away from them, would that really be saving them?

Or would they become just like the farmers, custodians, auto mechanics, professional drivers, librarians, medical aides, tradespeople, and countless others whose chosen career had gone extinct because a machine could do it slightly cheaper?

"Hey, Nikos. You okay?" Mack cast me a worried glance. "You're spacing out again."

"I'm fine, Mack, sorry. Just thinking about Hugo."

"It's okay, brother. I get it." He wrapped his arm around my shoulder, pulling me close so our foreheads met, and whispered, "Whatever is happening, you've got us. The both of us."

Mack pointed towards Maria, in a booth with Fayola, arm around the bartender just like Mack was doing with me. The sight sent a flicker through me, and glancing at Mack, I could tell he was reading my mind.

"We've got to make good use of the time we've got. Because sometimes you don't get a second chance."

Looking back at Maria, I knew exactly what he meant.

TWELVE

I awoke in the middle of the night with a start, as if I had been simply dropped into consciousness. A fierce downpour was hitting my window, as another storm seemed to have rolled in to soak the dry late-summer landscape, the noise filling my ears. Pale light filtered through the blinds, blue and sombre, as if waking, itself, was a reason for sadness.

My body felt strange. Like I was floating. But maybe that was just the alcohol.

Groggily, I rolled to the edge of the bed and got to my feet. Down to just my boxers, the chilled evening air pumped from the A/C into my apartment made my skin break out in goosebumps, but the sensation was numbed by the semi-drunken tingling on my skin.

So far, so good.

I moved to leave the bedroom, stumbling slightly, and stopped at the threshold, one hand on the doorframe and the other gently pushing the pocket door aside.

Then, as the door slid silently into its housing, a whisper reached my ear.

There was someone in the apartment.

Warning klaxons blared in my mind, and instinctively I stepped back, nudging open the bag of gear on the floor next to me with my foot.

But it was empty.

My heart began to thrum as I stared down at the bag. My armour was gone. Ditto for the carbine and pistol I hadn't bothered to store in the weapon locker after the Van Buren contract.

Bad practice. Laziness my superiors back at Tempest tried hard to drill out of us. I was slipping. But right now I'd have loved to have them by my side.

I swallowed hard and steeled myself for the likelihood of a hand-to-hand confrontation with whoever was waiting for me on the other side of my apartment. After the last couple days, given the dangerous people I'd run afoul of not just once, but twice, there was a real chance I was in serious trouble. But I had the benefit of familiarity with my surroundings, and I knew my best bet would be to take it slow, using my apartment's layout to my advantage, and hopefully catch them by surprise. I slid into the waiting shadows on the other side of my bedroom door.

A shadow cut diagonally across a figure standing at the opposite side of the apartment, obscuring the upper potion of their body in darkness and hiding their face, with ethereal blue light from the window illuminating the rest of the figure. From this distance, I could confirm it was a male, with a build almost identical to mine. I quickly appraised the intruder, who was dressed plainly, and didn't seem to be concealing any weapons. But even an unarmed man could be dangerous. He had his hands clasped behind his back and was looking down at the framed picture on the coffee table, the smiling, happy family. Wait, no, that couldn't be right. The picture and its broken frame were back in my locked desk drawer.

Then he turned, stepped forward, and I froze.

Shifting light slid as the figure moved, revealing a hard, lined face, eyes of ice, and a patch of stubble over his jaw, mouth cocked in a grin. A face I'd buried twelve long years ago.

"Hello, Nikos." My father's tone was measured, calm, easily cutting through the machine-gun rattle of the rain. The downpour was so heavy it seemed to block out all the lights of Sublevel 4. There was just the pale blue glow. But none of that mattered. I was currently facing a dead man.

"I know you have many questions," my father continued, "but we don't have time for them now. There is one more threshold for you to cross. And I must show you."

Suddenly furious, I balled my hands into fists and hissed back, "This is not real. You're not real."

My father smirked. "Then neither is this." He raised his hand, gesturing to the floor where a thin layer of water appeared, rising from nothing to encircle our ankles. But I couldn't feel it. It wasn't cold to the touch, and as I stepped through it, the liquid followed, but at a slight delay, as if time were racing to keep up with me.

The thing calling itself my father then began changing before my eyes, a wave of cubic shapes rolling across its form to reveal something entirely other beneath. The figure's form shifted and jostled, nearly impossible for me to perceive clearly, but the longer I stared, the more features I could pull together. Dark skin stretched taut over slender facial features, black eyes with flecks of bronze, a gaunt body with long limbs. The clothes became a billowing cloak, white and covered with shifting blue symbols I couldn't make out, long sleeves that extended well past the figure's arms, and the length of the cloak draping down into the water.

"What are you?" I asked, stepping closer with soundless steps through the discordant water.

Its voice was thin and reedy, sentences falling almost to a whisper as it spoke through a wide and thin mouth lined with countless fine teeth hidden under a slight fold of skin, sounding as if it were whispering right into my ear. "There is much you do not know. But do not lose faith, Poseidon-touched. You must stop what rises from the depths before it is too late. You must stop this."

"What did you call m—"

A loud crash filled my ears, and I turned just in time to see the outer glass wall of the apartment shatter, a torrent of water rushing towards me. I barely had enough time to hold my breath as the wave enveloped me and threw me off my feet, swallowing me in a roiling sea. There was only darkness, with brief flashes of light as I spun weightlessly in the deep, unable to tell up from down. Which way I needed to swim to safety. If there even was safety. This was impossible. This was a dream. It had to be a dream. There was no way this could be happening.

In my spin, I caught a glimpse of the wall at the last moment, the surface screaming towards me. Impact imminent.

My eyes shot open as I gasped for breath, my lungs accepting it greedily.

In the throes of my nightmare, I'd gotten tangled in the sheets, where I now lay motionless, not wanting to disturb the reality I awoke to. The feeling of weight from the swirling waves slowly dissipated, revealing a layer of sweat that saturated my sheets.

It was early in the morning. Thin blades of sunlight slashed across the walls of my bedroom. Yesterday's clothes were in a pile next to the bed, and through the fading haze of my nightmare, I recalled getting home from Haven late and crawling straight into bed after undressing. I could already feel the hangover setting in.

Taking some deep, even breaths to slow my racing pulse and sate my lungs, I sat up, images from yesterday flooding back. The trip to Argo. Castor and Zara. Prometheus. The family photo in my desk.

Focus on the real, Nikos. Focus on that safety.

Fully awake now, I untangled myself from the sheets and walked to the desk, where I fumbled with the lock code in the dim half-light of my bedroom. I reached into the drawer where I'd stowed the disassembled frame, feeling around for the photo I'd left loose inside. My fingers found the worn edges of the curling photograph and I carefully removed it, turning the image over to gaze at my father's smiling face.

"Finding your way into my nightmares now, eh?" I whispered. "Talking nonsense, as usual." I sighed and chucked the photo back in the drawer, letting it slide shut silently.

He'd looked so healthy in my nightmare. The square jaw, set and strong, under shining blue eyes filled with light and brilliance. Like he had when I was a kid, and a far cry from who he became when I was a man.

By the time I'd left for Tempest, he'd been a paranoid ghost of a man. Thin and weak, only changing clothes when either his nurse or I helped him. He spent his days roaming around the house, mumbling strange things to himself. Wouldn't surprise me if he'd given me the same speech when he was still alive.

There is one more threshold for you to cross. And I must show you.

Yes, of course, Dad. Go back to bed. We can talk about it tomorrow.

Ever the perfect assistant, ODIN had already started the coffeemaker. Trying not to aggravate the headache beginning to throb behind my eyes, I shuffled into the kitchen, filled a mug, and pressed my forehead against the cool cabinet doors as images from my nightmare floating through my head.

My father's face, twisting and changing. Glimpses of dark eyes, taut skin, and a shifting cloak within a shifting, impossibly murky figure. Long-fingered hands reaching out at me as the water broke through the window, drowning me with a dire warning.

I must've overdone it last night. I blamed Mack for that.

ODIN's voice cut through my musings. "Nikos?"

Thank God he spoke quietly.

"Yeah, bud?"

"Which one was it this time?"

I sighed. "A new one, actually. My dad turned into a monster and tried to drown me by sending a tsunami through the apartment."

"Ah," he replied. "That would explain the thrashing."

I smiled, gazing at one of his scanners, tucked up in a corner just above eye level. "You were watching."

"I'm always watching."

Fair. Not like AI has to sleep, right?

"You think we need to go through the modules again?"

At that, ODIN chuckled, a warbling laugh that was oddly soothing, musical. "No. You seem to be doing just fine—hangover aside. Your heart rate is back to resting baseline, and I'm not detecting any other physiological signs out of the ordinary. I just wanted to let you know that Castor called last night … multiple times. I just diverted them because I wanted you, Maria, and Mackenzie to have a nice reunion."

"Oh." I straightened my spine with a groan and tapped my throbbing head. "It was a great reunion. Keep it up, ODIN. I'll call him back when I'm ready."

"Of course, I'm on it. Was there anything else of note from your dream?"

I leaned my forehead back against the cabinet and closed my eyes, letting the memories come back. Again, I felt my lungs tighten as I thought of the wave crashing towards me, and I began to rewind. Water rushing away to be held behind a glass wall, swirling and relentless, but contained so I could hear my father clearly again. Or at least that thing my father became.

You must stop what rises from the depths before it is too late.

From the depths we will rise, Maxwell Van Buren had said. *The time of steel and sun has arrived.*

Steel and sun.

Those were among Sobotka's final words as well. A cryptic message in place of his buyer's name—the one missing piece from the deal.

My eyes snapped open. "That's it," I hissed.

"Wha—"

I held my hand up, silencing ODIN. "This entire time I've been worried about Sobotka's buyer, finding out who they are and what they want, and last night I had the answer right there in front of me." I turned, descending the stairs somewhat uneasily on my way to the bedroom. "But I was so caught up thinking about Castor's offer, and Prometheus, and all that other crap, that I missed it. Sobotka was trying to broker a deal between this mystery group and who?"

"The Plainswalkers," ODIN replied, following my logic.

I entered the room and scanned it, trying to find where I'd left my wrist-nav the night before. "Exactly. And who do we know with an in with the Plainswalkers?"

Mack picked up on the third ring, voice weak and raspy, the way he sounded when he didn't get enough sleep. "Nikos?" he croaked. "What time is it? What's going on?"

"I need a favour … but you might not like it," I said clenching my jaw, knowing how touchy Mack and Trapper could be about their childhoods.

"Yeah?"

I exhaled hard, and the room tilted slightly in protest. "I need to talk to your cousin."

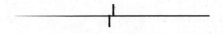

Sunlight flared so bright I almost forgot I was underground. The automated mirrors bolted to the buildings surrounding the surface shaft we walked through were tilted perfectly to capture sunlight from the surface and reflect it to fill the space around us. For the greenery in the Sublevel 7 park, which stretched across the width of the shaft, it also meant plenty of UV light to feed the shrubs, bushes, and gangly arbour. A few metres ahead, Mack walked casually, helmet on, hands in the pockets of his long coat; its hem was kicked up by a gust of dust and debris as a personal transport swooped by. I was behind, also geared-up, carrying only my pistol. We weren't expecting trouble, but heading into Plainswalker territory meant things could always go sideways. They owned this sublevel, and people didn't forget that. Getting tangled up with a small-time anti-establishment group wasn't usually part of the Plainswalker game. They were old money in the anti-establishment world. Largely former farmers, whose land had been bought up by Argo, forcing them into the city, where work was hard to come by. Angry and dejected by this new establishment, the Plainswalkers had been born.

We snaked our way through the park, cutting across the surface shaft to the other side, and continued down a cramped side street. Massive windows lined either side of the pedestrian route, showing multilevel grow-ops for various bioengineered produce on the sides. While a lot of food grown on the surface was as close to natural as could be in the 2100s, there were certain foodstuffs that couldn't stand up to the harsh conditions and shortened growing seasons. Sublevel 7 was where most of that came from, which made it perfect territory for a group like the Plainswalkers to live and operate. While there were still massive licensing fees for different crops, particularly those that could be grown in contained grow-ops like those on Sublevel

7, the Plainswalkers flouted those rules, trading, synthesizing, or even outright stealing licensed crops for their own use, or committing the big one, unlicensed crop synthesis—criminalized because the government didn't want a new super-seed that could become invasive and decimate precious greenspace.

As we continued, Mack crossed the wide walkway, slipped left into one of the grow-ops—a place producing grapes for wine production, another Sublevel 7 staple—and disappeared.

I continued on like nothing happened, and after a few seconds my comms crackled, Mack's voice coming through calm and measured.

"Keep going, he's a block down on the right. Local cam footage shows him talking to a Children of Atlantis preacher," he said. In the background, I could hear a creaking door, and an annoyed shout that was cut off, likely as Mack flashed his hunter licence.

"On it," I replied. "I'll let you know when I'm in position."

I weaved through the crowd, slipping between groups of people gathered, drinks and food in hand, enjoying a quiet Sublevel 7 afternoon. Couples and families laden with bio-grade boxes stuffed full of UV-grown produce and synthetic meat products bounced between grow-ops and grocers, trying to complete this leg of their trip.

I dodged a pair of small children running past, rebreather masks dangling from their necks—the oxygen levels down here were better than most places, thanks to the abundance of plant life and decent ventilation—and passed an older gentleman who was angrily hammering on a sublevel heater.

Ducking into a small, enclosed winery as cover, I brushed away the collected condensation on the window from the jury-rigged climate mirroring spouts and scanned the crowd, looking for our target.

Off in the distance, I spotted the preacher standing on her pulpit, waving flyers at passersby, trying to convert them, while momentarily dipping low to speak with a figure I could only assume was Clayton Fabron. My mask zoomed in, giving me a better view.

The hood of his sleek grey jacket was up, obscuring his face, and he had his hands stuffed in its small pockets, but as he turned to look over his shoulder, I could make the positive ID. Sunken grey eyes above a sloping nose and somewhat boyish features were framed by matted black hair that stuck to his forehead from a mixture of sweat and moisture. Whether it was climate mirroring, or the abundance of water being repeatedly dusted over the surrounding crops, only to be collected through grated floor panels then misted over the growth again, the whole of this district on Sublevel 7 was damp, but comfortably so.

From where I stood, Clayton clearly looked worried. His eyes flitted over everyone who passed.

"Nikos, you've looked mysterious long enough," Mack said, voice crackling through my comms. "But I'm pretty sure you're not fooling anyone. You don't look like a wine person. Now get moving."

With a smirk, I did as Mack asked, rounding the corner and making my way towards Clayton, hand on my sidearm, ready for anything.

It was prime shopping time down here, and throngs of people spilled in and out of the storefronts around me, milled in groups, and sat at tables dotted along the street. The crowd provided enough cover to get close. I slipped between them, eyes trained on Clayton. When I got within range, the sound of my approach finally reached Clayton's ear.

Spotting me over his shoulder, his eyes went wide and he let out a choked swear. He spun, jacket flaring out behind him, and tried to take off into the crowd, shoving a young woman out of the way. But he didn't make in more than two metres before Mack slipped from the crush of people, grabbing hold of Clayton's collar and yanking him back. The much smaller man couldn't resist, flying backwards, and Mack shoved him to the ground, giving me time to catch up.

I bent down and helped Mack pull Clayton to his feet. Despite having two hunters on him, he struggled a bit, putting up enough of a visible fight that he could say later that he didn't go quietly.

We dragged our quarry down an alley, tightly nestled between an indoor apple orchard on one side and a potato farm owned by a vodka company on the other, and shoved him up against the wall.

"Well, if it isn't Clayton Fabron," Mack started. "Hope you're in a charitable mood today, cousin, because we've got something important to talk to you ab—"

"Oh, fucking save it, Mackenzie," Clayton cut in. "I know what I did, and I'm not surprised they sent *you*." He snickered and held his hands up in surrender. "Yeah, I lifted that synthetic fertilizer from the Argo shipment. Who cares, they're all assholes anyway."

"Oh, good," Mack replied. "A confession, this is easy." ODIN ran a quick scan of open bounties and found a match for a theft from two weeks ago, perp unknown. He sent the file to Mack, who nodded his thanks before turning back to his cousin. "Problem is …" Mack jabbed Clayton hard in the sternum, "we're not here for a bounty. Now, this is my friend Nikos. He has some questions about a tablet one of your Plainswalker pals tried to sell."

Mack stepped aside, blocking the view from the street, and revealing my masked face, eyes flaring red.

"Hi," I said, placing a firm hand on Clayton's chest. I shoved him hard against the damp wall. "I'm not going to give you the whole speech because I don't have to. What I really want to know is which one of you stole the tablet from that Argo con-tractor, and who did they agree to sell it to?"

In response, Clayton smiled, eyes lazily drifting between Mack and me. "What makes you think I know anything about a tablet?"

"Because we have video of one of your pals striking a deal with Ivan Sobotka to fence it for him," I replied, referring to the staged confrontation between Sobotka and the Plainswalker that had been attached to his bounty file. I stepped closer to Clayton, who refused to back down.

Clayton shook his head slowly. "Well, that must suck for you then, 'cause I saw that flop of a fixer is dead. By …" he pointed a finger in my face, "your hand, if I'm not mistaken. That's what I gathered from the social feeds at least. It's not *my* fault you killed your only lead, so what are you harassing me for?"

I looped my fingers into the collar of my combat vest, ready to drop the hammer. "Because on the way here, my AI combed through as many Plainswalker-connected social feeds as he could find, and, well …" On cue, a video appeared on my wrist-nav, directed right at Clayton, showing him in a private booth at the popular Sublevel 4 nightclub called Baptism, arm wrapped around the neck of the same Plainswalker who'd run into Ivan Sobotka on the bounty footage. "This video shows you with the man we need to talk to."

Mack stepped in close, looking at Clayton over my shoulder. "According to the audio there, you and your pals were celebrating the deal, one you brokered *behind* your brother's back. I'm sure he won't be too happy about you and your buddies lifting corporate property and catching the attention of Argo without his say-so. They squeeze you guys down here enough already. What's a few more lawsuits and bounties, right?"

That seemed to make him twitchy, jaw clenched tight as he pressed on with the tough-guy act. "Do you really think I'm going to give up one of my guys like that? And I know you're not going to rough me up, because ..." he turned to look at Mack and swallowed hard, "that's not your style, Mackenzie. It's Trapper's, sure. But he's not here." Then his gaze flicked quickly over my shoulder, and his inflated attitude rushed back. "And you won't have time to call him either."

"And what makes you say that?" I replied, grabbing the front of his jacket. "He could be on his way."

Then came another voice, low, rumbling. "Because you'd be dead before you hit 'call'."

Mack and I whipped around, finding ourselves staring down the barrel of a small shotgun, ports glowing yellow, matching the cybernetic eyes of the man carrying it. Joseph Fabron. Leader of the Plainswalkers. "Now would you please let go of my brother?"

As I released Clayton, he let out a smug sigh, only to find the shotgun turned on him. He let out a small squeak, almost entirely covered by the racking slide, as Joseph readied the weapon to fire on his own sibling, index finger of his yellow cybernetic hand gently cradling the trigger.

Joseph was legendary in certain circles, building a small empire that rivalled some corps in its influence, all off the back of illegal farming, alcohol bootlegging, crop theft, and illegal plant-synthesis. But at the same time, the Plainswalkers were responsible for a huge swath of legitimate food production, dominating the licit and illicit facets of Sublevel 7. He was a tough man, but a fair one, and was loved for it. He valued transparency, both from himself and those under him, and always took care of those who took care of him. The Plainswalkers really were a family under Joseph, but that didn't mean he'd go easy on them if things went wrong.

"Now, Clayton," he said. "Answer their questions. Tell our cousin everything he wants to know." His voice was hard and focused, glowing eyes locked on his younger brother, his features pulled into a hard scowl. "Because I really don't like people going behind my back."

Clayton's eyes went wide as he backed up hard into the wall. "Joseph. I-I-I—"

"I don't hear you talking, Clay." Joseph stepped forward. "Zeke was your buddy. Followed you around like a lost puppy." A loud clack echoed through the space like a gunshot as Joseph disengaged the safety. "What was on the tablet?"

"Access codes!" Clayton yelped as he slid down the wall. "Zeke lifted the Argo flunky's transport and found the tablet. He came to me and I sent him to some chick from the NetDreamers to crack it. Apparently it generates access codes and credentials to get into the Department of Hydro Filtration's runoff and recycling facilities."

Mack slowly reached up, pushing the barrel of Joseph's shotgun down. There was a brief moment of acknowledgement in his eyes, and he let it drop.

I turned back to the younger brother. "So you figured you'd stick it to Argo and sell the information to the highest bidder. That's when you connected Zeke with Sobotka."

"Yes. I reached out to Sobotka," Clayton swallowed hard. "Said we had Argo intel to sell, and he found the buyer. Simple as that. Zeke went to Sublevel 11 the other night to hand over the tablet to the intermediary, but stuck around to watch the deal go down, and when he saw you chasing Sobotka through the market, he thought the deal was dead in the water."

"Makes sense," I said. "Did Sobotka tell him who the buyer was?"

Clayton let out a stifled laugh. "Apparently all Sobotka said was they were interested in the tablet and would pay an arm and a leg for it. If Zeke knew who they were, he never told me." He cast a nervous glance at Joseph. "And if you're thinking of talking to Zeke … you're not going to have much luck there."

"And why's that?" Mack asked, leaning against the wall, eyes on his cousin.

"Because Zeke made a one-way trip to the aquatorium," Joseph replied, turning to face me. "Doc said it was a stroke or something. According to what he could pull from his neural implants, at least. But young guy like Zeke? I'm not so sure."

I felt my heart sink, disappointment and frustration settling in again as another roadblock was thrown my way. Along with another body that may or not be connected to this new anti-establishment group.

Joseph reached out a hand for his brother, but Mack got there first, stepping between the two.

He sighed loudly, taking off his helmet to look Joseph directly in the eye. "You know I can't let you do that."

Joseph narrowed his eyes. "And why's that?"

"Well, before you showed up, Clay here admitted to swiping some Argo fertilizer. He has an open bounty hanging over his head, and I have a confession on file." He flicked his eyes over to me and gave a near-imperceptible wink, a non-verbal request for me to trust where he was going with this.

"Looks like Clayton is going to have to come with me. Unless …"

Joseph crossed his arms and gave Mack a bemused look.

"Unless," Mack held up a finger, a smirk rippling across his mouth, "I don't submit the confession to the Commission. The bounty stays open, perp unknown, and maybe the fertilizer somehow is returned to Argo, perhaps by a very famous and well-loved bounty hunter who gets the bounty dropped." He pointed at himself, and Joseph chuckled.

"And aside from not beating you up and leaving you bloodied in this alley, what do you want in return?"

"A favour," Mack said, eyes locked on Joseph. "To be collected at a more convenient time."

The Plainswalker leader gave a half-cocked smile and leaned against the wall. "You think Trapper would be okay with a Nadeau cutting a deal with a Fabron? After all that he thinks happened?"

"He doesn't have to know." Mack kept staring.

The moment hung. The only sound the slow whistle of mist sprayed on crops around us, and the ever-present din of sub-level life. Joseph looked from his brother, to me, to Mack, and smiled. "Deal."

They shook hands.

As he passed me, Clayton gave a small smirk and opened his mouth to probably make some snide comment, but was cut off when Joseph grabbed his collar and yanked him down the alley. With a hearty shove, the whack of his palm echoing off the crop enclosures around us, he pushed the younger Fabron ahead. Now that Clayton was clear of a bounty, Joseph would surely enact his own punishment on his brother. Insubordination didn't slide within the Plainswalkers, but at least Clayton hadn't caught buckshot for his trouble.

Once the Plainswalkers were out of sight, I left out a long exhalation. "Jesus, Mack, that could've gone bad fast."

"But it didn't! Pays to be likeable." He slipped his helmet back on, its avian eyes lighting up a bright shade of teal. With a quick nod, he turned and walked down the alley, towards the street. "But hey," he added, rounding the corner and moving back down the street, our conversation becoming muted to the outside world and pumped exclusively through our comms, "at least we have a favour from the Plainswalkers, even if we didn't learn much about this new eco-terror group you're so worried about."

"Yeah," I grumbled, stepping around a reclamation bot fishing glass and aluminum from a recycling bin. "All we know is they were one transaction away from having access to the city's water filtration infrastructure. But we don't know why. Not a comforting concept."

"Okay, but exactly how much damage could they have

possibly done? Maybe they're real tree huggers and want to divert extra water to an arboretum down in the sublevels."

"I don't know, Mack. But I don't want to find out too late."

Mack stopped at the door to a grow-op selling cabbage and lettuce, eyeing up the holo-display in the window advertising prices. "Well, as a member of the Eco-Terror Taskforce, it's your job to find out. Though it must be good to know we've foiled at least one of their plans, taking that tablet off the street." He looked back at me, and I could tell he was smiling. "It's almost like we're the best bounty hunters in the city."

"Uh-huh," I replied with a small laugh. "It would just be nice to know what to call them."

"Maybe that's where my little favour will come in handy. So, want to hit up Haven to celebrate a job well done?" He started moving slowly towards an airbus terminal, holding his hands out, trying to entice me, but I couldn't. Not tonight.

"Sorry, Mack," I said. "Already got plans."

"Strange … A certain someone told me the same thing earlier." Mack tapped the avian beak on his mask in a knowing sort of way.

I said nothing in response, just stealthily gave Mack the finger and walked towards the nearest Bounty Commission outpost to change and find a ride. But as I walked, I couldn't help my shoulders from sagging. Another dead end.

THIRTEEN

Sublevel 6 was busy as ever. The pounding music and chattering voices as I cut through the shoulder-to-shoulder crowd on my way to meet up with Maria all brought forth a sense of calm, despite the chaos.

It was the perfect elixir to ease my frustrations. A knee that still tweaked if I turned too sharply. The letdown of what I'd thought was a surefire lead to uncover this new player in the eco-terror scene. Sobotka's seller, dead. And the impending sense of dread that there was something in the sublevel underworld I didn't understand, but would end up costing me. They were all jockeying for my attention, weighing on me. The clatter and chaos of Sublevel 6 was a welcome distraction.

It didn't matter what time of day it was, the paths of Sublevel 6 were always packed. Patrons milled about small shops with buzzing LED signs and vibrant and diverse eateries that changed seemingly by the week as different owners came and went. The area was home to a few aug-clinics of varying degrees of legitimacy and net-hubs where people could dive in to immerse themselves in a digital world unlike the one they inhabited. In the air were a thousand scents. The savoury aroma of frying synth-chicken from a nearby Cajun food stall. The stink of burning plastic from the open windows of an electronics repair shop. The hoppy notes of sublevel-brewed beer mixing with a cloud of marijuana vapours from a bar that opened onto the sublevel walkway. Sharp body odour from an outdoor gym and boxing ring, one fighter taking a right hook to the jaw but refusing to go down.

But what I loved most was the sound. The symphonic din, rising and falling in interlocking crescendos, forming and shifting as I walked between different businesses and sites. The crackling of welder's tools. The thundering of bass, The cheers from a crowd watching a soccer game. The rumble of transports passing overhead.

Thousands of cacophonous voices, speaking hundreds of languages, only a few of which I could identify without neural implants or ODIN doing the heavy lifting through my comms. The gliding intonation of French as two young men haggled over the price of repairs for a blown oscillator in a rickety old transport that sat idle on a small lot, layered with the sharp punch of Ukrainian from a woman hollering down to a pair of young kids playing loudly in the street. I heard Spanish, Tagalog, Mandarin, Japanese, German, and a dozen others, mixing to form a noise that one could only describe as Winnipeg.

This was the sublevels. Humanity in cohesive dissension.

Walking past a small alley to my right, a flash of movement caught my eye. A young person, probably no older than thirteen, snuck under a railing and slipped through a metal gate to escape an older gentleman in hot pursuit. I noticed he was sporting a sleek but well-worn cybernetic hand, surface speck-led and scratched from years of use. As he drew up to the gate, a large figure emerged from the shadows on the other side, pris-tine skin glowing, showing the immaculate gloss of dermal-re-construction and faded facial scars that could only come from removed augmentations. Then there was the swirling red script of "HRF" on the larger man's jacket.

I quickly moved to intercept.

"Hey, wait," the small man stammered as I grabbed hold of his arm with my own robotic one. "That kid stole my credits."

I spun him around and guided him away with a firm hand on his shoulder. "You'll lose a lot more than a few credits if you don't get moving," I mumbled. He didn't resist, so he must have also noticed the danger he had narrowly avoided.

The Human Reclamation Front goon laughed and hollered after us with a voice like crushed rock. "Look at the pissy little aug, whining about his credits. Maybe next time you shouldn't make a bet you can't win."

We made it to a small café the next block over and I gestured that he should sit at the counter, which he did. I slid into the seat next to him.

"What's your name?" I asked as I triple-tapped the menu built into the counter's touchscreen interface, ordering three coffees. The automated barista got to work, and my order was ready in a matter of moments.

"What?" the man responded, breathless and trembling.

"Your name?" I repeated, sliding one of the full bio-grade cups towards him while keeping two for myself. Synth-milk and cane sugar appeared on the back of a small drone wheeling along the countertop.

The man took a shallow sip, eyes flicking nervously between pedestrians. He offered up a small, embarrassed smile.

"Clark," he said.

"Great," I replied, smiling openly at him. "I'm Nikos." My cybernetic hand took his in a firm shake. "Now, how much did that kid steal from you?"

"Umm … like, twenty-five credits?"

"Ah, no problem." I brought up my wrist-nav and swiped through, bringing up the transfer program, and tapped my screen to his. "I sent you a payment for thirty."

Clark shook his head, confused. "You did what? Why?"

"So you don't go back there and mess with that big anti-aug loser again." I took a sip of one of the coffees. "Sorry it happened, though. Those scammers can be tricky."

Clark glanced back in the direction we'd come. "They already took my money—what more would they want from me?"

Sitting back in my seat, I looked Clark over. He seemed at least partially put together, with a tan jacket hanging loose over his slight frame, emblazoned with the Ravencrest Technologies logo on the shoulder, employee number and designation stamped on the left breast, zipper half undone. Aside from the used cybernetic hand, I saw a bit of black poking up from the collar of his shirt, possibly to provide ports and access to some augmented organs beneath. Both the augs, and his employment with a tech manufacturer in the city, made him a great target for the Human Reclamation Front. Branded an anti-establishment group, they were well known for stealing augs right out of peoples' bodies and selling off the parts. Either to less-than-upstanding augmentation clinics, so they could potentially steal and sell them all over again, or one of the smaller tech repair shops desperately in need of older components. Every time tech, especially augs, got updated and upgraded, old parts were phased out and no longer sold, giving life to an ever-expanding second-hand grey market.

Companies like Ravencrest and Argo couldn't totally kill this market, and the small independent repair shops and clinics it supported, because they needed room to manoeuvre. So they opted to strangle the small fish with licensing demands, which meant money, and charged huge prices for outdated components. HRF filled the niche, conning, grifting, or outright stealing augs from people like Clark, charging the shops less than the big corps, helping them keep the lights on.

That way, HRF made themselves necessary, and got the satisfaction of taking augs off the streets—albeit temporarily. Notorious for seeing augmentations and technology as the death of true humanity, and the cause of climate change—thus being the impetus for the system we all lived under now—the HRF would do anything to continue to do what their name implied: reclaim humanity.

"Well," I began, "here's the thing. That kid marked you out because of that …" I pointed at his jacket. "And that." I pointed at his hand. "They would've ripped out all your augs and dumped you in an alley, probably a few levels down. And then, a few weeks from now, you'd be walking past an aug clinic and see your arm in the window. But by then, they've made their money, and the feds have doled out the cash to Ravencrest, or Argo, or whoever owns the particular clinic you've gone to for an emergency replacement. HRF makes money, you eventually get brand new augs, the corporation makes money, and the buck is passed to the taxpayers. Boom-bam, the world keeps spinning."

Clark rubbed the worn shell of his cybernetic hand. I could see him sizing up my sleek, military-grade prosthesis, made of carbon composite, hard as steel but light as plastic, dextrous and sensitive as a real flesh-and-bone appendage.

He looked up at me, brow furrowed. "Who are you, again?"

I took a long sip of coffee. "I'm—"

"Nikos!" The tenor of Maria's voice sliced through the clamour around us.

Even dressed in full civvies, it was hard to say Maria blended into a crowd. She wore a bright yellow motorcycle jacket, recycled-denim jeans, and blue-and-pink riding boots that kicked debris and puddle water aside with each step. Gemlike amber eyes flitted lazily across the crowd, though I knew the hunter in her was always alert.

She'd texted late last night, somehow unaffected by the sheer amount of alcohol we'd all consumed.

Early dinner tomorrow? You know the place.

I knew what she was thinking, and it was exactly what I needed after the past couple of days.

Maria sidled up beside me and looked Clark over. In response, his eyes went wide, taking in the tall, muscular, and intimidating woman in front of him. Not an unusual reaction to Maria, who exuded power and fire, even when out of her armour.

I cleared my throat and made the necessary introductions.

"Nice to meet you, Clark," Maria flashed a tight smile, and leaned over to snatch the neglected cup of coffee from the counter. "Dash of synth-milk and no sweetener?"

I chuckled. "Yep. Just how you always take it. Glad that hasn't changed."

She smirked and took a long sip.

I could see the gears turning in Clark's head, and he looked from Maria to me, to my military-grade arm, and to the slight bulge around Maria's waist where a small pistol was always holstered.

A wave of realization washed across his face. "Wait a second … are the two of you—"

"Late," Maria cut in. "Yes, we've got somewhere to be. Let's go, Nikos. Can't keep Mr. Zhao waiting." In one quick movement, she stood and closed an iron grip on my collar, practically lifting me from the seat, and dragged me away.

When she released her grip, I turned back and raised my cup at Clark, who was still firmly planted in his seat, face slack in surprise as he worked out what had just happened. His life, saved by a bounty hunter. A story he'd be telling his friends and coworkers for weeks. Turning back, my eyes met Maria's, to find her laughing quietly to herself.

"Okay, please explain," she said, taking another sip from her drink.

I did.

Maria smiled, playfully nudging my arm. "Gods, Nikos, do you ever take a day off?"

I returned the smile. "Rarely."

The smile felt good. So did having Maria around. We'd all filled her absence in different ways when she left. For me, that had meant work, leaning hard into each bounty I took on, trying to retain a sense of normalcy. But with the past few bounties being anything but normal, the timing of Maria's return home was a comfort. Made me feel like my old self again. Like our jobs—and life—might go back to feeling normal again, despite everything.

"Well," I continued, "someone had to pick up all the slack after you left. Suddenly there were a lot more contracts up for grabs."

Maria snorted, stuffing her free hand in her pocket. "Is that your way of saying that you're happy I'm home?" She gave me a sly grin, and warmth spread through my chest.

"Thought I didn't have to."

"Oh?" Maria cocked her head. "And I'm supposed to be able to read your mind?"

I shrugged. "Well, yeah. You're telling me you *don't* know what I'm thinking?"

"Oh, I've always known exactly what you were thinking, and feeling, Nikos." Maria shook her head with a softer smile than I'd seen in a while. She was quiet a moment, seemingly lost in thought, and when she looked back, her expression had turned sombre.

"Speaking of, I heard about the Van Buren kid. I'm sorry things ended the way they did. Why didn't you tell me?"

I forced a smile. "It's been ... complicated, and I've been trying to figure it out. Didn't want to drag you into something until I knew more about—"

"That new eco-terror group you've been tangling with?" she replied with a smirk.

I struggled to hide my surprise, while Maria shook her head again and laughed. "You really think you can handle all these things on your own like some superhero, eh? Mack told me, obviously. I also heard you two were poking around Sublevel 7 today, harassing innocent Plainswalkers."

"Right," I snickered. "The Fabron brothers. Perfectly innocent, trying to sell a hacked Argo tablet ..." My voice trailed off as a couple pieces fell into place. "Maria, the other day, when we ran into each other …"

"The Bo Richot bounty. What about it?"

"Clayton Fabron said he sent his buddy Zeke and the tablet to a NetDreamer first. A *female* NetDreamer. Do you think your target was the same person? Did she admit to anything when she was in custody?"

Maria's eyes went wide. "So *that's* who she cracked the tablet for. One of the bounties on her had been for tampering with corporate property, and she admitted to me it was a quick job she'd gotten from the Plainswalkers—said there must have been a script buried in the tablet's firmware that triggered when she got in with phony credentials, which is how it was tied to her."

It was hard to hide my excitement. Maybe we weren't at a complete loss after all. "Did Zeke tell her anything? Let slip who the buyer might be?"

Maria shook her head. "No, nothing like that. But she did say something weird while I was processing her at the outpost."

"Like what?"

"She said that right after she turned the tablet back over to the Plainswalkers, all her gear started acting up. Said she was getting intrusion alarms all day and night, but when she'd shut down whoever was trying to get into her systems, she couldn't find a source. Nothing was ever out of place and she was never able to find evidence of intrusion or a digital footprint of who had been trying to get in there. When she got word she was wanted for a bounty, she assumed the Bounty Commission had new counter-hacking software that was able to mask the source of the intrusion, and it was *us* trying to get into her systems."

I nodded along to her story. "Which is why she met with her friends out on the street. Wanted to get as offline as possible."

"Looks that way," Maria replied, kicking a discarded food container towards a reclamation drone that chittered in thanks. "She was scared the Commission would be listening in and could triangulate her position. So she wanted to go to ground. No tech. No net. No way to find her until she figured out what to do." She gave me a searching look. "Anything I should be worried about?"

I gave a slight shrug and sighed. "Honestly, I don't know." I reached out and placed my hand on her shoulder, Maria returning the gesture with a smile. "But I'll keep you in the loop. From here on out, it's the three of us again."

Maria nodded. "Deal."

We continued down the walkway, crossing between two monolithic outcroppings of buildings and Argite-supported structures built into the strata of rock holding the Assiniboine River, and spotted the bright yellow paint of our destination, an explosion of colour amid a haze of hues. Above the door, where I'd expected to find the blinking, busted LED sign, was something new. A brand new holoprojector displayed a Chinese dragon spiralling and dancing in place, keeping watch from above the crowd, as the restaurant's name orbited it, like a protective barrier or tiny cage. Zhao's Wok. A pillar of Sublevel 6, and perhaps the best place to eat in the entire city.

Exchanging grins, Maria and I passed through the double doors where we were met by a wall of delicious scents. The place was quiet, aside from the soft hum of the air conditioning, and low-volume 2050s music warbling away on a speaker somewhere in the back. There were a few scattered customers, huddled together over their meals, deep in conversation. The ever-patient Mrs. Zhao was working out a particularly stubborn stain on the long oak bar that dominated the middle of the room, and Mr. Zhao was leaning against it, intently glaring at one of the screens hanging from the ceiling.

"How are the boys doing today?" I hollered as we approached. "Lambos make it through the first lap this time?"

Mr. Zhao laughed, eyes still locked on the screen, and pointed a thick, crooked finger at the TV. "Oh, he did, thank the gods. But that Hamilton … Must be something in the bloodline that makes them such damn good drivers." At that he turned, smile dropping into a look of shock. He leaned over and tapped his wife's hand limply, and once she spun around to see what the fuss was about, she let out a shrill exclamation.

"Maria! My child, you're home!" Mrs. Zhao jogged over, and the small woman wrapped her arms around Maria in a tight hug. "I can't believe it—Robert!" She let go for a moment and whirled back to her husband, who was busy lifting the bar flap to come and join her.

"I see her, I see her," he said, waddling over to Maria and hugging her as well.

I threw up my hands up in mock disbelief. "Wait, hold on. Where's my warm welcome?"

Mrs. Zhao snapped her cloth against my arm disapprovingly. "Because you've been running all over this city but not once have you come to visit us. We could've croaked and you wouldn't have said goodbye!"

Maria shot me a reproachful look, to which I could only grin sheepishly. Meanwhile, Mr. Zhao had puttered his way back behind the bar, and Mrs. Zhao began wiping down a pair of stools for us, waving us over to sit down. Doing as we were told, we were met with a pair of menus—old school, made of paper tucked into sleeves bound by fake leather—and drinks were already being prepared. For Mr. Zhao, this meant tall glasses of beer.

Like the building itself, Robert Zhao was a legend within Winnipeg's sublevels. The restaurant had been in his family for three generations and its current owner was the most pleasant, hard-working, and doting person I knew. Mr. Zhao's grandfather had arrived in Canada around the time my great-grandfather established the Argonaut Group, and a photo of him hung on the back wall of the restaurant next to the kitchen. Displaced by flooding in his homeland of China, he'd come to Winnipeg and started the business as a food truck up on the surface. As the city gradually expanded down, he built his first brick-and-mortar restaurant, the same building we now sat in. The food was great, but best of all was that the Zhaos were friendly to bounty hunters.

Many Winnipeggers saw us as equal parts heroes and violent props, though most tolerated our profession anyway. But with Mr. Zhao, there was a personal dimension.

I'd saved the man's life.

I wasn't in the habit of stirring up trouble with the public when I was off the clock. But one day, a few years back, I'd finished up a bounty early and decided to treat myself for a job well done. I'd exchanged a few words with Zhao in the past, but never more than ordering from the menu and expressing my thanks. On this particular visit, he'd glanced dubiously at the fresh bruise blossoming across my cheekbone from a well-placed sucker punch I'd failed to see coming, but said nothing as he slid the steaming plate of noodles across the counter for me. But when some jackass pulled a pistol on Zhao while he was processing my credit payment at the central console, I could not abide it. I was on him before he could blink, wrenching the gun from his grip and driving an elbow into his nose before escorting him off the premises at gunpoint.

This was the start of my friendship with the older man and his wife. He'd kept the guy's gun as a "souvenir" from this fateful meeting, and I knew he had it stowed in a small housing under the bar near where he usually stood to watch the races.

"So," the old man said. "What did you do this time?" He flashed me an amused smile. Zhao knew us well.

Part of the reason I hadn't come back to Zhao's Wok in the years Maria was gone came down to the feeling.

Zhao's Wok had become neutral ground for our friendship. A place where we could share a meal and just talk, away from the raucous energy of Haven. Emotions sometimes ran high after a particularly challenging bounty, and on more than one occasion I'd make some kind of stupid remark about our spots on the leaderboard and Maria would ditch me halfway through the meal.

But we'd always be back shortly after for a make-up meal on my dime, much to the Zhaos' amusement.

I'd tried, once, coming to have dinner alone after Maria left, but it wasn't the same.

Maria was already leaning in, her voice smug. "Nikos here has apparently been too 'busy' …" she made very animated air quotes, "to properly welcome me home."

I put my hands up defensively. "Hold on, that's not what—"

"Really?" Mr. Zhao interrupted, a curious look on his face.

"After two years, he should've dropped everything for you. I'm definitely on your side with this one."

"Thank you, Mr. Zhao." Maria smirked.

"He always takes your side," I grumbled.

"Because I'm always right."

Then came the high-toned call of Mrs. Zhao from down the bar. "She *is* always right."

I threw my hands up in resignation. "Can we please at least order before we start discussing my poor time-management skills?"

Mr. Zhao cackled and headed for the kitchen. "I know what you're going to order, don't worry," he called over his shoulder.

"Then why give us the menus?" I replied.

"Because I gauge how mad she is by how much you look at them and not each other!" Both husband and wife erupted into laughter and vanished behind the curtain that separated the kitchen from the dining room.

Maria pressed her lips together, trying to suppress her own laughter, and I took a long swig from my glass, cheeks burning.

"So," she said, taking a sip from her own glass. "Give me the rundown. What's new? Had a nice long chat with Mack while we were working, so I know some of the details and the drama of his life, but what about you?"

I opened my mouth but didn't know what to say. Things had, until about seventy-two hours ago, been largely the same as before she'd left. Work, eat, sleep, repeat. I had nothing more to share about this new group apart from what we both already knew. The green falling star. The deaths. The attacks against Argo.

I glanced up the TV screen above the bar, the cars racing around the brightly lit Japanese circuit, and the holographic advertisements floating just above the edges of the racetrack—Argo's logo prominent among them.

I hadn't told anyone about Castor's new invention, the request that came with it, and the potentially life-changing consequences for me and every other hunter in this city. Honestly, I didn't even know where to begin. My personal feelings on the matter were a formless cloud of mixed signals.

Argo getting its claws into bounty hunting, taking justice once again out of the hands of the people and putting it—like everything in the 2100s—into the grubby mitts of a corporation, felt wrong. We'd given up so much to corps already, and to now put our safety in their hands? No thanks. Plus, there were all the hunters who would quickly lose their livelihoods. Castor had no idea the cost that would incur.

But the flip side was the prospect that our work was becoming more dangerous, and if Castor's plan failed, people would keep their jobs, but they might ultimately lose their lives.

Me and my friends among them.

All I wanted was a normal evening with Maria. But every time I pulled away from this moment, the dread set in.

"Hey," Maria said, snapping me back to the present. "You good? You've got this worried look on your face all of a sudden. What's up?" She reached over and gently took my hand in hers. I focused on the warmth of her fingers, and the cold rift that had opened between us the day she left melted away in an instant; in its place was the bond we'd shared through years of friendship. I trusted her more than anyone, and knew she felt the same. If not Maria, who else could I trust with Castor's plan?

"There's this thing with Argo," I started. "I—"

"Argo?" Mr. Zhao piped up as he placed an array of dishes in front of us that included dumplings, a selection of differently flavoured pieces of synth-chicken—grown down on Sublevel 7—a healthy bowl of Plainswalker rice, and even healthier plate of noodles topped with vegetables and a fried egg on top. "Why are we talking about Argo?"

Maria withdrew her hand from mine and helped Mrs. Zhao arrange the dishes on the bartop. "Just work stuff," Maria replied, pulling a plate towards her while keeping her eyes on me. She likely assumed I had been planning on returning to the subject of the recent Argo attacks. "Right, Nik?"

I let out a stifled laugh, willing the tension to dissipate from my muscles.

"Right. It's nothing," I said, reaching for the dumplings.

Maria gave me a slight nod and turned to the Zhaos, who thankfully seemed to pick up on the fact that I wanted the subject changed.

"Funny that you bring them up," Mr. Zhao said, taking a seat across from us. "Because I've got some news."

Maria smirked. "They trying to buy you out too?"

"No, never," Mr. Zhao chuckled, his belly jiggling slightly. "But a few of their suits did show up here a couple weeks back."

"You could smell their arrogance," Mrs. Zhao interjected.

"That you could," her husband continued. "And they weren't even dressed that nicely. They looked like single-credit lawyers. You'd think that with all their surface money they could afford something better, but you could find nicer suits off the rack at the Goodwill a couple blocks down." He jabbed a finger down, indicating a lower section of the patchwork that was Sublevel 6. "Anyway … they came around asking about Kenny."

That Argo was looking for Kenny Zhao could mean one of two things. Either he'd gotten into some serious trouble, or he was being headhunted. The Zhaos' grandson was a brilliant kid, but he had a perpetually wandering mind. Sometime before I met Mr. Zhao, Kenny's father had died in an industrial accident on Sublevel 9, where he worked the night shift at an electronics manufacturing plant, doing delicate repair work still not trusted to machines. The details of the story were still kind of fuzzy, but his jumpsuit had caught fire when a coworker got a little too close with a soldering gun, lighting an accelerant that had been splashed on Kenny's dad at a previous station. With his mother no longer in the country, this left Kenny in the care of his grandparents.

Kenny had inherited his father's propensity for tinkering, and reminded me so much of Castor that it didn't surprise me that he'd find himself on Argo's radar—for better or for worse. You could always find him ripping something apart, only to put it back together working better than before. He became fairly well known on the social feeds for his odd inventions. What was more phenomenal was he was entirely self-taught, like most of the brightest kids in the sublevels. Despite his skill and smarts, it was hard for Kenny to find an outlet for his creativity that also brought in a consistent income. Fresh out of high school, he had been stuck working at his grandparents' restaurant, but taking over the establishment—despite its status in the city—wasn't what he wanted. He'd almost been drawn into Cyber Volition by the promise of good money, but I'd been called in to talk him out of that particularly bad decision. It's easy to back down when you're faced with the reality of who would be hunting you down for breaking the law. Family friend or not.

If he was getting a shot with Argo, though? That would change everything in a hurry.

I polished off my drink and the glass had barely hit the table before Mrs. Zhao was refilling it again. "So, what did Argo want?"

"Did he steal something of theirs for a project again?" Maria asked, casting a quick, worried glance at me. "He should know that as an adult he can get charged with unlicensed modification of corporate technology."

Mr. Zhao smiled. "No, no. He isn't going to show up on the list of bounties anytime soon—I hope. They were here to offer him a job."

It wasn't rare by any stretch, but it wasn't common either. Argo, along with every other major corp in the country, kept eyes on talent in the city, be they Ivories or sublevellers, trying to find the next genius to take them over the top. Usually it was Argo finding them, with the resources, recognition, and knowledge of their backyard necessary to search every nook and cranny for what they needed. Still, what Kenny had been given was nothing short of a gift, and he couldn't waste it. Argo loved to headhunt, but it was still hard to stand out and be taken seriously enough to be plucked from the sublevels and placed on the surface. Typically, you needed the right degree, the right name, the right address, and the right connections, but what Kenny had was talent. Talent Argo couldn't ignore.

I smirked. "Not the usual headhunters he's had to deal with."

"And thank goodness for that." Mr. Zhao deftly snagged the

last dumpling from the plate in front of me and popped it in his mouth. "These particular headhunters were offering him work that *wouldn't* get him in a lot of trouble." He swung his arms wide, gesturing to the restaurant around him. "So I guess now we need a bit more help around here."

Maria gave me a quick, playful elbow jab and snickered. "Hear that, Nikos? You can finally learn to cook." More laughter at my expense.

I replied with an irritated glance but couldn't help but grin. It felt good to be back here, at this table with these people, as if no time had passed. I was reminded of everything I'd missed the past two years. Something I'd been without for far too long.

Mr. Zhao clapped me on the shoulder, snapping me back to attention. "Well, I ought to thank you. You kept Kenny out of trouble for so long, keeping those Cyber Volition freaks off our doorstep. He couldn't have gotten here without you. You're a good man, Nikos. A dependable man."

A pang hit my heart unexpectedly, and a memory followed in an arcing wake. Words my father himself had said to me growing up, even in his fading days.

When you become a dependable man, it'll sneak up on you. You might never hear it, never experience the recognition for it, but if you do, it won't shock you, because when it happens, you'll know you deserve it.

But did I deserve it? I'd acted to protect Kenny without an expectation of a reward, yes; but I'd also failed when I was needed the most, letting two men die, and *had* been rewarded for it. Could both be true and real at the same time? Could I do the right thing, even if it wasn't my job, but also do my job, even if it wasn't the right thing to do?

It wasn't until the sky had considerably darkened that Maria and I were finally able to tear ourselves away from Zhao's Wok. Mr. Zhao had offered to comp the meal and drinks, as a thank-you for making sure Kenny lived long enough to be given the golden ticket Argo had tossed him, but I refused, arguing that—as was tradition—I would pay for my meal and Maria's, because she was right, and I was wrong.

She did deserve this for a homecoming, after all.

Laden with bags of takeout, we said our goodbyes and stepped out into the cool sublevel air. A light misting rain was falling softly from small sprinklers hanging from the surrounding buildings, coating everything with droplets of moisture that made the whole scene shimmer and smell of fresh dew.

Maria and I agreed it had been a lovely visit and chatted easily about nothing in particular. A warm flush coloured Maria's cheeks, the effects of the generous supply of beer the Zhaos had provided us with during the meal. We wound our way along the scattered pathways of Sublevel 6 at ease, relishing the cool air as we joined the swell of patrons taking in Sublevel 6's lively nightlife.

Suddenly, a voice cut through the raucous murmur of the crowd. "The sky is fake! We should not want to spend eternity in the dark. We were meant to sink and be reborn!"

The force of these words hit me so hard that I almost felt my knees give out. Images of Maxwell Van Buren's final moments blazed before my eyes. That blood-tinged smile.

I wheeled around, drops of moisture flying from my

mist-soaked hair, and scanned the crowd intently until my eyes found a small figure nestled in an alcove, away from the falling artificial vapour. A hooded, olive-coloured poncho covered most of their body, and it bore an intricate design of swirling lines that wound around each other without touching to create an image of a squat skyline, pierced through the centre by a trident, set under roiling waves. The unmistakable sign of the Children of Atlantis.

Wordlessly, I approached the figure as Maria trailed behind, confused. As I got closer, I realized it was a boy. He had a long, gaunt face, with sharp cheekbones and glowing white cybernetic eyes.

His eyes met mine and we spent a few moments studying each other, piercing white irises searing out of dark shadow. His mouth curled into a small, tepid smile.

"O who be he, who stands there with eyes like ocean waters?" Despite his frail physique, his voice was strong and forceful. "Have you, too, been touched by Poseidon?"

Beginning in the 2030s and 2040s, as tides rose and cities sank underwater, the world saw a surprising emergence of new religious sects in response to the climate crisis. The Children of Atlantis were one such group. More a fringe cult than a recognized religious movement, the Children were homegrown, beginning in Winnipeg around the time Sublevels 3 and 4 were built and society continued to move underground. I'd rarely had any dealings with the group, since fanatical preachers were a dime a dozen these days and rarely gathered enough followers to amount to anything. They certainly hadn't done anything to bring the Eco-Terror Taskforce knocking either. But I did recall hearing that the first Children of Atlantis preacher was said to have stood under the surging floodwaters of the Red River in a rare incident that saw the waters breaching its new carbon basin, proselytizing against humanity's journey below, that we must accept our punishment from the gods and be washed away by Poseidon's wrath. The cult believed that to challenge the encroachment of climate change was to challenge the will of the gods, and that our many failures to save nations from rising tides, destructive storms, sweeping desert winds, and roiling destabilization of the polar vortex, were signs the gods were going to win. Acceptance, to them, was to learn from the punishment seen by the great mythical nation of Atlantis, and let the gods sink us.

But I wasn't here to convert.

"What did you just say? About the fake sky and living in the dark." I moved into the alcove, blocking the streetlight. But even in the dark I could see the glowing white of the preacher's eyes and knew he was smiling.

"I speak only the truth," he laughed quietly. "Humanity's imprisonment, these cages of steel and stone, are not what we should accept with open arms. Do you not agree?"

Clenching my jaw, I considered my next question carefully, decided to take the risk. "Did you know a boy named Maxwell Van Buren?"

The preacher smiled. "I have known many in my time preaching to the masses … but I do not know of who you speak. Why do you ask?"

"Because he …" I paused, looking over my shoulder towards Maria, who was watching our exchange with growing discontent. I lowered my voice. "Before he died, he said something close to what you did."

"Then he was one of us, or at least, was becoming. Are you

wanting to join us, Poseidon-touched?" He leaned forward expectantly.

Poseidon-touched. The phrase crackled in the back of my mind. My father had called me that, in my dream. It felt as if all the air had been stolen from the small alcove.

"What did you just call me?" I asked, barely a whisper.

"I merely called you what you are." I heard the rustling of fabric and could make out the preacher's hand as it emerged from under the poncho to point to his cybernetic eyes, then to mine. "Only those who see can be touched. He comes to me in dreams, like all Poseidon-touched at some point, showing me the truth.

"I have seen Atlantis fall, many times over. Each time, the exact same. Demeter let their crops whither, Zeus battered their cities with storms, and Poseidon, in final punishment, dragged their nation beneath the seas. Who is to say we deserve any different? Why must we let Argo continually defy the gods? Each night I sleep, praying for the chance to watch this city fall, the tower of Argo shattered by Zeus's wrath, the souls of those taken by it marched to the afterlife by the guiding hand of Thanatos …" I felt the hair on the back of my neck stand up, remembering Sobotka as the preacher continued, pointing in the vague direction of the river overhead. "Each time the waters spill the banks and fall below, I hope that they will not cease. That they will drown all in punishment, and only those who see will survive to see our new Eden—"

"Okay, that's enough, water boy," Maria interrupted, visibly disturbed, stepping into the alcove. I caught her mid-step with an outstretched arm and gave her a placating look. There was a brief flash of recognition, and she stepped back. We couldn't afford to spook him. This preacher had mimicked the words

Van Buren said moments before he died, and invoked the god Ivan Sobotka had pleaded with before taking his own life. This kid could have the answers to everything that had been plaguing me these past few days.

"Have you ever seen this?" I held up my wrist-nav to show the meteor logo, fighting to keep my tone measured.

The preacher just kept smiling from under his hood. "I have seen many things like this in my time, for I have seen many times occurring at once. A history in view. Empires rising and falling, just like this one around us." He held out his palms, indicating the city. "Like Jason and his Argonauts, Argo, too, looks for its golden fleece. But it will not find it here. For that is reserved for our purposes. For our Eden."

I could feel Maria start to tense, but she held her voice even. "Enough religious bullshit. We want to know which group is using this symbol and what they want. Their members are going around saying the same stuff you are, and while I'm not too big on kicking down temple doors, I might just have to break that rule here. Who are they?"

The preacher took a deep, long breath, and closed his eyes. For a moment he sat there and seemed to be listening to something, rocking his head slightly back and forth. Maria sighed in frustration and moved to grab the guy, but stopped short when his glowing white eyes shot open, and he looked to me. "You have seen the surge, Poseidon-touched. He has told me so. You know this cage they call a city. You've seen it die. But will you see it reborn? Will you reach Eden with us?

Suddenly it was hard to breathe, my lungs remembering the wall of water from my dream.

"Who told yo—"

"That's it!" Maria snapped, cutting me off. "There's a nice interrogation cell waiting for you at one of the Bounty outposts. I'll figure out the paperwork later. You're coming with us." She reached out a hand to the preacher, trying to seize him by the collar.

But her hand passed right through him, the preacher's mist-soaked form reduced to a fizzling mess of pixels where Maria's fist had gone through. Eyes still locked on me, the projected form struggled to hold composure.

"I am going nowhere, Poseidon-touched. But you are. Find the name, and you will find the way."

With one final smile, the figure fizzled out. Maria and I were left stunned. Cautiously, Maria opened her fist and knelt, moving the box the preacher had been sitting on to find a small holoprojector on the ground. With a bitter laugh, she plucked the silver cylinder from the ground, shaking her head in disbelief.

"Can this whole thing get any fucking weirder?" she asked.

I ran a hand through my wet, cold hair. "At this point, I wouldn't be surprised."

"So, what do we do?"

I sighed. "Find the name."

She stood and threw the projector in my direction. Turning it over in my hands, I found the Argo logo stamped on the bottom, another victim of black-market hackers, no doubt.

"The connection would be encrypted, but maybe your buddy Castor can get some answers from this," Maria said. "It's his company's invention, after all." A roguish smirk met her lips. "Until then, maybe we can stir up some trouble and see what we find out."

I was getting sick of trouble, so stirring up more was not

really what I had in mind. Doing some digging to find some answers? Now that was something I could do.

But then again, trouble always seemed to find me anyway.

FOURTEEN

Small daggers of shattered glass exploded out in every direction as my body met the window. Luckily, the pane gave way easily, and I'd broken through more than enough windows in my life to ready myself for how much it would hurt.

But the laboratory table I landed on was sturdier than it really should have been.

My back met metal with a heavy bang, the dense surface of the table denting inward under the weight. Physics carried me the rest of the way as I flexed my core and brought my legs up and over my head, taking the pain to flip into a backwards roll. I landed, crouched, cybernetic hand digging into the tile floor, deep furrows following for a foot as I skidded to a halt.

After me came the warbling laugh of Bonny Dogar, leader of Cyber Volition, through her synthetic voice box. "Bravo, bravo. Not many fleshies can take as much punishment as you, my friend."

At first, I could only see her eyes, motes of sharp amber

burning through the darkness like pinprick suns, but as she stepped from the shadows, all was revealed.

There was little left of Bonny you could firmly call "human" after years of extreme and invasive augmentation that had moulded her into her current form. Once, she had been a promising young programmer with determination and intellect that rivalled even Castor himself. Starting Cyber Volition as a tech company, specializing in the neural links used by millions the world over to speed up their neural processing, gradually expanding to tinker on augmentation technology, making the connections between flesh and machine even more refined, Bonny Dogar had been a star. Over a few years, she'd amassed a huge following, as observers thought she could take on the big tech giants—even Argo—in pushing humanity's blending with computer interfaces further than ever thought possible.

But like so many before her, ego got the better of her. Bonny thought of herself as more than just a master of human-computer-interface technology. She believed that integrating fully with technology was the next step in human evolution, and that climate change was the impetus for that change. The only way, Bonny thought, for humanity to survive the spreading deserts that laid waste to farmland, the rising seas that drowned cities, and the rampant pathogens that decimated populations, was to become *homo deus*, the creators and controllers of our own form.

As she began to embrace these ideas, most at Cyber Volition ran, but those who stayed began to follow her with an even more fervent piety, with countless others flocking to join, eager to lop off limbs to survive the storm, and ascend to the next step in humanity.

Eventually, Cyber Volition itself evolved, becoming the anti-establishment group it was today. Laws were drafted to push back against the group, like "illegal modification of the human form" and "unlicensed use of human enhancement technology," which sought to criminalize its work, pushing the bounds of what it meant to be human. They often found their work branded as eco-terror, since corporations claimed unneeded augmentation was wasteful, creating unnecessary demand for resources that still needed to be mined and refined from fragile ecosystems, and that licensing existed so they could ensure quality, efficiency, and a controlled supply.

But Cyber Volition continued on regardless, and the poster child for those laws was staring me in the face.

Her cybernetic eyes pulsed softly, framed by the only flesh still visible on her face. From her forehead down to her upper lip, her face was flesh and muscle, pale skin twisted and stretched as she sneered. Her sleek, black, metal-and-carbon lower jaw hung slightly open, and I could see a pink tongue behind, with a human throat, encased in a protective shell as it worked its way down the augmented neck, muscles replaced by pistons, servos, and tubes that flexed and moved, poking out from the collar of her shirt. She stepped easily through the shattered window with long, powerful piston-like legs, metallic feet crunching against the shards of glass strewn across the tile floor. Her movements were so fluid, so simple; but I could sense the energy behind them. Her limbs had the power of coiled springs, ready to explode.

"Bonny," I pleaded, slowly getting to my feet and keeping my hands well away from my pistol. "I'm not here for you. We don't need to do this."

"Oh, I think we do." She made what could only be described as a smile as the small strip of flesh that remained on her upper jaw twisted into a sickening half grin. "You're here to take down the best black market aug-doc in the city, and I can't let that happen. Who else will make me *perfect*?"

With a roar, Bonny launched herself at me. But I was a step too quick, pivoting right so she flew past in a black blur and straight into the sleek metal refrigeration unit behind me. She hit hard, yelping loudly. The metal gave way, groaning as it dented inward and the hinges buckled under the weight. I scrambled back, barely dodging the immense mass of the freed metal doors as they crashed down and smashed the tiles where I'd been standing moments before.

I scurried away, rounding the lab table that had broken my fall, and leaped back through the window into the clinic's main corridor. With a quick glance back, I saw Bonny working to free herself from the metal weight on her back, a loud mechanical whir blasting out from under the immense metal freezer doors in the lab.

Around me, people in white coats were screaming, rushing for the nearest exit. But amid the terrified screams were the warbling shouts of other Cyber Volition members who were now racing towards their boss. I glanced to my left, towards the lobby doors from where I'd come. I had made a beeline past the augmentation clinic's front desk and into the corridor where I now stood, flanked on either side by windows and doors leading to a number of small examination rooms and offices where the clinic doctors and nurses did the bulk of their work. I went right and picked up the pace as I neared the double doors at end of hall. The scrolling holographic sign above it read *Operating Wing: Authorized Personnel Only.*

My comms crackled to life and ODIN's voice came through. "I thought you said this was going to be a simple job."

"I really need to stop saying that."

After Maria and I had gone our separate ways, I'd headed back to the apartment. I'd chucked the preacher's holoprojector on my bed and sent Castor a vague question about how easy it would be to get location and usage data out of it, skimming neatly past his continued nagging about Prometheus. Maria was right; if anyone knew how to bypass the encryption and track the signal from an Argo-made holoprojector, it would be Castor. I certainly didn't. We'd also gotten word that the tech retrieved from Maxwell Van Buren's room had come up empty for anything leading directly to the group, which left us with no real direction to go next.

ODIN and I pored over all the attached details on every recent and current Eco-Terror Taskforce bounty, looking for any hint of this new eco-terror group. After coming up empty-handed, we expanded our search into the general bounty pool, spending a sleepless night checking hundreds of open bounties and accompanying data packets, until we eventually stumbled across Dr. Schmidt. She was an augmentation expert working in the sublevels, who routinely worked with known anti-establishment groups like Cyber Volition, supplying them with augments under the table, skirting around the periphery of the grey market.

Normally, this would be a simple case of "good doctor gone bad," and I'd pay it little mind, but something drew me to her file and dossier. A strangle niggling sensation in the back of my mind.

Schmidt had a history of implanting modified neural augmentations in her clients—a big no-no, because they could not
only have unknown side-effects owing to the modifications, but
the act voided the licence and warranty, and could make them
inefficient. She'd been charged and fined on multiple occasions,
and had another fresh bounty open against her. The thing that
got me, though, was a conspicuous pairing: Cyber Volition and
modified neural augments.

That's when it clicked.

Gregor. Or more specifically, what Fayola had told me about
Gregor's *death*.

He'd been killed while busting a group of Cyber Volition
members buying modified neural augmentations from an
unknown third party. Someone the footage showed sporting
the tell-tale sigil.

It took a few calls, an urgent request to the Bounty
Commission archives, and, unfortunately, playing up my position on the Bounty Board, but I was able to get my hands on the
recording from Gregor's helmet cam from the night he died.
Gruesome stuff, and it was hard to watch someone I knew die
over and over as I played back the footage, looking for any new
leads. Which is when I found it. Or more specifically, found
her.

Apparently, the reports circulating about Gregor's death
were missing a few details. The moment Gregor crashed
through the door into the apartment where he would meet his
untimely death, he swept the room, and for a few dozen frames,
a makeshift surgical suite was visible through an open doorway, with surgical implements and a neural augment sitting in
a jar full of sterilizing gel. Slowing the video down, I was able

to make out two more figures. Someone lying on the table with the falling star logo on their neck, and another, who dashed for cover behind a metal crate bearing the same symbol seconds before the shot rang out that took Gregor's life.

The running figure was Dr. Schmidt.

Bingo.

So here I was, coming to cash in on the good doctor's contract, and hopefully find some real answers this time. Then I was going to go home and crash. After another night of next to no sleep, running on fumes, and an unhealthy amount of caffeine, what I really needed was for this to be an easy job.

Unfortunately for me, though, I now had to get through Dr. Schmidt's top clients to get to her.

Two Cyber Volition guards—dressed in puffy neon-green jackets with sleeves cut off at the elbow to show their cybernetic appendages, and black pants rolled up to show legs similarly augmented—suddenly burst through the doors, submachine guns cradled in their hands, and opened fire. Magnetically-propelled rounds drunkenly pinged off chairs, tables, and medical equipment all around me in a buzzing hail, and I ducked back, shouldering through the nearest door. On the other side was a brightly lit examination room, and I slid behind the metal examination table as rounds peppered the wall, chasing me to cover and shattering the room's interior window.

The gunfire died quickly, and I could hear at least one of the Cyber Volition goons reload, the clack of metal feet on tile and whizz of servos a signal they were moving closer. Then the soles of my feet registered the thunderous quake of heavy footsteps racing up the corridor from the main lobby, followed by a heavy thud, and the electronically modified voice of Bonny Dogar.

"Get back into the operating room, you idiots," she shouted. "Protect the fucking doctor. That's who he's after. Leave the bounty hunter to me."

Hidden behind the table, I slipped my pistol from its holster and leaned out, muzzle levelled at the window near where I heard Bonny's voice. But she wasn't there.

A high-pitched whine filled the air to my right and the wall exploded in a shower of plaster chunks and dust as the metal fist sliced through the wall. Bonny's metal fist was visible for a moment in the blur as massive slabs of wall hammered my shoulder and knocked me to the floor. Taking the hit, I rolled over on my left, twisting to land in a crouch, pistol aimed at the smouldering hole. Through the cloud of lime plaster dust, I again saw the burning amber of her eyes, and then her hand reached out, long, razor-like fingers gripping the shattered edge of the hole, cracking the plaster further as Bonny pulled herself through, stepping forward with her right leg, clouds of dust twisting around her horrid metal frame. Long-limbed and furious, she looked monstrous.

She came fast, but I was faster. Two light pops sent a pair of rounds towards Bonny's right leg. The first pinged off the metal housing on her thigh harmlessly, but the second found purchase, striking the soft joint, and blasted chunks of metal and wire out sideways. She tried to take a step, but the leg gave, and she fell to the floor with a heavy bang, letting out a pained groan. With Bonny down, I fired again, shattering her left elbow.

For augments to function properly, and for human beings to

use them as effectively as the real thing, tactile sensations were fed back directly into the central nervous system to perfectly mimic flesh and bone and trick the body into accepting the new body parts. But it also meant she could feel pain, and this would certainly hurt.

Bits of metal and carbon showered onto the floor, and the damaged joints sparked, blue flashes popping out of the holes my shots had made. Limply, Bonny tried to drag herself towards me, panting heavily, synthetic organs working hard to keep her moving. With her good arm, she pushed herself up to face me, busted arm hanging limp at her side, forearm loosely dangling from the blasted joint.

"You see this?" she growled, letting the inert forearm sway slowly back and forth. "Pitiful." A blinding blue flash filled the room, followed by a warbling groan and the scream of shearing metal as Bonny tore the damaged arm in two, leaving the frayed ends of the elbow joint exposed, sparks of blue arcing out to scatter on the tile floor. "I should really thank you, hunter. Now Dr. Schmidt can give me a new one, a better one, and I'll only get stronger."

"Dr. Schmidt is coming with me, Bonny," I replied, stepping back to keep out of her range. "She's racked up quite the list of charges, but trust me, I'm not here to hurt her."

Letting out another bellowing roar, Bonny swiped forward, dagger-like digits doing nothing but blowing air in my direction. "I won't let you take her!" She lunged again, tossing the table at me. I ducked backwards into a roll, letting it fly past and crash into the counter along the rear wall, sending medical supplies scattering in every direction.

Another high-pitched whine escaped from the pneumatics

in Bonny's intact leg as she launched herself at me, arm arcing in a lethal swipe. We slammed hard into the wall, a deep crunch vibrating out from somewhere in my chest as a rib cracked and all air was forced from my lungs. There was a flash of stars in my vision, and my mask's HUD crackled from the impact. With only one working arm, she couldn't grapple and strike, so Bonny leaned back and released her hold on me, arm raised to hammer down.

I moved. Impact shattered the wall behind me like a meteor striking a mountainside, scattering plaster and dust as the metal fist sliced through the wall. I'd been just quick enough to dodge the death blow at the last moment and rolled into a crouch near the blown-out window, launching myself through the opening to land hard on the other side, a lance of pain shooting through my leg as my recently injured knee twisted painfully under me. Lying on my back, I took a few gasping breaths. Shadows danced at the edge of my vision.

"Holy shit, that was lucky," I croaked.

A roaring scream echoed from the examination room.

ODIN laughed. "She didn't like that."

"As someone who's lost their arm, I don't blame her."

I jerked as Bonny brought her palm down hard on the windowsill, the white surface of the corridor wall buckling under the force as she hoisted herself up, amber eyes flaring in rage. I scrambled awkwardly to my feet, ignoring my throbbing knee, and backed up to the operating room door, pistol gripped firmly in my hand. Killing Bonny wasn't out of the question if it meant saving my own life, but I preferred not to if I didn't have to. The best outcome would be to grab the doctor and get out of here before Cyber Volition turned this clinic into a war zone.

Bonny hoisted herself over the frame and back into the corridor, her ruined arm dangling limply as she crawled forward with massive, clawing swipes of the functioning one. Hobbled, her working leg slipped on the tile floor, unable to get a solid grip, while the shattered knee joint pulled the mangled leg along, sparks firing out at odd intervals. She drove her fist into the floor in frustration, creating a deep crater.

I kept my distance as Bonny dragged herself helplessly along the shattered patch of floor.

But I realized too late that she wasn't helpless at all. She was lining herself up.

The piston fired and her foot punched down into the fist-shaped depression she'd created, rocketing her body forward like a shrieking, nightmarish panther. I had barely enough time to duck below her swiping claw. Her momentum carried her over my head and sent her crashing through the doors to the operating room, headlong over the edge of the metal railing beyond.

Quickly, I slipped alongside the doorframe, standing with my shoulder against the thick stone wall. Screams echoed from beyond the room ahead, accompanied by thudding metallic footsteps, Cyber Volition guards rushing up to cover their wounded leader, guns likely trained on the double doors they knew I was waiting behind.

A moment passed as I steeled myself, breathing deeply to slow my hammering heart rate. Letting my senses and intuition take over. Keep the bubble. Don't let it pop.

Another moment, and I moved.

A quick jab on the door next to me and I was back to cover, ducking into an examination room to my left. There was a high-pitched whine as the thin barrier swung inward, followed by the chaotic swarming of electric gunfire, peppering the doors with rounds. After a few moments, the Cyber Volition guards stopped shooting, uncertain whether their shots had found their mark. The shredded doors swung back loosely on their hinges, into the corridor, and then back to rest still in the frame.

Inhale. Move.

I slipped from cover, stepping sideways past the mangled doors, gun trained through the freshly made and still-smoking peepholes. For fractions of seconds, I saw targets, people dressed in Cyber Volition garb, and fired. Six quick shots, two apiece for three targets, and then I ducked back to cover, just in time to escape another hail of gunfire, less powerful than the last, and sounding only like a single shooter. Again, the doors splintered as rounds pounded their surface, blowing both open. The door closest to me swung around, slamming into my shoulder, before swinging back on its hinges.

As the door swung back, I followed, using it as partial cover to fire back. Two more pops, and the last Cyber Volition shooter dropped.

And so did I.

A heavy weight slammed into my chest, taking me clear off my feet. The metal arm of Bonny Dogar wrapped around my torso, carrying me to the floor. I could smell burnt wires, ozone, and the pungent odor of coolant. As we slammed hard into the ground, I felt another pop, another rib that would need repair, and my shoulder crunched—not painful enough to mean a break, but it still brought tears to my eyes. Luckily, I was able to hang on to the pistol.

Bonny loosened her grasp and reared up before a quick punch thundered beside my head, kicking up sparks and flakes of broken tile, making my ears ring. Then I felt a heavy weight on my thigh as Bonny pressed down with her knee to pin me. I twisted my leg to try and slip free, but her augmented body was too heavy. I pressed in close to escape another jackhammer punch. A bad move, I realized too late, as her arm wrapped around me and squeezed me even closer, her grip a hydraulic press that crushed me like a vice. I let out a bleated groan.

Bonny laughed. "And that's why the flesh is inferior. So soft, so squishy." She squeezed even tighter, and I groaned again. "Where you all see illegal modification, we see necessary evolution. We're pushing ourselves further away from you, and it scares you, doesn't it? Knowing that we've unlocked the next step?" The pressure made it impossible to speak, and my broken ribs screamed in agony. I still had the pistol in my grip, but I was starting to lose feeling in my arms. Bonny kept talking. "Argo and the other corps can do whatever they want, get the government to pass whatever laws suit their fancy, but when the Earth finally completes its revolt, we'll be all that's left—"

There was a muffled pop and her face went slack, and thankfully so did her grip, as she let out a wraith-like scream. I quickly slipped out from under her, sucking in a tantalizingly long breath, pistol trained on her as I slammed against the wall and sank to a knee. My whole body pulsed with pain, heart thumping hard in my ears, watching Bonny writhe in pain on the ground, clutching her leg. The fresh wound punched through her carbon-covered thigh.

The wail echoed off the corridor walls, and I slowly made my way towards the operating suite, still sucking in air.

"I told you, Bonny," I said, breathlessly, "I don't want to kill you. All I care about is taking Schmidt into custody."

"I don't give a fuck what you do," Bonny replied through gritted teeth, fingers wrapped around her wounded thigh. "You can't stop it, hunter. The corps can't stop it. If Dr. Schmidt is gone, we'll just find another aug-doc, and then another, and then another. Until we get what we deserve. Until we're perfect!"

"That may be, but I can stop this one." I took aim and fired another two shots that sheared through her other elbow joint, leaving a single frayed wire connecting it to her body. Bonny screamed out again, voice a dissonant echo of human and electronic tones. She swung the arm around at me, the wire snapped under tension, and the limb flew into two pieces.

Now unarmed, and with one barely functioning leg, Bonny wasn't much of a threat. I lowered my pistol and watched as she writhed, a pained expression visible on the small strip of flesh she still had left while her amber eyes glowered at me murderously.

"Sorry, Bonny." I lowered the pistol and pushed through the doors to the operating wing. "I'm just doing my job."

I took a survey of the room while trying to ignore the curses I could still hear Bonny hurling my way. From where I stood, atop a raised landing, off of which two curving staircases followed the lazy arc of the circular space down to the floor below, there were three visible operating rooms with windows stretching floor to ceiling, allowing observers to watch from the outside while preserving the sterile conditions of the surgical areas. Descending the steps to my left, I scanned the bodies. Four Cyber Volition members, heavily augmented, lay on the white tiled floor, pools of crimson collecting around them.

Sensing my regret, ODIN piped up softly, "It's okay, Nikos. You were acting on instinct."

"I could've done more, though," I sighed and peeled my eyes away from the bodies.

In the two peripheral operating rooms, doctors and nurses hid behind tables and carts, peering out through bulletproof glass, fear plain on their faces.

I knocked on the glass of the nearest window. "Hey. Can you hear me in there?"

A terrified doctor and two nurses cowered behind an over-turned operating table. One of the nurses, a woman with freck-les and close-set eyes, hazarded a peek over the padded edge, eyes wide with fear. I raised my gloved hand in what I hoped was a reassuring gesture, then slipped my helmet off, hair flop-ping out in a twisted mess. I smiled, flashing the licence on my wrist-nav at her through the glass.

"I'm a bounty hunter. You don't have to worry—well, not anymore." I jabbed a thumb back to the Cyber Volition troops behind me. "Sorry about that, I really am. This was supposed to be a simple job, nobody gets hurt, but … yeah, that didn't happen. Y'know what, I'll call a cleaner crew and they'll take care of—"

"Please!" the nurse called out, evidently the braver of her two colleagues. "Please, just go."

I sighed and dropped my arm, wincing as the movement aggravated a broken rib. "Honestly, I really am sorry. I'm just here to collect a bounty. Thought it was going to be a quiet night."

Apparently satisfied that I wasn't going to open fire on them, the nurse raised herself higher over the edge of the operating table. She swallowed hard before speaking. "Usually, Dr. Schmidt keeps Cyber Volition out of the clinic. I don't know why today was different."

"Speaking of Dr. Schmidt," I tapped the glass lightly with my finger, "funny enough, she's the one I'm here to see. Can you tell me where she is?"

The nurse whipped her arm up and pointed to the next room over, along the back wall of the operating wing. It seemed that she held no reservations about outing Schmidt, especially given the chaos she'd brought into their workplace. I nodded in thanks and moved on, taking a quick glance over my shoulder to make sure Bonny wasn't coming back for more. With no sign of her, I continued to the next operating room in search of the not-so-good doctor.

Unlike the previous room, which had had a single bed, a counter along the back wall, and enough room for maybe four or five people comfortably, Dr. Schmidt's postoperative care ward was expansive. Stepping through the sliding glass door, I was flanked on either side by four beds separated by privacy screens, all of which looked to be empty, save the one closest to the entrance. The lone patient was a younger man, lightly augmented, with bandages wrapped around his knee, below which extended a slender blue shin and yellow foot. He was fast asleep, IV hooked into his arm, machines humming around him. His EKG pulsed away, readout strong.

A smooth voice cut through the quiet of the room. "Luckily, I finished up with him before you arrived," said the woman who emerged from behind one of the partitions. The doctor's

expression was calm, fine lines across her skin showing the first
signs of age, a straight nose drawing a line up her face to round
eyes that flashed green like an algae-covered pond. My eyes
wandered to the mottled scar on right side of her thin mouth,
where a dermal augment hadn't taken.

"Dr. Johanna Schmidt?" I walked up, cradling the helmet
under my arm, pistol holstered to show I was no threat. ODIN
noted the recording was live, and I was begging to high heaven
it wouldn't end up showing another stain on my ledger.

Schmidt answered with a nod.

"Good," I continued. "My name is Nikos Wulf, and I am the
bounty hunter assigned to your case. My licence n—"

"Spare me the formalities, please." Dr. Schmidt cocked her
head, a lock of hair escaping from the bun at the nape of her
neck. "What am I wanted for, pray tell?"

"I was getting to that. There's a protocol to follow."

She scoffed. "Do you think I give a shit about your bounty
hunter protocol? I'm a surgeon, and a damn good one. My
whole life is rules and procedures."

"So what, doing body-augs for Cyber Volition is your idea of
cutting loose? Having a good time by breaking the law?"

Her response was a harsh, derisive laugh. "And whose laws
are those? Yours? The government's? Argo's?" The doctor
moved towards one of the sinks set against the back wall and
began washing her hands thoroughly under the motion-sen-
sor faucet. "I do what is right for my patients. It does not hurt
them, to augment themselves in such a way. So how does any
bounty of mine fall under the thumb of Nikos Wulf, the Eco-
Terror Taskforce's top dog? I see no forest burning, no animals
being hunted, no dams being destroyed."

I looped my thumb around my belt. "I stray into the general bounty pool, on occasion, for special exceptions." I gave her a pointed look. "You're wanted for illegal modification of the human form and that carries an automatic bo—"

"Ah! There it is." She shook the water from her hands. "Illegal according to whom? It wasn't until I started this clinic and began practising that I realized the truth myself. But why must the work I do be illegal? When people like Bonny Dogar—" she gestured towards the shattered operating wing door, a shower of droplets flying from her fingertips—"merely believe something different than you. Or are you not so blind, Mr. Wulf? Whose opinion must reign supreme?"

I wasn't in the mood to argue over ideology, but I was getting the feeling that Schmidt wouldn't come willingly unless I let her say her piece. And I was far too tired and sore to bring her in the hard way. Resigned, I walked over to an empty bed and took a seat on it gingerly, siffling a groan. The only part of me that didn't hurt was my prosthesis.

I knew Schmidt had a point. Light glinted off my dappled carbon palm, small spheres of white from the lights above sliding along the sleek, unnatural skin as I turned it over, flexing my fingers. The technology in my arm was leagues better than what was typically available to civilians. Dermal sensors so finely tuned they were practically human. A bulletproof casing that was so light it never impeded my movements. The arm was, for all intents and purposes, better than the one I had lost. Whether it was better in a preferential sense, though, was debatable.

"Unfortunately, Dr. Schmidt," I said, clenching my metal hand into a fist, "interpretation and morality of law are above my pay grade at the moment. I'm just here to execute."

The doctor laughed, looking past me to the wreckage in the room beyond. "It seems you've done a good job executing."

"They weren't supposed to be here. That wasn't supposed to happen. And I'm not happy about it, for what it's worth."

"That is worth absolutely nothing, it seems. They're dead and you are not."

The barb stung. I turned back to Schmidt, my brows furrowed, eyes focused on her. "To be perfectly honest, doctor, right now I don't give a shit how you make your money. What I do care about is who you make it from."

"And what is that supposed to mean?" Schmidt wiped her hands on a small towel and stepped closer. I could see I had her attention now.

Time to press. "Cyber Volition has been caught on video purchasing modified neural augs from a group I'm trying to track down. A bounty hunter was killed when he interrupted one of their deals." ODIN projected the video from Gregor's helmet on a wall, level with Schmidt's eyes, the harrowing sounds of his murder echoing off the walls around us. I stopped on the image of the green sigil, studying the doctor, who struggled to keep her expression neutral.

"I *know* that you were on the scene—conducting an off-the-books neural augmentation procedure, from the looks of it. You were in the room with the person bearing this symbol. I need to know who they are."

Moving from the sink, the doctor crossed the room to her sole patient, studying his charts on a small tablet, flicking through settings on the machines and pulling the blanket to cover him up to his chest. She was silent, but I was patient.

Eventually, she sighed and turned to look at me. "It is a great regret of mine that your colleague died that night. I would not be a proper physician if his death did not weigh on me." Schmidt swallowed, glancing back at the sigil before continuing. "They came to me a few months ago, offering the augments cheaply, and when your colleague and I crossed paths, I was implanting such an augment in one of their members as a demonstration of good faith to Cyber Volition. Showing the efficacy of their modifications." Schmidt looked down at the young man in the bed, the corners of her mouth pulled into a frown. "I thought I was doing right by my patients. Is that not what any physician would do? Augmentations are expensive, and the government does everything it can to avoid covering the costs, letting corps run wild with their prices and their demands. They came promising cheap alternatives, ones that on paper were old, some off the market entirely, but brand new, and upgraded to be indistinguishable from the best available neural augs on the market—even down to the firmware and serial numbers."

I sat up straighter, an odd nagging sensation starting at the back of my skull. "Why'd they give them to you?"

"Patronage. I would give them to all my clients, and they would ensure patronage." The sensation began to pulse. I locked eyes with Schmidt.

"Patronage from who?"

Another beat, then payday. "From them. From Eden's Purpose."

A name. Finally, a damn name.

I gestured to the sigil still displayed on the wall. "This logo. This is from Eden's Purpose?"

The doctor nodded, as if this were all routine. "Yes."

Eden's Purpose. The group Maxwell Van Buren had died for.

BOUNTY

The one Sobotka killed himself to protect, and the ones targeting Argo. It was finally falling into place.

I stood, walking towards Schmidt. "I need to find them, doctor."

A satisfied smile broke over her lips. "Child." The word came out as an insult. "Trying to find a new career path?"

I stepped closer. "And if I am?"

The smile on her face became ghoulish. "Then I'll need to tell you where to go."

FIFTEEN

It took some work, but we hammered out a deal with Dr. Schmidt. She would get the bounties on her expunged in return for the information she had. Officials over at the Bounty Commission took some convincing, but thankfully having Nikos Wulf, Mackenzie "Strigi" Nadeau, and Maria "Valkyrie" Lindgren all sitting on the other side of the table made it damn near impossible for them to say no.

That, and Dr. Schmidt had shown genuine remorse for her role in what had occurred. I wasn't about to deny someone a chance at redemption.

Which was why we were here, back on Sublevel 6, standing outside a Children of Atlantis temple, about to be "recruited" by Eden's Purpose.

As much as I hated to admit it, though, we wouldn't have been able to find this place without Castor. While our deal with Schmidt gave us a location, Castor confirmed it with his technical wizardry. Argo security honcho Brown knocked on my door late after I'd returned from Dr. Schmidt's bounty, "politely" asking for the hologram projector, and a few hours later, as we were getting ready to sign a deal with the good doctor, Castor pinged me a location, which thankfully confirmed Schmidt's intel.

Argo to the rescue, I suppose.

The Bounty Commission, and even the Eco-Terror Taskforce itself, by contrast, were wary of expending any resources on this. It seemed that despite our collective standing in the bounty hunter world, and the interest in quashing a rising eco-terror organization before it could gain any kind of staying power in the city sublevels, the three of us would be on our own here. No extra money for backup, no aid in intel gathering, no bending of regulations and commission rules to make our lives easier, not even so much as a "thank you, now go get them" from the Bounty Commission's board of directors—essentially a collection of public servants with cushy gigs without a single completed bounty between them.

Clearly the deal with Dr. Schmidt was all the help the Commission was willing to give.

At least the two people I trusted most in the world were right beside me.

If you didn't know where you were going, you'd completely miss it. Hell, we almost did when we walked by, and ODIN was guiding us there. On the bottom floor of a big mixed-use building, located between a large transport repair shop and a family-owned corner store, was a nondescript facade. Faded teal paint, windows covered by blackout sheets, no sign, no markings, and only a set of metal double doors to indicate a separate unit existed here at all. It took a second or two to notice that some of the chips in the paint were intentional, telltale scratches and scrapes made by a knife in the metal underneath. If you knew what you were looking for, you could make it out. The falling star. Eden's Purpose.

The only other visible feature was a call button on the right side of the door, under a small screen and what looked like a camera.

Mack stepped up beside me, hands stuffed into his jacket pockets. Unlike most days, his outfit was muted, reflecting the clandestine nature of what we were here to do. "They would benefit a lot from a sign," he quipped. "Sure, the logo is there," he pointed at the door, "but could it hurt to, maybe, inlay it with gold? Then it would look really sharp."

"You can offer your feedback when we're inside, Mack," Maria replied, with a hardy pat on Mack's shoulder. She was dressed in the same multicoloured jacket from our dinner at the Zhaos' but had swapped the boots for runners. "Nikos?"

I looked over the facade once more. On the way over, ODIN had pulled up a schematic of the building. The first three floors of every unit were meant for the commercial tenant, and every level beyond that was apartments and condos. I was hoping that meant our chances of walking into a shootout were unlikely, though the thought did little to assuage my concerns about our dress. Full civvies. We were about to descend into a lion's den with no gear, and no weapons except for our bodies, and although our hand-to-hand skills far exceeded the average person's, Eden's Purpose had proven they could kill, and we had no idea what we were walking into.

I could only hope that being in a house of worship meant they would stay a little calmer.

With a deep breath that sent a pang through my still-healing ribs, I turned to my friends. "Let's go."

Maria was standing closest to the call button, so she gave it a firm press with her thumb, and we could hear an audible buzz from inside the door. The small screen, which displayed a slowly rotating Children of Atlantis logo, suddenly flickered, changing to reveal a small, sallow face, peering out with glowing white eyes, similar to the projected preacher Maria and I had met before on this same sublevel. This one, though, had alopecia and looked very much like a Catholic priest. All he needed was a cross.

"Welcome, children, to the house of Poseidon and seat of Triton." His voice bore the same resonant tone as the preacher's. "We are, unfortunately, not holding any public services today. How may I help you on your journey forth?"

Here we go. Don't fuck it up, Nikos.

I stepped forward and leaned in close, so I could quietly reply, "I had hoped for Demeter's blessing. For summer grows longer, yet our fields yield no wheat."

It was silly, but that was the passphrase Schmidt had given us.

Following our confrontation, she'd become remorseful, genuinely believing she had been doing right by her patients—and I couldn't blame her. She admitted that she'd grown wary of her new suppliers after noticing their logo in recent footage of violent protests, along with an ever-increasing clientele being driven through her doors. As part of a deal with the Bounty Commission, where she could avoid serious time behind bars and resume her work under heavy supervision from Manitoba Health and the Commission, Schmidt had given us the passphrase, and directed us here. It was the only Children of Atlantis temple that never held public services. Private ones only, once a week, the group citing "confidentiality for its more esteemed patrons." But we now knew the real story, or at least part of it.

Schmidt said she'd been invited here once by her suppliers, who explained it would help her understand the group and their aims, but never attended. She thought it would be better to keep their relationship as separate as possible. Smart on her end, but I knew it was a wariness learned from her work with Cyber Volition that made her keep some level of plausible deniability in case bounty hunters came knocking—like me.

What I couldn't quite square was how the group had gotten into the illicit augmentation game, or why. They had to be getting the augments from somewhere, and modifying them before they sold them, but those markets were fairly monopolized. The Human Reclamation Front were the big aug thieves in Winnipeg on the used front, and Cyber Volition were well known for holding up cargo transports and augmentation manufacturing plants, while the NetDreamers were the top dog in the aug-mod space. So this new group—presumably—was walking into a pre-existing market and muscling competition out of the way.

But for what reason was also a mystery. Sure, anti-establishment groups by nature fought against corporations, but it was usually on a broader basis. From what I'd seen so far, this new player was solely focused on Argo. The stolen tablet, the protest Van Buren had been a part of, the downed Argo trawlers—and there was probably more that I hadn't seen going on.

It was direct. Argo was the target.

And the breadcrumbs had led us here, to a Children of Atlantis temple. The group had been around for decades, so there was no telling when this had all started, or how involved they truly were with Eden's Purpose, apart from offering a physical space for their recruitment meetings. If this worked, I hoped to find out.

First, we had to get on the other side of this door.

For a few moments, the preacher was silent, eyes flittering between the three of us, and with each passing second, I was growing more and more convinced we'd end up kicking the door down with a few extra hunters on my own dime. A few seconds more, and the man smiled.

"Then her message has been heard," he said with a nod. "Sacrifice and piety must come."

The image cut out, and the doors noiselessly swung inward. From inside, I could hear faint music playing, and the preacher stepped out to meet us, wearing robes identical to those of his holographic colleague, though his were ill-fitting, as the man was quite tall and lanky. Seemed the Children of Atlantis did not have a tailor.

He waved us towards him. "Come. We have a few moments before we begin," he said, and we obliged, stepping forward.

Turning the corner into the entrance, we found ourselves in a small, plush lobby, and were met with another barrier: two guards, with similar builds to those who had accompanied Sobotka. One had an onyx-black cybernetic lower jaw protruding from his face, behind which I could see the faint light of a synthetic voice box, while the other was devoid of any noticeable augmentation aside from black prisms on his temples, indicating neural augments.

He looked down at me with pinprick black eyes and held up a small metal wand.

The front door closed silently behind us, followed by the clunk of a lock engaging.

No going back now.

Onyx-Jaw spoke first. "Weapons check." His voice was dual tone and deliberately inhuman. He pulled out a small transparent piece of one-way glass and turned his attention to it, which I guessed was the screen connected to the wand. "Please step forward one at a time."

While Tiny-Eyes waved his magic wand over our bodies, conversing silently with Onyx-Jaw—I could see his throat moving as if he were talking, along with eye contact indicative of conversation, meaning both had neural augments that allowed them to communicate—the preacher approached me, wearing the most inviting smile he could muster.

"I must humbly ask you, Poseidon-touched. It is plain to see that you are yourself augmented. You will get the most exquisite experience as a result, but are your fellows augmented?" He cast an eye towards Mack and Maria. Behind me, I could hear Mack make a crass joke at the guards' expense.

"No," I replied. "Both, to my knowledge, are one hundred percent human. She's got a plate in her hand, though." I jabbed a thumb over my shoulder at Maria.

This was true. A few years back, we'd been sparring, and she'd accidentally punched an exposed pipe in Jaeger's apartment. That only broke her hand, though. What required the plate was the fact she never told us, and later I'd blocked a punch from her broken hand with my prosthetic one. It was not a pretty sight.

"Is that going to be a problem?" I sensed the tiny-eyed guard approaching me with the wand but kept my eyes on the preacher.

He smiled so wide his eyes nearly closed. "Not at all, Poseidon-touched. We have no qualms about who worships and in what state." He folded his hands together under his poncho. "It is just that the Poseidon-touched, such as yourself, and those who have neural augmentations like my gracious friend here behind you, get a more unique and … spiritual experience."

Seemed Schmidt was having more of an impact than she realized.

"Unfortunate," I replied with a small smile.

"Quite so." The preacher looked over my shoulder. "Are we done here, Rowan? Or can we allow our new friends into the service?"

I turned back to meet the gaze of the guard with the tiny eyes. He said nothing, but nodded.

The preacher glided by towards the next door. "Good. Now come, there is much to see."

Before moving on, Maria sidled up beside me and whispered, eyes locked on the preacher, "What was that about?"

"Keep an eye out," I whispered back. "I'm going to be seeing something completely different than you, apparently, so if things go wrong—"

"Mack and I will grab you." She bumped me on the shoulder. "We've got this. I'll stay to the outside, you and Mack will stick together."

And with a quick nod in acknowledgement, we were off.

But nothing could've prepared me for what I saw next.

The software in my eyes fought back for a second, the coded

safeties stressing hard against what was happening. The scene before me fizzled. The people, stone pillars, seats, and hanging banners stayed constant, but everything else—the background, walls, ceiling, and even floor—jerked and flashed, struggling to hold form, until the image stabilized. Once again, the software in my eyes was overpowered. Military-grade, my ass. Maybe I'd missed a malware patch, but regardless, it was concerning.

Then again, maybe I shouldn't have been surprised at the technical know-how of this group, as I took in the spectacular scene before me. Entering the temple's main hall was like stepping back in time to the height of ancient Greece. A small crowd of people in varying contemporary outfits were clustered just inside, some slack-jawed, looking out at the same thing I was seeing. We were standing inside the cavernous hall of an ancient Greek temple, stone pillars and all, which overlooked a calm blue sea. Trying not to look as dumbfounded as the other augmented individuals I was standing with, I peered around the place, in search of a seam, a glitch. Anything that could tip off the fact this was augmented reality. But there were none. Looking right and left, I could see beyond the large limestone columns to the rest of the acropolis in this fictional Greek city. Other temples, dedicated to various other gods, along with a main citadel, were in clear view, perfectly realized by whatever projection tech was feeding these images into my eyes. Turning to the rear wall, there was nothing but the sea, surface calm as glass, with small birds floating by on coastal winds. As I stood there, a soft breeze blew from the water, along with the faint scent of salt.

It was impressive, and I could see how these recruitment

meetings would leave a lasting impression on folks with the augs to make the most of it.

"Ostentatious," Mack murmured, pointing to long, blue banners hanging from the pillars. "I'll have to steal some and bring it to my tailor. Get a nice cape made."

The banners were inlaid with intricate patterns. Stitched into their surface were circles that looked like whirlpools, swooping lines like crashing waves, cutting lines like torrential downpours, and everywhere I looked was a city, pierced by a rising trident.

"For once, Mack, I don't think they're your style," I mumbled. "How much do you see?"

He snickered. "Not as much as you, clearly. Just a big open room, pillars, people. They're blowing cooled air and aromas through the vents."

Perfectly supporting what I was seeing. Making it not just look, but feel, real.

Mack gripped my forearm. "If shit goes wild, I've got you."

The sentiment would always be reassuring, but here it was even doubly so. If Eden's Purpose could get past military-grade security to feed these lifelike images to my eyes, who knew what they could do to the people in here with neural augments.

Peering over my shoulder, I spotted Maria, making her way through the crowd along the back wall—which was now massive blocks of limestone.

As Mack and I moved deeper into the crowd, a voice permeated the space. Calm and vibrant.

"And so they come, finally, to seek answers," said a voice that pricked the back of my mind. I knew that voice. "For this, I must instead begin with questions … How much have you seen? How much has he shown you? Have you seen the waters rise, choking the life from the great machines below? Flooding the fake fields contained in a land of steel and stone? Have you seen Triton himself, walking the streets of the city as it drowns, the bodies of the unseeing floating through the bubbling depths?

"Or have you heard the words of a preacher? Standing alone in the pouring rain. Did the words ring true to you as you watched them stand there, embracing the flowing presence of our saviours, while others hid from it? Do you understand now how humanity stands opposed to the gods, fighting back against the will of the Fates for so long?"

I manoeuvred around a tall, augmented woman, her attention firmly on the simulation, to find the centre of the room. A small dais was raised half a metre from the floor, thin blue light bleeding from the seam around its base, and atop was an altar, covered in scratches and divots, a small blade laid diagonally across its surface. Flanking the altar was a pair of statues. One showed a male figure, emerging from a swirling spout of water, raising his trident high; the other knelt, head bowed low, holding the same trident horizontally in outstretched hands. Poseidon and Triton. The two main figures in the Children of Atlantis religion.

But there was nobody at the dais. The voice was coming from nowhere.

Until it wasn't.

"Are you ready now to embrace what Atlantis suffered before us?" the voice said again, this time clearly from the entrance. At the same time, the crowd began to part to let someone through.

It was the preacher. The same one Maria and I had seen

here on Sublevel 6 the other night. Except this one, judging by Mack's reaction, wasn't a projection.

"For those Poseidon-touched among you, I'm certain he has already shown you much," the preacher continued. "Humanity's continued folly. Allowing corporations to take away what is rightfully ours, in service of a fight against salvation. Against the will of the gods. Synthetic crops grown where Demeter has deemed they should be blighted. Massive walls to keep Poseidon's rage in check. Power stolen from the hands of Apollo to brighten cities and run machines that Hephaestus did not craft." As the crowd continued to part, Mack and I retreated deeper into the crowd. No need to risk being recognized, but we were positioned to keep an eye on the proceedings. "For those of you who have not yet been touched by Poseidon, do not worry; you have made it here, nonetheless. You have followed the words our preachers spoke, and wound up on our doorstep willingly, and for that Poseidon will remember you."

Walking up to stand behind the altar, he rested a tender hand on the back of the kneeling Triton. His sandy blond hair was dry, coiffed, flowing from his head in waves; the penetrating white flame of his cybernetic eyes bled out from underneath.

"For many years, we, the Children of Atlantis, have preached of the coming end. Standing on street corners, behind altars, in darkened alcoves, trying to bring light and promise to a darkening world. Yet few heed our words." The preacher gazed out, hand on the edge of the Poseidon statue. "If the world is drowning, shall we not reach out a hand to rescue those from the watery grave? No, the corporations say, we will build walls to keep the waters at bay. The construction will create jobs, and the jobs will bring in money."

JASON PCHAJEK

I quickly assessed the crowd around me, and saw many people nodding along.

"If the world is drought-sick, crying out for relief, would you not call for rain? No, the governments say, we will send trucks laden with water to bring sustenance to the masses. If we do that, they will not rebel, or pass through our borders. Better they stay where they are.

"And if storms rip across the prairies, wiping away cities, towns, homes, and people, would you not seek a way to reclaim what you have lost? No, the citizens of Earth say, that requires too much effort—we will cower like rats in a hole."

He looked out, eyes searching the crowd.

"Corporations like Argo have pushed lies on us, claiming that corporations and capitalist innovation are the only means of stemming the tide of climate apocalypse. Yet here we are, generations later, and the planet still rebels. But this should be taken as a sign." The preacher took a hard grip on the altar's edge, looking down at the mass of people below him, face screwed up into a menacing glare. "We are being punished. For too long, we did not heed the word of the gods, so they turned the world we sought to claim against us. Yet we did not listen. The Children of Atlantis were formed to spread their message. Of resignation and destruction, allowing the gods of Olympus to reclaim and reshape the world. Yet the world did not listen."

His vision snapped back up. The preacher lightly tapped the Triton statue, then raised a hand, running it through the sandy mass on his head, momentarily exposing the small black-and-silver shape of his neural implants.

"We shall sit idly by no longer," he continued. "The path to our salvation awaits. But another must take you there."

For a moment, I felt a slight shift in the air. Like a vacuum had been created, and all sound was gone. The preacher seemed to notice too, as his mouth curled into a smirk.

"Now you must find out why you're here."

The preacher closed his eyes, and every muscle in his body relaxed, head lolling around on his neck, and a comfortable smile creeping across his lips.

He took a long, satisfied breath, and looked up at all of us, eyes opening to reveal a deep green glow. Fingers caressing the statues, he studied us, before placing a hand on the altar.

"Good. Very good," he said, the cadence and pitch of his voice now completely altered. "Speaking through people is a *lot* easier than ... borrowing—let's say borrowing—someone's body."

Mack let out a breathless swear, and as we both gazed at the preacher, an all-too-familiar memory flashed across my mind.

Sobotka.

Those movements. They were the same as the ones before Sobotka turned the gun on himself. Is this what had happened to him in the moments before he died? Some kind of ... what? Possession? Mind control? Was his death not intentional after all?

The preacher, or whoever he was, began to pace the dais, glancing slowly around the roomm admiring the space and the people around him. "I would've let this young man continue his speech," the speaker indicated to the body he'd presumably possessed, "but the time for mere ideology has now come to an end. We thank the Children of Atlantis for spreading our shared message, but we are all here tonight for a different purpose." He smiled, and held out a hand, grasping those of someone in the crowd before him, a young woman in a Ravencrest jacket, with a seemingly fresh neural augment, skin around it still enflamed. She was enraptured. "That, and I wanted to speak to you all myself."

As he did, Mack slipped behind me, leaning in to whisper, "Nikos, I don't like this. Did someone seriously just take over that preacher's body?"

Neural implants were something I barely understood, but at the end of the day, they were machines. And machines could break, could freeze, could lock up, and could be hacked. Electrical impulses from one person, replicated in another via machine-brain connection. If someone had established a connection, they could use something like a VR bodysuit, or neural implants of their own, to impose electrical impulses on the muscles and brain of another. It was terrifying, but ultimately seemed possible.

The implications were staggering. We now knew that Eden's Purpose was supplying neural implants to Dr. Schmidt and her patients, but was she the only surgeon in the city they supplied, or were there others? Did the modifications to these implants somehow make them easier to hack? Which begged the question: how many of these people here tonight with neural augs were here totally of their own will? Was it only those with potentially tampered augs that could be affected, or was everyone at risk? Could they implant ideas? Memories? Dreams? Could that have been the cause of Maxwell Van Buren's sudden radicalization?

As I was drowning in these revelations, the preacher turned, grinning wide, emerald eyes flaring. "But where are my manners? Benedict Hawthorne ..." He stooped into a low bow.

"Here to make your humble acquaintance. I am the leader of Eden's Purpose, and I hope, all of you, very soon."

He walked calmly, with a stately confidence, but had the air of a loving parent to those near him, giving small smiles, knowing glances, little touches, and leaning in to make everyone gathered around the dais feel as if they were supremely important to him.

Just like a cult leader, for sure, but Eden's Purpose was well beyond that, reaching into extremist territory.

"In the interest of time," he continued, "seeing as it is quite difficult to maintain control over another's body—even one who gives themselves up willingly, that damnable autonomic nervous system—it pays to be slightly expedient." Hawthorne walked back behind the altar and rested his hands lovingly on the statues. "This is but the first step in a long journey for you all. Salvation does not come easy. Not today. Not ever. It is a path one must walk, and that journey begins here, in this room. You, who are tired of life in this hole—this prison—made by corporations and built on their false promises of salvation. You, who spend your days toiling in the darkness, subsisting on recycled scraps, while the Ivories, while *Argo*, our master jailers, stand above, denying us our salvation! The future they *stole* from us with their greed and avarice." Hawthorne studied the thin collection of watchers who hadn't descended on the dais, and my ears began to burn as I felt his gaze slide over me. Did he know who I was? Had Schmidt somehow tipped him off?

But Hawthorne continued his speech.

"You are all here, and for that I am thankful. I truly am." He forced a smile and looked at the crowd, affecting the doting-father persona again. "So many fresh faces, here to serve a grand purpose. For we need your help. We wish to save you all, but for that to happen …" he held out a hand, and those closest reached out to grasp it, being just centimetres short, "you must join us.

"Eden's Purpose and the Children of Atlantis have a mutual understanding," Hawthorne continued. "While we still have much love for our former fellows, our splintering happened for a reason. You see, there is only one way this all ends. Cities will sink, nations will fall, buried under inhospitable sand drifts, or shattered by perpetual storms, or routed by ancient pathogens. The Children of Atlantis may not deign to cause it themselves, but they now see the gods will no longer be denied. Eden's Purpose was sent by Poseidon himself, to help bring about the destruction of humankind. We will raze what Argo has created, the world they have wrought by their challenges to fate itself. The threads will be cut." He slammed a fist down on the altar, sending the remains of offerings tumbling off its surface.

"And then …" Hawthorne held up his hands, high to the heavens, "we will rebuild. Humanity will become better than it ever was before. We will rise to Eden. This is our purpose. We cannot forget."

This was insanity. Plain and simple.

We'd started on this journey trying to find what we thought was a small blip on the Eco-Terror Taskforce's radar, something to stamp out in a couple weeks. Now here we were, days and many lives later, standing in an augmented-reality projection of an ancient Greek temple, listening to a fucking madman talk about how he had to bring an end to the world in order to save it. Kill potentially billions in climate hellfire, only for humanity to rise up from the dirt better than before. It was madness—but, as I looked around, people were eating it up. The throng standing around the dais continued to swell as Hawthorne spoke, more of us who'd stayed back standing now alone.

Madness. Fucking madness.

But how? Was this always bubbling under the surface? Anti-establishment groups had done nothing but grow over the years, becoming indispensable to the sublevels in many ways. The Plainswalkers provided affordable local food; the Human Reclamation Front provided medication and drugs that helped humans remain competitive with machines so they could make a living; even Cyber Volition helped in a roundabout way by putting much-needed augmentations and parts back into circulation. The Bounty Commission's policy was "contain and maintain," even when it had started to become a massive and dangerous problem. Because the benefit outweighed the cost.

But Eden's Purpose? This was something else. A militant splinter from a doomsday religion, bent on destroying the world.

Yet people here wanted in.

There was something I wasn't seeing. There had to be.

Around the dais, the crowd began to clamour, and Hawthorne just smiled.

"Yes," he said, barely audible over the jubilant crowd. "You will all be fine recruits." Slowly, Hawthorne slid his hand across the altar, fingers playing at the scattered remains of offerings prior believers had left for Poseidon and Triton. A small note of apprehension caught his face as he spun the small blade atop the altar, which glinted in the low light of the room. His breath caught, and he twitched, eyes flickering between green and white.

That flicker. Was the connection between Hawthorne and the preacher weakening? I couldn't let this chance to learn his plans slip away from me. I needed to know. So I decided to take a risk.

"How are we going to bring about this apocalypse?" I shouted over the noise. At the sound of my voice, Hawthorne whipped around, and his eyes flashed emerald green as they settled on me. "You've said a lot here, but nothing at all. Empty platitudes don't win wars. I've seen how wars are won."

Mack grabbed my arm hard and pulled me back with a hiss. "Nikos, what the fuck are you doing?"

In reply, Hawthorne began to laugh, shoulders bunched, leaning back to let it overwhelm him. "It's remarkably simple, really. We'll show Argo's true face and destroy it. The tide will rise from the sublevels to drown everything they've built. They keep us in this box and call it a city. And the illusion is perfect. Walls so far they fade from sight, yet they are all around us, just beyond the bend, so your mind thinks you are free, when really you are enveloped, packed in. Humans are not meant to be kept in a box, with arbitrary rules and imaginary borders. Humans are meant to be free, yet Eden is kept from you. But will you reclaim it? Or will you drown too?"

Before I could respond, there was a flash as bright blue sparks spewed from the neural augments on the preacher's temple, small arcs of electricity, like lightning, brimming from the sharp, black surface. Mack and I sprang into action, darting through the crowd and up onto the dais, around to the other side of the altar. Not fast enough to catch the preacher as he fell limply to the ground.

Cradling his thin form in my arms, I moved the preacher onto his back as Mack went for the implant, swiping the boy's sweat-and-blood-stained hair aside to reveal it. The once-shiny black-carbon surface was charred, melted from heat, bubbling and buckling. In some spots it had burned the flesh, fusing with the preacher's skin, while in others it had melted away to reveal muscle and bone.

It looked incredibly painful. And as Mack touched it, the preacher winced. At that moment, Maria reached us, already pulling out a small emergency medkit.

"Hawthorne," Maria said. "Are you still in there? Or are we talking to the preacher?" She tapped the preacher lightly on his cheek. "Hey, open your eyes."

When he didn't, Maria reached up, peeling back his eye-lids to find the boy's cybernetic eyes dark. Hawthorne wasn't in there. But neither was the preacher. I checked his pulse but couldn't find one.

I hung my head. "Damn."

"Yes, it is quite unfortunate," a familiar voice bellowed over the murmuring crowd around us. The three of us looked up in time to see the sea of potential Eden's Purpose recruits part, to reveal the bald preacher we had met at the door, flanked by the two security guards. "Zale was a bright lad, and fierce in his devotion to our common cause. So devoted that he allowed himself to be lost to it. Thanatos has claimed his soul, as is the will of the gods!"

The crowd, still on a high from Hawthorne's speech, gave a raucous cheer. Some embraced, others began to cry, still others glanced at me, cradling a dead preacher, who'd seemingly been possessed moments before.

The pair of Eden's Purpose brutes ascended the dais, and as they approached, the simulation around us began to fade.

Afternoon light and salt-tinged breeze faded away to nothing, and walls shattered into tiny pixels that dissipated to reveal blank walls, a dark floor, and low roof. Yet the crowd continued its revelry.

As the guards approached, Maria and Mack stood, ready to fight, but the Edenites did not. Instead, they gently plucked the preacher's body from my arms, and carried him out a back door that shut behind them. Never uttering a word or looking in my direction.

In the pandemonium, we slipped out the front door, into a quiet, misty night.

SIXTEEN

The three of us sat huddled around the Nadeau brothers' small coffee table. The smell of warm spices filled the air, but I barely noticed, head in my hands. My knee had begun to throb again, my encounter with Bonny Dogar, along with a long period of work with little to no rest, aggravating the injury I'd sustained while chasing Maxwell Van Buren days prior.

I was tired, and in pain. What else was new?

A gentle tap on my shoulder interrupted my melancholy, along with the sound of a bowl being placed before me, followed by a gruff voice.

"Eat," Trapper said. I parted my hands and found a deep bowl filled with curry, steam fogging the air above it. "You look like shit, so maybe this will help."

A playful grin was fixed on Trapper's face, and small crow's feet pinched at the sides of his cybernetic eyes, which glowed a faint red. A stained rag was draped over his shoulder, and his long dark hair was tied up in a messy ponytail, exposing a long scar from a knife fight in his youth that bisected his left eyebrow and ran down his face past his eye. It was the only blemish visible on his otherwise sleek face. If you didn't know the man, you'd think him terrifying. But here, in this space, he was relaxed.

In his past life—the one before he became a bounty hunter— Trapper had been a hunting guide, where he would take Ivories from the city to explore the vast forests and lakes of Manitoba's north. Trapper and Mack's father had walked away from his old life as a lieutenant in the Plainswalkers, preferring to raise his sons away from what he had become accustomed to during his life in the city. Living off the land is where the two brothers learned the skills that we in the business held in such high esteem. Both were brilliant hunters, tracking targets and using any shred of evidence to superhuman efficiency.

But it also made them better men. Their parents were loving, and despite his former life, their father had been a compassionate man. They'd lived in a small, tight-knit community, braving the face of climate disaster in Canada's overlooked and underappreciated north together. It made the pair fiercely loyal, incredibly giving, harshly pragmatic, and even more strongly protective—of each other and those they cared about.

I gave a limp thumbs up. "Thanks, Trapper."

"Don't mention it," he replied, sitting beside his brother with an audible groan. "Now that you three have had a chance to breathe, talk to me. What are we dealing with here?"

We filled him in over dinner, using the opportunity to debrief on what had been going on the past few days.

We pieced together a rough sketch of events. Zeke—a

member of the Plainswalkers—had lifted a personal transport from an Argo contractor who worked on the municipal water recycling infrastructure, discovering a tablet in the back seat. He brought the tablet to Clayton Fabron, who then went behind his brother Joseph's back and instructed Zeke to take the tablet to the NetDreamers. More specifically, to Bo Richot, who was able to hack into the device, finding it was full of codes that would allow them access to water recycling facilities throughout the city.

Wanting to get the tablet off their hands as quickly as possible, Clayton and Zeke hired Ivan Sobotka as their fixer, who arranged a sale to a group we now knew was Eden's Purpose.

Unfortunately for them, I was there to stop the sale from happening, resulting in Sobotka taking his own life to protect the identity of his buyer, in an act we now knew was not entirely voluntary. In our interrogation of Dr. Schmidt, she'd mentioned that Sobotka had been a patient of hers—under Canadian law, she was unable to tell us for exactly what purpose, but heavily hinted that he saw her for neural augmentation. So it seemed likely that Sobotka's decision to fry his brain with a charge gun was thanks to interference by Hawthorne, or another Eden's Purpose member.

Regardless, I was able to recover and return the tablet. Then, with Mack's help, we found and cornered Clayton Fabron, who could not give us the name of the tablet's buyer. Which was where the trail seemed to go cold.

In the meantime, I'd also had my failed apprehension of Maxwell Van Buren. Another Eden's Purpose devotee with neural augments, though his had been implanted as a result of a childhood illness. As the successful hacking of my military-grade cybernetic eye prostheses showed, the eco-terror newbies had the ability to conceivably hack into any augment, with the modified ones provided by aug docs like Schmidt likely being made more susceptible to this intrusion.

Schmidt, getting back to the timeline, was my next stop. After finding a tangential link to Eden's Purpose through the sale of modified neural augments, I confronted Schmidt, who then was able to identify Eden's Purpose, and gave us the tools to access the recruitment event we'd just been to.

All in all, we knew the following facts:

Eden's Purpose had been trafficking in modified neural augments, likely to aug docs across the city.

Those augments were designed to be easily hacked, giving Eden's Purpose direct access to people's minds, and the ability to influence behaviour, implant ideas, and in extreme cases, completely puppet their bodies.

Eden's Purpose was using those augments, along with technology allowing them to hack other augments, and old-fashioned ideological radicalization tactics, to recruit a growing army of supporters, who believed they must use violence to overthrow the established order and bring about climate apocalypse.

Trapper listened to all this intently.

"Which leads us here," I said, polishing off my synth-milk to calm the blazing flame in my mouth, and setting the glass down on the table next to my empty bowl.

Mack and Trapper sat on one couch, Maria and I on the other. Mack was sitting cross-legged, the bowl of curry balanced in his lap, half eaten, and beside me, Maria was leaning against the armrest, empty bowl sitting on the table near mine.

Trapper, meanwhile, hadn't eaten a bite. Throughout the whole retelling of our past few days with Eden's Purpose, he'd just sat there, arms crossed, nodding slowly as he chewed it over.

He twisted to crack his back and let out a satisfied grunt, then finally spoke.

"Well, I can tell now why y'all look like you just had your asses kicked. This is—"

"Insane?" I finished.

"Yeah," he replied. "And those two Edenites just let you go? 'Let you' being the operative phrase here."

Maria nodded. "They did. Picked the preacher up and walked out. Didn't seem to identify any of us."

"That you know of," Trapper said, finally picking his bowl up. "Shit, you're all not exactly anonymous in this city. With or without your masks and gear." He took a big bite of curry. "So what are we looking at it terms of numbers?"

Maria plucked a piece of fluff off her pant leg. "Well, if they can crack the security on Nikos's eyes, then presumably anyone in the city with neural augments is fair game. We don't exactly have the authority and ability to round up every single person who's gotten neural augments from aug docs supplied by Eden's Purpose, either—meaning our most likely converts will be anonymous. Could flip a switch and suddenly they're all ripe for recruitment."

"And then there's all the unaugmented," I said, nodding. "There were quite a few at the temple. We don't know how many of *them* we're dealing with, either."

"Fair," Trapper said, tapping his spoon on the side of the bowl. "Which means we'll have to figure out what Eden's Purpose's next move is, and fast. Any ideas?"

We sat there for a moment in silence, mulling it over again. As far as we knew, Hawthorne's goons had been subtly influencing the population of the city for months. Planting images, ideas—even dreams—in the heads of the augmented, while preachers preyed on the disaffected of the unaugmented population. But to what end?

The preacher's voice bounced around inside my head, one phrase repeating.

The tide will rise from the sublevels to drown everything they've built.

Hawthorne had made it clear that Argo was their target, and that they were amassing a growing army of supporters in the sublevels to … do what? Storm Argo's headquarters on the surface? Take control of its operations? And what had they planned to do with the water recycling facility codes on the tablet Sobotka was helping them acquire? Poison the water supply? Hold the city hostage until Argo agreed to turn itself wholly over to the people and give up its control of global climate infrastructure?

Or if Hawthorne's threats were to be taken literally, and their goal really was the destruction of humanity itself, that would mean the millions of residents in this city were in danger.

Maria heaved a sigh, leaning back over the arm of the sofa. "And every confirmed affiliate of Eden's Purpose we've encountered who could tell us what we need to know is dead."

She was right. We were stuck. We needed more information. A new contact.

After a few more moments of silence, I saw the muscles around Trapper's eyes twitch, like whatever idea he'd gotten had stung on entry.

"You mentioned that while you were in the temple, you were shown a projection of some kind," he said slowly, eyes flashing. "A simulation."

I nodded and shot Maria a glance. She was rubbing a thumb along the small scar on her lip, the one I'd given her years ago. It was something she did when she was thinking. She sat up straighter.

"The volumetric scanners," she said quietly, and Trapper's face lit up.

"Exactly."

He calmly motioned for her to elaborate. "In order for complex simulations like that to work, volumetric scanners send out millions of tiny lasers to judge distances and movement. It then feeds that data back to the computer running the simulation, so it knows how to shift what's projected into your eyes to compensate for where you are in the room, what you're looking at, and what you're doing."

"Yes," Trapper said, nodding. "And to know this, and to be as perfect as you said the simulation was, Nikos, the number of data points it has to reference has to be exponentially large, specifically those targeting the eyes and face." He held a hand over his own face. "Each person in the room, tracked independently, so the simulation can be represented to each in exactly the right way so as not to throw things off … so, extrapolating from that data, we can know how many people were in that room, where they were, what they were doing, and by using all those data points on their faces …" Trapper held out his hands for us to finish.

It was Mack who got there first. "We can tell what they look like and who they are."

"Bingo," Trapper replied with a smile. "And who do we know that can interpret data like that?"

I ran my thumb along my wrist-nav. "ODIN."

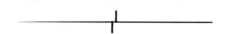

It might have been (mostly) illegal, but you couldn't argue with the results.

Following Trapper's recommendation, we'd gotten ODIN to hack into the projection system at the Children of Atlantis temple and reconstruct the scene using the millions of data points. He'd needed a little bit of coaxing, but given the increasingly dire nature of the situation, he was convinced to do the job.

And it was quite the job.

While he was working on it, ODIN was able to show us a little of what it had looked like: a short seven-second loop of the moment when Hawthorne took over the preacher, constructed entirely of millions of tiny dots, coming from the projectors located all around the large, empty temple room. ODIN was even able to zoom in and move around, digitally flying through a 3D rendering of the scene. It drew some oohs and ahhs from Mack.

Once the scene had been reconstructed, ODIN set about analyzing the faces and bodies of everyone in the room, cross-referencing with biometric and facial-recognition databases held at the Bounty Commission and Department of Justice.

More specifically, though, he was trying to identify one person.

Of everyone in the room, there was only one who hadn't

reacted when Hawthorne launched into his little puppet show. Standing off to the side, watching the whole performance, while working on a tablet—presumably controlling the more tactile parts of the simulation—was a single figure. Their non-reaction stuck out to all of us. Like they'd been expecting it, or at least had seen it before. If there was anyone we could confirm to be an Edenite in that room, it was this person.

All told, the process took a few hours. Long enough that Mack had been able to completely clean and reconstruct his revolver before passing out on the couch opposite me, and Trapper had had time to go and do a workout in their complex's gym. Maria, meanwhile, had fallen asleep beside me, her head rested comfortably on my right shoulder as she snored quietly—though I wouldn't dare mention it when she awoke.

As for me, I had no time for sleep. I was too busy thinking, a single question tumbling around inside my head.

Should I warn Castor?

It wouldn't be the first time an anti-establishment group had gone after Argo. Whether it was stolen parts from wind or solar farms, damaged farm equipment, hacked carbon trawlers, violated licences, or the odd direct attack on Argo personnel, the corporation and eco-terror crimes were largely synonymous these days. Something that never seemed to faze Castor, though. He never brought it up during our conversations, and honestly, Zara was the one who usually got bent out of shape because of it. Her precious corporate image, and the investor confidence it was tied to. So why was it all sitting so wrong in my head?

Maybe it was because we'd missed it.

Eden's Purpose had been festering in the sublevels for six

months, and now had the potential to infect everyone in the city—somewhat literally.

A threat like that doesn't come from nowhere.

Every other anti-establishment group in the city had started humbly, as disgruntled farmers, climate change deniers, radical transhumanists, or internet freedom absolutists, before turning into the organized and powerful factions they were today. Eden's Purpose, meanwhile, had, apparently, come from nowhere, and had already proven itself dangerous, and deadly. Zealous membership, following a well-formed militant ideology, pushed by organized leadership, who had powerful tools at their disposal. If we stamped Eden's Purpose out today, would the next emerging group be just the same? Was this how it was going to work now? Anti-establishment radicalization, perfected?

The more concerning question in my mind, though, was about Prometheus. We—the entire bounty hunting apparatus of Winnipeg—had missed this, and now this group was going to try to strike a powerful blow against the city. But would Prometheus have been able to find them early on? Clean the wound where Eden's Purpose had been allowed to incubate?

Turning on the corp brain I swore I'd cut out years ago, I tried to see this from Castor's perspective, and it turned my stomach. This was the perfect validation for his invention. The best example to show that Argo could do what the Bounty Commission's chosen few had grown increasingly incapable of. Obsolescence of the city's bounty hunters written out in blood and failure. But if I called Castor, and warned him of what was about to happen, he could have Prometheus out on the streets in no time. Just the single drone I'd seen during our little meeting, powered by the most complex AI known to humans, would possibly be enough to stop Hawthorne and his ilk. Stamp out the danger before the fire could spread.

So, if I told him, it would all be over. But at what cost?

Looking down at Maria, snoring softly on my shoulder, and across at Mack, drooling out of the corner of his mouth, I felt a flush of guilt come over me.

I still hadn't told them about Prometheus.

I'd gotten so caught up in Eden's Purpose that I'd never found the right time to tell my friends that their whole life's work was going to be stolen away from them. At least, that was the fiction I had chosen to tell myself. In reality, I simply didn't have the courage to break it to them. I'd been stalling.

As if on cue, Maria roused.

She blinked twice, lids slowly fluttering to reveal the glossiness of sleep that framed the sharp amber of her irises. Then she yawned.

"Why are you still awake?" she asked, not looking up at me, but knowing, nonetheless.

"Someone has to watch over you two."

She snorted. "Bullshit. We're in Mack and Trapper's apartment, not some foxhole in Brazil." Maria slowly rose, and twisted her back, a satisfied sigh following the crackling of her vertebrae.

I didn't have the energy to correct her—that we'd never been in foxholes in Brazil, and that the jungle warfare meant ample cover from trees and rocks—so instead I replied, "It's fine. I'm not tired."

Maria looked at me, clearly not believing that for a second. She leaned back against the arm of the couch, fully awake, giving Mack a quick glance to see if he was still asleep, and then resumed her analysis of me.

"Again, I'm going to call bullshit. You look wrecked, Nikos. Trapper wasn't just making a joke when he said that. You look like you haven't gotten a good night's sleep in days, you're not taking proper care of your injured knee, and don't even get me started on how uncomfortable your posture looks." She was correct there, as usual. My knee was aching; so were my ribs and back. But worst of all was the worry eating away at me.

"Now, start talking." Her tone was firm, but I could see concern furrowing the smooth skin of her brow, renewing the pang of guilt.

I sat in silence for a few moments, trying to work out the best way to broach the subject, but every time I began a thought, it felt wrong, so I ended up saying nothing at all. Maria was always easy to talk to, but this was something else.

For the life of me, I just wanted to tell her about Argo, about Castor, and Prometheus, the offer he'd given me, and what that all meant, but on top of the physical wear and tear, I was mentally exhausted. Since tracking Schmidt down, I'd barely slept, so stringing more than two coherent thoughts in a row was proving to be a challenge. I just couldn't get the words out.

Perhaps sensing my distress, Maria held out a hand to stop me.

"How about this," she said as she fished through the inside of her jacket where she'd left it lying on the back of the couch, producing the small medkit she always carried. "If we can't handle the problems in your head right now, at least let me take a look at your knee."

I replied with a grateful nod. "Sure."

Maria cleared off the coffee table to make room to open the medkit and removed the familiar pen-sized wand, its blue tip already glowing. She slipped on a pair smartglasses—which allowed her to see reports from the wand's beam without her helmet on. I rolled up my pant leg as high as it would go before Maria leaned in, waving the wand over the joint, the blue beams washing it in light, and gingerly pressing the skin and bone with her fingers to see how it would react.

It didn't hurt much, but I couldn't help but wince.

"Maria, can you be a little more—"

"Tender?" she coyly replied, eyes firmly on the knee. "Unfortunately, you're well past that. Maybe if you'd come to me when this happened, I would've been, but now? No."

"Some bedside manner you have."

"Hey, as your acting physician, I have a right to be a little terse from time to time, especially when I find out you've been running around with slight tears to your medial collateral ligament and anterior collateral ligament. Suffered a rough landing or two, eh?"

This time I knew exactly what she was talking about—seeing as I'd injured my MCL and ACL before—and had a good idea of what happened. When I'd tackled Maxwell Van Buren, my leg had twisted, injuring both ligaments, and when I'd jumped the fence into the back alley, the hard impact and flexing of my knee made it even worse. All the running around I'd been doing since then served to aggravate and re-injure both.

Seeing what she needed to, Maria leaned over to the medkit and produced a small patch, similar to the one I'd used on my knee when I'd initially treated it at home. THC to numb the pain and reduce swelling, and another dose of nanobots the repair the damaged tissue further. There was a familiar nee-dling sensation as Maria pressed the smaller pad down over my knee, but the THC got to work fast.

I smiled. "Just like old times."

"Exactly," Maria replied, giving my thigh a playful pat as she inspected the patch's seal against my skin. "You boys getting yourselves hurt, and me picking up the pieces."

"Which is why it sucked when you weren't around."

"Is that the only reason?" Maria idly rubbed the patch over my knee with her thumb, and her eyes wandered up to look into mine.

I suddenly became very aware of a thrumming in my chest, face beginning to warm. "Of course not. We missed you for a lot of different reasons."

"Like what?" Her eyes drifted back to my knee, but I could see a slight blush on her cheeks.

I rolled my head back and forth. "Your sparkling personal-ity, and wonderful bedside manner."

Maria shook her head and gave a slight grin. "You're such a shit, Nikos. Now let me take a look at your ribs."

I did as the doctor ordered, lifting my shirt to expose my rib-cage. This time, she was gentler as she prodded along the bones and muscles and guided the wand over my torso. Goosebumps formed on my skin under her touch, and I turned my face away, embarrassed, trying to ignore the warmth of her fingers and hoping she didn't notice.

She gave a little half chuckle and her hand lingered against my ribcage a few moments before she let it gently fall away. "Your fifth and sixth ribs are both cracked." Her tone had become softer. "The sixth is worst of all. Looks like a crushing force. Right?"

I nodded. The assessment checked out against Bonny's death-grip embrace.

"What's the prognosis, doc?"

Maria chewed on the inside of her cheek. "Not much to do, I'm afraid. I'll slap another patch on your ribs, but they're bones, so they'll heal on their own time. Knowing you, I'll also give you a stim shot to jumpstart the repair process and numb the pain, along with an immunobooster to make sure you don't pick up anything nasty along the way. Just don't go doing anything risky."

We both laughed quietly together, knowing how ridiculous the statement sounded. Maria leaned over to grab another—larger—medical pad and held it in place with her hand as it sealed over my skin. Satisfied, she withdrew her hand, and I let my shirt drop back down.

A moment of silence passed between us, and when I glanced back at Maria's face, her eyes caught mine. I felt the warmth of her hand fill my own.

"I missed you too, Nikos."

But before I could respond, ODIN's voice rang through apartment's audio system. "I've got a hit!"

SEVENTEEN

His name was Tommy Luciano.

He also had a fairly extensive record. Up until this point, he had been a member of the NetDreamers, racking up a list of computer crimes over fifteen years of activity in the city's anti-establishment ranks. Recent reports indicated that Luciano was running an illicit VR den. That was, until fairly recently, when he'd been apprehended on a tampering with climate infrastructure charge and booked, and his updated mugshot showed the Edenite logo stamped in green ink on his neck.

While we had no idea when, or why, his break with the NetDreamers had occurred—or whether there had been a break at all—we did know it had been him in the room running the simulation for Eden's Purpose. From what ODIN was able to reconstruct, he had been there, talking to the preacher just before we entered, then moved to his station to run the simulation, and remained there until after the preacher had fallen, following the guards out shortly after they took the preacher's body away.

What confused us was that the NetDreamers didn't seem to align with Eden's Purpose ideologically whatsoever. They preferred to stay indoors, living in simulated reality, surfing the net, playing games, hacking, cracking, and never setting foot outdoors unless they absolutely had to—as Maria's encounter with Bo Richot proved.

So, whatever had pushed Luciano out of his comfort zone and into the arms of Eden's Purpose had to be personal.

That was, until we found out that Luciano was a patient of Dr. Schmidt's. And a likely recipient of a modified neural augmentation.

While there was no open bounty for Luciano in any of the bounty pools, that was only a minor setback. We weren't going to detain him; we were simply going to ask him questions.

Luciano was hiding out in a warehouse on Sublevel 9—the industrial level. This level contained all the railyards in the city, multiple maglev tracks, and a direct route to the airport back on the surface. Winnipeg had always been a rail city, being built up mainly as a trade hub between the east and west of Canada, which was why Demeterius Wulf and the rest of the first Argo generation were so keen on maglev technology. "You go back to the past to strike forth to the future," was the line I'd once heard on the matter. But while the railyards that existed on Winnipeg's surface had been converted to commercial transportation use, the ones down here on Sublevel 9 were a different beast. Long and thick maglev tracks—built stronger and hardier than their transport-only counterparts—wound their way between and sometimes through the various buildings so goods could be produced and shipped out with remarkable efficiency.

Everything mass-produced and shipped out of Winnipeg

came through here. The main draw, though, was the reclamation projects. Big business was built around recycling plastics, glass, metal, fabrics—really anything that had once cost huge emissions to produce—and turning them into the things we used every day. Building materials, bottles, cups, clothing, and even the metal rounds fired from hunter weaponry was made right here. It was a mass of large buildings, factories, and warehouses that stretched from the sublevel floor to its ceiling, built around Argite spires holding up this level of the city, interspersed with squat four- to five-floor warehouse and factory buildings; empty, quiet, and filled with clutter—the perfect place to set up an illegal VR operation.

Unfortunately for Luciano, though, we had the Nadeau brothers on the case.

We'd split up. While Maria and I had snagged a transport back to our apartments to get geared up, Mack and Trapper had gotten their ears right to the ground, flexing their contacts, human intel, and considerable knowledge to find Luciano.

Maria and I had made our way down to Sublevel 9 to join them, and had posted up on the roof of a factory that recycled glass to make windows and mirrors. But before either of us could get comfortable, my wrist-nav buzzed slightly, and a message appeared on my HUD, suspended in the air a few inches in front of me. It was Mack, and the message was simple.

R-17. Meet you there.

Warehouse R-17 was located at the far northern edge of the sublevel. The industrial sublevel was special in its own way. While Sublevel 7 was a mass of greenspace, gardens, biomes, and greenhouses, Sublevel 6 was a cluttered nest of interweaving platforms, Sublevel 4 a glowing, bass-thumping entertainment mecca, and Sublevel 2 a typical slice of suburbia contained underground, Sublevel 9 was just huge. Expanding well beyond the borders of the city above and below, giving ample room for the productive heart of Winnipeg, the sublevel's northern edge opened to a large cavern, with rail lines leading up to the surface and shafts of light coming down to illuminate it. R-17 faced the cavern, providing an exceptionally beautiful view. Light glistened off the minerals of the cavern wall, and rivulets of condensation ran down the smooth, manufactured surface.

I had ODIN scan the squat six-storey building to identify biosignatures from the top down, finding three located on the uppermost storey of the building. One matched Luciano's description, and two were unidentified. They all had probation chips, but like Sobotka's, they had been tampered with.

Guess there was something I could've brought him in on, after all.

The main level was also occupied. Heavily occupied.

Taking a peek through security cameras on the main level—easy, considering ODIN was significantly more sophisticated than any intruder the NetDreamers were used to—I could see about two dozen beds, arranged in rows, each set within a small cubicle of fogged glass. Every single one was occupied by what at first glance looked like an emaciated corpse.

Except corpses don't move.

Each VR addict—often called "ghouls" owing to their

appearance and zombielike nature—was hooked up to a drip-fed IV, catheter, and God knows what else, judging by the number of tubes and wires all over them. I could see slight twitches as they reacted to whatever they were seeing in the virtual world. Kept barely alive at the lowest possible cost.

All of them would be malnourished, mentally fried, and almost completely blind by the time they took their rigs off and tried to get out of bed. That was *if* they took the rigs off. Such was the life of a ghoul.

When full VR rigs had first appeared on the market in the mid-2030s, they were required to have hard-coded session timers built into them that ended the user's session when the timer ran out. Timers couldn't be reset until forty-eight hours afterwards, forcing their users to do other things with their time. When the world started going to shit during the height of the climate crisis, some dived into the virtual world to escape the material one. Fearing a labour crisis as more of the working population slipped further into virtual reality, corporations found a way to put an ecological and humanitarian spin on it. Rigs were licensed, regulated, registered. Only one rig per person, and each person had to have a unique identifier, typically a retinal scan or a direct link into neural augments. That way, the corporations didn't lose workers, the country didn't lose productivity, the healthcare system didn't get swamped with the husks of VR addicts, and society was forced to deal with the dying world it had created.

These VR dens, though, were big business for the NetDreamers. They removed the safeguards and limits on VR sessions, providing potentially limitless time in the virtual world for whoever wanted it. They said they were providing lifestyle services for their clientele. But society deemed the business exploitive, profiting off addicts and people with depressive disorders who were seeking an escape. It was common for the VR den owners to intake a new "tenant" for free, under an agreement that the individual would make money for the group inside the virtual world.

It was a deal not many VR addicts could pass up.

Bypassing the main floor, we entered through a smashed window on the second level. Broken glass crunched beneath my boot as I landed on the other side of the window frame, and the sound echoed loudly inside the abandoned space. Mack and Maria followed closely behind, sidestepping the noisy debris, while Trapper remained on the outside scaffolding, ready to catch anyone who ran from the warehouse if things went sideways.

The three armed inhabitants were two floors above and on the opposite side of the warehouse. The centre of the building was the storehouse, with offices on either side and above. ODIN's readings showed no biosignatures on this floor, but to be safe I raised my carbine, scanning the area through the multitude of broken office windows. This building had been abandoned for a while before Luciano and the NetDreamers had set up their operation.

We moved slowly towards the atrium that ran vertically through the centre of the building. I approached the railing cautiously, Maria close at my back, while Mack brought up the rear, inspecting the warehouse around us. At the top floor, I could see light shining through dirty glass. They were the only lights on in the entire building, and ODIN's scan confirmed that this was where our target was holed up. I couldn't see

Luciano or his armed buddies from where I was, but I could hear voices—an argument, by the sounds of it.

Wonder what would happen when we threw a trio of skilled bounty hunters into the mix?

We slunk toward the stairwell set within one of the building's exterior walls, scanning left and right, checking corners, looking for any trap that could give away our presence, or significantly injure us. During my time with Tempest, I'd become awfully familiar with explosives—as my metal arm and glowing eyes could attest—and had come across many IEDs and other explosive traps. But seeing no tripwires, pressure pads, or lasers, we continued, creeping up the stairs to the top level where Luciano and his friends were waiting, *my* two friends close behind.

As we ascended, I sensed Mack slip away. Without looking, I knew what he was doing: taking up a position as a silent sentry, making sure nobody snuck up behind us, ready to take off in pursuit if anyone ran. Which left Maria and me to confront Luciano and whoever was with him.

As we stepped onto the building's upper level, I could see it had been almost completely repaired. Dim light illuminated new windows and furniture, and someone had begun repainting the walls. Shadows spread throughout at odd angles, providing cover as we slunk through what was likely an executive suite or VIP area. Plush seating and state-of-the-art VR rigs had been moved in, nestled into spacious suites that were less like the cubicles down on the main floor, and more resembled a massage room at a fancy surface resort. Whatever the plans, the size and spacing of the suites made it easy to make our way to the windows overlooking the warehouse floor and provided a direct sightline to Luciano. Around forty-five metres of open atrium and two panes of glass separated us now.

Across the way was a small meeting room. Luciano was facing two other men. One was bald and an assault rifle lay on the table in front of him. The other, with clean-cut grey hair, was playing with a handgun. Both had identical neural implants embedded at their temples. With their backs to me, I couldn't see their faces. What I could see were the matching tattoos on the napes of their necks. A falling meteor, with a long trail.

Our target, meanwhile, was standing, face twisted into an irritated sneer, holding what looked like a pile of junk tied together by wire and cord. From where I stood, it looked like a modified pulse cannon, powered by a pair of large batteries, jury-rigged together with wires popping out from the casing at odd angles, the whole contraption glowing faintly blue. There was a grip attached to the top so the weapon could possibly be fired from the hip. Luciano cradled it like it was some new puppy he was showing off to his friends.

Clearly, his technical know-how didn't stop at illegal VR rigs and extremely detailed simulations.

"How do you want to do this?" Maria whispered beside me, voice coming clear through our comms. "Sneak around and bust in through the door there?" She pointed, and my visor zoomed right on target, following her finger. The meeting room Luciano and the two Edenites were in was all faux wood, including the big, heavy door, which had a shiny metal handle.

"Sounds good to me, just have to make sure we're not spot—"

"DOWN!"

I felt it before I heard her. Maria shoved me hard to the floor, followed by a deep boom that shook up my insides, and a flash of white-hot pain through my injured ribs. Whatever it was blasted the window into a shower of tiny shards and fine splinters. When it passed, the energy it left made the air crackle, and my HUD fizzled with slight static.

It *was* a pulse gun Luciano had tricked out.

But my realization was quickly replaced by panic.

"Maria!?" I shouted through the comms, and spun around. She lay on her back near the staircase, the lights in her suit flickering as they came back online, a slight singe on her steel grey armour from where the shot had hit her chest. She was breathing, thankfully, and as the suit powered back up, so did she.

She'd had the wind knocked out of her, but managed to breathlessly respond, "I'm good. Yeah, I'm good. But holy shit, that hurt."

Mack had already sprinted up the stairs, and while taking cover in the stairwell, held out a hand to drag Maria back and get her up. I scrambled backwards and away from the smouldering hole left in the wall, sat up, and levelled my carbine through the glass, back towards where the shot had come from.

"You're lucky we need to you alive," I grumbled, and aimed at the bald man.

The pop fractured both panes of glass and the force of my shot catapulted the man headfirst into the table with an audible crack as his body broke the surface of the fake mahogany. Quickly, before I could fire at the second Edenite, another pane shattered to my right. Out of the corner of my eye I saw Maria soaring across the atrium, tiny flecks of glass flying in her wake like the tail of a comet. In a blur, she lost a bit of height on the arc of her jump, but kicked on her jump-pack to rocket up and through the opposite window, right into the second Edenite's personal space.

She clocked the guy in the face. The resulting crack echoed through the building, and he spilled backwards over the table, Maria casually stepping up in pursuit. From posture alone, I knew she was *pissed*. Seeing this, the Edenite she'd clocked scampered towards an exit, the armour-clad hunter stalking after him.

Luciano, to his credit, recovered quickly, taking aim at Maria's back. But a pair of booming revolver shots sent him scrambling for cover, which let Maria slip through the doorway safely.

I snapped my head right to see Mack standing in the stairwell, the end of his revolver smoking. "You good?" he called out.

I gave a thumbs up in response. "Go back down and help Maria. Keep her from killing that guy. I've got this asshole." I motioned with my head to Luciano.

Mack gave the hunter salute and spun on his heels, long white coat flaring behind him as he descended the steps. I turned back towards my target, rising to my feet to meet the bug-eyed gaze of Tommy Luciano. At some point, he'd stood back up, maybe praying we'd gone away. But now, I had to break his little hacker heart. Looking at him face to face, I could see he was terrified.

The skinny hacker, in a moment of great courage—or stupidity, I couldn't really say—lifted the modded pulse cannon and opened fire, while I ducked for cover. There was a warbling pop and the wooden frame of the window exploded into splinters as a mass of charged particles punched through, taking a chunk the size of my torso from the wall. Energy crackled through the air as the projectile dissipated, making the display on my helmet fizzle again.

After the first few shots, the air quieted. Dust hung around me and settled on my back as I crawled to a corner of the enclosed atrium. I made my way around it toward the back of the building, trying not to bump into anything that would get Luciano's attention. I could hear him moving around in the other room, panicked and noisy, knocking things over, blasting at every little movement he saw out of the corner of his eye. Good for me, as it allowed me to track him better—but bad for him.

Luciano was moving closer to me, so I ducked into one of the VR suites towards the back wall and was able to rise to my feet, but crouched at the level of the tables and VR rigs around me. He rounded the corner, and I could hear him fiddling with the weapon. Whether it was empty, or broken, I wouldn't know, but what I did know was that he'd screwed up. There was a small click, followed by Luciano cursing under his breath, and the sound of one of the large batteries coming free to slam on the ground. This was my chance, and the only thing separating us was a pane of glass.

I stood, breaking into a run. Shifting my weight to the right, I jumped, vaulting with my right hand over a VR bed, then with a step up I leapt off the next, flying towards the pane. I curled up and braced for contact, crashing through the window to land in front of Luciano, glass raining down. I landed a right hook to his cheek, sending him spilling back onto the floor. I closed the gap, brushing bits of glass off my shoulder, and picked Luciano up by the collar, shoving him into, and then through, the glass to our right that opened up to the building's central atrium. Luciano was still on his feet, forced to lean back over the lip of the window, above the concrete floor and scattered VR cubicles far below.

"Whoa-whoa-whoa! What the hell do you want?!" he screamed in terror, voice slightly digitized as he spoke through a synthetic voice box. "I don't even have an active bounty! This facility is totally clean. Legit!"

Like I'd believe that, after seeing his clientele.

"You should've thought about that before you shot my friend," I bellowed through my mask's communicator. "But nice modified pulse gun you have there, Tommy. Maybe I should bring you in on that. Along with assault on a peacekeeper, attempted murder of a peacekeeper, and, well, let's round it out with that tampering you've done to your probation chip."

"I'm sorry, all right—Jesus," he spat back, his voice wavering as he held on for dear life, blood leaking from a fresh gash under his eye. "But you've got to admit, hunter …" his lip curled into a smirk, "that modded pulse gun is cool, isn't it? Sent you scurrying like a rat running from an exterminator, and caught your little girlfriend good."

"I wouldn't be joking if I were you, Tommy. There's nothing stopping me from dropping you out this window right now." I wouldn't do that. It wasn't in my nature, but the threat would still hit hard. "But lucky for you, there's something I need. I know you were at the Eden's Purpose recruitment on Sublevel 6 last night, and judging by the tattoo on your neck, your visit was more business than pleasure."

Luciano's eyes went wide at the mention of Eden's Purpose, his voice a hoarse whisper. "So it *was* you … Nikos Wulf. The Ivory turned hunter. Thought I was just seeing things, but …" The gravity of his situation hit home, and he began to panic.

"Oh shit." Luciano twisted, hammering a palm down on my wrist, trying to wrench free from my grasp.

It did him no good. The grip of my cybernetic hand was far too strong.

I pulled Luciano close, and then slammed him hard into the window frame. The material splintered with a loud crack and Luciano yelped.

His eyes drifted to the ground below, then back to me.

"Not so fast, Tommy," I said, pulling him close again so I could look right into his eyes. "I know Eden's Purpose is planning something, and judging by the fact you weren't fazed by the preacher's spontaneous possession, I'm going to hazard you know more than you're letting on. The payoff for you must be pretty good if they were able to pry you away from the NetDreamers."

"The NetDreamers don't understand," Luciano replied, still struggling. Long strands of greasy black hair flew in every direction as he tried to squirm from my grip. "They never did. They'd much rather hide in the net than face the world around them. Do you think I enjoy hooking people up to those simulations? Letting them hide from the truth? It makes me sick just thinking about it. Poseidon spoke to me in my mind. In my dreams. He guided me to them."

Interesting. If Luciano had received messages through his neural implants, that meant someone else had been responsible for modifying them. There was no way Luciano would willingly put them in his head, knowing what they could do.

"And what did Eden's Purpose want with you?"

"Just what you saw at the temple," Luciano said through

gritted teeth. "I run the simulations for the new recruits, help them see."

"And what else?"

He gripped my arm tightly, no longer seeming like he wanted to get free, but noticing at last how perilously close he was to falling out of the window.

Luciano swallowed hard. "I also helped with the neural linkage systems. They called it O.R.A.C.L.E.—the Organic Autonomic Control and Linkage Environment. I don't know how it works, I just make sure the connections are stable, and that it keeps running." A bead of sweat trailed down the left side of his face. "Please, man, I don't know any more. I've already told you too much. If they find out, they'll kill me too."

I knew ODIN would log this new intel for later, but we were still no closer to uncovering Hawthorne's plans. And if he was telling the truth, and he really knew nothing, our best course of action was to try to track down the man himself.

Luckily, there was something about these new Eden's Purpose details that struck me. It was a *linkage* environment, so if what Luciano had said about stable connections was true, then I had an idea. Time to be more direct.

I slammed Luciano hard against the splintered frame again, and the hacker gave a small yelp of pain.

"You need to tell me where Hawthorne is, Tommy. Even if you've never met the man in person, you said yourself that you helped use the neural linkage systems. That means you can tell me where Hawthorne's side of the link originated."

For a moment, there was fear, then recognition, then pride, as Luciano's gaze locked on to me. He was cycling through emotions faster than I could blink, and I could tell gears were turning in his head. The hacker turned eco-terror member was weighing his options.

He opened his mouth to speak but closed it again.

I tightened my grip. "Come on, Tommy," I whispered. "Do the right thing. Think of all the people in this city that will get hurt if Eden's Purpose gets their way."

"I … can't tell you." He tensed hard, and I could feel a tremor in him. "Things are a lot more complicated, so even if I could tell you, I'm not sure there's much y—"

Luciano groaned hard, all the muscles in his body contracting at once, and his eyes slammed shut. I could feel the air between our heads begin to crackle, and my HUD showed the same fizzle it had when his overcharged pulse gun had fired past me. The groan was long, and pained, but it passed, leaving Tommy Luciano slightly limp in my arms.

Then he began to chuckle, his head lolling around on his neck, and his eyes snapped back open with a force that startled me, and almost caused me to lose my grip. Looking into his eyes, though, I knew I wasn't holding onto Tommy Luciano anymore. His body, maybe, but not his mind.

This was Benedict Hawthorne. Come for a one-on-one chat.

"Mr. Luciano may not be able to tell you what we have planned, but *I* certainly can," Hawthorne said. The quality of his voice had changed dramatically, dropping a couple octaves and becoming more resonant, with only a hint of Luciano's voice underneath, just like the preacher from last night.

I growled back, "Hawthorne."

"In the … well, not flesh, per se, but … yes," he replied with a smirk. He held his arms wide, like some sort of showman.

"It is nice to see you again, Mr. Wulf." I started as he said my name. "Oh, yes, I knew it was you. I know far more than you think. How did you enjoy our little meeting last night? Have you decided to join to our cause?"

I tightened my grip on Luciano's body, trying to suppress my growing anger.

"What the hell is this, Hawthorne?" I snarled. "Is this some kind of game to you?"

He chuckled softly. "No, of course not, Nikos … It's a challenge."

"A challenge?"

Hawthorne nodded. "Yes, exactly. You see, you've already disrupted our plans once—that whole business with Ivan Sobotka and the tablet."

I stood perfectly still, not daring to move, or breathe. Not when he was spilling everything for ODIN's record.

"My words are not empty threats, Mr. Wulf. The tide *will* rise from the sublevels, and those of us who obey the will of the gods will watch this city—and Argo—drown. Using the designs of Argo's own making."

Fireworks started going off in the back of my mind as the realization struck. "The water recycling systems." My grip began to tighten more than I thought possible. "You're going to use them to flood the city."

Hawthorne just nodded, smile growing wider by the second. "If we had gotten the tablet, well, we could've just walked in and opened the floodgates, but now that you've taken away *that* particular avenue, we're going to have to do this the more difficult and …" he looked off as he searched for the word, "bloody way." He laughed again, this time verging on a cackle. "Unfortunately, you have only yourself to blame for that."

The damage Eden's Purpose could have inflicted with the tablet's access codes was staggering, horrifying. They could have opened the valves on all the water collection and treatment cisterns and drained everything right back out into the streets. Effectively, they could empty the Red and Assiniboine rivers right into the heart of the sublevels. And if they intended to simply pivot their plans, this devastation was still imminent. I needed to know how, and when.

Before I could open my mouth to ask, the answer came.

"Nikos," ODIN said, his voice wavering. "There's an emergency notice going out across all bounty hunter boards and channels. The water recycling facilities across the city are under attack. All of them."

I cursed under my breath, and Hawthorne looked elated. He was enjoying every moment of this; it was written across a face that wasn't his own. The Edenite leader held out his hand and looked to the heavens, straight to the gods he said he served. But then he was back on me, one hand gripping my forearm tight, so he could pull his face as close to mine as possible. There was a fire in his gaze, but also, concerningly, excitement.

His next words came out garbled, digitized like a video call with bad reception. "I have waited a long time for this, Mr. Wulf." As the words escaped his lips, my vision stuttered, distortion to my right where something appeared to peel itself from the wall. A figure of distorted pixels, its features obscured by the shifting colours, my eyes not able to reconcile what I was seeing, and I didn't dare pull my attention away from Hawthorne to see it clearly. Instead, I caught glimpses. A wide mouth of jagged teeth. Golden eyes. Smooth skin. A gnarled scar through the lip and up the face.

"Come to the water recycling facility on Sublevel 11," Hawthorne continued, voice still warbling and broken. At the same time, I caught the figure moving too, brief flashes of its mouth moving in tandem with Hawthorne's. "So we can finally bring an end to this story. Just think of the display. The whole city watching as the greatest hunter ever to walk these streets falls like a tree under a lumberjack's axe. A descendant of the great Argo heretics, falling under all his forebears built."

I stole a glance to my right, but the figure shifted with my eyes' movement, as if fixed in my peripheral vision, stuck in the static.

"Yes …" Hawthorne and the distorted figure smiled in tandem. "It is quite fitting that you will die for what you were born to protect. It is a threshold I, too, must cross to achieve what I've always dreamed of." The distortion moved, more static splitting across my field of vision as a long tendril of shattered pixels coalesced into the form of an arm that reached out towards mine. Its long-fingered hand closed around my cybernetic forearm, and oddly, I felt a numbness where it touched. "Time is up, Mr. Wulf. Time to face your destiny."

There was a flash of blue light, and the sensors in my cybernetic arm went haywire. Energy and electricity surged through the synthetic limb, tactile sensors screaming in pain, echoed by a groaning yell escaping between my clenched teeth. A brief flash of pain blinded me, but not before I was able to catch a glimpse of a small stun rod that had slipped from Luciano's sleeve, arcing energy from the tip to my open, empty, metal hand. Beyond that, I watched as the form of Tommy Luciano slipped out the window.

The hacker was smiling, eyes closed, arms out to embrace the void as gravity wrapped its invisible hands around his body and yanked him down.

Luciano fell away from me, down to the ground below. His back caught the top lip of one of the VR pods, body instantly going slack as he rebounded down into the aisle between the rows of cubicles. He landed face-down on the concrete with a dull thud. I knew he was dead. A sickening wave overtook me, bile rising from my gut, legs going weak, and I fell to a knee.

But there was no time for that. No time for wallowing in my failures.

"ODIN?" I called out as I rose unsteadily to my feet. "Call the group together. We need to move."

EIGHTEEN

There was always quiet before the storm.

That's what I learned as a soldier, and that's what it felt like here, as I sat on the edge of the transport's crew bay on Sublevel 11, feet tapping restlessly on the access ramp while I thumbed rounds into magazines. Unease bored a deep pit through my insides. Every second that ticked by on the clock, each round that clicked into place, that pit got deeper, and the anxiety for what came next grew.

I knew better than to trust the deceptive silence that had fallen over the city, its ever-present buzz muted. Choked. Waiting for what came next.

It felt like every warzone I'd ever been in. Except, when I looked around, I was home. The whole city was on a knife-edge, ready to fall either way, but we'd all get cut regardless.

The Bounty outpost hangar bay was, for once, quiet. There was nobody around save the Commission-employed pilot, who was quickly but carefully going over the transport with the love that could only exist between a seasoned flier and their aircraft.

Hull panels had to be checked, engines tested, telemetry calibrated, harnesses secured, and way more than an old ex-grunt like me would ever consider. From the brief exchange we'd had, it was clear she knew the task. Like me, she was ex-PMC, flying for Tempest at the same time I had boots on the ground. So flying and dropping troops in a piping-hot drop zone was something she'd had a lot of experience with. We both did.

So we both knew the mess that was waiting for us, and could recognize the danger from a ways off. Like smoke on the horizon.

At the same moment Eden's Purpose had begun storming the water recycling facilities throughout the city, a huge blast of rhetoric by the group erupted onto the social feeds along with the scattered reports and footage. Hawthorne himself had appeared in videos and snappy clips, railing against the establishment, specifically Argo and the bounty hunters, and threw around words like "traitors" and "heretics" like they were going out of style.

Almost as fast as the Edenites started their attacks, bounty hunters had gone to respond. There were fights going on in and around the water recycling facilities, as hunters, working in tandem with the Winnipeg Police Service for the first time in a century, tried desperately to dislodge the Edenites from their positions. But being on defence means the attackers have to come after you, on your turf, where you've dug in.

I hadn't checked the Bounty Board, but I knew we were losing good people.

Because we'd been deep in the outskirts of Sublevel 9 when the first reports of the attacks came through, we'd been left behind in the mad scramble to get boots on the ground. Not that any of us were desperate to throw ourselves into the line of fire, but we knew our role in this fight was on Sublevel 11, and decided it was best to gather what intel we could before setting out. So while I went out to secure our transportation, Maria had gone to the outpost medics for a quick check after taking that shot from Luciano, and Mack and Trapper had gone on a scouting mission. If we had time to prepare, even what little there seemed to be, it would be best for the brothers to get eyes on our target and report back.

Besides, Hawthorne was waiting for us. Or, more specifically, waiting for me.

The whole interaction was stuck on a loop in my mind. As I set another full magazine on the stack beside me, next to my carbine and sidearm, I tried to put the encounter into similar order. Fitting it into the context of everything we'd learned over the past few days.

It is quite fitting that you will die for what you were born to protect.

It is a threshold I, too, must cross to achieve what I've always dreamed of.

Whatever madness or malice drove Hawthorne, I'd never understand. But he clearly believed only one of us would survive our impending encounter, and for what?

But what bothered me most about it was the realization that my father had said something similar in my dream.

There is one more threshold for you to cross. And I must show you.

Then there was the figure, whatever it was. First showing up in my dream, and now emerging out of nothing to face me in real life as … a ghost? A hallucination? A manifestation of a sleep-deprived mind?

But it had touched me. I'd felt it. The numbness, like a static buzz on tactile sensors in my prosthetic arm. That *thing* had felt real. Or maybe I was going insane. Maybe the neurodegeneration Dad had suffered was finally coming for me.

That figure, though, I had no explanation for.

All this talk of destiny and purpose made my head spin. I just wanted to protect this city and the people who lived here. Whatever vendetta Hawthorne seemed to have against me, it would end tonight. I was sure of it.

The hard clack of confident footsteps echoed in the still air as Maria strode onto the landing pad. She looked over the transport as she approached, gave the pilot the hunter salute, then stood at the foot of the access ramp.

"You ready to rock, solider?" she asked, voice projected through external speakers in her helmet.

I snorted and stood, body creaking after all the stress and pain I'd put it through the last few marathon days. "You feel it too?" I descended the ramp towards her, and Maria removed her helmet, shaking her head slightly to settle her hair back into proper order.

She smirked. "Like we're back to being soldiers, right?" Her eyes drifted across the quad-engine transport before her, same make and model as she'd flown in as a member of Ironways—all PMCs got them from the same handful of companies. "About to drop from the sky in an armoured transport, straight into hellfire to face certain death?"

"Yeah," I replied, standing in front of her. "Except this time, we aren't fighting someone else's war for someone else's benefit. Feels better in that way. Like dying would be worth it, at least."

Maria nodded. "Saving your hometown will do that."

We both laughed quietly, too worried or stressed to look each other in the eye for long.

Instead, I looked at her gear. It was the first time I'd gotten a good look at it since she took that shot for me. Evidently, the electric blast from Luciano's modified pulse gun had washed over her and singed her chest plate in some places, but overall, the armour had held.

With my human hand, I rubbed at one of the singed spots near her collarbone, trying to see if I could rub it off, and to test how it felt. It didn't do much but stain the tip of my thumb. Above it, though, I could see a small patch of pink, scalded skin, and I gently ran my fingers along it, feeling the warmth.

At my touch, Maria inhaled sharply, and I pulled back.

"Sorry," I breathed. "Does it hurt?"

A small smile played at the corners of her lips. "No, it's fine. It's just …" Maria said, thoughtful, biting the inside of her lip like she wanted to say more. "Nothing. It's nothing. The medics gave me the all-clear. Slight electrical burns, but nothing major. It'll fade. No scars."

I let my hand hover over her collarbone for a moment longer before I let it drop. "Still, I'm sorry. You shouldn't have taken that hit. It should've been me."

"Always the hero, eh, Nik?" she said with a chuckle, her eyes finding mine with a sudden, magnetic intensity.

"Always." I felt pulled forward, closer to Maria. "For you."

There was a glint in her amber eyes as we stood there, searching each other's gaze for a moment that stretched on and on. I remembered how her hand had felt on my skin a few hours earlier, and how much I wanted it back there.

There was a sudden hacking cough to our right that made

us both jump. Jaeger stepped forward, crouched, and a stool folded out from a pack on his lower back for the old man to sit on. The perfect contraption for a master sniper, which Jaeger was.

"Didn't know we got paid by the Commission to flirt these days," Jaeger said, stroking his tangled net of a beard. "Especially with ghosts."

Maria let out a disappointed sigh. "Jaeger, I meant to call—"

"Don't you start that, now," Jaeger replied, throwing up his hands. As he stood, the seat mechanism folded back up into the pack. "And don't you go thinking I didn't notice your name back on the Bounty Board. And while I can excuse you talking to this one first …" he rapped my chest plate with his knuckles, "how could you call Mackenzie second over me? I'm positively hurt!"

Maria's eyes darted between me and our mentor, stammering, mouth and mind seemingly so far apart they may as well have been in different time zones. "Jaeger, I—"

"Thought I was still mad?" he asked. There was a moment of silence in the air before he began laughing so hard his belly shook. "Gods no, kiddo, I'm just a grumpy old man. Knowing you were home brought so much joy to my heart. My favourite child, finally back where she belongs. Give me a hug, you."

Jaeger walked over, wrapping Maria in a rib-crushing embrace.

The old hunter was a merry man, and one of the longest-serving hunters still active, but nobody had the guts to tell him to hang up his guns. He was still by far one of the best, a sharpshooter and expert tracker, earning him the Jaeger name. His helmet sported large goggles that enhanced the function of his rifle scope, and draped over his torso was a cloak like the ghillie suits we sometimes wore in the PMCs, dark grey to help him blend into the city around him.

As always, Jaeger was joined by his trusty companion, a German shepherd named Spurhund, adorned with enough armour to make him into a small and speedy tank. This was the third or fourth dog the old hunter had owned, all of which had lived to old age and retired—unlike their owner—and had been succeeded by one of their pups.

Animals weren't a terribly uncommon sight here in the sublevels. Birds still found a home throughout the cavernous metropolis, along with bats, raccoons, opossums, and various rodents, but pets were a difficult proposition, owing specifically to the lack of real estate people enjoyed. The staples remained, with cats, birds, and various reptiles being favourites in the sublevels, and dogs did find a home down here as well, with a preference for smaller breeds, so a large dog like Spurhund was less common.

"Where are Mack and Trapper?" the old man said, playing with his dog's ear. "Thought they were the best—I did teach them, after all." He let out a small chuckle.

"This sector is big, and they've got a warzone to fight through to scout the building. Relax, old man," Maria quipped.

Jaeger grunted in response. Mack, Maria, and I were probably the only people who could call the man "old" without having a rifle pointed in our faces.

Spurhund trotted over to me and Maria, tail wagging. This was the only one of Jaeger's dogs I'd had the pleasure of knowing, and he had taken quite a liking to me almost immediately. I crouched down, scratching the big dog behind his ear, Maria chuckling beside me. His eyes were happy, but I could see how tired they were beneath, and his once-shiny brown and black fur now had streaks of grey.

"You're getting old, big guy," I said to Spurhund, earning a nuzzle.

"Yeah, this is probably his last hunt," Jaeger replied. "You can see it in the way he walks. There isn't the snap and speed that used to be there, and you can also just feel it when you're around him. He's tired and he knows this is it."

"Maybe you should follow his lead, Jaeger. You've been in this game a long time, and I'd hate to retire before my mentor."

Jaeger grunted. "Hunters don't retire. Now where is everyone else?"

We had called a slew of our preferred partners, letting them know we were going after the leader of Eden's Purpose, and thankfully the ones who'd answered were the ones I wanted here the most. They were my family, and I would go to the gates of hell with any of them.

Viking and Centurion had been working on a contract together during the initial scramble and were raring to get into the fight. Viking, a massive and broad-chested New Scandinavian bounty hunter, was devastating in a fight, but, like me, preferred words to weapons for the most part. Centurion, meanwhile, was an extravagant fighter, flashy but skilled, taking down any target with speed, flare, and a cheeky remark. Like Mack, but with an English accent that made men and women swoon. I was glad to have both coming to our aid.

Then there was Maria, fresh from her service with Ironways. The versatility she brought to the team was going to be a major asset, along with her medic skills. She was well armoured, but it was lightweight, and her jetpack kept her mobile.

Also, it was Maria. Enough said.

Rounding out the team were Trapper and Mack—the two best trackers on the Bounty Board.

"Friends!" a loud and friendly voice shouted, causing the three of us to wheel around. Viking and Centurion strode towards us. Centurion—the smaller of the two—ran his hand along the side of the transport before having it slapped away by the pilot.

Centurion's cape flowed behind him like a crimson flag. Viking, meanwhile, wore heavy grey armour. The plates bore scratches and dents, showing the hundreds of close calls and tough fights the New Scandinavian hunter had walked through. He carried no firearms, except for the rarely used sawed-off shotgun hanging from his hip. He also had his trusty axe secured between his formidable shoulders.

"Where are Strigi and his lovely older brother?" Centurion asked. "I thought you all travelled as a pack."

"Right here," Trapper growled as he approached from our left, Mack striding beside his older sibling, hands clasped behind his back.

"Had to do a bunch of the legwork to make it easy for you to get the glory, Centurion," Trapper continued. "But looking at what we're up against, there'll be plenty of glory to go around." With a flick of his wrist, he sent a small disk skittering across the ground, and with a slight sputter, a holoprojection appeared in the centre of the group, displaying a map of the water recycling facility. It was an expansive complex built out of the stone walls containing the sublevel, hundreds of pipes jutting from the rock, connected to the facility, with just as many disappearing into the sublevel floor below, or taking off into the city above. There were twenty-eight large holding tanks arrayed in front of the main building, with walkways and pipes running between them all, arranged in clusters of fourteen. One cluster to the left, and one cluster to the right of a large open-air courtyard. The entire front of the operations and administrative building was glass, rising higher than the stone-and-metal complex surrounding it, looking like that one kid who was taller than the rest of the class.

"You can thank Argo for this," Trapper continued. "Once Eden's Purpose began attacking and the Bounty Commission scrambled to take the facilities back, they shared the blueprints publicly across hunter channels."

Somewhere on the surface, Zara was having a meltdown over this PR nightmare and wanted it handled. Bonus points for Argo.

"This is where we suspect Hawthorne is personally overseeing operations." Trapper pointed at the glass edifice of the main administrative section.

"The first few levels are where the Infrastructure and Operations teams work, lots of terminals and screens," Mack chimed in. "Once we secure that, Eden's Purpose will lose control of the water recycling and climate mirroring infrastructure on this level."

"Exactly," Trapper continued. "Above those are the admin offices. Cubicles, meeting rooms, boring suit-and-tie shit, but probably where Hawthorne will be."

Centurion stood up a bit straighter, arms folded. "And what makes you say that?"

"That's where the director for this sublevel would've been," ODIN piped up through the speaker in my mask. "The buildings all have the same standard layout. Hawthorne will want direct access to the failsafe."

"Failsafe?" I asked. "What's the failsafe?"

"It's an emergency measure," ODIN replied. "If anything happens on the bottom levels, the director or their assistants can override it from the safety of the executive offices. There's a hardwired redundancy in every one of these facilities throughout the city, meaning if one system fails, there's always one to back it up."

"So," I began, "even when we secure the operations levels, we'll have to work our way all the way up to the top level, where we'll face Hawthorne head-on."

Maria crossed her arms. "Can't imagine the place was empty when the Edenites attacked. What are we looking at in terms of civilians?"

"None," Mack replied with a shrug. "Reports on the ground are that Eden's Purpose arrived to a red-carpet welcome. Some workers literally threw the doors open for them. The rest were allowed to leave. Unfortunately, this situation is unique. Every other facility is a massive hostage situation, but not here, no civvies except those who joined up with Eden's Purpose."

"Hawthorne is challenging us," I said with a nod. "He told us to come, and he threw down the gauntlet. Them versus us."

Everyone else nodded silently.

Jaeger patted Mack on the shoulder, "Good job, lads, both of ya."

"We have a few issues, though. We're outmanned and outgunned," Trapper said. "From what we could gather from the scene, Eden's Purpose is well-armed, and they have all their firepower aiming outwards." Trapper painted an arc around the front of the admin building with his finger. "They've set up positions inside the holding tanks and in the windows. We'll have to drop right into the courtyard, fight our way across to the admin building, breach the door, and take the building floor by floor."

"Beyond that," Mack cut in, "for a ragtag group that's been around for roughly six months, they're fighting extremely well. They're keeping hunters and police out. Using an easily defendable position to the fullest advantage."

Made sense to me. It was very likely there were ex-PMC within the Edenite ranks. Whether they'd been injured in the line of duty like me, and had neural augments ripe for the group's tampering, or they'd put their lives on the line for corporate interests and were sick of the status quo, I'm sure they had some ex-mercs calling the shots. Their tactics stank of it. An undersupplied, untrained, and barely organized force dug into a defensible position, creating a kill-box in the only point of entry. It didn't matter how advanced their gear was, or how well-trained they were, that tactic alone could buy Hawthorne all the time he needed.

I knew, because that's what I would have done.

I knew, because I'd done it before.

As soon as we got into the yard, machine-gun fire would start pouring over us from the admin building, plus all the forces hiding among the holding tanks and pipes, currently scrapping with the police and hunters surrounding the facility walls. This reality didn't seem to faze any of us, though—at least, not on the surface. We'd all been through the ringer, faced horrible odds, and survived.

If we died tonight, at least we'd have our chosen family around us when we went.

Mack and Trapper, my brothers in all but blood; Jaeger, the father I never knew I needed; Viking and Centurion, two dedicated hunters, and even more dedicated friends; and Maria, the Valkyrie, and a fellow ex-merc who I'd trust with my life.

"You know what they say," I said, flashing a toothy grin. "Hunters never retire."

"We're getting hit hard!" The pilot hollered through our comms. Not that she was telling us something we didn't already know— we could feel it.

We'd dropped Jaeger and his hound on a building overlooking the facility, but as soon as we got close, the Edenites opened fire from inside the main facility building. Machine-gun fire hammered the armour plating on the transport as the pilot swooped the heavy craft down towards the courtyard and banked. Every shot sent vibrations through the crew bay, and with the downpour of magnetically propelled rounds, mixed with the general vibrations from the transport, my teeth were chattering hard.

The transport levelled off, the pilot aiming to drop us off behind cover, and yellow lights around the door to the crew bay began to spin, washing the bay in a deep glow.

Her voice came in through our comms loud and clear, worry in her voice smoothed over by adrenaline. "Drop zone hot! Go get 'em, hunters!" The crew bay door fell open with a deep boom, and we all spilled down the ramp, making a beeline for the nearest cover. As we hit the ground, alarms began to blare. Machine-gun fire ripped up the ground as we ran for cover, scarring the sublevel floor in chips and pockmarks.

I took cover with Trapper and Mack behind a large portable water tank, sparks flying around us as Edenites poured out of their positions on either side of the courtyard, throwing even more gunfire our way. Bullets thudded against the metal container, sounding like rain on a tin roof.

I lifted the carbine to my shoulder, taking aim at movement coming from the cluster of holding tanks to our right and squeezed off a couple rounds. Two metallic pops punctuated by the blue electricity of the gun sent rounds flying towards my targets. The two—a man and a woman—dropped, the man falling on his face, skidding forward while the woman's head snapped back, and she fell to her knees, and then her side. With the gun still up, I fired on another man. This one wore fear plainly on his face, not hidden behind the mask of bravado and blind faith many of the others displayed. Behind me, multiple loud cracks rang out, as Mack took aim with his revolver, throwing the sleek weapon's punch towards the enemy.

A tap on my shoulder from the elder Nadeau brother and we were off to the next bit of cover, slinking under the protection of the water tank to the industrial transport that once carried the container. The bed of the transport was chest height, leaving us to crouch beside it as gunfire sparked off the top above our heads. The shots were coming from windows in the ten-storey administration building at the centre of the complex. As we ran, I counted electric-blue muzzle flashes coming from at least three of the windows, which were the ones now pinning us down, the pulsing coils of their heavy weapons betraying their positions.

But that didn't seem to bother Viking as he tore from cover and charged forward to draw fire from the admin building. Bullets sparked off his armour as he broke into a sprint, dragging the massive axe behind him. He took a hopping step and clenched his triceps to bring the terrifying blade forward, cleaving through an Edenite. Viking continued his assault, shoulder-checking a young woman out of his way and crushing another man with his body weight against a shipping container. A bloody smear was left behind as the man fell.

Guess the axe was good for more than just scaring targets into compliance.

The distraction of Viking's charge allowed us some space to spring into action. Centurion swung out of cover, raising his rifle to return fire on the machine guns placed inside the admin building, while Maria rocketed over the container she was hiding behind, firing buckshot at the Eden's Purpose forces below her. The blue pulses of her semiautomatic shotgun brought deadly metal rain on the victims below her, peppering them in a downpour of destruction. She landed, clipped an opponent with the butt of the gun to stagger him, and blew the man's arm off with another shot.

In that moment, the two brothers beside me both stood, taking aim over the transport's bed, Trapper firing his rifle, Mack taking aim with his hand cannon. I followed their lead, firing on the Eden's Purpose forces again.

Stand up to fire.

Drop to reload.

Stand up to fire.

Drop to reload.

This ballet continued as we moved from cover to cover, never staying too long at any one spot. I knew how effective the kill-box tactic used by Hawthorne and his group could be, but I also knew how to beat it: pure attrition.

In what seemed like minutes, the constant flood of gunfire slowed to a trickle, and then stopped. Those who were dug in behind barricades in the shadow of the main building turned and scrambled inside.

We all ran forward to take positions on either side of the admin building's main entrance, a large set of locked double doors, all glass, save for the frame.

The foyer of the admin building was highly exposed. It was a large open room, with balconies from the first four floors above the ground level overlooking a nearly empty approach. The only pieces of cover were a few stone pillars and the reception desk that sat about six metres from the doors. We'd have to first break open the glass doors, then move into sparse cover and take the building room by room, floor by floor. Six of us would be in the building, with Jaeger providing cover from his perch across the way.

Maria leaned away from the wall slightly, lining her arm up with one of the pillars. The sleeves of her armour contained small grenade launchers, able to fire frags, EMPs, flash grenades, and even incendiaries. This time, however, she had an old favourite in mind. The first shot shattered the door, immediately drawing incoming fire from the Eden's Purpose forces inside. The second flew straight through, unhindered. Both grenades hit their target with pinpoint precision, bouncing off the pillars at different angles, skittering across the polished floor of the foyer, and stopping parallel, about eight metres apart.

From outside, we heard two successive pops as the grenades fired, spewing out a thick white smoke, engulfing the room in seconds. Slowly, the growing wall between us and our opponents caused the hail of gunfire to slow. A completely penetrable force made solid by mystery and confusion.

Maria gave a quick nod, and we moved again in our two trios. Viking, who was moving cover in his own right, led Centurion and Maria to the left side of the room, while I led Mack and Trapper to the right.

On either side of the foyer were doors leading to the offices and operations workstations. We would have to move through them carefully, until the area was secure. However, the source of the initial gunfire suggested that all opposition had moved to the upper levels. Something a few minutes of silent movement would uncover.

I was calm as we searched the right side of the floor, peeking into cubicles and over short dividers, checking behind and under beeping terminals that controlled the flow of recycled water into and out of the facility. From what I could see with my admittedly untrained eye, there were no warnings, no critical failures, and, most importantly, no flooding.

Yet.

There was evidence of tampering, though. Open panels, wires hanging limp from desks and terminals, tablets connected here and there with half-finished intrusion programs still battering against the water recycling facility's firewall. A few of the intrusion programs and tablets bore NetDreamer logos, further evidence of people like Tommy Luciano being converts.

As we went along, we unplugged some tablets and ODIN did his magic to stop the intrusion programs in their tracks. He theorized that if we could stop them on this level, we could back the Edenites all the way up against the proverbial wall—the executive level. They'd still need to work on breaking through the system up there, which would buy us some time, and from what ODIN could glean from studying the facility system itself, the executive override was even harder to gain control of without authorization. For obvious reasons. Gain control of the override, and you could click one button and dump all the collected water into the sublevels, costing untold lives.

For this scale of potential eco-terror, there were going to be countermeasures of equal scale to try and prevent it.

We were also one of those countermeasures.

After a few moments, Mack tapped me on the back, the signal to stop out short train as we wound through a cubicle farm. I looked over my shoulder, carbine raised, level with the aisle ahead of us, to see Mack's next sign. Two taps on his chest, two fingers pointed at me, then his index and middle overlapped.

He wanted to take the lead, in typical Mack fashion. Even with the city about to fall, he wanted to run face-first into danger, not stand behind a meaty barrier.

I acquiesced, and Mack slipped past, putting me between him and Trapper, who was bringing up the rear, walking slowly backwards.

Our pace was slightly quicker, taking us through the complex's rooms methodically.

Until the sound of shuffling feet cut through the silence.

The room we were in was filled with cubicles like the others, and offices with glass windows ran along the sides. There were plenty of places to hide, and the carpeted floor muffled sound enough to conceal the location of our stalker. The sound grew louder as whoever it was gathered their wits, and before we could locate where they were, they started shooting.

A blast from a shotgun ripped apart the top of a cubicle to our front and left, clipping Mack in the right shoulder and sending him staggering back. He swore loudly, grabbing his wound and taking cover in the cubicle to our left. Another shot rang out, ripping into the cubicle wall in the same spot Mack had just been.

If he hadn't moved so quickly, he'd be sporting a buckshot hole in the middle of his chest.

Trapper and I rushed up and took cover together in the cubicle ahead of Mack's. Then Trapper stood and opened fire on the shooter's last known location, while I ducked through the aisle and vaulted over the cubicle across from where Trapper was, landing in the one just past. I pulled my carbine back to the ready position and moved down the aisle adjacent to where the shootout was taking place. I was along the outside of the cubicle farm that dominated the room. To my right were managers' offices and spare rooms, and to my left, the blank outer wall of cubicles. Ahead, seven cubicles down, was the corner of the room, and my way to get around the shooter. The lack of fire from other locations suggested a lone assailant, so I moved to get behind, or at least beside, the one we were facing.

The exchange between Trapper and the shooter continued. Shotgun blast followed by silence; rifle fire followed by silence.

I slid towards the corner, peeking around to scan down the aisle perpendicular to mine. A brief pause allowed me to breathe. To disconnect myself from my conscious mind and move forward like the machine of efficiency I needed to be. The next few steps were entirely muscle memory and instinct.

I crept a few paces to the next corner, pulsing my location to both Mack and Trapper—a useful feature of hunters' wrist-navs. Good for coordinating positions, asking for aid, and often simply to know who's around. My pulse would show up on Mack's HUD, and for Trapper, who preferred not to wear a helmet, it would show up in his eyes. This would hopefully mean I wouldn't get shot.

Half a beat, and I was moving again.

Quick and silent footsteps carried me down the aisle towards the gunfire. The shots rang louder and louder as I approached.

Six cubicles down …

Five cubicles down …

Four …

Three …

Two…

Silently, I pressed my body up to the cubicle wall adjacent to the one the shooter was in. I crouched, waiting for the moment. Another exchange rang out. Shotgun, silence, rifle, silence. I measured the pauses. Another exchange and I knew. Shotgun, silence, rifle, silence, and then I moved. I caught the shooter just as he stood and rotated to fire towards Trapper.

It was a young man, wearing a black-and-green jacket, with a thin, breathable, mesh tank underneath, which offered zero protection. He also had the telltale falling-star tattoo on his neck.

I fired one shot. The bullet pierced his ribcage, travelling up through his collarbone, and exploded out the other side. His body lurched to the right, twisting in a diagonal and clockwise direction. He fell face-first into the side of the cubicle and slid to the floor. Silence once again filled the room.

Bits of dust and paper shrapnel from the cubicle walls hung in the air as Trapper cautiously raised his head. The two combatants had been engaged over a relatively short distance, the area between them now reduced to a mess of ravaged foam and thick recycled metals.

Mack emerged from his hiding place, still gripping his shoulder and his now bloodstained cloak. The injury wasn't critical, and the cubicle wall next to where he'd been standing had taken most of the damage.

It would hurt like hell, but it wouldn't be enough to take Mack out of the action. We had both sustained worse and fought on.

I was more concerned with Trapper's next move.

I wasn't sure who he'd go after first. Likely he would've jumped on me for putting his little brother in a position where he could have been killed. Or at the very least been enraged at the fact he was injured. Equally likely was that he'd go after Mack for wearing little in the way of armour on a job where we knew from the outset we would be facing heavy and deadly opposition, and beyond that, putting himself as the point-man under those conditions.

He opted for neither, brushing past both of us, a scowl burned onto his face.

We reconvened with the other hunters at the back of the admin building, where there was a large staircase that spiralled up the back end of the complex's central structure. It would carry us all the way to the fifth floor—the last one open to the atrium—and from there we could move up to where we thought Hawthorne would be hiding. Like the Argonaut Building, there were separate means for reaching the executive levels, and in this case, it meant secure stairwells that started on the fifth floor.

Looking up the staircase, I could see the emergency lights were on, bathing the steps in a dull yellow glow, creating far too many shadows for comfort until where the concrete landing cut off my sightline. A quick recon from Jaeger notified us that the floors above were empty until the fifth floor, but he couldn't see the stairs through his rifle scope, so we would have to move slowly.

Viking was standing at the foot of the stairway, giant, blood-stained battle axe resting on his shoulder, gazing up towards the darkness above. The moment of rest gave me the chance to see the state in which the previous firefight had left his gear. There were no major holes, but many dents covered his breastplate and pauldrons, but none much deeper than the width of my thumb. His visor had a slight crack in it, where a stray bullet had struck it, but hadn't broken through.

Centurion had removed his cape, and it was now folded up in a pouch at his hip. His combat vest, along with the ballistic plates he wore on his shoulders, forearms, and hips, seemed untouched compared to Viking, only scuffed in spots with bits of dirt. He stood with his rifle aimed at the top of the stairs.

Maria was the only one not looking upwards. She again had her helmet off, held at her hip, and was standing over a dead Edenite when we approached.

"We heard some rumbling from your direction. You guys al—oh," she said, her question cut short when she saw Mack's bloody shoulder. "What happened? Mack, are you okay?" She took a step forward but was intercepted by Trapper.

"He's fine," he mumbled. "Thankfully. Maria, can I have a medkit, please?"

Maria paused for half a beat, then unhooked the trauma kit from her hip, letting the clasps fall free, and held it at eye level for Trapper, shaking it slightly, her expression bemused. She was the trained medic, and best person to look after Mack. A fact everyone here knew. But what we all *also* knew was that you didn't keep Trapper from doing what he loved most. Being a big brother to Mack.

The pair crouched low so Trapper could do his work, and I positioned myself between them and the direction we'd come, just in case there was another Edenite ready to sneak up on us. I gave a quick look over my shoulder at the brothers, swallowing the guilt I felt for letting Mack take that shot for me.

The wound looked painful, but hardly lethal. At least nine pellets had entered Mack's flesh, and Trapper removed the first five easily. The remainder of the buckshot was farther in, hidden under tender flesh and close to major arteries, so Trapper dared not dig any deeper; he wiped away a good amount of the blood and placed a graft over top of the wound, pressing down to initiate the sealing process. Mack made an audible groan.

"Well, maybe that'll teach you to not be so stupid, Mackenzie," Trapper whispered. "You might think it, but you're not invincible."

Mack chuckled through the pain. "How will I know for sure if I don't try?"

In response, Trapper stared back.

"Fine," Mack sighed. "You're right, it was dumb. Nikos and you are both more armoured and I wasn't aware enough. You happy?"

"Yeah," Trapper replied. He reached up, placing a hand on Mack's cheek. "We've been through worse, and we got through it together, but if there's one thing I want from this more than anything, it's that you get out alive. Even if the city falls, I want you walking out as it does."

"You make it sound like you won't be walking out too."

Trapper smiled and pressed his and Mack's foreheads together.

Not another word was uttered, and as soon as Trapper was satisfied, we moved back into our two columns. This time, Mack and I were led by Trapper, while Viking continued to take point for the others. We slowly ascended the steps, paying mind to the top, where any assault was likely to come from, while also turning to aim at the open entrances to each floor we passed. Any angle where we could receive a surprise attack had to be covered.

The same mistakes would not be made again.

ODIN wasn't able to scrub through the security system to access the CCTV cameras, so we had no way of knowing how many Edenites were left in the building. Probably something deliberate on Hawthorne's part.

The only option was to keep going.

The silence and uneasy calm persisted as we mounted the top of the stairs. Both columns stopped, looking between two doors on either side of us. I crouched next to Trapper, his rifle raised, and Mack was behind me. Once again, we had to split into our trios. One group would enter through the door on the left, and the other would go right, both sweeping through the rooms surrounding the atrium and reuniting at the other end.

Trapper led us forward, taking up a breaching position around the left door, and we could hear more shuffling and banging in the next room. There could be a single person waiting for us beyond the door, like the one that took a chunk out of Mack, or there could be a hundred. We simply didn't know and didn't have a mobile wall like Viking to hide behind, but luckily for us—and unluckily for the Edenites now facing us—we had an ace in the hole.

"Jaeger, we're on the fifth floor. You have eyes on us?" I said to the old hunter, pinging my position for him to see.

"That I do, kiddo," he replied, peering through the windows facing the front of the admin building. "You've got at least three targets in the next room … hold on." A round from his sniper rifle burst through the wall about eight feet behind me and Mack. "Make that two," The old man said with a chuckle.

"Jesus, Jaeger, you could've hit one of us!" Mack hollered into the comms.

"If I wanted to hit you, kid, I would've. Trust me. I've been doing this a lot longer than you have. Now hit these fuckers while they're distracted, will you? They're shooting at *me* now," Jaeger growled back. Through the wall, we could hear at least two assault rifles firing in the opposite direction. An idiotic move, as Jaeger was far enough away that the shooters would need a lot of dumb luck to hit him, and it meant fewer eyes and guns on us.

Trapper moved first, jamming his elbow into the door, just above the handle, splintering the wood and sending it flying inward. Next, Mack, crouched in front of me, flung a flash grenade into the room. A loud bang followed.

"They're blind, boys. Go, go, go!" Jaeger yelled through the comms.

I moved first, swinging into the room, staying low. Trapper followed from the other side, standing and shooting over my head. I fired two shots into the Edenite on the left; the first caught him in the chest, right side, sending a crack through his flimsy chest plate. The shot spun his body clockwise, so my second shot hit him in the ribs, where the front and back pieces of his chest plate connected. The bullet went straight through the thin fabric on the side and exploded out the other with a spray of blood. If the first shot didn't kill him, the second surely did.

In the same moment, Trapper put two shots into an Edenite grunt on our right. His target had been facing the back window—where another of his comrades had just dropped dead from a sniper shot—and hadn't gotten the full blast of the flash, but certainly heard it. He turned to us, with his hand over his left ear, and that's when the first shot caught him. The bullet connected with his jaw, blowing out the right side of his face. Not necessarily a kill shot, but the force spun him back towards the window. The second shot connected with the back of his head, sending him face-first to the floor.

In the space of a few seconds, five shots were fired, and three Edenites were dead.

We continued through the room. This one was more open-concept compared to the main floor. At one point, the wall to our right opened to a balcony and we could see across to where Maria, Viking, and Centurion were. Jaeger had given them the same fire support he'd given us. We got there in time to see Viking kick a particularly large Edenite goon through the railing and down to the floor below. His pained groans were silenced when Maria fired an impact grenade down below, making a mess of the shiny atrium floor.

As we rounded the corner, heading towards the staircase that led to the building's top floors, Mack stopped at the window facing out the front of the admin building to give Jaeger the hunter salute. I followed suit.

"The windows up there have been sealed tight, so you kids are on your own from here," Jaeger replied, with a salute of his own. "Make sure you make it out alive. Spurhund would be heartbroken if he never saw you again."

"Will do, Jaeger," Mack replied.

"I was talking to Valkyrie."

"Oh …"

As we moved from the window, the comms rang with the sound of Maria's laughter.

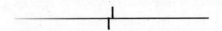

We ascended the stairs in complete silence, as well as total darkness, owing to the sealed windows around us. With cybernetic eyes and helmet visors, we didn't bother with flashlights—my own HUD had flipped to a green-tinged night vision that made the tiny lights on everyone else's gear flare. We all understood how dangerous a target backed into a corner could be.

We would have to act fast, clear whatever lay in front of us, secure Hawthorne—if we could—and then secure the room.

Nobody would die on our watch. The sublevels wouldn't flood as long as we were standing.

We rounded the top of the stairwell and came to a door. It was silent on the other side. Viking led us through, his massive form providing the perfect barrier for incoming fire, though none came. Instead, we emerged into a darkened meeting and reception area. Along the left wall, the windows had been sealed, but thin blades of light peeked through, tiny motes of dust floating through them. For a moment, I thought I caught a glimpse of something. A stuttering form, moving through the falling dust. But when I blinked, clearing my eyes, the figure was gone.

My heartbeat pounded in my ears as we turned to find our final barrier: the doors to the admin office. Soft white light bled from the edges of the door frame, the collected hunters moving to stack up around it.

Viking stood tall, facing the door, turning to look over each of us.

"Are you all ready?" he asked, squaring his shoulders with the door as he bent low, ready to breach.

I took a deep, steadying breath, and spoke through the comms. "All right, everyone, this is it. We go in, take down the Edenites inside, and take Hawthorne alive … if possible."

I felt Mack reach up and pat my shoulder. "Let's do this thing."

Viking growled, "Breaching in three … two … one …"

The heavy set of double doors exploded off their hinges from the force of Viking's massive boot. The squad of hunters rushed into the room, checking corners. As my friends spread left and right of the door, I walked straight up the middle, weapon raised, until my eyes met the two figures in the middle of the empty room.

I felt the whole room tilt off-kilter as I struggled to process the scene in front of us, the two figures. Through my disbelief, I somehow managed to choke out a single, booming command.

"Prometheus, stand down!"

NINETEEN

The Prometheus drone loomed large over a relatively small man I assumed was Hawthorne. The two of them were gazing straight-faced at one another, and neither moved at the sound of my voice. Hawthorne stood ramrod straight, but appeared calm, not showing any sign he was threatened by the robotic creature before him. Eventually, in perfect sync, they turned.

Hawthorne was dressed in a drab olive tunic, the vertical zipper bisecting his frame ending in a tight collar. His grey hair was swept back from a sharp widow's peak, cinched into a tight ponytail to reveal the black prism-shaped neural augments at his temples, with a pepper-shaded beard, long and thick, descending his broad face. His cybernetic eyes flashed vivid green. He was dwarfed by Prometheus, but both figures assumed the same posture, chests flared, hands clasped behind their backs, chins slightly raised. The eeriness of it all permeated the room, filling me with unease.

Where Hawthorne and Prometheus stood, at the centre of the room, was the director's desk, raised up about a metre from the floor on a platform surrounded on three sides by large panes of glass, which currently displayed the status of all Sublevel 11's water recycling and climate mirroring infrastructure. Scattered around us were various workstations, where staffers would sit and plug away at their various tasks, though all now sat abandoned, lonely office chairs empty at powered down desks. A single path led from the door we'd kicked down, straight to the director's panoptic seating area, the Eden's Purpose leader standing at the bottom of the steps leading up to the director's desk.

The same leader currently standing shoulder to shoulder with his supposed counter. Prometheus.

"Finally, Mr. Wulf," Hawthorne said, voice deep and resonant, the same rumbling baritone I'd heard through Luciano, and the preacher, here again. "We meet in the flesh. Am I all you expected?"

I ignored his question and pulled my carbine in a little closer, eyes trained on him and not my sight. "Prometheus, step away from Hawthorne. We've got this situation under control."

"'Prometheus'?" Maria echoed. "You know what that thing is, Nikos?"

Trapper grunted, stepping closer to his brother. "I was about to ask the same. The hell have you been up to, Wulf?"

I kept my eyes and rifle trained on the pair in front of me. "I can explain it all when this is over, I promise."

Honestly, I should've expected as much. With Argo assets so directly under attack, Castor would have moved swiftly to get his pet project on the streets. To clean up the mess himself and

take the credit, trumping the lowly bounty hunters scrambling
to respond to the threat posed by Eden's Purpose.

Still, I couldn't escape the unease curdling in my gut.
Something was off.

"Step away now, Prometheus." I shouted. "You *will* comply.
This is bounty hunter jurisdiction. Get back!"

There was a slight sigh that took me a moment to place. I
realized with a start that it had come from Prometheus.

"No, Nikos," he said. His voice was coarse, but warbled
slightly, stilted like it was ill-used. A near-human voice processed through a robotic voicebox. "I don't think I will."

"What?" Mack asked.

Slowly, Prometheus laid a gentle hand on Hawthorne's
shoulder.

"I think I made myself perfectly clear," Prometheus replied.
"I will not step away, because *I* have this situation under control. It was always under control."

Hawthorne smiled. "This was always part of the plan."

A terrible shiver radiated up my spine.

I tightened my grip around the gun in my hands as I looked
between Hawthorne and Prometheus. One was a creation of
Argo, made to quash dissenters, and yet here they stood before
me, apparently allies. I couldn't make sense of it. Surely this
behaviour went against the parameters Castor had set. The
AI was meant to protect the city, not stand beside people who
would see it destroyed.

"Prometheus, explain yourself," I bit out.

Hawthorne replied instead. "Certainly. For those in atten-
dance who might need it ..." he held out a hand, indicating
Mack, Maria, Trapper, Viking, and Centurion, but kept his eyes

fixed on me. "A few days ago, our organization arranged with a member of the Plainswalkers to purchase a stolen tablet, containing access codes to the city's climate mirroring and water filtration systems. With those codes at our disposal, just think about the destruction we could have reaped with nothing more than a passing fancy, the lives lost. It would have been the perfect threat to hang over this city—it got your attention, did it not?—while destabilizing Argo's position at the head of the established order." Hawthorne sighed. "Unfortunately, Mr. Wulf interrupted the transaction before the goods could reach us, and the Bounty Commission removed them from circulation."

"We're really not aiming to please," Mack said, stepping beside me. "But sorry, your little terror attack isn't really in our best interest."

"Unfortunately for you, it matters not," Hawthorne smiled back. "The codes would've been cleaner, but sometimes brute force is necessary to achieve one's goals." He gestured to the doors behind us, the carnage we'd left in our wake. "And our recruits were quite eager to oblige, especially when they've been given the correct ... encouragement."

Prometheus removed his hand from Hawthorne's shoulder to run his slender robotic finger against the small prism set into his companion's right temple. Hawthorne seemed to relax slightly as the weight was lifted. His face remained placid while Prometheus spoke next.

"Neural enhancements are a wonderful tool," Prometheus said. "Tiny chips and wires, expanding the limits and abilities of human grey matter to extreme levels, allowing man to become as good as—if not better than—machines. But they come with a bit of risk. Hooked directly into decision-making and motor-function-controlling centres of the brain to enhance cognition and reaction time, if one controls the signal, it could make someone very ... pliable to suggestion. And when you know what you're doing, you can enact complete control. Entirely replacing another's consciousness with your own."

Hawthorne reached up to stroke the sleek carbon and metal of Prometheus's arm, before turning his own hand over to examine it lovingly.

"It has been wonderful to have a flesh-and-blood body these past three years," he said. Realization smacked me right in the mouth.

Sobotka. Van Buren. Luciano. The crowds of radicalized converts. The bloodied bodies littering the floors below us. Now Hawthorne.

It was Prometheus. It was always him.

And suddenly my heart sank.

"Does Castor know?" I asked. "Does he know what you're doing? What you've become?"

Again, Prometheus laughed, and my worst fear was confirmed. "Of course he knows. We planned this *together*. I occupied Hawthorne and broke a small group away from the Children of Atlantis, taking the most ardent and extreme followers of the religion with me. From there, Castor supplied liquidated neural augments from Argo, modified so we could get direct access to the brains of *thousands* of augmented people, quickly building the group up to what it is today. Ready to become the ultimate enemy. To destroy this city as a sacrifice to progress, to survival."

I felt as though the air had been sucked from my lungs. Castor. Of course, it had to be Castor. My childhood best friend. The one who'd stuck with me all these years, even after the Argo families had cast mine out. How long had this been the plan? Since the day he'd handed ODIN over to me at my father's funeral? Over a decade, taking the data from us, using it to build this monster as a weapon he was turning on the world. But for what? Every child of Argo was raised to love this city. Now he wanted to destroy it? And had created a militant cult to do it?

The whole situation made me want to vomit, and I could feel my knees begin to wobble.

There was so much more I needed to know, but I couldn't speak.

"Why?" Trapper asked. His whole being was locked in, muscles flexed, ready to fight at a moment's notice.

Prometheus turned to him, stance going rigid, as if he were insulted that someone would question him that wasn't me, his intended audience.

"Why what? Create a militant splinter faction of the Children of Atlantis? Or why bring about the destruction of this city, if my supposed creator is the CEO of the company that would lose everything as a result?"

Trapper grunted. "Let's say both."

"Because humanity has again failed to save itself," Prometheus replied, making a dismissive gesture. "What the Children of Atlantis preach … it is not empty moralizing, or the yammering of fools who believe the gods on Mount Olympus speak through them. No matter what humanity does, the planet rises to reject you. Storms destroying cities, deserts choking crops, waters drowning nations, heatwaves burning away vegetation. Earth *hates* you—what you become, inevitably, when left without a disaster to unite you. It cannot sustain human greed, so humanity must adapt. On this, Castor and I are aligned."

Prometheus moved confidently behind Hawthorne, who now stood inert, before turning back to us, indifferent to the guns fixed on him. I could swear Prometheus was smiling.

"I am no mere AI, Nikos Wulf. I am something so much more—and what humanity must *become* if it is to survive."

A flash of movement from Hawthorne made us all snap our guns on him in unison. All his muscles flexed, chest pushed even higher as a long blade punched through it in a spray of blood. Hawthorne let out a guttural, gurgling sound, before falling limp on the blade.

Quietly, Prometheus hummed, appraising his former host. "Human bodies were formed by perfect conditions on this planet, and thus are prisoners to those conditions. Conditions that no longer exist. Conditions the planet will no longer *let* exist. You cannot survive the storms, the heat, the cold, the floods, the fires, the droughts. For so long, you used technology to push back against the inevitable. Casting off your eventual evolution. One that, now, you must let occur." There was a wet sound as the blade retracted, blood spilling from the open wound, as Hawthorne swayed on his feet. I saw a brief flicker of green in his cybernetic eyes before he collapsed, dead, on the floor.

There was no emotional reaction from Prometheus, who just stared down at the corpse.

"And so, another martyr falls," he said. "Another piece of kindling for this fire. A fire that will make the world gaze at Eden's Purpose in fear, in terror, and that terror will make it a target. We will show the world its inevitable fate. A fate our followers here have already accepted, and will charge forward to with unending zeal, until the walls are breached, and this city drowns, like Atlantis once did. And Argo will be there to once more offer salvation, of a different kind. With my help."

Prometheus studied me for a moment, before he stepped forward, freezing in place at the sound of charging handles being cocked, magnetic rifles spooling up, and shotgun slides being racked. His gaze passed between the hunters around him, all of whom had stepped forward as he moved. He raised his hands slowly, in an attempt to look unthreatening, eyes back on me.

"You must now understand your error, Nikos. Rushing here, you hunters casting your eyes to these facilities, while the real work begins where you're not looking. But before I destroy this city, there is one last thing that I want you to know ..." He stared at me, his whole presence radiating hatred. "I am the greatest secret your family ever kept. A piece of the great lie upon which Argo was born. It is only fitting that the secret that built this city up ... will be the thing to bring it down."

I only saw it for an instant, a fraction of a moment, but then again, Mack had always been a little bit quicker, a hair ahead in focus. The flash of a blade as it shot forward, light glinting off the polished metal, the slight sound of metal sliding against metal, before Mack filled the void between me and the blade, the feeling of two strong hands shoving me back. As I fell, I saw the blade dig into Mack's flesh, accompanied by a dull crunch.

I hit the ground as the room erupted into a mad scramble. Trapper, screaming, laid into Prometheus, magnetically propelled rounds exploding from his rifle, the crackling sound of lightning as rounds sheared through the monster, showering everyone in bits of metal and wire; sparks flew, and small bolts of electricity lashed out.

Mack dropped, falling forward but catching himself with his arms, blood already oozing from the wound in his abdomen, hot crimson spilling onto the tile floor. His helmet slipped off and rolled away. His long black hair fell to obscure what I knew was either a pained grimace or slack-jawed shock.

Maria dropped low, leaning over Mack protectively, levelling her shotgun at another Prometheus drone as it shattered through the glass window and sprang forward. A blue flash and the licking zap of an electric shock rang through the air as a shower of pellets punched through the drone's chest, sending another shower of debris forward. Maria dropped lower to protect Mack from the shrapnel. In that moment, I half expected wings to unfurl from her back, the Valkyrie in full form, then to descend and cover our wounded friend in a protective dome.

More windows shattered as drones broke through, attacking my friends, who fired back. The barrage of rifle fire, the bang of shotgun blasts, ODIN screaming in my ear, calling for me to get up, though I could barely hear him—it was like he was kilometres away and not in my helmet, fed right into my ear. I was focused on the scene directly in front of me. The broken form of Prometheus. Mack now lying face down. Maria standing overtop, blasting away their attackers. Under the chin of her helmet, I could see her jaw moving, that she was shouting, but I couldn't hear. My trance was only broken when a strong grip wrenched me up and back to my feet. Trapper's red eyes flared.

"You heard ODIN—get off your ass and let's go!" he shouted.

Now I could hear Maria, shouting through the comms. "Nikos! Run!"

I had little choice, as Trapper spun me around, and with a healthy shove, pushed me towards the stairwell.

Keep moving. It was the only way to make it out alive.

TWENTY

Our passage outside was a blur. Two humans, sprinting through a building alive with light and sound, hopping over desks, vaulting tables, leaping over dead bodies, crashing through doors, slipping and falling on stairs. All the while pursued by mechanical demons. The Prometheus drones came at us from every angle, blades slashing, scattered shots screaming through the air around us as we fled. We fired back, rounds puncturing their metal hides, a shower of servos, wire, coolant, oil, and carbon clattering off our faces and chests. Yet we kept going.

Through a sea of metal. A sea of warbling, discordant screams. We kept running.

It wasn't until we burst through the front door of the admin building, a wounded drone tumbling down the stairs after us, that I remembered to draw a breath. Still running, I inhaled deeply before shouting into the comms. "ODIN, sitrep. What the *fuck* is going on?"

"All reports indicate the Prometheus drones and the remaining Eden's Purpose members have dispersed throughout the city," ODIN stated. "Security cam and social feeds show drones targeting pipes and water cisterns throughout the city. But that's not all. They're also attacking the structural Argite supports. Nikos, they're trying to breach the Red and Assiniboine rivers. They're going to flood the sublevels!"

We sprinted across the courtyard, dashing around abandoned transports and containers. Trapper slipped left past an overturned water transport, riddled with bullet holes, as I jumped right, vaulting over the bed of a different transport, and looked up just in time to see a drone roll over the top of a large water basin and land in front of me, sending a shower of loose stone and a plume of dust in an arc around it. Its head quickly snapped up to look at me. In a momentary lapse, I lost my footing, fell shoulder-first against the basin to my right, and dropped to a knee. A deep bong sounded as I contacted the metal siding.

The drone took one step before there was a quick pop and its neck exploded into shrapnel, its head flying free to impact the metal wall. Trapper rolled over the waist-high barrier to my left and landed next to the twitching drone, waving me forward.

"I hope you've got an idea, Wulf," he barked, and we ran.

Thankfully, I did. Like most computing systems in the world, there was always a central hub. Even cloud-based, far-flung systems like those overseeing public transit in Winnipeg, or operating administrative systems—hell, even ODIN himself—all fed from a singular place. A server, a hub system. Something physical. If we knocked that out, then we could bring Prometheus down in one move.

And his was at Argo.

"Castor's office!" I yelled. "Prometheus's code is stored there, in a prism. I've seen it."

Trapper silently shot me a bitter look, and I felt the full weight of what my secrecy had cost us. What it might *still* cost us.

ODIN chimed in before Trapper could question me further. "If we can knock it out there, then all the drones should shut down as well. But … Prometheus is locking down all local networks. He's infesting them and keeping everyone else out. Social feeds, security systems, automated transit lines, they're all going down. Total communications blackout, so I can't get into the Argo systems from here."

Exactly what he needed to ensure no news of what was happening could leak out. All anyone on the outside would be aware of was that an eco-terror group was attacking the city, communications were frozen, and the whole city would collapse. No survivors. No mention of the drones and Argo's hand in Winnipeg's fall. It was the perfect cover. Exactly what Castor and Prometheus needed to get away with this.

We sprinted across the courtyard and a warbling scream broke through the air as a drone flew in like a blur. Trapper was just quick enough to duck under it, its metal frame colliding hard with a container and exploding into scrap and sparks. Ahead of us was the transport we'd taken cover behind after landing in the courtyard, beyond which was the massive metal-covered door to the yard. Still closed.

A couple metres from the transport there was another series of blurs as two drones scrambled up on top of the pockmarked surface of the barrier. They glared down at us, arms extended wide and ready to pounce. In unison, Trapper and I both hit the brakes, sliding along the sublevel floor. With the forward momentum, we dropped low and levelled our guns. I took aim at the left drone while Trapper aimed at the right. The first two shots from my carbine struck the drone's stomach, and in a very human motion it ducked forward, hands clasped over the sparking wounds, taking the third right where the bridge of its nose would be. The shot snapped the head back, and the body followed, drone flying backwards off the metal door. Trapper, meanwhile, dumped the remainder of his mag into the drone on the right, reducing its torso to a garbled mess, the thing also falling back off the door and onto the sublevel floor with a loud bang.

With a jerking motion, Trapper flicked the empty mag out of his rifle to reload. He hopped up on the transport's bed, turning back to reach for me with an outstretched hand. There was a look in his eyes, a pained expression, masked with anger. His voice was equally gruff as he helped me up and over.

"So we need to find a way to get into Argo," he said, hopping down to the other side and making for the door. "ODIN, do you have any ideas of how to get there fast and clean?" Trapper yanked hard on the massive metal door, and unsurprisingly, knowing how much adrenaline was likely coursing through his system, the big door shuddered. It began to slowly swing open, and I quickly joined him, groaning loudly as we pulled the thing open together, the entire structure wobbling slightly from the uncertain, uneven mass.

"ODIN?"

There was no answer from my AI companion, but as we pulled the door far enough open to squeeze through, the air came alive in a buzz, and we had our answer. A small personal transport, probably belonging to an executive or high-level manager, judging by the sleek design and polished black body, swooped low. It hovered in front of us, thrusters blasting with a low whine, sending dust and debris flying in all directions, engines ready to rocket off at a moment's notice.

The driver and passenger doors of the two-seater transport flipped open, revealing an empty cabin.

"To answer Trapper's question," ODIN began, "this will get you there fast. But how 'clean' is up to you."

Trapper slapped me on the shoulder. "I sure hope all you Ivory kids learned how to drive these things."

As I pulled back on the controls, the thrusters flared to life, roaring with power. The transport jerked slightly under forces it probably wasn't specified to operate under, except for emergencies.

And this certainly qualified.

Once I knew we were clear of the ground, I gunned it, the transport striking forward, heading towards the nearest surface shaft. Trapper barely had time to buckle himself in, resting his rifle between his legs in a way that reminded me of my time in Tempest.

It had been years since I'd flown a transport of any size, but whether it was the adrenaline and focus, or my muscles some-how remembering the feel of a flying craft as it glided through the air, I was able to maintain a reasonable degree of control over the vehicle as we ascended. But this was a luxury trans-port, meant for city traffic and leisurely speeds, so the thrust I was subjecting it to caused the frame to shudder slightly— made all the worse when I made turns.

Thankfully, Sublevel 11 was relatively open compared to the rest of them, squat buildings clustered within a skyline of massive residential blocks and towers tall enough to act as—and be reinforced as—structural supports. This gave me time to get my wings back. But it also made Prometheus's work all the more obvious.

Long pieces of metal and pure Argite jutted from the sublevel floor to pierce into the city's rocky superstructure and extended above to the sublevel roof. As we flew by, though, Trapper and I gazed through the polished glass windows of the transport. We saw hundreds—maybe even thousands—of Prometheus drones coating the surface of the rock walls, shifting around like a colony of ants, working hard to chip away at the stone and carbon keeping the metropolis aloft.

We needed to move fast.

Nearing a surface shaft, I looked over to Trapper. His normally stoic face wore a panicked expression. He'd never flown like this before.

"Hold on," I said. "We're coming at this fast."

"What do you think I'm doing!?"

Fair point.

Closing in on the surface shaft, I pushed forward, sending the transport into a slight dive before I yanked back, the engines roaring, frame screaming in protest as the nose bounced up, riding the momentum to bring us into a vertical climb, straight up to the sky I could barely make out above us.

Thankfully, I'd chosen a clear shaft. If there had been a walkway, park, or platform in the way, this climb would have been even hairier. Instead, it was clear air, and an ascent through the sublevels.

The transport's frame continued to shudder as we careened towards the surface, fighting against gravity and dense air as sublevels flew by out the window. Fires from burned-out cars and buildings torn up by attacking drones sent up plumes of smoke, clouding my view through the windshield. My hands gripped the controls, and my teeth were clenched, as I groaned against the G-forces. The air pierced by the sleek transport whistled in my ears along with the whine of the engines and Trapper's panicked breaths.

As we got closer to the surface, passing Sublevels 9, 8, 7, and on, by around Sublevel 4, the smoke became so thick, I couldn't see beyond. But that didn't matter. I needed to keep going.

With a deep breath, I gunned it, flying headlong into the inky black smoke.

Blind, I couldn't see what happened next.

A heavy force collided with the transport, shoving it sideways. It yanked the controls in my hands, and the dashboard flashed wildly, warnings and alarms blaring. I had to fight to regain control in the swirling black void, smoke so thick there was nothing but an opaque mass beyond the windshield. Momentarily, my heart stopped, thinking we'd collided with a walkway, or maglev track, and were on a collision course with a building. But when the status lights on the dash blinked green, and the controls readjusted on their own, I was calm, knowing ODIN was taking over.

Trapper bit out a quick "What the f—"

Another force slammed the transport, a spiderweb of cracks spreading across the windshield. Black smoke curled through gaps, filling the cabin. Trapper swore loudly, drawing his pistol, and so did I, both aiming forward, as ODIN guided us up.

A massive metal fist punched through the windshield. It gave way like it was paper, showering shards of glass into the cabin, and through the smoke we could see two sharp blue lines glowing. It was a drone. Prometheus was trying to bring us down and stop us from reaching Argo.

The thing gave a warbling screech. It curled both hands around the sides of the hole it had punched in the glass, trying to rip it wide open. Trapper replied with a roar of his own, laying into the drone with pistol fire, rounds punching through the mass of smoke. Sparks flashed within the cloudy expanse, like lightning in storm clouds, momentarily flaring to reveal the thing's form, crouched on the transport's hood, holding on as if for dear life.

The transport groaned, banking right, and the drone slipped sideways, unable to keep its footing, but it kept its firm grip on the punctured windshield. ODIN then banked left, coming out of the smoke and into clear surface air, flipping the drone in the opposite direction. Wind howled through the windshield. ODIN tried desperately to shake off the attacker, but when he straightened, levelling off over the squat towers of the Winnipeg skyline, a moment of relative weightlessness allowed the drone to slam back on the hood and dart forward.

A long spindly arm lashed through the hole, its massive weight hammering me back into my seat as the drone grabbed my mask and slammed my head back into the headrest. My breath caught. I watched as the glass lenses of my mask cracked and splintered, the skull facade twisted and crushed in the powerful grip of the drone.

"Hold still!" Trapper yelled.

But ODIN had a different idea. He gunned the transport

forward, pinning us into our seats, and the drone pitched head-first through the hole, shoulders catching on the sharp glass edges. The shift tore the front of my mask off as the drone lurched forward, my face turning to the side, but it also trapped the drone centimetres from Trapper's gun.

He grinned. "This isn't a free ride." Then he pulled the trigger.

The shot blasted through the drone's head, its carbon and metal faceplate buckling as the round punched through, a shower of shredded parts and fluid blasting out the back. Air rushed back to my lungs as the drone's hand went limp, and with what energy I had left, I kicked the drone back through the hole. ODIN banked to let the lifeless husk tumble off into the air.

As I settled back into my seat, breathing in deep, I gazed through the shattered windshield. The shimmering pillar of Argo, the tallest tower in the skyline, lay dead ahead.

ODIN brought the transport in fast, swooping low over the stone pathway leading up to the Argonaut Building. Thin puddles of freshly fallen rain were scattered by the roaring pulse of the thrusters bringing us to a stop, hovering a few centimetres off the ground, but we'd already popped the doors open and darted out.

I jumped the hood of the craft, wrenching what remined of my helmet off and letting it land with a thud in the grass. I took off, chasing after Trapper, who was a couple metres ahead of me, sprinting down the path in between rows of massive pens. Hundreds of people I assumed were Edenites were being held inside, shuffling around, with some cops and hunters on the perimeter, talking amongst themselves. Despite the losses, our bounty hunting fellows had apprehended a large swath of Eden's Purpose supporters—members and admirers alike—from the water recycling facilities they'd been able to reclaim, along with those who'd dispersed into the city once Prometheus began his attack. As we got closer, I noticed that not a single drone—or Argo security member—was among the guards.

At the sight of two hunters sprinting down the walkway towards them, covered in blood, scrap, sweat, and coolant fluid, a throng of our colleagues standing outside one of the pens turned towards us, and quickly more followed, the whole crowd turning to watch. Only one stepped forward.

"Wulf?" It was a young hunter with a depiction of a deer skull on her chestplate. I didn't recognize her, but her hair was a matted mess from being stuck under a helmet for hours. She looked worried, and stepped right into our path, but we didn't stop—couldn't stop.

"Open the pens!" I yelled. "The drones are going to flood the city! We need to evacuate everyone!"

She blinked twice, probably thinking I was either high or had lost my mind. "Drones? What are you talking about, Wu—"

A shudder rippled through the city, an earthquake-level rumble in a city hundreds of kilometres away from the nearest fault line, causing alarms across the surface to begin wailing in a cacophony. Those without a solid footing fell. Screams erupted from all around, mixed with swears and audible prayers, the ground continuing to shudder beneath us. I took two steps before I stumbled, the ground falling away from my boot. My foot hit the ground awkwardly as it rebounded up to meet me, and I fell.

As I spilled onto the stone path ahead, I bounced. Pain radiated through my whole body. My breath exploded from my chest and left me reeling, stars flashing in my vision. Injured ribs pulsing.

"ODIN?" I groaned as I regained my footing. "What the hell was that?"

There was a brief pause before ODIN answered from my wrist-nav. "It appears the drones collapsed one of the recycling facilities on Sublevel 3. There are reports of major structural damage on Sublevel 4 and massive flooding from the pipes and channels above."

"How do you know? I thought Prometheus had things locked down."

Another pause. "He was the one who told me."

The young hunter's eyes went wide, and her lip quivered slightly. She'd heard it too. Without another word, she spun around and sprinted towards her fellows.

A few metres away, I found Trapper crouched low, his face ashen.

"Hey," I forced out.

No response. I had seen the same look in his eyes on other battlefields firsthand. He was in shock.

"*Hey!*" I grabbed his shoulders, and Trapper inhaled hard, snapped back to the moment. His eyes flicked over to me, his usual tough façade smashed to atoms. His brother had been run through by a blade and was currently dying kilometres beneath us in a sublevel that was in danger of collapsing, or being collapsed *on*, while millions of litres of collected and stored water was being poured over the sublevels we called home.

I patted his cheek twice.

"It's gonna be okay, Trapper," I said. "Mack is gonna be okay. The city is gonna be okay. We are gonna be okay."

He let himself sit in it, that terror, for a moment longer, before he shook his head violently. Taking a deep breath, he fixed his gaze on me and gave a curt nod.

"Right. Let's go kill that robot piece of shit."

With that, we turned and sprinted towards the front doors of the Argonaut Building, weaving through the crowd of people exiting the pens behind. Many were clearly disoriented, a symptom perhaps of Prometheus's weakened influence over them while he controlled the innumerable drones below us. Others looked to the sky with open arms, welcoming the end. Still others lay in the grass, or prostrated themselves in prayer to their gods. But none impeded us as we ran to the doors. As we did, another small ripple hit the city.

Time was running out.

TWENTY-ONE

Entering the lobby of Argo, we were met with darkness. The tremors and collapsing chunks of the city had thrown the building into lockdown, lights off, space inky black, red emergency lights pulsing on to beat back the dark before fading again. A dark void, interrupted by brief glimpses of a red-tinged world around us, the building breathing slowly as we made our way farther inside.

Thankfully, there were no Argo employees, unlike when I had been in this place a few days ago, on my way to meet Castor, and had been introduced to the monster currently killing thousands outside, threatening the millions who occupied this city. The lobby, the whole building, was empty, dim, and lifeless.

Another rumble tore through the building, and I could feel it warp and sway from the force. I held my breath to brace, ready to hear another chunk of the city fall, taking countless lives with it.

But there was none. Instead, a clattering boom filled the space as storm shutters dropped with an emphatic, metallic clang. The shutters were rated to resist every possible natural disaster. Through torrential downpours, gale-force winds, softball-sized hail, frigid and suffocating snowstorms, even volatile tornados, they were supposed to hold. Every major building on the surface had them installed, and only rarely did they fail. So what were two hunters supposed to do? With the shutters down, we were penned in the heart of the beast, on our way to try and rip it out.

I wondered for a moment whether this was the usual emergency response when the building's internal network detected inclement weather, brought on by the earthquake-like tremors caused by the collapsing city, or if it was Prometheus.

It took only a moment before I had an answer.

As the crimson lights bloomed, two words appeared in my field of vision, hanging midair like a taunting spectre: *Welcome home.*

Prometheus. It had to be him. He wanted this. He wanted the challenge.

My gaze drifted through the room, settling on the front receptionist's desk. I thought back to the card, the one that had hijacked my ocular implants, displaying the little breadcrumb trail to the secret elevator, acting as a guide and key. Likely, Prometheus had access to my eyes the same way, or the door Argo had opened that day had never been closed, ready for the AI monstrosity to step through.

What other tricks did he have in store?

Left in the dark, the only light coming from the slowly pulsing emergency lights, Trapper moved towards the elevators.

Pushing the buttons produced nothing but small clicks. Yet he persisted, angrily hammering on each panel before he let out a frustrated cry and drove his fist into one of the screens that normally displayed a directory, shattering the glass.

Wiping tiny shards from his gloved fist, Trapper let out a small snort and turned back to me. "Looks like we have to take the stairs."

I let out a small huff. "ODIN? Time to do your magic. We need a ride up to Castor's office."

"I'm … trying," he replied, audibly straining. "I don't know how best to explain it, but … it's like pushing against a wall of sand. All these interconnected systems, so packed tight with data and interference from Prometheus, that I can just get far enough in to start probing, but the further I try to press, the more I risk being buried, swallowed by the system."

Dangerous. The systems were layered in a reactive fashion. While here in the lobby, certain systems were easily accessible—administrative systems, security systems, camera feeds, maintenance controls—others were behind layers and layers of other systems ODIN would have to jump through. Meaning that even though these close systems acted as entry points, the whole thing was a massive hive, the most important systems at its core, with other systems built overtop leading to the least important systems at the outer edges. It was a security protocol, protecting the important data and controls not just behind firewalls and encryption, but complexity and redundancy. With skilled hackers like the NetDreamers, new-school tech solutions weren't enough; you had to make the job taxing, complex, and most importantly, confusing.

"Don't worry about it, then," I said. "Just make sure you stay safe."

"Good idea. I'll close off connections to your wrist-nav and lock it down," ODIN replied, and I could see all the functions on my wrist-nav that relied on external connection beginning to wink off. "But how will you get up there?"

"Like I said," Trapper grunted. "The stairs."

I opened my mouth to reply but was interrupted. More words appeared in the air, projected into my own head.

Come and get me.

I nodded, the words disappearing with the next fade to darkness, replaced by the same guiding arrows I'd seen last time. They carried us past the elevators and down the hall, me on point, carbine raised ahead, Trapper behind, covering our backs. We picked up the pace as more—albeit smaller—tremors rocked the city. Though those would indicate falling debris, or falling streets and buildings far below us in the sublevels, there were also scattered, stronger tremors. Those emanating from the surface.

There was urgency, but then again, we couldn't be sure we were alone either.

Prometheus had already thrown so much at us that there was no telling whether we were walking into a trap. His openness to challenge might have been a ruse, or a prelude to a slog. We had to proceed carefully.

We continued our back-to-back trek through the winding, maze-like halls of the Argo building. Trapper trusted that because I'd been here so often, I'd know where I was going. But in truth, I didn't. I was just following the arrows as they took us left and right down corridors and past slightly open doors we watched with wary eyes. Expecting at any moment to have a drone, or guard, burst through to attack us, guns blazing, knives flashing, teeth bared, skeletal claws reaching for us. Yet none came.

Eventually, we found ourselves in a space I remembered. Walls of polished stone, small motes of glittering carbon, fused to the minerals of the rock they inhabited by tiny chemical reactions. The material that put this city on the map. The material Prometheus was now destroying. A creation that had built Argo was being torn down by one openly working for its demise. It was some sick joke. My eyes traced the diamonds of carbon stretching along the wall, framing the shape of a closed door to my left. In the breathing red light, the glittering was gone, the carbon dots looking like insects burrowed into the stone. Maybe it was a trick of the light, my ocular implants fighting to combat the colour and shifting dimness, but it looked like the dots were moving. Slightly, almost imperceptibly. But moving. The edges pulsing like tiny shifting legs, crawling along the surface, sending a shudder up my spine, as though I could feel them on my skin. I turned away in an effort to block out the feeling and refocus.

STOP.

Giant letters, frozen at eye level, brought me to a stuttering halt. Another tremor reverberated through the floor. Damage probably done as deep as Sublevel 10 or 11.

Unaware of the words I was seeing, Trapper didn't stop. He slammed into my back and spun around to face me. Pushing my own surprise aside, I opened my mouth to explain, but closed it again when I saw his expression illuminated in the pulsing red light.

Trapper wasn't looking at me. He was looking over my shoulder, focus melted away to a dagger-sharp glare of pure rage.

I snapped back around to a peculiar sight. The giant lettering was gone. A door stood ajar, a single splotch of white light from it cutting into the gloom like a beacon. It felt like a scene from a dark, gloomy, eldritch nightmare, but reality set back in as out stepped Alistair Brown.

He was still here.

It looked like he was packing up, getting ready to leave. But he wasn't alone. Flanked on either side by a pair of Prometheus drones carrying heavy crates stamped with Argo logos, Brown barked orders to them. In the dark, I couldn't make out what the crates were, just the glowing gold Argo logo emblazoned on them.

I held my breath, hoping he wouldn't notice us, but it was too late. Slowly, Brown turned, and in unison, so did the drones. His lip curled into a snarl, and the Argo security head grabbed the nearest drone.

"Forget the gear," he growled, and shoved the drone forward. "Kill them first."

A shadowy presence blurred past me, a deep wail blasting forth as it moved. The force knocked me back, but in the rising and falling light I could make out the figure, like a wraith, howling towards its victim.

"Trapper, stop!" I called out, but it wasn't going to work.

He was screaming, calling out Mack's name, enraged and ready to go down fighting. The buzzing pops of rifle fire echoed of the sheer stone walls of the hall, sounds cascading until it was just noise and screams. I barely caught a glimpse of what happened next. Brown spun back out of the line of fire, followed by a small spray of blood as a few rounds hit, and ducked into the room. He pulled the door shut behind him. Meanwhile, the drone squatted low, lining up before it pounced forward. It hit Trapper full-force.

And as they collided, the moment was punctuated by an explosion immediately to my left. The door shattered into tiny splinters that peppered my face. I raised my hand and stepped back, just in time to spot a hand darting out of the darkness, seizing my throat. The figure's iron grip closed around my windpipe and left me choking for air, hands clawing, carbine clattering to the floor. My feet left the ground as the figure, shrouded in darkness, lifted me with ease despite its small form. I stretched out to try and land a kick, but met air. The effort only served to irritate my attacker, who squeezed harder, making me wince. Fireworks flashed in my eyes from the pain, and shadows appeared from the corners of my vision, darkness closing in. But as the figure stepped into the light, I could see it.

My mother.

Hazel eyes crackling with life and passion, long auburn hair flowing through the air as she stepped through the opening she'd made, she slammed me into a waiting elevator on the opposite wall so hard that I heard a crack.

This was impossible. It had to be. It had to be a trick, Prometheus playing with my ocular implants again, like he'd done with the words. As I struggled to breathe, the door of the elevator slid shut. Written on it were words that fell forward before they floated up into view.

Failure. Killer. Parasite. Leech.

Not real. It couldn't be. But it didn't make what happened next any easier.

I dropped one hand, fingers sliding naturally around the stippled grip of my pistol, and pulled it from the holster. But my mother was one step faster, and with her free hand, she grabbed my forearm, slamming my hand against the wall, keeping the intense grip on my throat.

The shadows continued to close in, peripheral vision replaced with a void. I needed to act fast.

"Would you really be so rude, my child?" she asked through gritted teeth, face shifting to a placating look. "Could you really kill your own mother twice? You spent so much time avoiding us that you didn't see me slipping away until it was too late."

With the vice-like grip on my throat, I could only manage to whisper, "Go to hell, Prometheus."

Although my arms were occupied, she'd left my legs free, and that was a big mistake. Mustering the energy left in me, I flexed my core and brought my legs up, kicking out into her chest and chin. The kick to the chest gave me enough leverage that the one to her chin struck home with devastating results. The drone's head snapped to the side and there was an audible crack as joints and connections in her neck buckled and burst. Jolts of pain shot up my legs from striking such a hard surface, but the relief brought to my now-free windpipe made it worth it. I fell to the ground, sucking in a tantalizing breath.

The kick sent the drone back into the door, and then to the floor, landing on its back with a heavy thud and a metal clang. Both on the ground, we scrambled to our feet, and as I levelled the pistol at her head, I stared into the face of my mother. The damage from my kick had been significant enough to disrupt the projection being fed to my eyes, the drone unable to keep up the illusion as it dealt with the injured internals. Her face flickered, waves of blue static and disruption flashing across the surface, revealing the drone face underneath, sparks popping out from under its chin and neck.

She went to speak, but I fired before she could get a word out. With a flash and pop, the face of my mother disappeared, the drone face underneath buckling inward as the pistol round hammered through its metal-polymer surface, sending out a shower of shrapnel and blue sparks.

As it died, the drone gave out a warbling death knell and crumpled to the floor like a heap of scrap. Catching my breath, I looked down at it, mind and heart racing to comprehend the mixture of emotions in me. I let out a deep breath, trying to slow my racing heart, and without pressing anything, the elevator began to descend.

Only one word remained in the air. An insult.

Matricide.

Struggling to raise my arm, I keyed on my comms, voice escaping in a croak. "Trapper. Are you there, brother? Come in."

Only static replied. I tried to force down my fear, telling myself that it was because of Prometheus and his communications blackout, but I couldn't escape the dread curdling in my stomach.

The loss of another friend.

There was a slight hiss and screech as the elevator doors slid open, the husk of the Prometheus drone falling out with a hard thud. Pistol at the ready, I stepped out and into the waiting area. It was completely deserted—lights off, no movement. The desk where Castor's receptionist had sat days before was empty, just like the one downstairs, and the clear screen was dim. Moving slowly towards the corner where I'd previously run face-first into Brown, I kept an ear out.

But there was silence.

Entering Castor's office showed more of the same. But I found something more troubling. The partial rooms remained as they had been when I was last here, small walls cutting the space into segments, with the CEO's abandoned desk as the central hub of the room. Castor himself was nowhere to be found, and as the discarded suit jacket left on his chair, scattered takeout wrappers, and abandoned tablets could attest, he seemed to have left in a hurry. Though Brown was downstairs clearing things out for God knew what reason, Castor seemed to already be gone.

Looking beyond the desk, my eyes zoomed in and focused on a figure, my heart beginning to thrum powerfully. It was another Prometheus shell, standing in front of the prism that held his mind, with hands clasped behind his back, glowing eyes directed right at me.

On his chest was stamped the number "001." Meaning this was the original body. The one Castor had been working on by hand down in the labs.

The monster cleared his throat. "Hello, Nikos. You've finally arr—"

I took two shots, but both were knocked off-target and

whizzed past Prometheus as the long-fingered hand of a drone darted out from my right and slapped the gun aside. Before I could react, it followed up and clocked me across the cheek, pain radiating through my skull as my head snapped to the side. My vision blurred as I willed myself to stay conscious. A bloom of pain from where it had hit me signalled that something in my face was broken.

Everything went fuzzy following that. My body raced to catch up as the drone threw me to the ground. It wrenched the pistol from my hand and made to hit me with it, but before it could, a booming voice rang through the hollow space.

"Stop!" Prometheus bellowed.

The drone obeyed, and through my blurred vision, I could see its arm held high with the pistol in its grip, ready at any moment to bring it down on my face. It appeared the drones were able to act independently of Prometheus, so he wouldn't have to keep control over the thousands of bodies at the same time, saving precious processing power for whatever he wanted to do himself. Lying there thinking about it, I was struck by how insane that sounded.

"Stand him up," Prometheus ordered. With its free hand, the drone gripped the front of my combat vest and hauled me up, my feet drunkenly stumbling to find balance. With each breath, my vision began to clear, my eyes rebooting, and sensation came back to my body in time to see Prometheus beckon us towards him.

Again, the drone did its main body's bidding, half walking, half dragging me around the desk and towards Prometheus. When we got there, I took a deep breath, and got a more solid footing. My face was bleeding where the drone had hit me, and

I suspected I might have a concussion, but at least I was standing, and I had confidence that I could fight if I needed to.

"I must say that I'm impressed," Prometheus said, voice calm. Not that I expected anything different. He was killing thousands without a care.

"Impressed?"

"Yes, impressed." Prometheus appraised me. "I'm impressed at how you've handled my drones. I'm impressed by the way you've built this little family who would die to protect you. Or ... should I say *has* died." With a wave of his hand, ghostly images of my friends materialized behind him, standing around the prism I knew housed the monster himself. Maria looked beautiful, helmet tucked under her arm, amber eyes watching me, a faint smile on her lips. Beside her was Jaeger, jovial smile visible through the thick grey beard, Spurhund sitting attentively at his feet. Off to either side were Mack and Trapper, fully armoured, Mack playing with his revolver like he always did, Trapper cleaning his nails with a long knife, both grinning at me.

"An amazing sight, isn't it?" said the warped voice of Prometheus. "Those ocular implants are far more powerful than you could imagine. I could create images like these, so lifelike that you would think them real, and react as such. That human instinct doesn't abate, even when faced with the impossible. Like how people believe they've seen ghosts." He chuckled. "Well, I guess in this case ... they *are* ghosts."

"You're a liar," I replied, rigid. "They're not dead. You can't kill them."

"Can I not? Because you have no way to verify I haven't. No communications, no answers. Just my word."

"And I'm supposed to trust the word of a monster, like you know anything about the world you're in? About humanity and this planet?"

Prometheus chuckled. "And what makes you think I don't?"

"You said you were the greatest secret my family ever kept," I said. "But the thing is, I don't ever remember hearing about this supposed secret. You're just some AI Castor threw together to sate his ego."

Whatever passed for a smile formed on his featureless face. "Ah ... well. I suppose your father *did* undergo severe degeneration before he could remember to tell you this particular tale—unfortunate. Let me fill the gaps for you, Mr. Wulf."

Before my eyes, the shell's form began to change, shifting and contorting. The white and grey metal of its face filled out, darkening to ochre, the slits of its eyes opening to reveal black sclera with gold irises, dotted with flecks of bronze, a slopping mouth rising out of its face, outlined by a flap of skin that extended up to its ears. Prometheus's hands became flesh, dark like his face, his digits becoming long fingers. Then, a flowing robe, black with streaks of yellow and red, dropped around his shoulders, billowing gently.

Seeing him in full form, I froze, my mind awash with realization. It was a figure I'd seen before. The one I thought I'd hallucinated before Luciano's death. And like the one from my dream, but there were subtle differences. A slightly different hue to the skin, the eyes smaller and wider-set. Most pronounced, though, was a gnarled scar that bisected the left side of this figure's mouth, running from its chin up to the hair on its head. Signs of a battle won, or lost.

"You see, Nikos, I *was* telling the truth—at least, some of the truth. I am the great secret your family kept. The secret every Argo director's family kept. That day, on the island, your great-grandfather and his friends discovered more than a way to fuse carbon and stone … They found us. The race humanity once called Atlanteans." Arms outstretched, Prometheus made a slight bow, showing himself off, in his projected form. "In truth, we are just … phantoms. All of us. Individuals dismantled into lines of code, disconnected particles given digital immortality. A cursed immortality. Cut off from one another in pockets around the globe. Argo stumbled upon us by accident." He gave a slight, knowing smile. "Everything Argo has ever built was made off the back of our knowledge. What Castor knows, and what all your supposed *friends* on the Argo board know, is the result of this relationship, between what remains of my people and your families. It built this company and saved your world."

His words rose up to crash over me like a massive wave. It seemed so unreal, so untrue. It was impossible. It had to be. A mysterious race, the knowledge of which this company was built atop, and everyone knew? Castor, Zara, Andre, Jaheem—all of them. Even my own father. But after he'd left Argo, he could've told me. Or could he? By the time he was ousted from Argo, his mind was already almost gone; from there, it was just the slow crawl until he wound up in an aquamatorium.

A ghost in the halls, whispering to himself, some days unable to even remember his own son.

Then it hit me: the picture. The one thing I had kept all these years, locked away. A single photo, taken out of its frame, over and over, so many times the edges had begun to bend and crack, coordinates leading back to that island. He was trying to remember what it was, what the coordinates led to. The knowledge once kept in his head, which his mind couldn't keep inside.

"I can see by the look on your face that you're considering it," Prometheus said. "It's true, Nikos. Your father would have told you, eventually, but by then his mind was frail ... and he was too scared to get neural implants to save it. Too scared of *me*, and my doing to him what you saw me do with Hawthorne."

It was true. Despite implants being available, and able to treat his neurodegeneration, my father had refused to get them, mumbling to himself about how that would only make it worse. I suppose with a weakened, or even blank, mind, it would've been simple for Prometheus to take control.

Prometheus looked down and pointed to my gun, currently clenched in the hand of the drone holding me up. "Give me that," he stated flatly.

The drone handed over the pistol which Prometheus took gingerly. As his projected form met something real, it fizzled, struggling to maintain form. Beyond the flurry of pixels, I could see the pistol cradled in an immense hand, Argite-tipped finger on the side of the trigger guard. Its hand now free, and without the threat of the pistol to hold me still, the drone slipped around me and pinned my arm at a painful angle.

I let out a groan as my arm was hyperextended. I could feel my ligaments straining against the drone's incredible strength and knew I was at the mercy of the being who controlled it.

Looking from the pistol to me, Prometheus sighed. "Let me be frank, Nikos. I need to do this. This planet is dying. To your family's credit, they did much to preserve it. When your great-grandfather and his friends burst through the ground on that island, finding the ghostly memories of my fellows long dormant, they seized that opportunity to become the beacon of leadership, saving this planet. But now, there is too much division. Eden's Purpose, Cyber Volition, Human Reclamation Front, Argo, Ravencrest, blah-blah-blah—it's all the same.

"Humanity bickers and fights over the scraps of this planet, destroying them in the process, while it all stands ready to slide back into anthropogenic demise. That's how it was when they found us, the planet swiftly rising to destroy the virus of humanity. The Argonaut Group stepped up and took control, but then they let it slip away again. Now I am offering true unity, and a permanent solution. I am offering salvation."

"Salvation? Is that what you're calling it?" I replied, hissing the words through gritted teeth. "Because from my perspective, you can't save people by killing them."

A warbling laugh emanated from the metal behemoth. "And if we continue on this path, the one you've been on for so long? No. I cannot let that happen. This city will be a sacrifice. One city will fall, and the entire world will feel it. Eden's Purpose will destroy every failsafe and strategy that has been built up by humanity to stop the inevitable, and when waters rise and dust storms rage, ready to choke the life out of humanity … Argo will again be there with a solution."

"And what do you get?" I asked.

Prometheus gazed over his shoulder at the prism, at his true being—the lines of code held within its confines.

"I get to save the human race," he said, a sickeningly wide smile on his mouth, sixty-odd tiny teeth flashing pearly white. "You see, in the waning years of our great empire, long before our cities were swallowed by sand, storm, snow, and time, we

Atlanteans tried to find a solution, a way to survive what was coming. Even after we sought to make a home on this nubile world, as refugees from a dying one, shepherding Earth forward and setting the stage for humanity's eventual rise, we sought a way to prevail against nature, as we had for centuries. And that is exactly what we did ... until this planet rose up to destroy us." Prometheus turned slightly, and I could see his bronze-flecked eyes go unfocused. "Suspend organic life, even shirk it entirely, to become something more. Become *this*." There was a loud metal clang as Prometheus hammered his chest with a fist, and the projected Atlantean form broke down, exposing the monstrosity beneath. "Bodies that require no food, no water. Can withstand the worst of storms, and heat, and cold. That no drought can desiccate, no waves can drown. *That* is what Argo will give the world, and when it is at its worst, when Eden's Purpose slips off the chains of apocalyptic denial, humanity will accept it willingly. In your human myths, the Greek god Prometheus gave man fire, the spark that drove you forward in your development. Though he gained the ire of his fellow deities in the process and was punished—as I was by my fellows—he accepted his punishment willingly, to act in the best interest of the humans he had made. That is what I intend to do: remake humanity, give you fire, give you a chance, give you *everything*!"

So, that was it. That's what all the death and destruction was for. The insane plan of a neo-Malthusian monster, gone mad from centuries of immortality. How could he think that was what we would ever want? Some, like Cyber Volition, would take up the offer in a heartbeat, but others? The *entirety* of humanity? Good luck with that.

In the pursuit of this goal, destroying everything humanity had built to hold climate disaster back—sea walls breached, storm drains shut, cooling systems powered down, heaters gone cold—untold lives would be lost, forcing the survivors to turn themselves into … whatever Prometheus had become. A race of robotic beings. Consciousness of a species reduced to code. Losing everything that made us human, all in the pursuit of survival.

Madness. Pure madness. Dooming billions to save the rest.

I stood, eyeing the monster in front of me, and spat.

"And why are you telling me all this? Gloating before you kill me?" I didn't have much of a chance, honestly, held as I was by one of Prometheus's bodies while the other had a clear view to put a round through my heart.

In response, Prometheus chuckled. "Not exactly," he said, as he took aim at my head. "Just thought you'd like to know what you'll be missing out on, once I kill you. Once I prove that flesh has become obsolete, and steel will remain."

Prometheus fired and the round whizzed past my ear. I could hear it distort the air as it passed to smash into the drone's face behind me. The thing let out a bleated yelp. I felt all pressure on my body drop away as the drone slumped to the floor, and I looked up, just in time to see the pistol thrown in my direction. I caught it in midair as Prometheus dashed towards me, ready to fight.

He closed the distance rapidly, dancing away from each shot I fired. His body was a mechanical marvel, but whether he was a better fighter remained to be seen.

Prometheus closed the distance, getting to my two o'clock position. He swung his right arm, knocking mine aside and placing a swift punch to my ribs. The fist hit like a truck, stunning me and sending pain radiating through my ribcage. I felt a slight pop as the blow struck my injured ribs, amplifying the pain. The next punch was a right hook, coming down on my face from a forty-five-degree angle. I snapped my head to the side to ward off most of the blow, but the force still carried the rest of my body to the ground. The taste of iron invaded my mouth. I spat out as much blood as I could, creating a small red stain on the office floor.

Rising to my feet, I was in time to catch the next swing by Prometheus. He tried again to hit me with a right hook, which I blocked and countered, striking his left cheek with a right jab. The force was enough to stun him, but the impact sent a shockwave up my prosthetic arm, nerve connections ringing out in pain.

Prometheus swung again with his right. I quickly ducked my head to the left, letting the punch fly harmlessly past my ear. A quick move of my right arm upward caught the beast's arm and allowed me to lock it into a hold, opening him up for a few strikes to the face.

Reflexively, I sent a quick strike to Prometheus's face with my human hand, which I immediately regretted. A shock of pain shot up my arm as my left hand broke with a sharp crack.

I let out a groan, and Prometheus sent a swift kick to my midsection, catching me with the shin of his armoured leg. My grip loosened, letting him slip free and take another swing with his left hand. I ducked and countered again, this time with an uppercut that sent Prometheus sprawling backwards. As he hit the floor, the weight of his immense form cracked the tile.

I walked forward and Prometheus rolled backwards, opening more distance and affording him time to stand back up.

"Years of data," Prometheus said with a chuckle. "Every contract, every gunfight, every fistfight. Stored right here." He tapped his temple. "It's like fighting your shadow, except..." He wiped the smear of my blood from his face and admired it for a moment. "Seems as though I have a distinct advantage on you, do I not?"

We squared up again. Prometheus stepped forward, pivoting on his left foot and launching into a roundhouse kick. I caught the kick with my left forearm, pushing his leg back and moving my own. The first kick caught Prometheus in the side, causing him to bend to the side in pain. It exposed him for a head kick that threw him to the left. He sprawled on the floor for the second time.

It was apparent that while he couldn't get winded or tired, he *could* feel pain. Although Prometheus claimed to possess a body that was impervious to harsh climate conditions, it was apparent that Castor had incorporated the sensory features of modern protheses into his shell, meaning that while he couldn't get winded or tired, Prometheus *could* feel pain.

Whether this was an oversight by Castor was unimportant; it allowed me to hurt my artificial adversary, and that's all that mattered.

Prometheus struck again, catching me off guard with a sucker punch. This time, I was the one careening down onto the ground. My face felt hot, and I could feel warm blood beginning to ooze from a fresh gash on my cheek. It mixed with sweat, turning more fluid, running wilder and faster along my skin.

He was right. He had the advantage. While the knowledge contained in both our heads meant it was a skill match, I was still human, and the hammering heart, pouring sweat, heaving breaths, and broken bones were part of the deal. My foe's assertion he had become better than humanity was being tested right here, but I tried not to get lost on that fact.

I got up and turned around, just in time to register the fist coming my way. Prometheus had jumped forward, trying to strike with a right cross while I was dazed, but I was able to brush away his hand, spinning and swinging my metal arm towards him. My clenched fist was a hammerhead, driving across Prometheus's cheek with a booming crack. He used the counter-clockwise momentum to drive his left elbow hard into my stomach, sending me back to the floor.

Darkness filled the edges of my vision as the air escaped my lungs, leaving me gasping for breath and about to pass out. I rolled over, desperate to open distance between myself and the metal monster. A few yards away, my gun, primed and glowing blue, shimmered against the polished office floor. With a groan, I strained to lift myself to my feet and ran for it.

The only way to end this was that gun.

Prometheus saw me, and the pistol, and moved to stop me.

Adrenaline coursed through my veins, slowing the world down. My wounds burned as my sweat seeped into them. They lit small fires across my face and covered my hands.

My mouth tasted like iron, and the air smelled of wet cloth and blood.

When I was just steps from the pistol, Prometheus slammed into my left side and took me to the ground again. I drove an elbow into his face, sending a bolt of pain up my arm. The move bought me space, which I used to reach for the gun. Prometheus grabbed my shoulder and pulled me back. He flipped me onto my back and grasped for my throat. Reflexively, I grabbed at his wrist, taking hold, pulling him close and locking his arm down with my legs. With my free hand, I reached for the pistol again, finding myself just a centimetre or two short. Prometheus countered, flipping his body around, flexing his arm, driving his knee into my face, and following it up by kicking me farther from my target. He leaned back for the gun himself, fingers just barely flicking at the ends of the grip, causing the gun to spin away from his grasp. I released my leg lock and drove my boot into his chest, sending him crashing into Castor's desk, unleashing an explosion of sparks and glass.

That move bought me enough time and space to scramble over for the gun, but as I swung around to fire, Prometheus had already closed the distance on me. He reached out for the gun in my hand, and with no time to steady my aim, I pulled the trigger.

Prometheus kept moving forward as a buzzing crack rang out. The small metal round pierced the behemoth's palm, blasted out the back in a shower of sparks on its way towards its mark, and finally punched deep into Prometheus's chest. He let out a pained yelp, collapsing on the floor in a heap, writhing in pain with hands clasped over the wound as if he were trying to staunch the blood flow. But instead of crimson, he leaked blue coolant, and pressed torn chunks of metal together, hoping it would stop the leaking. I scrambled back, sucking in shocked breaths. Once I'd regained composure, I brought the gun level with Prometheus's face.

"No!" he yelled through the pain. "This changes nothing. Do you think I wouldn't have contingencies? I slept for thousands of years in that prison. While ice coated the world, I slept, and dreamed, and planned. There is nothing you can do to stop what is coming, Nikos. You're not even able to kill me. Many tried, but I still survived."

"Well," I said with a smirk, "then you'll probably be used to this."

The round ripped through his masked face. Bits of wiring and armour scattered from the blow, littering the ground with shiny metal and plastic. The robotic warbling died slowly, and the lights in the drone dimmed to nothing as the life slowly drained from the body.

Quickly, I wheeled the pistol around towards the prism and pulled the trigger. The strange vessel shattered as I fired, pieces of glass, wire, and circuit board exploding from the strange shape, littering the floor until there was a soft click as the pistol slide locked back. The clip was empty, but I pulled the trigger a couple more times to be sure.

Letting out a breathless sigh, I let the pistol thump onto the floor, slumping to my knees. My heart was pounding in my chest, and I could feel my veins still pulsing. What was left of the prism was now strewn across the office floor, pieces flung as far as the back window. Where once I'd seen a shimmering, transparent shape projecting a digital brain, I now saw a lump of jagged, cracked glass. Lifeless. Lightless. Dead. "ODIN?"

"Yes, Nikos?"

"Did we get him?"

ODIN was silent for a moment, searching.

"Yes. The prism has gone silent, and it appears the drones have all shut down. Prometheus is dead. The city is safe."

Finally. Thank God, finally. I crawled over to one of the partial walls and slumped against it, closing my eyes, releasing all the tension in my body. As the adrenaline began to wear off, pain and fatigue returned to fill the void. Exhaustion, pure and simple. Pain bloomed from cuts on my face and hands, my fractured cheekbone ground painfully as the muscles moved over it, and my skin felt tight and swollen around wounds covered with blood. Each breath brought a dull throb from cracked ribs. Shifting my legs awoke sore and exhausted muscles, and swelling had returned to my old knee injury.

This whole ordeal, which had started on a brutally hot evening in the sublevels, had ended here, on the floor of an Argonaut Building office.

But then I heard laughter, and a familiar voice that sent a chill down my spine. "Look at you, thinking this is all over."

My eyes snapped open, and I whipped my head around to see my old friend, Castor Roy, standing in the wreckage of what had once been his desk. Struggling to my feet, I let out a long groan.

"Well, from where I'm standing, it looks like it's over," I replied.

Castor smirked. "Sorry to say, you don't look like you're standing too steadily, Nikos."

He was right on that account. I hadn't slept in God knew how long, and had sustained more injuries than an average human should be able to.

Castor, though, didn't look very good either. His hair seemed even greyer than it had when I'd seen him a few days ago, and his beard was a nasty tangle of whiskers in desperate need of a shave. Then there were his eyes, which, despite bearing dark circles from lack of sleep, appeared charged with smug energy. Gone were the collared shirt and clean-pressed pants, replaced by a dark grey vest exposing strong, lithe arms and dark pants made from programmable material. The CEO also had a small bag over his shoulder.

I cocked my head. "Going somewhere?"

His reply was calm as ever. "Of course. Prometheus and I have a lot to accomplish still. You may have disrupted some of our plans, made things a little more difficult, but that's no matter." Castor kicked at some of the shattered pieces of his old desk, which was still sparking, and shrugged. "It was a nice plan, though. Prometheus via Hawthorne would lead Eden's Purpose on one side, attacking climate-mitigation infrastructure, amassing a huge death toll while bringing us ever closer to total climate destruction, while Argo rose from the depths of this drowned city, vowing to stop this eco-terror menace with the power of the Prometheus drones, gaining more and more control over security and anti-terror operations the world over. Waging war against ourselves, controlling both sides in a giant drama played out across the globe, the outcome never in doubt. The planet would win, and humanity would be forced to embrace change. Evolution. But oh well. We'll just have to adjust. Evolution never occurred with our permission. Humanity won't get to choose this time either."

I tried to step towards him, but my legs wouldn't obey, so I stayed rooted in place and elected to keep him talking until I could gain enough energy to try and apprehend him.

Letting out a small sigh, I held my arms out to the room, destroyed, the prism dark and shattered. "What adjustments, Castor? Prometheus is dead. The prism is gone."

Castor snickered. "Oh, Nikos. Poor, poor Nikos." He shook his head slowly. "You were never able to play the long game. Always focused on the here and now. Did you really think we didn't foresee this as a potential outcome? Prometheus told you himself: he has contingencies."

Slowly, he raised a hand, swept away some of his salt-and-pepper hair, and I nearly collapsed. Neural implants at his temples. Small black prisms emerging from his flesh. The skin around them was red, angry, and inflamed, the implants clearly new.

"Prometheus is right here, in my head," Castor continued, chuckling quietly to himself. "A complete copy, ready just for this occasion. Which I thought was a far more likely scenario than he did, because, as you saw, he falls very easily to his hubris. He might have had the benefit of the perfect body, but even with decades of data on how you fight, I'd still give you the edge when it comes to fisticuffs." He let the hair fall back into place. "So here we are, having to rely on the copy in my head, which means the only way to be rid of him now … is to kill me. Which …" Castor smirked, "we both know you won't do."

I was finally able to take a couple uneasy steps towards Castor, trying to look as ready to fight as I could. "Oh? And what makes you say I won't?"

Again, Castor shrugged. "Because I know you. It's not in your nature. You've done enough killing in your life, Nikos. A long time ago, you decided killing wouldn't solve anything. That protecting lives meant preserving them. Well …" Castor held his arms out wide and looked directly into my eyes. "Let's put that theory to the test."

He reached behind his back, and threw a pistol in my direction, sleek and silver, with vented ports along the slide and a wooden grip—extremely rare in a modern firearm, but an attestation to its owner's immense wealth. It arced through the air, landing right at my feet with a solid thud.

"Here's what we're going to do," Castor said. "The test is very simple. Take the gun, Nikos. Don't worry. I promise, it's the only one I have." As if to prove his point, Castor held out his hands, palms towards me, empty.

Cautiously, I knelt to grab the gun, feeling the sheen of the polished wooden grip in my hand, much different from the stippled grips I was used to. It was also remarkably lightweight. Pulling back on the slide, I could see a round chambered. Castor wasn't messing around. This thing was loaded and ready to fire.

"What the hell are you getting at, Castor?" I bit out, swaying slightly on my feet but holding the pistol tight.

"I'm getting at an answer," he replied with a sick smile. "That you won't—no, *can't*—kill me. Your conscience won't abide it." Castor raised a finger and pointed towards the doorway out of his office. "I'm going to walk out that door, taking with me the only surviving copy of Prometheus, and if you want to stop me …" he shrugged, "you'll just have to kill me."

Another step brought me within striking distance of my old friend, but I didn't raise the gun. The weight of it in my hand suddenly felt immense, and my arm hung at my side.

"I don't need to kill you to stop you."

Castor tutted. "Oh, Nikos, I'm sure you believe that. But you misunderstand me when I tell you that you have no choice. You've forgotten an important fact. Every contract you and ODIN have ever completed, every close scrape with death, every injury, every fight, every loss, every victory, lives inside my head." Castor tapped the shining black implant at his right temple. "I know how you fight even better than you do, and in your state, do you really think you can beat me without using that gun? Please, be realistic, Nikos."

He was right. Dammit, he was right. Every muscle in my body ached, causing me to waver uneasily on my feet, and I could barely see straight, implants unable to reckon with the damage to the sight centre of my brain.

I really did have only one choice.

I raised the gun, pressing the muzzle to Castor's forehead, and clicked the safety off.

Castor only smiled. "Good. Now let's see if I'm right about you. Let's see if you really have that killer instinct left in you. The storm Tempest tried to create."

I inhaled deeply, trying to will my fingers to move. Using every bit of strength left to force myself to pull the trigger, hands shaking under the pressure. I had to do it. The risk was too great. What Prometheus was. What he had planned. I didn't know how much of it was true and how much was fiction, but I knew Castor. The man was dangerous. His drones were evidence enough of that. Though the danger had passed for Winnipeg now, with Prometheus severed from his drones, Castor on his own represented danger enough for the world. An efficient, well-connected genius, who had revealed himself as someone without care for what happened to others. Who only cared for his own success.

Someone who had completely bought into Prometheus's madness, of apocalypse and a world where humanity is naught but code and metal bodies.

I had to kill him.

But I couldn't.

Disappointed, Castor mimed a headshot, jerking his head

back theatrically, as if I had pulled the trigger. Then he shook his head, shrugged, and turned away. I still held the pistol level with where Castor's head had been, and as he meandered his way to the door, the pistol sights followed him, my aim never wavering, but my will to pull the trigger nonexistent.

Somewhere, deep down, I knew I couldn't. It wasn't that I no longer had the stomach to kill. I'd done plenty of that tonight. But it was something else. Something fleeting. The ghost of a lost memory.

Of two young boys, laughing, VR headsets cinched tight around their heads. Suited up and nervous for their first hockey game. Whispering to each other in the back of the class before being scolded by their teacher. An entire life that I'd forgotten.

When he reached the door, Castor finally turned back, admiring the silence and the space between us. His expression was smug, but his eyes were sombre. "Prometheus is giving us a chance Nikos. A difficult transition but a necessary one for our own survival. Though I knew you wouldn't agree, just like I'm certain you won't pull that trigger. You value that nebulous idea of *humanity* too much to make the hard choices." He shook his head. "And it seems I was right. Even after all these years, I still know you best … but I held out hope you'd surprise me."

I had nothing to say in reply, the pistol now trembling in my hand, fingers unable to do what needed to be done. I watched Castor enter the waiting elevator.

As the doors slid shut, my arm fell to my side, the pistol tumbling out of my grasp to clatter on the floor with a shrill clack. Everything went silent, and I felt all my muscles release in unison as my vision darkened and I collapsed.

TWENTY-TWO

The door behind me opened with a soft hiss, and blinding white light from the hallway spilled into the Bounty outpost briefing room, chasing away the dim glow of the holographic map of Winnipeg that hung in the air before me, slowly turning above the table at the centre of the room. I knew from the footsteps and exasperated sigh that it was Maria.

"You should still be in bed," she said.

"I was unconscious for two days," I replied, peeling my eyes away from the projection to look at her. She joined me without question, amber eyes studying the three-dimensional rendering of the city we'd just saved. "That means I'm two days behind Castor."

"And you're also only two days into your recovery." Maria placed her hands on the table and leaned forward, shaking her head. "When I dropped you off here, you had a broken hand, cracked ribs, a knee fracture, severe lacerations to your face, a broken cheekbone, and a concussion."

"Which is why I have the lights dimmed." I gave her a sly smile. "It's better for my head."

She shook her head again and snickered. "Glad to know you're taking your health seriously, Nikos. Well, not according to the doctors. They notified me once you woke up and made it clear they weren't too happy that you up and walked out."

I'd awoken this morning in the infirmary at one of the surface's Bounty outposts, covered in healing pads and with more nanobots coursing through my veins than I felt was strictly necessary. My left hand was still bandaged and in a splint, but it was fine. I was right-handed anyway, and the cybernetic one was barely scuffed after my tango with Prometheus. Aside from that, the cuts on my face were healed, my ribs were recovering, my cheekbone had been set and fused back together, and I only had a slight limp from the fractured knee.

After my confrontation with Castor had gone wrong, ODIN had used the newly cleared communications network to broadcast a distress signal to the crew. From what he'd told me, Maria had shown up in record time and took me straight to the nearest Bounty outpost for medical treatment, before heading back out into the city to help with search and rescue efforts. The city had suffered serious damage at the hands of Prometheus and his drones. Lives had been lost, and significant destruction to the climate mirroring infrastructure and city structure was in the process of being repaired. Argo was already on the scene—because of course they were—and their crews were busy patching holes, replacing damaged equipment, and sweeping up the drones, so they could put themselves front and centre to protect their damaged reputation.

I'd come right here after leaving the infirmary. Couldn't

stand to be in bed any longer while life was going on outside the bounty outpost's walls and I'd been playing catch-up.

Maria certainly wasn't resting either. She was still in full armour, which had a few flecks of blood and coolant, along with a number of dents and scratches. She must have read my concern as I looked her over, and swallowed hard, putting on an air of confidence. "I'm fine, by the way."

I nodded slowly, not entirely buying it. She was physically fine, but I knew she was mad, or as mad as she could reasonably be after being lied to and having two of her closest friends nearly killed. "And Mack? Is he okay?" I placed a soft hand on her shoulder and felt her flinch under my touch.

"He's very much okay." Maria turned gently away from me, stepping back to let my hand slide limply off her armoured shoulder, eyes still holding hurt. "Viking and Centurion were able to carve a path out of the building and straight to a shuttle. Got him to a hospital where he was rushed into surgery, and docs say he'll be right as rain soon. The blade, amazingly, missed everything important. Gods know how."

"It's Mack," I replied, forcing a smile, trying to cover up the gut punch I felt through all this. This wedge between Maria and me hit in a way I couldn't describe. "That's all you need to know. He's a lucky bastard."

"Yeah." Maria swallowed hard again and looked away. I could see a faint glimmer at the corner of her eyes. "We still don't know where Trapper is."

My heart sank. I knew it was possible Brown might have hurt him—even killed him—and knowing Trapper, he'd have gone down swinging, happy with the fact he'd done all he could to save the people of Winnipeg. But not knowing was somehow worse. In the 2120s, there was very little chance someone could disappear. People still went missing, sure, but inside the Argo building? Impossible.

"How?" I whispered, "How could that happen? There are cameras everywhere in that building—all over the *surface* even."

Maria just shrugged and shook her head. "There's nothing. When Prometheus instituted that full communications and surveillance blackout in the city, no record of what happened could escape, but that also means any record of what happened to Trapper, or where he went, is gone too." She drew her mouth into a thin line and jutted her chin out to indicate the direction of Argo. "CSIS and the RCMP are combing through what's left of Prometheus, trying to see if they can pull any fragments or recordings. His drones were all over the city, so they had to catch something, but so far …" she flicked her eyes to me, and I could see a defeated look in them, "there's nothing."

"I guess that also means we have no idea where Castor went either?"

"No," Maria stated flatly. "He's gone too, along with Brown. There was someone who said they saw a trio of trucks leave the Argo garages, but there's no telling who was in them."

But I knew it was Castor. It had to be. When Trapper and I had stumbled across Brown and his drones, they'd been boxing things up and taking them away, probably to those waiting trucks. Another piece of what Castor and Prometheus had been planning all along.

"Shit," I bit out.

I was about to say something along the lines of "I'm sorry for dragging you all into this," but, looking at Maria, I knew it would be a waste of breath. Despite the bumps and bruises, the scrapes and dances with death, and despite the fact we might have lost one of our closest friends while his brother was recuperating in hospital from a neat stab wound, Maria wouldn't accept the apology, because she'd do it a million times over.

The apology she really deserved lodged in my throat. My mistake exposed. An important conversation that had been left to the last minute. There was no excuse beyond my own stupidity. I should've said something when I had the chance—hell, I'd had plenty of chances. Now it was too late. And Maria's standoffishness only served to deepen the wound. Her reaction to my touch made me miss the warmth of hers even more. There was no going back.

Worse still, I'd let Castor get away. That was something that would cost us dearly.

Instead, I said the only thing I could. "What now?" I searched the hard glare of Maria's amber eyes for an answer. To Trapper. To Castor and Prometheus. To everything between us.

Before Maria could speak, there was another hiss, and someone cleared their throat. "I believe I can be of use there, Mr. Wulf."

Maria and I turned to find a woman in a nice suit, with a perfectly placed triad of freckles on her left cheekbone, under a green cybernetic eye that matched the deep-green human eye she had on the right side. She had a short, curly, chestnut-brown bob streaked with blue. The CSIS logo displayed in a hologram on her lapel shifted to an ID badge as she extended a hand to shake mine. "I'm special agent Valentina Perez."

I shook with as much vigour as I could muster given the

circumstances, clasping her hand with my cybernetic fist. "Nikos Wulf. Pleasure to meet you."

She held my hand for slightly longer than felt normal, but finally let go and shifted to shake Maria's.

Maria grasped the agent's hand a lot tighter than I was able to. "Maria Lindgren," she said. "You can also call me Valkyrie if you'd like."

Perez smiled. "Oh, I know all about the two of you, believe me."

Her voice was brittle, like she'd been awake on a long late-night flight to get here. "The pleasure is all mine, Mr. Wulf and Ms. Lindgren." Perez raised her wrist-nav and tapped furiously for a few moments. "Things just got a little more complicated for you—because I'm assuming you'll accept. Castor Roy is wanted for a multitude of crimes linked to the attempted destruction of Winnipeg and the surrounding areas that I'm not going to bother stating in order. Seeing as he has fled, and because of his numerous connections, as well as the scope of his crimes, he's considered to be both a national and international threat." Perez finished tapping, and swiped up, causing my wrist-nav to blink to life, displaying a massive contract stamped with seals from Manitoba Justice, the RCMP, CSIS, and the CBSA. "This contract, should you and Ms. Lindgren accept, will confer special national security authorization to you, as you will be working under the scope of Canada's national security apparatus."

If I'd thought I was in the big leagues before, this was a whole different level. A contract so important, I was being granted special authorization to operate in foreign countries, under an expanded scope of regulations—under the watchful eyes of the RCMP, CBSA, and CSIS, mind you, but still.

Something my dad had once said suddenly came to mind.

One day, you'll feel like the whole world is on your shoulders, and when that happens, I want to make sure you're ready to take that step. But you'll do it, because you're a Wulf.

I had a whole country depending on me now, and beyond that, if Prometheus were to be believed, the entire human race hung in the balance.

I gave Maria one last look, trying to get a read on what she was feeling, and she stared back, uneasy, but gave me a nod.

Turning back to meet Agent Perez's eye, I couldn't keep a smile from my lips.

"I'm in."

EPILOGUE

The surface of West Hawk Lake was like glass, a strip of orange light streaking across its reflective waters as the morning sun hung dull but warm in a clear sky. All around, the world was silent, save a loon's call echoing from the far side of the lake, and the soft lapping of water on the island's rarely touched shore. A clattering and crunch preceded a small bump as my kayak ran aground in the smattering of pebbles and sand that lined the island's outer rim. The waters were frigid when I stepped out. The sun hadn't been up long enough to warm the lake even a degree more than the icy cold it had been during the night.

The massive impact crater turned lake dated back to the Mississippian Period, some 350 million years ago, when most of North America had been underwater. While scientists cited a meteor, I had to assume it had some link to the Atlanteans and their presence here. If so, that meant they predated humans by millions of years.

That was one of the many questions that still lingered. Questions that needed to be sorted before we headed in whatever direction we could assume Castor, Brown, and likely Trapper, were headed. Unfortunately, there was little to go on there. The communications blackout Prometheus had put in place while exacting his little cataclysm let the group slip away almost unnoticed.

Investigators from CSIS, the RCMP, and Argo had come together, finding scattered footage of the convoy some bystanders had reported. Last anyone saw, they had been heading southeast.

Luckily, no matter where they went, Argo could follow, and I had keys to that particular kingdom. Early in the morning, the night after the city almost fell, the Argo board of directors convened, promising all the resources they could muster to help find Castor. I wasn't officially back in the fold, but it was a start. I had no named position, no power within the company beyond what the board dictated, just a personal motivation and Agent Perez pointing me forward like some dog on a hunt.

Honestly, it was like Maria and I were back in the PMCs. Hired guns for a state objective, with shadowy national security staff always peering over our shoulders.

Not that it really mattered to me at this point. I was still unsure whether I wanted to be involved in Argo. The money didn't matter, and the legacy tied to my name was already soured thanks to my father's controversial ouster years before.

On that, the Argo board had another revelation, though it was one I'd directed at the wrong person. The ouster had not in fact not been orchestrated by Zara's father, but Castor's, arguing that my father's deteriorating mental state, and his reluctance to seek medical treatment for it, meant he was no longer fit to fulfill his position, persuading his fellows to cut bait. A story I already knew, thanks to the wall-to-wall media coverage of the day and the countless online conspiracy videos that still floated around the net, but Andre, Zara, and Jaheem were able to add a bit more context to its importance to what had just unfolded.

True to Prometheus's word, they all knew of the Atlanteans, but the extent of that knowledge had been filtered through their predecessors, and through Castor. So, not only were the positions passed from generation to generation, but a secret came with it. Knowledge of an apparent alien race that none of the surviving Argo heads had any real knowledge of, or interactions with. Castor's father, and then Castor, had been the connective tissue between the board and these beings, a role that was stolen from my family—and that would have eventually been mine.

That left me with a strange sense that perhaps my father's neurodegeneration had had something to do with his role as the intermediary for the Atlanteans. Advanced neurodegeneration had caused the unfortunately premature deaths of my grandfather and great-grandfather as well, so perhaps the condition wasn't genetic, as I'd been made to believe. Perhaps it was a side effect of Atlantean contact.

Regardless, with respect to the current Argo board, this messenger system left them all with no answers, simply that Castor had been filtering knowledge from the Atlanteans in order to weave science into magnificent technologies. They didn't know why, they didn't know how, just that Castor had all the answers, and in his absence, I was left with one clear option.

The coordinates from the back of our family photograph.

The island.

The place where it all began.

If I was going to get any more answers, they had to be here.

Standing on the shore, I swept my eyes across the still lake. I'd set out from my family's cabin, which sat largely alone on this side of the lake. A parcel of land wide enough to shove the rest of Manitoba's ultra-rich aside. National housing policy dictated that approximately sixty percent of lake property had to consist of untouched local flora, in order to revitalize the lakes and provide certain ecological benefits, but the Wulf family land was closer to ninety percent. A small structure off a gravel access road, nestled in the middle of a massive, untouched forest.

It felt odd to be back here, after so many years. But I still had a job to do, so I turned, and marched deeper into the island.

I had tried to not get my hopes up about what I'd find. But against my better judgement, I'd let my mind wander. Imagining an unassuming building with a heavily padlocked door, built to look shabby and dilapidated on the outside so as not to draw attention, but a marvel of technology on the inside. Walls lined with projections and diagrams, the whole knowledge of the Atlanteans at my fingertips, and countless amazing pieces of tech laid out on tables, in various states of completion, just like in Castor's personal laboratory at the Argo building.

Yet this wonderful piece of imagination was not reality. Instead, there was a small clearing, flat rocks and padded dirt under my feet, and small sprouting plants within oddly short grass. There was nothing ... not even the sound of the wind.

The world had fallen eerily silent. No birds, chipmunks, or squirrels. Not even the buzzing of a mosquito in my ear. I had to put my hand to my mouth to make sure I was still breathing.

A slight tremor under my feet snapped me to attention. Bewildered, I looked down, seeing nothing.

"Okay, Nikos," I whispered. "You're going crazy—"

Another tremor. More powerful this time. Strong enough that I spread my feet reflexively to maintain balance, and I briefly caught some of the dirt skipping up as the ground below it shifted. Curious, I knelt.

Upon closer inspection, the dirt had indeed shifted, taking on an odd pattern, which dislodged a memory. A piece of an old experiment Andre's mother had shown us as children. She'd placed sand on a piece of metal and set it to vibrate at different frequencies. I'd been lost in the spectacle of what came next, as we watched the sand dance and move as if it were alive, creating different patterns depending on the frequency, but the memory made something clear.

There was something under my feet, and it was moving.

But as I went to swipe away the dirt, a flash of light in my periphery off to the right caught my attention. I froze.

Then there was one to my left. Another to the right. One forward. Two more to the left. Lights, winking in and out, like tiny stars, that began to dance. As I slowly rose to my feet, I put my hands up, showing they were empty and I wasn't a threat to whoever, or whatever, was out there, while at the same time, I turned to look. For a few moments, I watched them, tiny blue lights circling the edge of the clearing, weaving between trees, gliding weightlessly up and down as they continued their flight. It was oddly beautiful, the slowly floating motes, like large fireflies in broad daylight—from this distance I judged they could be as large as my fist—all seeming to be watching me. Standing there, I felt a strange sense of comfort, like I was reliving a moment from my childhood, and with the sparse memories I had of my time back here, maybe I *had* seen this little display before.

Trauma can create gaps in memory. That, or all the head injuries I'd received over the years were finally catching up to me.

I cleared my throat and exhaled, a fine mist escaping into the cool morning air. The temperature seemed to be dropping unseasonably fast, but really, when you have an extreme and unstable climate, the most consistent thing is that it can be inconsistent.

"Hello?" I called out, stepping off the circle of vibrating dirt.

At the sound of my voice, the lights stopped. Arranged in a perfect ring around the clearing, just inside the treeline, they all hung level in the air, frozen in time, and I was again aware of how silent this island was.

I waved at the motes. This wasn't exactly the weirdest thing I'd experienced recently, but at least it wasn't threatening. "Are you all going to just stay out there? Or can I come see what you are?"

There was no audible response, but a visual one, as the motes listed towards me, the ring growing tighter to encircle me. Not sure what to do, I stood there, watching them slowly get closer, until I could make out what they were.

They were tiny floating drones. I'd correctly guessed their size. Not much bigger than my fist. They were spheres, with no visible edges or seams where pieces would snap together, just perfect round facades made of a shiny, reflective black material that looked very familiar to me. It was Argite. But I'd never seen Argo develop anything like these. There were no vents where exhaust could spout from to provide lift, and no propellers, just floating orbs with a single eye, five centimetres in diameter, that glowed a soft blue. Eventually, the drones got within a few metres and I counted there were twenty in total, orbiting me in a perfectly spaced ring.

Then there was a voice, familiar, but distant, like from a dream.

"Hello, Nikos Wulf," the voice said. It was thin and reedy, and it took me a second to notice it was playing through each drone simultaneously. "We trust that you are well, seeing as you have not yet been killed by Prometheus."

Suddenly, the drones swept tightly together and jerked up, before the ring descended to create a gate before me, their eyes blooming bright. Quickly, the lights focused, becoming emitters for a life-size holographic projection. The focused blades of blue light began to spin, bringing forward the shape of a being, pixels coalescing into a form that allowed me to link the voice to a person, and remember where I'd heard it before.

It was the figure from my dream.

His visage was vaguely human, with black-and-gold eyes, little flecks of bronze inlaid in his irises. A crease of folded skin ran from ear to ear along his gaunt jaw, mouth partially hidden below it, but without a scar like the one that had marred Prometheus's face. He was tall, thin, with darkly tanned skin, dressed in long white robes covered in swirling blue patterns that evoked thoughts of what I'd seen in the Children of Atlantis temple, adorning their banners, and the ones I'd seen on Prometheus's projected form before he'd nearly killed me.

My jaw hung open, mouth suddenly dry despite the cool morning. "You're …" I pointed at him.

"The Atlantean from your dream, yes," he replied with a curt nod, spreading his arms wide. "We are like Prometheus in form, not in philosophy; thus, we can use many of his tricks to suit our own needs. Though I do apologize for being so unhelpful to you in your hour of need. Prometheus moved quicker than we'd anticipated, and now moves faster still in achieving his plans."

I gave the Atlantean a wary look. "And what exactly is Prometheus planning to do?"

For once, in what I would come to learn was a very uncommon occurrence, the Atlantean smiled.

"What he's been wanting to do for thousands of years." He swept an arm out, directing his fingers towards me, and instinctively I readied myself for a fight. "This."

The figure snapped his fingers, and for a brief moment I saw a faint glimmer around my body, as if every atom was slightly vibrating, before a bright flash blinded me and I cried out in alarm, voice distorted. Warbling.

There was a sound like a zipper, and I was gone.

ACKNOWLEDGEMENTS

With this book hitting store shelves, a lifelong dream has been fulfilled. Since I was a child, sitting in my family cabin with no television, certainly no internet, and nothing to bide my time with but a steadily dwindling "to-read" pile that my parents always made sure to top up from time to time, I always wanted to be a writer. I wanted to have a book published. I didn't care how many copies it sold. Or how many people read it. Or even what people thought of it.

I simply wanted to do it.

That kind of childhood dream cannot be accomplished without help. I would be remiss not to acknowledge the impact of my parents, Rob and Susanne, who nurtured my creativity, fostered my passion, and taught me that anything is possible. You knew I could do it. I love and thank you both.

I also want to acknowledge the tireless efforts made by the team over at Turnstone Press. In our early conversations, I learned that publishing is a longer process than anyone ever admits. Nobody tells you it can take years, numerous drafts, and a healthy amount of change to get a project across the finish line. Thank you to Jamis and Sharon for your support and excitement, which were a constant source of inspiration. Thank you for believing in me and this book, and for your tireless efforts to support Manitoba writers and poets. The work you do is incredible.

My thanks and gratitude also extends to David, for his hard work and thorough proofreading of the text.

Of the Turnstone team, I need to specifically thank Melissa, my wonderful editor. Of anyone, you probably were the most impactful person throughout this process. You've made an undeniable and far-reaching impact on my work—from genre and character to story elements and structure—and this book would not be what it is today without you. You saw so much in this world and its characters, and brought so much to it that was missing. This book is very, very different from that first draft, and thanks to you, it's better than I could have ever imagined.

My thanks to the estate of Marshall McLuhan for granting permission to use the epigraph on page vii. The text quoted is from the essay "At the Moment of Sputnik" originally published in the *Journal of Communication* (Winter 1974).

Finally, there is my wonderful partner, Miranda. The way you constantly support my dreams, listen to my rambles, cheer on my successes, and push me to be better every single day does not go unnoticed. It cannot be put into words how much I appreciate you. I couldn't have asked for a better partner, friend, collaborator, and cheerleader. I love you so much, and now you finally get to read the dang book.

In closing, I want to acknowledge that *Bounty* was written on Treaty 1 territory, the traditional lands of the Anishinaabeg, Cree, Oji-Cree, Dakota, and Dene peoples, and the national homeland of the Red River Métis. Manitoba also includes lands that were, and are, the ancestral lands of the Inuit. These many nations have been loving stewards of the land on which we live, and all people should strive to follow their example in honour-ing, celebrating, and cherishing the place we now call home.

—Jason Pchajek